The Visitor

Tony Harmsworth

Get Tony Harmsworth's Moonscape Novella FOR FREE

Sign up for the no-spam newsletter and get Moonscape and other exclusive content, all for free.

Details can be found at the end of THE VISITOR.

Copyrights and Thanks

Thanks to:

Rosie Amber, Wally Andrews, Mark Dawson, Wendy Harmsworth, Annika Lewinson-Morgan, Louise Lilley, Stephanie Parcus, SFF Chronicles Forum, SP Formula, Melanie Underwood, Alison Williams, Sharon Zink, Writers' Workshop, & Wattpad

KDP ISBN: 9781076834966

Cover by Juan J Padron
Doctored star image in chapter 15 © 2009 NASA
Alien symbol and text © 2016 A G Harmsworth

A G Harmsworth has asserted his moral rights.

Published by:
Harmsworth.net
Drumnadrochit
Inverness-shire
IV63 6XJ

Part One
SCAFFY WAGON

[Note for non-British readers – if any spelling, punctuation or grammar seems strange, it is because Tony writes using UK English.]

1 Window on The World

What a ride!

As if a switch had been thrown, the deafening roar of the rockets ceased and silence descended upon the three of us. We were in freefall. The Soyuz capsule had achieved orbit.

Moulded to my body, the seat had been made-to-measure to protect me from the forces experienced during blast-off and re-entry. The straps no longer dug into me, and now loosely restrained me, stopping me from floating away. Mind you, the view captivated me more effectively than the restraining belts ever could. I was transfixed by the panorama from the small circular window.

Intermittent Russian chatter and the crackle of the communication system were now the only sounds. The unpleasant falling sensation confused my inner ears which insisted I was on a roller-coaster careering earthwards. It overwhelmed my senses. Dizziness and nausea were battling for dominance. How could I tolerate freefall for seven whole months? Had I made a dreadful mistake? Too late to regret it now.

I opened my visor. The claustrophobic nature of the Soyuz capsule didn't help. I'd never have been selected if constrained spaces seriously bothered me, but the bulkiness of the pressure suits, the helmets, the proximity of the walls, instruments, and my fellow cosmonauts was oppressive and didn't diminish my queasiness.

I had to control it. *I must.*

The beauty of the view compensated for everything else. Earth's curvature seen first-hand was awe-inspiring, the vista stunning – the land verdant and fertile, surrounded by sea of the most vibrant and azure blue, all visible through pristine swirls of snow-white clouds. Despite growing nausea, I couldn't stop smiling. The surrounding jet-black of space threw our unique haven of life into stark relief.

I felt sick. I pulled a bag from a pouch beside me. Don't be sick. Don't be sick. Control it. Control yourself.

'Вы все в порядке, Ева?'

I snapped out of my self-pity. Yuri, our bullish, shaven-headed commander in the seat next to mine, had sensed my discomfort and asked if I was okay, 'Yes. Да.'

I eased his concern, telling him the view had stunned me into silence. Concentrating on speaking Russian helped relieve the nausea. He laughed, then, in his less than perfect English, said, 'It is to amaze the first time, Eva. Enjoy.'

I managed to say, 'Yes, amazing, Yuri. Mind blowing!'

The pageant of scenery drifted past my porthole. I cast my mind back to my first plane ride to Tenerife as a ten-year-old girl. That magical moment when we punctured the clouds and the thrill of then seeing them beneath me. But this – this was on a whole new scale. The only known refuge of life in the universe stretched out beneath me. My space mission promised to change me forever. The nausea diminished a little.

More Russian radio dialogue between Roscosmos and the ship. Russian was an essential part of our training for a Soyuz launch, but I had struggled to achieve fluency. I have no affinity for languages. At thirteen, my fail in French and a disastrous nine per cent in German saw me confined to the science labs. Fondness for mathematics morphed into fascination and university beckoned with the promise of astronomy and space. I was a scientist, not a linguist.

Yuri Bulgakov switched back to his thickly accented English, 'Hello, ISS. Soyuz MS-one four seven here. Over.'

'Is that the Sahara?'

Yuri leaned over to see. 'Yes, deserted,' he quipped.

I couldn't stop my grin as I watched Africa moving into the wings and the Sahara taking centre stage. Its vast, scorched expanse of cloudless desert was, in turn, displaced by the sparkling blue of the Mediterranean. I listened to the communications, but the view seduced me absolutely. I could no more turn my gaze from the porthole than I could slow my racing heart. My queasy stomach made me wish weight might return, but there'd be only spasmodic weight from now until I returned home for Christmas and could share the thrill with Mario.

The radio sprang into life, 'That you, Yuri? Mike here. How're you guys doing?'

'Hi, Mike. Yes, me again. Bringing two beautiful ladies to the ISS in my classic spacecraft!'

A chuckle emanated from the speakers. 'That's what you're calling that ancient heap of junk, is it?'

'Tried and tested. Tried and tested.'

The smiling, dough-faced Russian told me it was normal for the Americans to wind them up about the antiquity of the Soyuz crafts. Most astronauts travelling to the ISS now flew the Dragon Crew or Starliner Crew – both commercially operated. NASA's Orion spacecraft was being exclusively used for the moon project, not for low-Earth orbit work.

'About to change orbit. See you in few hours.'

'How did the girls enjoy blast-off, Yuri?'

'Eva and Zinaida are still glued to windows, of course. We soon have to winkle them out of seats, I think. Get hot dogs ready for us.'

'I just got some.'

'We help you eat them soon.'

'I've waited a month for these. You can keep your thieving Cossack hands off them!'

'Just look for my ten per cent. Yanks no understand free trade?'

'Extortion more like.'

'How you say, "sticks and stones..."?'

'Okay, we'll see.'

'Roger that. Speak soon.'

'He hot dog mad,' a beaming Yuri said to Zinaida and me. 'Always hot dogs eating.'

I laughed. I'd discovered Mike's predilection for hotdogs a few months previously in Houston.

'I know about his obsession with hotdogs,' I said. 'Mike took a few of us out for dinner a while back. I dressed for a gourmet restaurant, but we went to a hot dog stand and stood in the street, drank beer from bottles and ate giant dogs with overflowing relish. Never did get the ketchup stain out of my finest blouse.'

Zinaida laughed at my story.

Yuri depressed a couple of buttons, switched back to Russian and told Roscosmos he was in contact with the ISS.

Roscosmos acknowledged his message as a cloud-streaked Russia passed across my field of view. I tried – and failed – to pinpoint the location of Korolyov Mission Control in the scene below. The broken cloud cover defeated me. Further east, the shroud of night and clearer skies approached.

The ship lurched! 'What was that?' I gripped my armrest resolutely. What had happened? Anxiety now fought with nausea for my attention.

'Just the injection burn,' said Yuri.

The third crew member, Zinaida Sobolevskaya, a more rotund version of myself, had fired the rocket to raise our orbit to the next level. I had weight again for a short while. It reminded me to pay closer attention to their Russian chatter. I'd missed the warning.

At this stage in my mission, which was to eliminate space junk, I was merely a passenger. My time would come. For now, Yuri and Zinaida were commander and pilot, but they surrendered most of their authority to the precision of on-board computers. I was launched in this Soyuz because my mission was part Russian and part European. In fact, roles would soon be reversed – I was to command my own craft and Yuri would be my pilot.

A succession of thrusts caused more disturbing movements of my internal organs but when they'd ceased, I felt a huge relief, because my nausea settled too, thank goodness. Suddenly, freefall was not so bad after all.

'Feeling better, Eva?' asked Yuri.

'Yes. Yes. The view's out of this world.'

Yuri laughed then checked an instrument and depressed the transmit switch. 'ISS. We have aligned. On course. It is excellent trajectory. Copy?'

'Looking good, Yuri,' Mike said.

Another burn pressed me back into my seat. I'd expected this course correction. A vital, short side burn taking the Soyuz out of the ISS's plane to prevent a collision if the retro jets failed.

'Side burn complete,' confirmed Yuri, his piercing blue eyes flashing at me with the excitement of the launch achieving its orbit. As a veteran Soyuz commander, I think he got a thrill from seeing my enjoyment of the view.

'Copy that,' said Mike.

I peered anew at the night side of Earth and the amber-tinted necklaces of sparkling jewels illustrating the nocturnal ebb and flow of mankind. The spangled clusters were towns and cities along rivers and highways beneath.

Celestial jewellery. In Russian, Zinaida said, 'Wow, beautiful.'

'Yes, and so clear,' I agreed.

'KURS locked on,' said Yuri, confirming a positive lock on the ISS which allowed the approach to be completed automatically.

'Copy that.'

'Rotational burn complete.'

'Copy that.'

'Docking probe unlocked. He is extended.' The final item on his checklist.

'Copy that.'

Now we faced a long slow approach, taking an hour or so. Gratefully, I accepted the extra time to indulge myself with the view. I poked the barf bag back into its pouch. I wouldn't be sick now. I began to feel much more myself.

'Eva, Zinny, look at here. You can see ISS,' Yuri said, pointing at his main screen upon which a tiny bright spot sat at the centre of a pair of dotted cross-wires.

We both gave it a glance, but light suddenly flooded into the cabin and I was immediately drawn back to the view of the sun breaking over the curvature of the planet. Amazing. Sixteen sunrises each day.

'Good morning, Earth,' I said.

'Захватывающий (Spectacular),' said Zinaida.

The Soyuz approached the gigantic, spidery framework of the International Space Station. My porthole was filled with the structure. Several supply craft were attached to the docking nodes. Yuri pulled out the manual docking controls from his console. If anything were to go wrong with the automatic system, he would take over and dock us as if playing a sophisticated video game. I'd watched him doing this endlessly in simulation. I'd even practiced it myself many times in preparation for some emergency, simulated

11

by Roscosmos, in which I was the only conscious crew member. The ISS now filled Yuri's viewscreen.

A series of automatic burns changed our attitude to align the Soyuz with the docking port.

'Thirty metres.'

'Copy that.'

The minutes passed. Yuri said, 'Three metres.'

The docking hatch on the station grew larger until it filled the screen. The whole ship shook and stilled.

'Have contact,' he said.

'Copy that, Yuri.'

There was a further push from behind, plus a judder. The docking probe mated with the matching hole in the hatch and the clasps gripped its shaft, acting out a bizarre mechanical copulation.

We still faced an hour of sealing procedures to ensure all the clamps were properly tightened. Yuri monitored the process from the upper module of the Soyuz. Finally, the hatch joining the Soyuz to the space station was pulled away. My ears popped as the pressure equalised, and Yuri asked, 'Permission to come aboard, sir!'

'Permission granted,' Mike Wilson's American accent sounded much more human now it no longer passed through the communication system.

Zinaida waved me through before her. Grabbing my small pouch of personal items, I pulled myself into the Soyuz orbital module and Mike's familiar, ebony-skinned smiling face greeted me on the other side of the constricted access hatchway.

'Welcome to the ISS, Eve,' Mike offered a hand and pulled on me to help me through into the Russian docking module.

I followed Mike's lanky legs as he moved through the space station towards the international modules. I did my best to keep up, while Zinaida brought up the rear.

I couldn't believe it. I was here, aboard the ISS at last. It had taken a huge chunk of my life. A couple of years dreaming and hoping, three years hard work and another year of detailed planning and intensive training.

What the hell? What was happening? My reminiscing was rudely interrupted. We were drowning in the painful decibels of sirens crying out throughout the space station. Alarms and flashing strobe lights surrounded us. Fear was instinctive. Would I die on my first day in space?

Mike shouted, 'Quick, follow me!'

Within a few seconds, we were pulling ourselves rapidly through the cramped passageways of the ISS from the Russian to American sectors.

My training kicked in as I recognised the sequence of this alarm. It meant we were under attack, and the enemy was invisible. We needed shelter urgently!

2 International Space Station

Within a minute, all seven of us floated in the United States Destiny module. Claustrophobia rose again with so many in the one location, all in bizarre positions watching Mike.

The commander counted us and hit a large green button on the wall. The sirens were silenced, but the threatening flashing continued to remind us the emergency was still in progress.

Our invisible enemy comprised neutrons mainly but also protons coughed out by various high-energy sources in the galaxy. Geosynchronous satellites gave warnings which were relayed to us from NASA who triggered the alarms. Several ISS modules were now protected, but the safest was Destiny. Its new water-jacket absorbed many particles before they could do damage, but some would inevitably pass through both it and us, potentially damaging our DNA and causing future cancers, cataracts, and other medical problems. Everything was done to minimise the risk, but space was inherently an unsafe place in which to work and we'd need to be monitored for the rest of our lives.

The ISS needed replacing, but it had been reprieved, expanded, and its structure improved on an ad hoc basis. The planned new Orbital Station would incorporate far better radiation protection, but none of the agencies wanted to scrap the current set-up.

We whispered among ourselves while half listening to Mike's conversation with NASA and Roscosmos.

The call ended.

'Okay, guys. We're stuck in here for about forty minutes until we enter the Earth's shadow. The danger will be over by the time we emerge. Sorry to the newcomers. Not much of a welcome for you. We get two or three of these a week.'

'Just our luck,' I said to Yuri.

14

'Well, Eva. You wanted meet everyone. Now you have time,' he replied and laughed.

It's true. The emergency gave us the opportunity to relax, have a coffee, and talk about current ISS projects. In such fascinating company our temporary imprisonment quickly passed and the induction action for Zinaida and me began once more.

I'd met most of the astronauts during training but it was good to encounter them again in this environment for which we'd been preparing. As with most visitors to the ISS, few were taller than Mike's five foot ten inches. When it came to moving around in the space station, smaller was more convenient. My slim, fit, five foot five was ideal, but I wished I'd not kept my hair shoulder-length. I hated stunted ponytails and pigtails, but it was either that or I'd have to improvise a couple of hair bands or print some on the 3D printer. Currently it escaped from my head in virtually every direction. If it was curly it would be an afro!

Our induction continued with fire extinguishers, emergency lockers, and equipment stores. We'd done it all before in training, but freefall, with its variable ups and downs, added a whole new perspective.

After the induction, Mike and I floated in one of the largest empty spaces on the ISS, the Kibo Japanese module.

'Just want to catch up with your mission plans. How'd you get involved in this space junk project?' he asked.

We already knew each other from training in Houston, but we'd never really discussed the space débris mission, mainly because it was a Euro-Russian project.

'Long story short, I had no career path towards becoming an astronaut at all but joined European Space Agency mission control in Darmstadt in a science role. Somehow got side-tracked into space junk, then onto ESA science missions at Noordwijk.'

'And that led to this mission?'

15

'Yes, a Scottish scientist called Angus MacBeath took me into his team and we designed the Space Débris Investigation Vehicle. I still didn't think I'd get to command it though, yet here I am. I guess I ticked all the right boxes. Can't wait to get started.'

'What sort of qualifications does a space refuse collector need?' he asked.

I laughed. 'Ha, there's never been one before. I took Astronomy and Sociology degrees; followed that with a Master's in Mathematics and PhD in psychology.'

'Phew! Impressive.'

'Don't know, Mike. Doubt I'll ever use most of it.'

'You worked with Yuri for long?'

'The past twelve months simulation training together at the Johnson Space Center and in Space City. Did you know this is his eighth ISS stint?'

'Yes, no one's been up here more often.'

'With the complexity of our missions, he'll be my security blanket. He's such a cool, matter-of-fact personality. He says the Soyuz is boring. Too automatic. He's looking forward to flying what he calls a *real* spaceship. Very reassuring having him as my pilot.' I looked around myself. 'Can't believe the ISS will be decommissioned. Doesn't seem possible.'

'Well, it's had several reprieves, but it's holding up well. The structures are gradually deteriorating, but we're pretty good at running repairs. I think it'll still be here in a decade. It was supposed to be replaced by 2020 and here we are in 2035 with no real end in sight. In fact, over the last five years, Russia have added four new sections and ESA, with Japan and Canada, have added another three, so it has almost doubled in size.'

'Hope you're right,' I said.

'I think NASA thought that when they stopped funding, it would soon become too expensive for the others, but they almost seemed to see it as a challenge. Don't suppose your missions will be affected.'

'No, we can work out of any orbital base.'

'No one thought the ISS would last over thirty years, so it's outperformed all expectations. Did you always want to come into space?'

'Always dreamed of it, but never thought I would. It just happened somehow. You piloted the shuttle, yes?'

'I did. Nearly twenty-five years ago, now. This is my third and last gig, so shuttle, Dragon, and Starliner.'

'You missed the delights of the Soyuz then. Which was best?'

'Oh, the shuttle, definitely. Was like flying a plane.' Mike moved towards a circular window in one of Kibo's walls, around a foot in diameter. He said, 'Guess what's outside this porthole.'

I gave him a puzzled look and pulled myself over to it. The entire reason for my being at the space station was right outside.

Wow! There she was.

'The Scaffy Wagon,' I said. My baby. The reason for me being in space, berthed at the Harmony node docking station was my Space Débris Investigation Vessel. I couldn't wait to get started.

'Scruffy Wagon? Where'd it get such a name?'

'Scaffy, not *scruffy*.' I laughed. 'It's a strange story, really. The designer, Angus MacBeath, is a Scottish Highlander and they call refuse collectors "scaffies" – meaning scavengers. A refuse collection vehicle in Scotland is called the scaffy wagon. QED.'

'Ha-ha, but if you use the name in a broadcast, it'll go viral for all the garbage trucks in the world. We've great influence over trivia up here.'

We both laughed.

Mike despatched me to find Yuri and to retrieve my belongings from the Soyuz. In my sleeping space, off Destiny, I unpacked them quickly. I wanted to call Mario and Mum and Dad once I was organised. How wonderful to just release things and leave them floating until you worked out where to put them. Mustn't make the mistake of doing that when I got home or there'd be some breakages.

I went to the ISS toilet where there was space to strip out of my flight suit, get rid of the soiled Soyuz diaper, freshen up and put on my ISS kit – cotton top, Bermuda shorts and socks.

I returned to my personal space, finished unpacking, and Blu-Tacked a picture of my partner, Mario, to the wall. I'd taken it on the London Eye with Big Ben in the background. I loved his beaming smile. Seeing his dark curly hair and bushy eyebrows made me feel lonely. I paused to think about him. I'd almost turned down astronaut training because I couldn't stand the thought of separation. Now was to be the best and worst of times. Best because of being in space and worst because it meant seven months apart, without even the odd naughty weekend we'd had during training. I unwrapped a small gift he'd given me for my birthday. A beautiful engraved ballpoint pen. How lovely.

I had to thank him and logged into Skype.

'Eve, you're there? Happy birthday.' His smile was so comforting.

'Can't believe I'm thirty-three.'

He laughed. 'How are you getting on?'

I released the pen in front of my face. 'Thanks for the pen. It's lovely.' I gave the personalised silver stylus a spin along its longitudinal access. It drifted, so I stopped it and left it floating almost stationary beneath my chin. 'Love you,' I said softly.

There were a couple of seconds' lag, so I assumed we were going through a relay in the southern hemisphere. 'Love you too. I was a bit restricted on weight with the present.'

'It's beautiful.' I gave it a touch and it began to tumble. I laughed and retrieved it again.

'Tell me then. What was it like?'

'Well, brilliant flight up, although a bit scary at blast-off. God, the Soyuz is claustrophobic, but it gave me a birthday ride I'll never forget.'

'But it was okay, really?'

'More than okay. Once I relaxed and we cleared a few miles in altitude, I had the window. Stunning. You wouldn't believe the views. You think all the videos from space would prepare you for it, but no, it is spectacular. You could see every detail, field, lake and forest. Wish you could see it.'

'Sounds wonderful.'

'Mike showed me around the station and did my induction.'

'Say "hi" to him for me. He was pleased to see you?'

'More concerned that Yuri might want to share his hot dogs.'

'Ha-ha, I bet. You feeling space-sick at all?'

'Oh, Mario. When we first hit zero-g, I felt awful. Worse than the vomit comet. To be honest, I was worried that I wouldn't be able to do anything up here.'

'You knew that it would settle though.'

'It is one thing knowing and another thing feeling you might throw-up any second. Awful.'

'Were you actually sick?' he asked with a sympathetic expression.

'Thank God, no. It soon wore off and, I'm fine now. Don't tell your parents I felt ill. They'll tell mine and that'll make them worry.'

'No, I won't,' he said and gave me a lovely smile. God, I was going to miss him.

'Keep bashing myself on things, though.'

'Sounds painful.'

'Not too bad. Strange talking to you while floating in my private space.'

'Wish I was there with you.' He mimed a kiss.

'Yes, that'd be an interesting birthday experience,' I flushed at the intimate scene which flashed through my mind.

'Wonder if anyone has made love in space,' he said quietly, putting my thoughts into words.

'Shut up! Someone might be monitoring this.' I said, and chuckled. I was going to miss him and our closeness. We'd known each other several years, love had grown, and we'd lived together for some time. The next seven months promised to be a trial.

'Don't forget to call your parents.'

'I won't. Better go. I'll call you later in the week.'

'Okay. Be careful.'

'I promise,' I said, we blew each other kisses and I cut the connection.

I followed the call to Mario with one to Mum and Dad. Pride has a strange effect on parents. My dad had always loved anything to do with space and he remembered staying up, aged seven, to watch Neil Armstrong's giant leap for mankind. Now tears ran down his cheeks as I performed zero-g tricks for him. Mum, much younger than him, called him a silly old fool and told me to wrap up warmly for some strange reason only mothers can explain. I tried not to laugh at her concern and told her I would if I went outside. I don't think she got the joke.

Afterwards, I switched off my light and tried to accustom myself to the hums, clicks and noises of the space station. The sleeping area wasn't particularly restful. A laptop stuck out of the wall on a bracket, and it was like trying to sleep in a shower cubicle. On top of that, disorientation made me feel dizzy each time I opened my eyes. It wasn't unexpected and would settle down in a few days, but it wasn't conducive to sleep. However, sleep eventually searched me out.

«‹o›»

'Eve,' a quiet voice said. 'Evelyn.' A little louder.

I gasped and grabbed a strap to stop myself falling, then laughed at my stupidity. I'd done that a couple of times during the night. Why wake me? My alarm hadn't gone off yet. Was there another emergency?

'Yes, what is it?'

It was Brian's voice, another American. 'Think you might have overslept.'

The digital clock in front of me said eight o'clock. Good God. I must have slept straight through my alarm. I'd set it for seven.

'Yes, thanks, Brian.'

'No problem. It often happens to newbies.'

I stretched, blinked several times, climbed out of my bag, and moved the door cloth to one side. I could see Brian working on something inside Destiny.

'Gave me a fright. Thought I'd fallen out of bed when you woke me,' I said and laughed.

'Yes. Takes a week or two to get used to it,' he replied.

Pyjamas were allowed until nine, I'd been told. After nine it was considered bad form. I flew through to Tranquillity

21

for my ablutions, returned to my compartment and pulled the door closed to dress. The relaxed ISS environment and temperature remains constant so shorts, top, and socks was fine. I wouldn't need shoes except on the exercise machines, although the specially adapted socks had thick instep-pads to prevent sores when working with your feet hooked under grab handles.

I shot back to Tranquillity for some breakfast, choosing cheese and fruit juice. There were cereals, but I'm not a great fan without real milk. I reconstituted some egg with bacon. Delicious. As I finished my coffee and munched on an energy bar, Yuri flew in.

'You're late,' I said with a laugh, guessing he'd been told about my failure to rise.

'Ha-ha, oh yes? I was being generous. Brian told me you had sleep beyond your alarm. I will have coffee with you while you are still making yawns.'

'Ha. Wide awake and ready to go! Been waiting for you!'

We sucked our coffees through straws as we talked over the plan for today. Coffee finished, we did pirouettes in mid-air, then passed through Destiny and into Harmony, where the SDIV was docked.

Yuri swung the hatch back out of the way to give us better access, but it was still tight for space because of cables and the air-conditioning hoses. We wriggled between the internal docking mechanism and the frame of the docking port. Easier for me than Yuri.

Now the Scaffy Wagon opened up before us. Wow!

'Oh, Yuri, it's amazing,' I said, rotating to take in the whole craft. Yuri did the same.

'Much better than just the front half,' he said. Our simulation training had all been in the business end. Seeing the whole thing made it so much more real.

Two seats faced forward with a huge compartmentalised window in front of them. I wound back the protective shutters. Spectacular. 'Look at that!' I said. The Kibo module and some of the extensive ISS solar arrays filled much of the view. Yuri pulled himself over towards the seats to see.

Behind them, we had a compact toilet and storage cupboards for equipment and food. Two floating spacesuits were attached to the ceiling above. These were not the full EVA suits used from the space station but similar to the suits worn by the early Gemini astronauts for spacewalks. They had umbilical cords and were fed with the necessary environment directly from the SDIV. They were for emergency use only and we doubted we'd ever need them. The manipulator arms were extremely flexible in their abilities and I'd undertake most fine work on satellites using them.

Also to the rear, was the SDIV's life-support and propulsion system. We had a main motor for orbital work and several thrusters for positional use. The back-up engine, smaller than the primary rocket, would be sufficiently powerful to get us back to the station's orbit if the main engine failed for any reason.

In front of each seat were truly space-age consoles. Yuri's dashboard, on the right, was for flying the Scaffy Wagon. My commander's seat had a bank of sophisticated computer screens which gave me access to radar, lasers, and navigation aids for locating, vectoring to, and pinpointing space débris. Sensors and probes could provide information on radiation or leaking gases from satellites. Yuri and I were after the big stuff initially, future crews would eventually eliminate smaller material using nets. We both had sophisticated joysticks, mine to control the manipulator arms and Yuri's for flying.

The Scaffy Wagon's prime objective was the collection of large space junk from low-Earth orbit to protect not only

23

the space station but also other satellites. Our precinct, so to speak, was between one hundred and three hundred miles above the Earth.

This morning's task was mundane. Stocktaking. Every cubbyhole and drawer was to be checked against our inventory. It took us nearly four hours. We returned to the station for lunch.

'How's it going?' asked Mike as I rehydrated some beef casserole and vegetables. Yuri chomped on some Russian fish dish I didn't recognise.

'Fine,' I replied. 'We've finished the inventory. Will be attaching the manipulator arms and testing the engines this afternoon. We're a couple of hours ahead of schedule, actually.'

'Can't wait to see it with its arms,' said Mike.

'Yes, it'll look like a flying lobster,' I said, and laughed.

'Cannot wait to fly her,' said Yuri, miming joystick hand movements.

Boris, another Russian cosmonaut, asked, 'Do you have specific pieces of junk to destroy?'

'Yes,' I replied. 'Four items of a substantial size to deal with on the first actual mission. Tomorrow will see them aligned. We know one's an old unidentified satellite from the sixties. The plan is to give it a nudge earthwards and it will burn-up on re-entry. We also have three unknown objects which are probably parts of early satellites or other space items no longer in use. We think one is a housing from a satellite launch, but another has a puzzling shape and is surprisingly large – bit of a mystery. Can't wait to find out what it is. NASA is pretty curious about it. To be honest, it looks like a missile in long-range images.'

'Take care,' said Brian, the scientist from Caltech.

'Too small to be a real missile,' I said. 'It'll be something much more mundane, I'm sure.'

During the afternoon, we wore flight suits for the test flights.

After separation our first task was to collect our remaining tools, ropes, chains, a variety of extra arm extensions, plus ninety-six blast cylinders. These were officially "de-orbit burn modules," but we all referred to them as *deorbules*. They varied in size from the smallest – no larger than a domestic aerosol can – to the size of a large fire extinguisher. We would attach them to débris which was too large for us to knock out of orbit with a push, and fire them remotely. We stored them under the Scaffy Wagon's belly. It was so exciting to finally be equipping the Wagon to make it mission-ready.

During the test flight, target four, the mystery object, was about to pass thirty miles beneath us and produced a clear speck on my monitor. I zoomed in on it and saw an odd shape. Right enough, it looked similar to a missile or fat torpedo, but with one smooth and one irregular side. It didn't match any on our list of known orbiting equipment. I examined it as best I could, and radar pinged it a few times which told me it was metal, but I couldn't make out anything else. Intriguing. It was soon out of range because items in lower orbits travel at higher speeds. Dealing with four items on the first mission needed detailed planning as they would only be in proximity with each other for a few hours. The missions had been planned weeks previously. Any mission which failed, couldn't be simply postponed for a few hours or a day. It would be completely rescheduled. For this reason, each mission had specific targets.

After the test flights, we docked to the ISS and Yuri went off to help with unloading our Soyuz. I was alone in my spaceship.

I fed the power cables and air conditioning hoses through the hatch, reconnected the power, then relaxed in my commander's seat, still needing to pinch myself that I was actually here. This was not the simulator. This was the real thing. The window in front of me was not showing a video projection as it had been in Houston, it was space itself.

This wasn't how I'd seen my life. Being in space was an unexpected career move, a sort of climax, but at a young age. I might make two or three trips to orbit, but also had to fit having a family into it. I guessed I'd end up back at ESA Mission Control eventually as some sort of mission planning consultant or manager, but I really had no idea. I intended to thoroughly enjoy the excitement of the moment. My career would look after itself.

I flipped off the lights and was plunged into almost total darkness. Only the glow from my instruments remained. The Earth was eclipsing the ISS so it was night outside. Kibo and some solar arrays were illuminated by moonlight, but the right side of the window was inky black and sprinkled with stars like Christmas glitter. So intense. Much more distinct than even on the blackest night back on Earth and no twinkling. I dimmed the instruments further to intensify the star fields and marvelled at the vibrant, glowing centre of the Milky Way. Wonderful.

While in training I was often asked if I got excited. Astronauts always seem so cool and level-headed. We are trained to keep our emotions, hopes and fears under control as they can impact unfavourably upon the mission and compromise safety – but it doesn't mean that inside we aren't bubbling over with excitement.

At two hundred and sixty miles above the Earth's surface, only a reinforced window stood between me and the deadly vacuum of space. At any instant, a sufficiently large meteoroid strike could kill me faster than I would be able to shout for help. I'd not even know what had happened, but Mario and my parents would never see me again. Astronauts do think about these things. What would go through your mind in those few seconds before the brain gave up its struggle to make sense of what had happened to its body? That it would be quick, was certain. Would it be painful? Who knew whether the pain receptors would have time to pass their message to the brain before the cold and vacuum destroyed their ability to function?

It was funny. While I was helping design the Scaffy Wagon, going into space was still a dream. It couldn't really happen, but when the prospect of being part of the mission was casually mentioned by the ESA, that was it. Nothing else mattered. I had to qualify and threw myself into astronaut training. I mustn't lose the opportunity now it had become real.

Only a select few had experienced this privilege of weightlessness and seen the vibrancy of the star fields from orbit. I loved it. I loved the scariness of it. Loved the thrill of having a unique career. Loved knowing I was part of a great adventure – mankind's exploration of a universe so enormous the light from some of its galaxies of hundreds of thousands of millions of stars took countless millions of years to reach us.

Surely, we were not alone in this vastness?

Somewhere out there, a being, perhaps beyond imagination, was thrilling to its own adventure in the cosmos, but so far away neither of our civilisations would ever know of the existence of the other. I had no inkling I was to encounter one on my very first mission.

Was I excited at being in space? I was so excited I wanted to explode with the intensity of it. In silence, I marvelled at my incredible luck. Being here at this very moment thrilled me. I reminded myself to enjoy every single instant of my space adventure.

Reluctantly, I forced myself out of my daydream, closed the window shutters and squeezed through the hatch.

Back in my personal space, I found my old physics teacher's Skype identity. I'd toyed with the idea of this call for weeks. I wanted to avoid communication lag – which is a dead giveaway – so waited until we were heading northeast over the Atlantic, dialled him, and positioned myself to hide the background. I put a baseball cap on my head to keep my hair from floating around too much. I wasn't entirely successful. My hair still frizzed wildly.

The screen sprang to life and a lady who I presumed was his wife appeared.

'Mrs Peabody?'

'Yes, and you are?'

'One of your husband's ex-pupils. Am I able to get a word?'

'What name shall I say?'

'Can I surprise him please? If you can listen in, you might enjoy it.'

A puzzled expression crossed her face. She shrugged and stood up, disappeared from the screen, and I heard her shout, 'George!'

Twenty seconds later he sat in front of the screen. How much older he seemed. I'd not seen him for fifteen years. His hair was no more than silvery wisps, but the same distinctive half-moon glasses perched on the end of his nose. He must be long retired.

'Hello. Who are you?' he asked in his usual gruff manner.

'An ex-pupil.'

'Which one? I don't recognise you.'

'I want to thank you for interesting me in physics. If it hadn't been for you, I would not be calling you from here.'

'From where? Who the devil are you? Don't play games with me, young lady.' His grumpiness took me instantly back to my schooldays. He could be so disagreeably impatient.

'Watch!' I released a large globe of water from a squeeze pack. It floated and shimmied in front of my face.

His expression changed to one of total shock. 'Good God! Slater?'

'The same.'

'How wonderful! A long-distance call, indeed.'

'Not really, we're passing over you about now. Only a few hundred miles, probably.'

'Yes. Yes, how incredible.'

I broke up the globule of water and swallowed some. 'It was you who convinced me to do Astronomy at Exeter.'

'Yes, I remember. I knew you were up there, but never expected a call. I didn't recognise you. I should have known from your hair.'

'Ha-ha. It does behave strangely up here. I tried to hide it in the hat. Can't do a thing with it,' I removed the hat and every hair on my head seemed to execute its own personal escape plan.

Then something happened which I hadn't anticipated. He began to cry just as Dad had. Sobbing, pulling off his spectacles, and hiding his face.

'Oh, Mr Peabody. I didn't mean to upset you.'

His wife put her arm around his shoulders and he was obviously lost for words, wiping his eyes. Eventually, he struggled to reply, 'Evelyn... I'm sorry. You spend your entire life... wondering if you've done any good with your pupils and one suddenly calls you... from outer space, of all places, and tells you it's all because of you. I am flattered... and grateful. Thank you.'

He soon stopped sobbing and we talked for almost half an hour. I performed some tricks for him and left him far more cheerful by the time we'd finished and said goodbye.

3 First Mission

This was it. Our first space junk disposal mission. We strapped ourselves in tightly, cleared our departure and Yuri applied thrusters to take us a kilometre away from the space station.

I'd already done the necessary work to vector us into the proximity of target one. After the checks were made, Yuri asked for a go to change orbits.

'Wait two minutes from my mark and you have a go,' came the voice of Gerald, our European Space Agency mission control director for the day. A few seconds later he said, 'Mark.'

We waited the two minutes so that we'd be in the correct position for target one, then Yuri said, 'Firing on four, three, two, one, fire.'

Relativity played havoc with our senses. Instead of looking out of the front of the ship, we were now on our backs looking upwards through the same window. All the effect of the thrust coming from behind. Weird.

Although the jet was slowing us in the higher orbit, as we fell, we gained velocity. Essential, so that when we were in the same orbit as target one, we'd be doing a similar speed.

I counted down our distance to orbit. Yuri stopped the engine.

'Okay,' I said shortly afterwards. 'Orbit achieved.'

Yuri leaned over and we checked the instruments together. Correct altitude. Correct speed.

'Gerald, orbit confirmed,' he announced.

'Rotate us, Yuri,' I said.

The craft swung through one hundred and eighty degrees.

'Go for adjustment burn,' said Gerald.

The timing of the adjustment burn was calculated to leave target one behind us but catching up. Our new orbit was slightly out of the plane of the débris, so it wouldn't accidentally run into us. At the correct moment, Yuri fired the engine.

'Orientation correct,' I said after just a couple of seconds and he cut power. Apart from a few hums and clicks, we were in silence once more.

Radar showed target one ten kilometres behind us, we turned through one hundred eighty degrees to watch the target approach. It was catching us at forty kph.

As the object closed on our position, Yuri fired thrusters to match speed and orbit.

It was now off to our left and the gap closing much more slowly. Yuri applied thrusters to make final adjustments and there it was, sitting right beside us, only ten metres away. Such a thrill to have found this object in the vastness of space.

'We're beside it, Gerald,' I said. It was astonishing to be looking at a real satellite after all of the simulations.

'Copy that. Well done, guys. Excellent.'

'You wouldn't say that if you saw it.'

'What's the problem?' asked Gerald.

'It's spinning and tumbling.'

'Ah yes, I see it on your video feed.'

Target one was almost a cube, about the size of a domestic washing machine, with part of one solar array attached. The spin must have caused the solar array to tear apart. The other array was missing, assuming it had two originally. Most did.

'It is one of ours,' said Yuri.

'Typical Russian, staking a claim without proof,' I joked.

'Ha, I show. Top right on face coming around... now!' And there, clearly visible, were the red letters CCCP.

'Oh yes. Do you think it has any fuel on it?'

'No. Seems old. Maybe Breshnev era. I not recognise from list.'

'Wonder why it's spinning so fast?' I asked

'Probably thruster stuck until fuel exhausted.'

We both pored over the array of satellites on the central console. I did a search on cubic ones and it didn't give us anything like this, either.

'Hi, Gerald. This is an unknown USSR satellite. Not emitting any signals. Weighs about one hundred kilos. One broken solar array and the other missing. Very dead.'

'Юрий . Как вы думаете, мы должны сохранить его?' Roscosmos broke into the conversation asking if it was worth saving.

'нет', we both replied at the same time.

I'd been told Roscosmos listened in, but this was the first time they'd made their presence known.

'Hello, Ivan. Glad to know you are on the line,' said Gerald.

'What do you want to do, Eva? Can you stop it?' asked Yuri.

'Tricky. This bottom corner seems to be the slowest moving part.'

'Yes.'

'Pull back a few metres. Let's keep ourselves safe.'

Yuri fired thrusters and we moved to about fifty metres. Using my arm console, I unfolded the left arm. Each of the two main lengths were about six metres and I stretched them out to a total of about twelve metres.

'Okay. Bring me in so the claw is about twenty centimetres from the slowest-moving corner.'

Tiny jet manoeuvres let the Wagon close on its quarry.

'Change the aspect so we're facing the corner, please.'

Again, minor thrusts moved us around, so the satellite was turning with the slowest corner directly in front of us.

Using my controls, I opened the maw of the claw to about twenty centimetres, extended rubbery nodules within the grips, and rotated the claw until it matched the spin of the satellite. Fifty-five revolutions per minute. No wonder the arrays had sheared off.

With the stealth of stealing a chocolate from plain view, I eased the claw forward until it made contact. I snapped the grip shut and a slight judder passed through the ship as the difference in momentum transferred to us. The robotic hand and satellite revolved as one, and I slowed the rotation gradually as if deceiving the satellite into being unaware it had been captured.

It took fifteen minutes to bring it to rest in relation to the Wagon. Now we all travelled around the world at thousands of miles per hour as a single entity.

It was time to put all my training into use. With the precision of a surgeon, I drilled holes in the satellite's casing, attached a small deorbule rocket and primed it ready to fire. Meanwhile, Yuri photographed the satellite for identification purposes. I'd filmed the whole process for my educational talk for schools.

With both arms, I manoeuvred the satellite so when I fired the deorbule it would slow its orbit. I released the grip, folded the arms and tucked them neatly back to the sides of the Wagon. We were running short of time if we were to rendezvous with target two.

'Right, Yuri, get us out of the plane of this thing and a distance of about four hundred metres, please.'

Using thrusters, we soon reached the prescribed distance. Yuri rotated us, so we could watch the fireworks. We were motionless with target one stationary in the distance, highlighted by the setting sun against the blackness of the Pacific at night.

'Hello, Gerald. I think we need fifteen minutes to ensure any residue falls into the Atlantic. Give me a go to fire the de-orbiting module,' I said.

'Confirm fifteen minutes, Eve. You're going to be tight to catch up with target two, so leave as soon as you can after the deorbule fires.'

'I'll orientate in readiness,' said Yuri.

We gazed at the Earth beneath, the bejewelled coast of South America approaching while we waited. A tropical storm was passing by the Galapagos Islands and we knew the serenity we were enjoying was not being felt by anyone visiting the famous archipelago. I double-checked our position in relation to target two. We should be okay. It showed why the advanced planning was so vital.

The wait was over, 'You have a go for that when ready, Eve.'

'Three, two, one, fire.' I tapped the red fire logo on my screen.

The briefest of flames during ignition was followed by a cloud of almost transparent exhaust from the deorbule and the satellite moved away from us, backward in its orbit. The jet fired for about twelve minutes. Anything over eight minutes would have been sufficient for the mass of this object. They weren't meant to be too precise. Yuri used the thrusters to keep it in sight and I could monitor its deceleration. There was no sign of any pitching so I must've got the deorbule smack bang on an axis through the centre of gravity. Very satisfying.

The deorbule fuel was exhausted and my console confirmed the trajectory was perfect. The satellite was falling out of orbit and would burn up over the Atlantic, somewhere east of Rio de Janeiro.

'Job done,' I said. Fascinating to watch it disappearing into the distance.

'Excellent,' said Yuri.

'Well done, you guys. We're monitoring it from Durban. I'll let you know when it's gone.'

'Thank you, Gerald,' I said.

We set off, not too late, for our second target which turned out to be an almost complete solar array from target one. I held it in the arm at full stretch and Yuri gave us a vector opposite to the orbit. Once we reached the correct velocity, I released the array and Yuri backed us off using thrusters. There was no way any of this array would survive re-entry. We were back on schedule.

We were fascinated by the third target. Such a surprise. NASA thought it would be a housing from a satellite booster, but it was part of the command module housing for Apollo XII. How this great chunk of moon history had remained in orbit for sixty-five years was a mystery. Its orbit must have been deteriorating for years. It was a large enough piece of metal for us to need to check where it might fall. Its irregular shape meant that it would be impossible to use a deorbule without setting it spinning, so, once we had approval, we gave it a really energetic shove in a retrograde direction and released it.

'Some pitch, Eva.'

'Ha. The Earth's a pretty huge target. Can't miss!'

We watched the housing disappear into the distance with some sadness, knowing none of the Apollo moonwalkers remained. Could I, perhaps, get the job of clearing up some of the space junk on the moon's surface working out of one of the new moonbases?

'Only the mystery job to deal with now,' I said.

Target four required another fifteen-mile descent to match speed and orbit. We rotated, and Yuri adjusted our orientation. It was really odd. I pulled my binoculars towards me and stared at it. It was in the distance, approaching us quite slowly.

At a kilometre range, it was obvious to me it was not any run-of-the-mill space débris.

I let out a gasp as I realised what I was seeing. Surely impossible.

We'd been taught to keep cool if anything untoward occurred and I instantly knew this was as "untoward" as anything could ever be.

I took a deep breath and said, in a deliberately flat monotone, 'Hello, Gerald. This is a type thirty-two sat.'

Yuri glanced at me sharply and grabbed his own binoculars. We both switched our communications to a secure channel. "Thirty-two sat" was code meaning the conversation should not be overheard – the media and lots of enthusiasts listen in to our chatter. Calling a "32 sat" also meant the public video feed was cut. It ran five minutes behind the live feed. ESA, NASA, JAXA, CSA and Roscosmos had the ability to continue monitoring us, while preventing the feed going public.

'Gerald, do you copy?' I asked while zooming in on the target on my forward-facing monitor.

'Yes, Eve. Why the cloak and dagger?'

'This is not one of ours,' I said, realising that sweat was forming on my brow.

'What, Chinese?'

'Guess again. This is from no nation on Earth. Seriously. I've just zoomed the camera in on it. You'd better give us some advice what to do.'

'You're joking! Will do, Eve. Stand by.'

Again, Yuri and I exchanged anxious glances. Yuri adjusted our orientation and, whatever it was soon sat a few metres off our port bow, rotating slowly.

'Will you look at that?' I said quietly.

'Alien?' asked Yuri – in a deathly whisper.

'Must be,' I said as I saw the writing on its side.

We stared at it in sheer amazement.

4 Artefact

It was nothing made on Earth. For all these decades, humanity had been searching for intelligent life somewhere else in the universe, and Yuri and I had found it on our own doorstep. This was no more man-made than I was delivered by a stork.

In the manner of a miniature spaceship, its vaguely egg-shaped form rotated along its major axis. The main body seemed to be some sort of iridescent material. The front resembled burnished gold. Deep grooves ran the length of the object from the gold collar to the blunt rear where funnel shapes gave the impression of a propulsion system. Stubby fins completed the resemblance to a mini-spaceship. The funnels and fins looked as if they had grown out of the fuselage. There was no sign of any rivets or other construction methods.

The gold collar at the front, as brilliant as Tutankhamun's casket, had a matching central node the size of a large half-melon, evenly dotted with pure silver, two-centimetre blisters, reminiscent of thimbles, right down to the crowded regular dimples on their surfaces. Simply stunning. From the centre of the node, a long, tapering golden rod pointed forward, adding an extra metre to the object's two and a half metre length. Its diameter at the widest point was about one and a quarter metres.

It revolved, sedately, once per minute permitting us to examine the damage to its unworldly symmetry. An entire side was smashed and distorted, showing it had been the victim of a cosmic collision. Perhaps the guilty party was a meteor, gathered by Earth's gravity, moving too fast to be detected, and smashing into the object as it plunged towards the surface of the planet. A billion to one accident.

Its electronic entrails had spilled into the void, with wires and components trailing behind the direction of rotation.

Some of the material was hanging out more than two metres, the furthest item being an iridescent cylinder the diameter of a test tube, but over twenty centimetres long. Two strangely coloured, uninsulated wires held it captive. In the fore section, similar tubes formed clusters of various lengths and all with different coloured wires leading to and from them. Had fire burned off the insulation? Inside at the rear were a dozen marrow-shaped, steel-coloured spheres which might contain fuel. Two of them were split open, one with a jagged gash and the other a broken shell. What gas or liquid had these vented into space? Fuel was the most likely answer. What sort of fuel did it use? Was it dangerous?

'Oh, my God!' I said as a sudden panic overcame me. I manipulated the right robotic arm and brought the small claw to within thirty centimetres of the object.

'Touch it not, Eva,' said Yuri hurriedly, grasping my arm.

'No. Don't worry. Checking radiation.'

'Блядь! Yes. Of course.' It was rare to hear Yuri emit a Russian profanity.

After a few taps and slides on my computer, we had a reading. Marginally radioactive, but only slightly stronger than the background radiation in this orbit. I reported it over the secure channel.

'Sorry, you guys. We should have thought of that,' said Gerald.

'No harm done. Can't think of everything,' I said.

Yuri's skill with the thrusters gave us the opportunity to circle and film it from all angles. Strange symbols on one side, gave the impression of a name followed by a sequence of dots. The first column of dots was three, followed by seven followed by two. If I'd been a gambler, I'd have said this was number 37'2. Was it to base eight, ten, sixteen or some less predictable sequence? Base nine or ten was hinted at by the central block of dots. Surely no creature would choose base nine, divisible only by three.

What did the apostrophe represent? Or maybe it wasn't an apostrophe, but a comma and we were viewing it upside down? 2,73 something?

'Are you seeing this, Gerald?' I asked.

'Yes.'

'Да,' confirming Roscosmos was still with us.

'Permission to stop its spin, Gerald?'

'No, Evelyn. Wait. We have people who want to consider your options and there are more on the way. Presume you've people arriving, too, Ivan?'

'Да. Us too,' confirmed Ivan using English for the benefit of the numerous non-Russian speakers who must be arriving at NASA, ESA, JAXA, CSA and Roscosmos. The trivial game of testing the Americans with the use of Russian forgotten in the excitement.

'Don't touch it, Evelyn, until we know what we're dealing with,' said Gerald.

Off air I said to Yuri, 'That could be an extremely long time.'

'Indeed,' Yuri agreed, with one of his disarming smiles while raising his eyebrows.

I switched communications channel, 'ISS. SDIV here. You copy us?'

A few seconds passed, and Brian answered, 'Hi, Eve, copy you.'

'Could be a while on this one, Brian. Let Mike know we'll be late back. Difficult spin on it,' I lied. 'We'll have to analyse and recalculate our trajectory.'

'No problem, Eve. Be careful.'

'We will,' I switched back to the secure channel. We were now going to be very isolated. Our orbit and that of the ISS would quickly diverge.

Yuri manoeuvred us, so we were facing directly towards the artefact from the side. The mess of wiring and circuitry was much clearer as we approached to within a metre.

There was no way this was of human manufacture. The wires were multi-coloured but not insulated, almost as if the metal had colour built-in. They entered the components at seemingly random locations. One was broken in half and appeared to be an empty tube. Whatever had been within it was long gone. Although we could see the wires entering the exterior of the tubes, there was no sign of them inside. The inner surface of the broken tube appeared smooth.

'See wires, Eva? They like hairs growing out of it.'

'Yes, and they disappear inside.' I felt a gut-wrenching sickness in my abdomen. 'Looks hellish advanced,' I said.

'What we stumbled across?'

'Don't know, Yuri, but I've a feeling simply finding it will change our lives.'

'Да.'

I opened the microphone, 'Gerald, this had a serious impact at some time. Are you seeing these wires and cylinders?'

A different voice replied, 'Hi Evelyn. Peter Wright here. NASA's taking over for a while and I'll be your liaison with target four. Gerald will look after the unscrambled communications. We're re-designating it AD1 for Alien Device One. Stand by while we assess the video. I take it you're sure it isn't a hoax.'

41

'Copy that. I'm looking around for the mother ship as we speak!' I said. I'd met Peter Wright a few times at the Johnson Space Center. He was a very cold individual with apparently no sense of humour.

'Ha,' I said in an aside to Yuri, 'they're talking about us behind our backs. You got plenty of images?'

'Yes.'

'I'm still recording continuous eight K video,' I said. I didn't want to stop recording in case it reacted to us and I had plenty of memory cards.

'What is this thing, Eva?'

'Something more advanced than us. I'm glad we can see inside. At least we know it's not a bomb.'

'Our mission parameters will take drastic change of direction, I am thinking.'

'Yes, no doubt.'

'It seems only mechanical thing.'

'Yes, Yuri. No little green men arrived in this.'

'Evelyn?' Peter's voice.

'Copy.'

'We'd like you to camp out beside it there. We want some time to discuss this Earth-side. Any problem with that? Resources? Air?'

I looked at Yuri and he shook his head.

'No problem, Peter,' I said.

'Hello, Evelyn, Gerald here, copy?' came over the insecure channel a few minutes later.

'Yes, Gerald?'

'We want to think about whether we want you to nudge this one to burn it up or whether it might be worth cutting off and keeping the array. Are you okay to stay with it until morning?'

'No problem, Gerald,' I said, knowing the conversation was for the benefit of the ears of the listening public.

'By the way,' continued Gerald, 'We've lost your video feed. Can you check out your end?'

'Copy that, Gerald. I'll examine the connections. When did it go down?'

'It was broadcasting fine then suddenly cut. Happened about forty minutes ago.'

'Copy that. Might be the antenna. I'll get back to you,' I said.

The main reason for the security delay was in case we had a catastrophic accident, but it was also useful if we didn't want the public or media to catch sight of something until we'd examined it, exactly as had happened here. Those who designed the system were thinking "military" not "alien". Having to conduct some subterfuge was not that unexpected. The nature of our discovery, however, was of Earth-shattering proportions. It had Area 51 written all over it.

'Early dinner, Eva?' asked Yuri, unstrapping himself and moving over to the storage lockers.

'Any roast chicken in those supplies?'

'Да.'

'Could murder a gin and tonic.'

'Sorry. Bar's dry,' he replied.

We both moved to the back of the craft to eat, floating in mid-air watching an alien artefact from God knows where, rotating before us. One side incredibly alien and the other seriously trashed. What was it and why was it here? The questions were mounting.

After dinner, I reported back to Gerald on the open channel that the video dropout did appear to be a fault with our antenna, so we'd have to replace it when we returned to the ISS. That would explain to the media and public why there was no video feed.

I had come to space to help rid low-Earth orbit of worrying space junk and now I was becoming embroiled in the most incredible adventure. The significance to the world of our discovery of this alien wreck, would be enormous. We finally knew, once and for all, we weren't alone in the universe.

Our current aspect had the artefact spinning slowly in front of us with the majesty of the rotating Earth beneath it. Earth had been the only place we knew of which supported life. This object proved not only that life existed elsewhere, but much more importantly, *intelligent* life.

After dinner, Yuri backed us off to a safe distance, I shut down unnecessary systems and put on my harness. I set the laser rangefinder to ping the object silently once a minute and set off an alarm if the gap opened or closed by more than a metre. I tried to sleep, but with AD1 spinning in front of me I knew sleep wouldn't come easily. I wished I could tell my dad.

5 Secrecy

Yuri speaking Russian on a secure channel woke me.

It took a moment to become fully alert and check our alien friend hadn't done anything unexpected.

'Yes, sir,' said Yuri in Russian.

Who was he saying "Yes, sir" to? I'd missed the bulk of the conversation. A voice I didn't recognise sounded from the intercom. It was ending the transmission, thanking "Captain Bulgakov" and telling him Roscosmos would keep him informed. I knew Yuri was still in the Russian military. Were they trying to muscle in on our find?

Yuri thanked the speaker and called him "sir" again. The slight hiss of the encrypted channel faded.

'Who was that? Didn't recognise the voice.'

'He, dear Eva, is President Gorelov.'

'You're kidding?'

'No one kids about our glorious leader,' he said seriously then laughed.

'I only overheard the end where he said Roscosmos would keep you informed. Are you permitted to tell me the rest of it?'

'Yes, it okay, Eva. Classified obviously, but Americans want to keep lid on this and ...'

'The *Americans*?'

'Yes, it is them who want classified. We, Russians that is, are going along with it for time being. I've been ordered to not discuss it with anyone except encrypted space agency connections.'

'But why was it President Gorelov calling you?'

'They taking this very serious indeed. Bet you get special call in morning.'

My dashboard indicated four in the morning GMT. Moscow would be getting to work, but not Britain yet.

'You think they will try stifle this news?' he asked.

'Sounds like the sort of thing governments would do.'

'Area 51? Even Russians heard of it!'

'Good God! With that thing sitting in front of us, I wonder whether there *is* something in Area 51. Maybe they really do have an alien spaceship there.'

We exchanged more serious glances. Given the nature of our discovery, the possibility was no longer a joke. No astronauts I knew of believed in UFOs – or so they said. Maybe this wasn't the first alien object to be found. Had our governments been lying to us all these years? Was this object just one of many, including alien creatures and entire flying saucers?

Still guarding its secrets, revolving silently, it was revealing nothing but its extra-terrestrial innards.

I took a sip of water and slipped out of the harness to brace myself, stretch, and do some exercises.

'Want a coffee?'

'Please, Eva.'

We floated over our seats with our hot pouches, observing this piece of alien scrap and wondering how much was already known in the corridors of power about alien devices.

Coffee in the middle of a night period was a soon-regretted idea, but I did manage to slip back into a fitful sleep a while later.

«»«O»»»

My alarm awoke me at seven. It hadn't been a dream. An alien artefact revolved only a few metres in front of me. I metaphorically pinched myself to be sure it was real.

What about the secrecy? I wished I'd heard Yuri's full conversation with Gorelov. It seemed weird that the Americans wanted secrecy. I would've expected it to be the Russians. Surely with such an international situation, no one could keep a lid on this. All those space agency scientists and communicators in America, Canada, Japan, Europe, and Russia knew about AD1. How could it possibly be hushed up?

I opened the general communication channel.

'Good morning, ESA, we're up and about, over.'

'Good morning, Yuri, Evelyn. What's the weather like up there?' came from Gerald.

'You're in early, Gerald. Black sky but no rain! Made your minds up about keeping the array from target four yet?'

'No. I'll let you know as soon as we can, Eve. Someone's trying to unearth the spec from the archives. I go off duty at eight.'

'Copy that.'

'Hello, NASA secure,' I said using the encrypted channel.

'Good morning, Evelyn, Yuri,' said Roger Watts who was standing in for Peter Wright during the US night period.

'Any thoughts about how you're going to get it to Area 51?' I said glibly.

'Ha-ha, yes. That would start the tongues wagging, wouldn't it?' he said with a Texan drawl.

'That wasn't an answer, Roger.'

He ignored my jibe. 'We'll get back to you as soon as we can. It's still the middle of the night down here so the boffins won't be up and about for several hours.'

'Okay. We'll stand by.'

I looked at Yuri and raised my eyebrows.

'Breakfast, Eva?'

'Sure. One of those ham and mushroom omelettes, please. They're delicious.'

'Coming up,' he said, removing his harness and gliding to the rear storage area.

Breakfast was consumed while watching AD1's inscrutability with the night side of the Earth as a backdrop, only our own lights illuminating its iridescent hull.

'Do you think we've been visited by aliens, Yuri?'

'No idea. Understand why it kept secret to stop panic.'

'You think ordinary people would panic?'

'Possibly, Eva. Ignorant majority. A sensational headline could make boil over into panic. Like Orson Welles Martian panic.'

'What was that, Yuri? Who was he?'

'Ha. Thought you sci-fi mad. You never heard of?'

'No. Spill the beans.'

'In America, hundred years ago, Orson Welles reading *War of the Worlds* by Jules Verne. Was live radio broadcast. Caused panic as he described destruction by Martians moving across US countryside. People thought real. Surprised you not heard of it.'

'I'll do a search. Can't imagine it causing panic. Didn't H.G. Wells write that?'

'Yes, Wells, but caused much panic, Eva.'

'So they're keeping a lid on it for that reason?'

'Probably. You the psychologist. What you think?'

'I think secrets never come to any good.'

'Yes. You right, I think also, Eva.'

'Wonder what it's made of?' I mused.

'Nothing I recognise. Anodised aluminum is similar in appearance.'

'Aluminium,' I said, pronouncing every syllable.

'There no second i in it.'

'There was. The Americans cut it out for some reason. Why they cut it out of aluminium and not iridium, plutonium or the other 'iums is a mystery.'

'Alu-min-i-u-m,' Yuri said slowly as if conjuring a spell with the word.

'Wonder how old it is?'

'Metal pristine, even forward-facing gold area. Some pitting on main body though.'

'Yes,' I said. 'No abrasion at all on the gold nose cone. Must be extremely resistant or new.'

'Cannot be real gold then. Gold is soft.'

'Yes. Unless it's very new.'

'Hello, Evelyn. Do you copy?' the ESA secure line cut in.

'Copy you,' I replied.

'Call for you.'

I raised my eyebrows to Yuri.

'Hello. Doctor Slater?'

'Yes, it is.'

'This is Roger Clarke.' Fuck me, it was the Prime Minister! I wished I'd had more time to think on the psychological aspects of this discovery before such an important call.

'Yes, sir.'

'I'm calling you over this encrypted channel about the object which has been designated AD1.'

'Yes, sir,' I didn't know how to address him but guessed *sir* would be safe enough.

'We want to learn more about it and are putting the investigation into the hands of NASA at this stage. I'm afraid I need you to consider the whole subject classified.'

'I understand, sir. Might I enquire for how long it might be classified?'

'We're concerned an unprepared announcement could cause panic. It needs to be thought through when we've more information.'

'Sir. Permission to speak freely?'

'Yes, Evelyn, please do.'

Ha, first name terms now.

'I was wondering last night about all the conspiracy theories over UFOs, Area 51, and the like. If you slap *Secret* on this device and the news leaks, it'll be like a confirmation all the UFO nonsense was true after all. It could be incredibly damaging.'

'Evelyn, Area 51, flying saucers, and all the other UFO conspiracy rumours really are just that. As far as we're aware, this is the first alien object ever encountered and we need to be careful how we handle it.'

'Are you sure, sir? I'm aware of the Official Secrets Act so won't talk about this or anything else without permission but would hate to later discover I'd been misled and all the UFO stuff was true after all. It would be good to know about it now, sir, if that were the case.'

Yuri's piercing blue eyes widened at my forthrightness. I could be very opinionated sometimes, but Mr Clarke sounded measured in his response, 'Evelyn, I understand your concern, but I promise you, as far as I'm aware personally, this is the first alien artefact ever discovered. I promise you. We do, however, need time to consider all the implications of this thing. You do understand that, don't you?'

'Yes, sir. Thank you for taking the time to explain, Mr Prime Minister.' Perhaps it was better than *sir*.

'So, you'll work with NASA on this and keep it classified?'

'Of course, sir. I merely wanted to express a view on the possible dangers of unnecessary secrecy.' I'd no choice about complying. I didn't fancy prison or being grounded. 'Can I mention something else about the discovery?'

'Of course. Go ahead.'

'Just something to consider, sir. If news of the device were released soon then the world will be able to get used to the fact there are other people in the universe. Then, if we actually get to see or meet with them in the future, that can be introduced bit by bit, defusing xenophobia or horror... at their appearance, perhaps. Drip feeding information soon after it's discovered could prevent more serious problems at a later date. Have you seen *Arrival*? I hope the military can be kept on a leash.'

'Yes, I saw it as a youth and understand your concerns. You've a psychology degree, yes?'

'My doctorate, sir.'

'Thank you, Doctor Slater. You've made your points well, and we'll consider them. If you can work with Peter Wright on this for the time being, I promise you'll know before anything is released. You've made a great discovery and credit will be given to you and Captain Bulgakov when the time comes. Pass on my regards to him.'

Yuri spoke, 'Thank you, Mr Prime Minister.'

'Excellent. I'm sure you'll both get great satisfaction from this discovery. It's exciting for all of us. What's it doing right now?'

'Just revolving in front of us. We're both still in some shock, sir. It's so obviously alien.'

'Quite. Hopefully we'll find a way to move forward with it. Thank you for your cooperation, Doctor Slater. Goodbye.'

'Goodbye, Mr Prime Minister.' The encryption static dropped off the connection.

'Good God, Eva! Cannot believe you speak to your Prime Minister like that.'

'I was polite.'

'Yes, but how you question him. Gorelov would go into a rage. I would sure be vacationing a while in Siberia as soon as I return.'

We both laughed, and it relieved the tension.

'I have strong opinions about this, Yuri. The world has been fed lies and distortions by its political and religious leaders for millennia. I believe in truth in all things. I want this truth to be opened up and talked about,' I lowered my voice conspiratorially, 'and frankly I won't stand by and allow it to be "covered up" if they try to do that.'

'You cannot speak of it, Eva. Classified means classified.'

'I'm also thinking about how to stay involved. I was glad he asked about my degree as now he knows I'm qualified to discuss cultural shock. Maybe I can get on a committee or something. Anyway, I'll go along with it while it's being investigated but, if it becomes a permanent secret, I'll blow the lid off it.'

'And you will be as all, how to say, conspiring theorists.'

'Conspiracy,' I corrected. 'Yes, you're probably right. *"That nutter Evelyn Slater who believes the Earth has been visited by aliens."* Ha-ha. That's exactly how they'd label me, but I've ideas up my sleeve.' I winked at him.

'Be careful, friend.' He reached over and squeezed my hand firmly.

»«O»»

Débris collecting was off the agenda for a while as AD1 was sure to be the priority. There were so many questions mounting.

What fuel was in those spheroids? What had been inside the cylindrical tubes? How come the wires didn't require insulation? What caused the iridescent glow of the main hull? Why hadn't the gold area been damaged at all by space dust? What was the purpose of the craft? Where had it come from? Surely there was no civilisation in the solar system which could have made this, yet it didn't seem to be equipped to travel light distances. Could I believe Roger Clarke?

Surprisingly, I did believe him. I'd never believed in UFOs and Area 51 having a flying saucer, but there was always a lingering doubt in the back of an inquiring mind like mine.

How sure was I that NASA didn't have something in Area 51? Might my outspoken approach even put my life in danger? These questions and many more ran through my mind. I was annoyed with myself for not making a better case for an early release of the news of what we'd found. More coffee was needed.

I was floating with my face inches from the front windows, studying the detail of AD1's interior, when Peter came online.

'Good morning, Evelyn, copy?'

I returned to my seat. 'Copy.'

'We want to use your small claw camera, so we need to stop the rotation. How can you stop it without damaging the nose assembly?'

Yuri and I had already assessed possible places to hold the device. I didn't dare grip the gold rod and there was nothing else to grasp at the front other than the melon-shaped node, which was probably going to slip through my grasp. It also had those thimble-like structures and I didn't want to damage them.

'I think it must be the back. What do you think, Yuri?'

'Certainly. But want not be behind jets in case activated.'

'Why not park off to one side? I could grip the jet nozzle closest to the two damaged spheroids. If they're fuel containers it'd likely mean those jets would be unable to fire. We'd also be more than ten metres away from any trouble. I can't imagine why anything would fire.'

'No, but rather safely than sorry.'

'Okay. Move us back ten metres and towards the rear of the object so I can observe the rear assembly again.'

The Wagon's thrusters fired and, within a minute or so, we were stationary once more. The alien craft was now off to the left of us and we were looking straight across its rear.

I unfolded the left arm and pointed it forwards to maximum extent.

'Forward a metre or so, please. I want the claw central to the rear assembly.'

The Wagon moved forwards slowly and stopped exactly where I wanted it. I turned the mechanical hand in towards the craft and rotated it to match the object's spin.

'I can't grasp anything but the central nozzle. Not ideal.'

'I have idea, Eva.'

'Go on.'

'If park directly behind AD1, leaving ten metres, could put us in a spin to match it. Then you reach forward and grab any nozzle. Spin will be uncomfortable.'

'Great idea.'

'Ah. Problem! If it fires jet, we directly behind. Not good idea after all,' he added with disappointment.

'Okay. Do it in front. I can reach around and grasp one of the damaged rear jet nozzles.'

'If it fired a jet, golden rod could pierce our front.'

'No. Once I've got hold of it, it shouldn't be able to move. As soon as we drop out of the spin, we can turn it sideways on.'

I used my computer and calculated the stresses which would likely be applied to the joints.

'Should be okay. With it being hollow, the mass can't be too great. We just need to take care and stop the spin as quickly as possible so that we can move to the side.'

'Right. Let me work maths a minute,' Yuri said and began attacking his keyboard.

The rear angle showed me the top of the inside of the object where there were bunches of the test-tube-type cylinders.

There was an unexpected thrust from my side and the Wagon moved to face the alien object and pulled back.

'Making us error space, Eva. Get NASA clearance.'

'Okay,' I affirmed and continued on the secure channel, 'Peter, can we have a *go* for Yuri to put us into a spin along AD1's axis? It'll allow me to hold any part of the rear assembly. Yuri will use his thrusters to slow the spin, saving too much stress on the claw arm interface which I can lock solid during the manoeuvre in case it reacts.'

'Give us a moment,' said Peter.

There was obviously quite a team at mission control now and they were double-checking everything to do with this alien object.

About three minutes later, 'Okay, Evelyn. You've a go for that.'

'Copy that, Peter.'

'Right. This going to be for sure disorientating as put in angular momentum,' Yuri said, tightening his harness. I did likewise.

There was a distinct kick from underneath and behind. The effect on my stomach was worse than at any time since lift-off, and we started to spin. The Earth was rotating in front of us. We were no longer weightless and were being forced outwards. There was some nausea, but I managed to control it. I closed my eyes but that was worse. I concentrated on AD1 and tried to ignore the fact the entire universe was now revolving around us. Copernicus would have had a fit. I knew Einstein would have had no problem with it. What about Newton?

'Not good sensation,' said Yuri.

'No. You okay, though?'

'Yes. Can tolerate. You?'

'Okay. Did you know Neil Armstrong got into a dreadful spin when they were trying to dock with an Agena during the Gemini program. He almost blacked out and someone else would have been the first man on the moon.'

'No. Had no idea. How'd it happen?' he asked.

'Rogue thruster, I think.'

Another two or three minutes passed with numerous small thruster adjustments and Yuri moved us forwards so that we were just a few centimetres from the golden rod.

'Peter?' I said.

'Copy.'

'Peter. Yuri has put the SDIV into the appropriate spin along AD1's axis. Most uncomfortable but we're almost there and I'll be able to grab one of the thruster cones which is positioned by the split spheroids. Hopefully that'll be safe.'

About a minute passed.

'God, this is uncomfortable, Yuri.'

'Damn right,' he said.

'Go with that. Your call,' said Peter.

'How's that?' asked Yuri.

'Perfect,' I said. In relation to AD1, we were now stationary, despite our sickening spin.

'NASA, I'm going to grasp it.'

'You've a go for that.'

I made some delicate motions with the manipulator arm to bring the claw in and around the object. I opened the jaws to about forty centimetres and extended the silicon grippers inlaid into the jaws. I hit the "instant grip" button which closed the claw upon one of the jet nozzles attached to a broken fuel container. Yuri must have the spin absolutely spot on as there was no transfer of any momentum.

'Got it. Feels firm. Pressure five kilos per square centimetre. No sign of any distortion of the nozzle,' I said to

Yuri, then to Peter, 'NASA. I have hold of the jet. Are we go to slow the spin?'

'Go for that.'

I increased the grip to ten kilos for security and locked the hand, arm, and joints rigidly into position.

'Go, Yuri,' I said.

A kick from in front and behind reduced our angular momentum. I kept a close eye on the object. I thought it was dead, but I knew Yuri was worried about it reacting to us.

'Slowly does it, Yuri.' God, I felt sick. I told myself to control it.

'Yes.'

Gradually our spin reduced, and we all came to a halt, including our stomachs.

'Spin halted,' I reported and felt my pulse returning to normal.

'Copy that. Can you reposition and get your high-res camera inside?' asked Peter.

'Roger that, but give us a minute. That was most uncomfortable,' I said.

Yuri and I relaxed and breathed deeply for a minute or two, then I relinquished my hold and Yuri flew us around to the gash. My right manipulator hand eased its way to the entrance. The top finger concealed a high-resolution close-up camera designed to let me undertake delicate electronic repairs to any satellite which might be worth saving during our mission. It was now dead centre of the hole.

'What would you like to do, Peter?'

'I'm sending you a profile of Doctor Reginald Naughton, Evelyn. Have a read.'

'Will do, Peter.'

Almost instantly my console showed a picture of a mid-thirties scientist. The blurb told me he was a professor emeritus at MIT in astronomy, exogeology, and theoretical exobiology. An expert in the study of the geology and biology of other planets. There was an extensive list of scientific papers he'd written and books he'd published.

'Okay, Peter. I've got the gist and Yuri's reading it too.'

'Copy that, Evelyn. I'm handing over to him.'

Damn it all – that was a bit of a surprise. I hadn't expected him to hear me saying "I've got the gist" – it sounded dismissive. I should've been more flattering.

'Doctor Reg Naughton here, Doctor Slater. I've got some checks I'd like you to make.'

'Copy that, Doctor Naughton. Pleased to be talking to you. That's an impressive profile you have.'

'Pleased to be talking to you too. I'd like to change that theoretical exobiology into the practical version sometime and this offers the best opportunity. You can't see any little green men inside, can you?'

'Ha ha. Not a chance!' I replied.

'Ah, well. Back to reality. Can you see the broken cylinder hanging on the end of the purple and red wires?'

'Yes.'

'I'd like to examine the inside. We can't make out what happens to the wires. They appear to blend with the surface of the cylinder, and I want to see if there's any sort of continuation inside.'

'Copy that. You've got a good picture?'

'Yes, Doctor Slater.'

There didn't seem to be anything protruding into the inside of the cylinder. I moved the claw to the left and approached the broken tube, retracting the other fingers from the grip and telescoped the camera from the top finger. It now extended on a two-millimetre diameter tube which I pushed into the open cylinder and slowly scanned the interior.

'Odd. Nothing. No hole or blister on the inside,' Dr Naughton said quietly.

'Yes. Strange,' I agreed.

'Doctor Slater. Can you come out of there and give us some close-up views of the outside of the complete cylinder to the right of the broken one? We want to examine where the wires attach to it.'

I directed the camera to the next cylinder. The wires seemed to become part of it, unlike human hairs which emerge from a follicle. Even the colour of these wires blended into the cylinder's base colour where they joined it.

'Amazing,' said Dr Naughton. 'Can you close in on the node on the far side of the interior which has the huge cluster of wires emerging from it? Let's call it the control hub for now.'

'Copy that.'

Avoiding trailing wires, I pushed the claw slowly into the cavity towards what was reminiscent of a durian fruit with dozens of pointed protrusions, each of them being the terminal for three or four wires of different colours.

'Doctor Slater, using your eyes on the real thing, can you count how many different colours of wires there are going into that thing?'

'No. Not with eyeballs. I'm about four metres away from it and from here not one wire is the same colour as any other. They all seem to be different. Any similar colours are our human inability to separate the visible wavelengths.'

'Yes, I was thinking the same.'

'The colours on the camera are pretty damn accurate, Doctor Naughton. Probably more accurate than our eyes.'

'Yes.'

There was a movement. Something had happened. My claw was being pulled in to the craft.

'Back off,' I shouted.

Yuri hit a thruster and we pulled away, my claw hand ripped several wires with it as it came out of the gash and scraped against the opening on the way. I retracted everything in double-quick time to try to save the delicate camera shaft.

'What the hell?' I said.

'It fired thruster,' said Yuri.

'What's happened?' asked Dr Naughton.

Peter said, 'Quiet. Let them concentrate.'

'What? *It*? The artefact fired a thruster?' I asked.

'Yes, it's back to original rotation,' said Yuri.

'Peter. Are you there? Did you see that? This thing isn't as dead as we thought!'

'Yes. We saw it,' said Peter.

I moved my claw around to the other arm and checked the camera was okay. I eyeballed it through the window.

'Peter, the camera is still usable, but we've damaged the stalk section. It won't fully retract.'

'Copy that.'

'We also lost a cylinder. It's floating away. Yuri, pursue it.'

The Wagon turned and chased after the cylinder. It was amazing how quickly the gap opened, and it was difficult to see against the Earth. A few minutes and almost a kilometre later I managed to grasp it.

'Got it, Peter.'

'Well done.'

'I'm going to tape it to our outside store.'

While Yuri flew us back to AD1, I busied myself with both arms, collected some gaffer tape from the underneath store and taped the escaped cylinder next to the deorbules.

'Secure,' I said.

'Copy that.'

'What do you want to do now? Something in that thing realised its rotation had stopped and restarted it,' I said, as we returned from our chase and took up a position facing the side of AD1.

'Yes. Copy that. Sit tight you two.' I heard the encrypted line cut out.

Only Yuri's quick reverse thrust had saved my right claw.

The crippled alien artefact was fighting back. What other tricks would be in its repertoire?

6 Capturing the Artefact

It was a while before discussions began again. We were all shocked that the alien device was still active, considering its damage.

I had an idea, 'What if I reached forward and grabbed the top edge of the damaged side?'

'It would put a lot of momentum into the SDIV, Evelyn,' said Gerald, who was now back on duty. Peter had deferred to Gerald's superior knowledge about the Wagon.

'Could ride with it instead of resisting,' suggested Yuri.

'Wouldn't it fire the thruster again?' asked Peter.

'We have to face the possibility,' I said, 'but if we hold on, wouldn't it run out of fuel eventually?'

'What about trying to disconnect those spheroids?' asked Peter. 'They're almost certainly fuel containers.'

'I'm sure that would help, but I can't do something so delicate while we're spinning. It's best to grab it by the hull and find out how it reacts. I can release, and Yuri can back us off if necessary. If we can't stop its rotation, we can never get it back to the space station's orbit. It's vital we find a way.'

'Give us a minute to consider this, Evelyn,' said Peter.

'Copy that.'

I switched to the unencrypted channel and called Jean, who was one of Gerald's team at ESA.

'Jean. You there?'

'Here, Eve.'

'Can you give Mario a call for me and tell him we're safe and have got a problem with detaching the array on this satellite?'

'No problem, Eve.'

'Also, I was supposed to be doing a live schools' broadcast at eleven. Can you contact them and postpone? Better make it a week hence to give us time to resolve this.'

'No problem. I'll get onto those, Eve.'

'Thanks, Jean. Out.'

The secure channel came to life immediately, 'You've a go. Do what you think best, Evelyn,' said Peter.

'Copy that,' I replied, pleased that Peter was finally realising I was more than just an interface with the Wagon.

I extended the heavy-duty left arm and slammed the jaws shut. They opened, and I practised again.

The biggest danger was not knowing how much mass was involved and, as the artefact rotated, it would put a considerable torque on the arm joints. There was, without doubt, a danger of breaking the arm off.

Yuri and I discussed our options.

'Hello, Peter. Just be aware we could lose an arm in the worst scenario.'

'Copy you, Evelyn. As you say, we don't have a choice,' said Peter.

'We're going to have a try at this.'

'Copy that. Sounds good.'

'Ready, Yuri?'

'Ready.'

I watched the object rotate and moved my main jaws into position facing it, about midway up its side.

I observed a complete revolution and, as the damaged area disappeared, I said, 'Next time, Yuri.'

'Right.'

The gash spun into view. The jaws jumped forward and I slammed them shut. The moment they closed, Yuri fired a counter thruster which almost instantly stopped the artefact's spin. The Wagon's system of gimballed gyros whined into service, counteracting the rotation imparted to us as we stabilised our combined mass.

We sat in space, the jaws firmly locked on and holding the object stationary. The stresses on the arm joints were well within tolerance.

'Peter, we're stationary. Did anyone keep a note of the time before it fired its thrusters last time?'

'Copy that. I'll find out.'

We kept still and held our breath. What would AD1 do?

A minute later Peter called back, 'Hello, Evelyn. It was twenty-three minutes fifteen seconds stationary before it reacted. That doesn't mean it'll do the same this time, of course.'

'Copy that, but I'm hoping we're dealing with an automatic system. If we are, it should fire on schedule. We're staying in readiness anyway,' I replied, checking my chronograph.

Four minutes and fifty seconds had passed since I grabbed it. I set a countdown timer on my computer and we both watched the countdown. While waiting, I used my other arm to relocate the cylinder we'd captured onto the artefact so that everything was kept together. The tape seemed to adhere to the inner surface of its hull without a problem.

Ten minutes. Nothing. Twenty minutes. Nothing. The timer was now counting down from fifteen seconds. Yuri gripped his thruster control more tightly. Ten, nine, eight, seven, six, five, four, three, two, one.

There was a tug on my mechanical arm. Yuri applied a tiny reverse thrust and we held it.

'It fired dead on twenty-three fifteen, Peter,' I said, 'Yuri has countered it.'

'Copy that.'

I was hoping it was going to continue to fire its thruster as the fuel would then eventually run out. That it only used a tiny thrust was a disappointment. I set the counter again and we relaxed.

Dead on time it fired again. Once more Yuri countered the motion and we held it fast.

'And again, Peter, dead on time,' I said.

'Copy that.'

'Any ideas, Yuri? We could mess about like this for years. It only uses a tiny thrust, so the fuel is not going to run out any time soon. I thought it might fire continuously to try to get back to speed.'

'Would arm hold if fire orbital burn to take us to station orbit?'

'It shouldn't be a problem if it doesn't fire its main motors to change back.'

'Hmm, yes.'

'What're you thinking?' I asked.

'Get it back to ISS. Attach to Japanese open-to-space platform. Once secure you can work on fuel cylinders and disable it,' said Yuri.

'I don't know if NASA would want it so close to the station.'

'Hey, it's not fired,' said Yuri.

'Peter. It's twenty-six minutes since the last burn and no sign of any more.'

'Copy that. Continue to monitor.'

Another two hours passed without any further reaction.

'Peter, we'd like you to consider taking it back to the station orbit.'

'Copy. Let's have your calculations.'

I put my vectors into a transmission and we waited for confirmation. Another hour passed. Still no sign of life from our companion.

'Evelyn, we're a go on that, but we'd like you to have a break first for lunch and a drink et cetera. It'll put you in a better vector position for the ISS if we wait fifty minutes,' said Peter.

'Copy that.'

'I've put automatic thruster program into console, Eva. I pay rest room visit and make my lunch. If it moves, hit alt plus F-seven on your console.'

'Okay. Got that.'

Yuri unstrapped himself and I monitored our friend. He returned with coffee, spare water flask, and hot meal. Once he was back in his seat and in harness, I reminded him of the emergency detach button and paid my own visits. We tried to relax for thirty minutes, watching our captive closely for any sign of life.

'Ready for orbit burn?' asked Yuri.

'I'll bring it in to the side of the Wagon first.'

I used the arm to bring AD1 parallel to the Wagon and retracted the elbow joint to hold it tight against us. We didn't know what sort of jets it might deploy once the orbit changed.

'Evelyn, Yuri. We'd like you to wear suits and helmets, please,' said Peter.

'Copy that,' I said. It seemed a sensible precaution in case AD1 did something unexpected and damaged the Scaffy Wagon.

We both climbed into our pressure suits, turned on the environmental systems, and closed the visors. These suits would protect us if our hull was breached.

'Suited up, Peter. The moment Yuri completes the burn I intend to move it away from the hull for safety.'

'Roger that, Evelyn.'

'Firing in three, two, one, fire,' said Yuri.

Once again, we were on our backs as the burn increased our altitude and slowed our orbital velocity. We were soon in orbit a hundred kilometres ahead of the station.

I pushed my left manipulation arm out and forward to position the object ahead of us and facing obliquely to our left, so we weren't in direct line of fire of its jets or the object itself if it broke free under power.

'Burn complete,' reported Yuri.

'Copy that.'

'AD1 back at arm's length,' I said.

'Copy that.'

'Any ideas, Peter? I'm concerned about bringing this thing too close to the ISS.'

'Yes, copy that. We're making plans.'

'Would be good to listen in.'

'Mainly diplomacy, Evelyn. I'll get back to you.'

To Yuri I said, 'What do you think?'

'Think have America, Europe, Russia, and Japan trying agree. We have to enact when finalised. Could be some time,' he said and laughed.

'I guess you're right.'

'Our friend's still being obedient?' asked Peter.

'So far,' I said.

'Okay, you guys. Relax as best you can. This might take some time.'

'Is Doctor Naughton still there?' I asked.

'Hi, Doctor Slater. Yes, I'm still here.'

'I'm bringing AD1 around in front of the ship at right angles to us and I can use the camera on it. Tell me what you'd like to see.'

'Okay, I'll move to the monitor.'

The second arm approached AD1 and I manoeuvred the camera to the jagged entrance. I programmed a retraction movement to enact on the F16 key.

Under Dr Naughton's instructions, but using my own initiative too, we surveyed the interior of AD1 and particularly the section which he'd designated the control centre. We found we were a good team and were soon on first name terms. He was happy for me to examine the spheroids at the rear of the interior, just keeping him advised as I made measurements. It was good to be undertaking some real science.

Stopping for a coffee break, I examined the hieroglyphs. They were so alien. Even their alignment was alien. We were not sure if they were meant to be read from right to left, left to right, top to bottom or bottom to top.

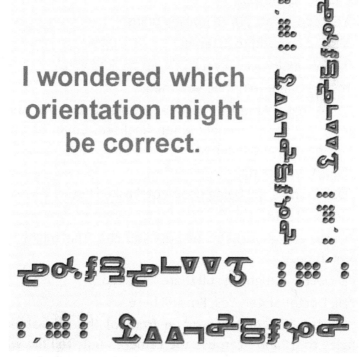

I wondered which orientation might be correct.

Deciphering would be a major problem and, in that moment, I knew my involvement would cease. If I were

68

going to stay involved, I'd have to charm and cajole my way into the inner circle of whoever began to examine it.

AD1 made no attempt to rotate again, nor change its orbit. That, in itself, was interesting. Did it *know* it was being manhandled by an intelligent species or were its undeniably damaged, automatic systems failing?

The hours dragged on. Twenty kilometres from the ISS was the closest we were allowed. There was nothing for us to do until they formulated a plan. It was frustrating being kept out of the loop. We hung up our pressure suits and helmets and both of us tried to do some exercises, hooking our feet in storage cupboards and conducting sit-ups and bicep-pumping with improvised weights, but always with one eye on the visitor.

While in our makeshift gym, we discussed options. We couldn't park the object here because it could start up again if unattended and, because of its damage, it might drop out of orbit and be lost forever. If it was being restrained, its automatic systems perhaps recognised it was being studied. Was that why it was inactive? Maybe the makers intended it to now be communicating with us, but the damage was preventing it. I'd already run radio frequency scans and detected nothing from minimum to maximum frequencies. The ISS crew, who were now aware of our discovery, were also watching us through the entire electromagnetic spectrum and there was nothing of any description being emanated. No calls for help to some mega-ship in the outer solar system which would come and annihilate us for stealing its baby!

Yuri and I couldn't sit out here indefinitely as muscle and bone wastage didn't take long to have an effect in microgravity. Our improvised gym was no substitute for ISS equipment.

This all led me into formulating a plan, but in GMT it was already night. Houston would be approaching evening.

'Peter, you there?' I asked over the secure link.

'You just caught me. I was about to leave and hand over to Roger,' Peter responded.

'I've had an idea.'

'Fire away, Evelyn,' he said with a sceptical tone of voice. It almost sounded as if he knew the idea wouldn't be of any value but didn't want to sound disinterested – or maybe he was just late to his kids' football game, or something. Had Yuri and I become a couple of plebs now the designated scientists had moved in? Had they forgotten my scientific background? I could be doing him an injustice, but it bugged me.

'We've emergency supplies on board, but we can't exercise in the Wagon and we should try to get back to the ISS. Why not bring the Progress craft, currently attached to the Russian sector, over here? I can strap AD1 to the Progress. I know you can control those things at a far greater range than twenty kilometres, so if AD1 plays up, the Progress can keep it under control.'

'Sounds interesting.'

'Also, I surmise you've already decided it can't be returned to Earth owing to possible contamination, or being destroyed en route, so I've a further suggestion.'

'Continue, Doctor Slater,' came Dr Naughton's voice – ah, I'd an interested audience after all.

'I'm assuming nothing is a greater priority than investigating AD1. We can't take it to the ISS in case it causes a problem. It can't be taken back to Earth, so a structure is going to have to be built within which it can be studied. A prefabricated pressurised sphere, sent up in sections via Ariane Eight, could be assembled by the Scaffy Wagon a safe distance from the ISS. The scientists would then have their own environment in which to study it.'

'Yes, yes, we'd considered a variation on that,' said Dr Naughton, 'but we'd veered towards bringing the artefact down in a Dragon re-entry vehicle and taking it to Antarctica, but we were still concerned about contamination even there, and, as you say, the danger of losing it on re-entry.'

'Yes. I see the benefits of what you're suggesting, Evelyn,' said a much more positive Peter.

'Plus, while we're waiting for the parts, Yuri and I could get back to work and offer shuttle facilities to and from the research dome and the ISS if it were done up here.'

Ivan spoke in Russian and Yuri translated for Dr Naughton and Peter. 'Ivan says it is a good idea and they'll discuss it at Roscosmos.'

'Okay, Evelyn, Ivan, Yuri. I'll consult with the others and get back to you, but it has great merit,' said Peter. I was glad he'd taken the idea on board.

'Oh, and Peter ...'

'Yes.'

'I want to be involved,' I said firmly.

'I would hope you could be,' said Dr Naughton.

'Well... it's not in my gift,' said Peter, 'but I'll pass it on. Now if I'm going to catch the powers that be tonight, I must go. Good thinking, Evelyn.'

The connection broke and Yuri said, 'You brilliant, Eva.'

'No, only determined. If we can keep it up here, I've a better chance of remaining involved.'

'Well, do not be forgetting your Russian friend when you famous person.'

7 Enacting the Plan

At the speed space agencies usually engaged, my seven months in space would be long over before my spherical research lab was built. Once we strapped AD1 to the Progress it might be the last time I ever saw it. I had to assume my involvement would only be on the fringe and I decided to make personal decisions based upon that.

The next morning, I copied video of the object onto one of the 8TB microSDXS cards I had for the cameras. I said nothing to Yuri, but I intended to hide this item for posterity. It showed the discovery, the stopping of its spin, the investigation of the interior and the bringing of it back to ISS orbit. The memory card was so tiny I should surely be able to find a way to conceal it on return to Earth. I wanted a record of humanity's greatest discovery away from government's hands. Keeping it was illegal, but the risks were outweighed by the importance of the record being secured in case AD1 were ever to be hushed up permanently. Hopefully, Mr Clarke would be true to his word and make an announcement eventually. The discovery was so exciting. We'd been contacted by aliens. Creatures from another world were interested in us and planet Earth. I couldn't allow that to be buried in some anonymous government bunker.

Late on the third day of our isolation, the Progress craft was given the go to approach us. We were about to be very busy indeed. I'd gone through our plans with mission control and had all the materials I needed among our accessories already strapped beneath the SDIV.

Progress vehicles are, outwardly, identical to a Soyuz, but didn't have any of the life support systems. Together with several private supply vessels, mainly based in the US, Europe, and Japan, these craft were the workhorses which kept the ISS supplied. They would blast off from Russia laden with supplies for the space station and would remain attached until the next craft was due. Each would be sealed up, filled with garbage from the ISS and would burn up on re-entry. The Progress wasn't reusable.

On board, it had an automatic docking system and could be flown remotely from the Russian sector of the International Space Station, which was what was happening now.

'One hundred metres,' said Yuri.

'Roger that,' replied Boris, another Soyuz pilot, who was remote-piloting the Progress.

It came to a halt about ten metres from us and we'd be responsible for completing the task.

AD1 had no hoops or loops anywhere for anchorage to the Progress so I would strap it tightly to the supply craft's hull to keep it in position. Its egg-like shape would be problematical, but the damaged section would allow straps to be tied together around it securely enough.

Yuri manoeuvred us to within a few metres.

'Hello, Gerald,' I said.

'Go ahead, Eve.'

'I need to let go of it now and change the robotic hand on my right arm. I'll grab it again as soon as I can. Yuri is going to keep a sharp eye in case there is any motion. I can swap hands in fewer than ten minutes so hopefully it won't realise it's been released.'

'Okay, you're go for that.'

Taking a deep breath, I opened the claw on my left hand, withdrawing the arm simultaneously.

Yuri gave a short burn and we withdrew about ten metres, so I had room to manipulate the arms under our belly where my accessories were stored. Faster than I'd ever done in simulation, I managed to remove the delicate hand from the right robotic arm, stow it, and attach a second heavy-duty claw, similar to the one on the left arm. Yuri brought us back in towards AD1 and I grasped it once more by the broken opening.

'Phew!' I said as an aside to Yuri then, to Gerald, 'Second heavy-duty robotic hand attached and AD1 reacquired.'

'Copy that.'

I took a strap from the accessories pallet and uncoiled it.

'Okay, Yuri, push AD1 tight to the waist of the Progress.'

'Roger that.'

Slowly the Wagon nudged the alien vessel up against the natural waistline between the two forward spherical sections of the Progress craft.

'Contact,' he said.

'Copy that,' from Gerald.

'Releasing the grasp,' I said, and the left arm released its grip on AD1.

Using both hands on my controls, like playing a video game, I manipulated the straps until AD1 was securely attached to the Progress. The process took a lot longer than the telling of it. Probably about ninety minutes.

'Secure, Gerald,' I said with some satisfaction and not a little relief.

'Copy that. Well done. You're go to return to ISS.'

'Copy that,' said Yuri.

««o»»

Back on the ISS, I headed straight for my personal space, picked up my small personal diary, and examined its cover.

Using a scalpel, I slit open the leather binding at the bottom of the back cover and slid the 8TB microSDXS card into the space between the cardboard binding and the leather. I used the end of the scalpel to push it into the top left-hand corner beside the spine. It was so small it didn't show through the leather cover at all. I used a drop of glue to reseal the cut. Not an invisible mend but good enough to fool anything except a forensic examination. Had I become the first ever space criminal?

Next, armed with some space shampoo, water, and body wipes, I headed to the loo. What a pleasure to clean myself – well as best one can ever do on the ISS.

Refreshed, I put on a change of clothes and Skyped Mario.

Oh, there he was. His smiling eyes searching my face for signs of stress or strain. Now I had to lie to him and he mustn't suspect anything. Was I up to it? I had to convince myself that what I was saying was the truth.

'I was worried, honey.'

'Love you. Sorry to cause concern.'

'What happened?'

'Oh, we had a dreadful spin on one of the satellites and it took ages to stop it. Then they didn't know if they wanted to keep the solar array or junk it with the satellite. Meant we had to spend two nights in the Wagon. Sorry.'

'You couldn't call me from there?'

'It wouldn't have been very private. Jean did let you know?'

'Yes, she did, but it's hardly like an assistant relaying, "She'll be late home from the office". It's worrying. You're in that tiny craft halfway round the world from the space station and anything could happen to you.'

'Mario, I wasn't in any danger. It was all under control, but it would've been ridiculous to come all the way back to the ISS without having resolved it.'

'And your video was down. Did you know? It meant none of us could see what was going on.'

'Who was us?'

'Well, I know your mum and dad, your sister, and my parents were trying to log in and the image was blank.'

'Yes, the antenna failed. Couldn't be helped,' God, I didn't like all of this lying and knowing one day he'd find out I wasn't telling him the truth. How would he feel about that? Was I jeopardising our love?

'Horrible not talking to you or being able to watch what you're doing. Especially knowing you were having trouble with that one.'

'Mario, I love you and I don't want to spend our precious time talking about this. What've you been up to?'

'Just work, really.'

'Right. Same as me!'

He knew I'd trapped him. 'Damn you, Eve, you always get the upper hand with me.'

'Any hand would do right now! I fantasise caressing your stubble and kissing you. I'm lonely up here, you know, and it's only been a few days. We've got months of this.'

'Sorry. I'll try not to worry, but the thought any second you could be gone in some accident...' His voice trailed off.

'Yes, and you might be in a train wreck or car crash. It's not easy for me, either darling.'

'I know.'

Neither of us spoke for a minute. Then he broke the silence. 'We're getting married as soon as you come back.'

'Oh, yeah? I haven't seen you on one knee yet.'

His face ducked out of view, a hand turned the monitor to a downward angle, and he was obviously on his knees.

'Doctor Evelyn Slater, BSc, MSc, MA, PhD, and space superheroine, will you marry me?'

'You always take the easy way out. Doing it in a video call! I want the real thing... in a crowded restaurant... with a diamond ring... and champagne... and everyone watching!'

'Damn you, Slater. You like seeing me suffer.'

'And I mightn't say yes then, either.'

We blew kisses and continued to talk a while with the inquisition now on hold. I felt more relieved about the deception.

Later, I had to go through a similar trial by lies with both my own and his parents. Dad was suspicious. This "classified" situation didn't make life easy.

8 How Time Flies

The following day, I did my schools' broadcast from the Scaffy Wagon and it was huge fun, with live questions from all ages between eight and eighteen. A later press interview was also enjoyable, but I'm afraid I got ratty with a journalist. I'd be told off for it later.

He asked, 'How do you do your make-up in zero-g, and what hairstyle do you prefer in orbit!'

In fact, I rarely wear any make-up and certainly not on the ISS. 'What has that got to do with the mission?' I griped.

'People will be interested,' he said.

'And did you ask Yuri how he manages to shave his head? It's irrelevant. I'd have thought this discriminatory attitude towards astronauts would've disappeared by the second quarter of the twenty-first century. Don't be so sexist! Mission questions only or this interview is over!'

The schools' event was much more satisfying and gave me a welcome break from the churning within my mind which AD1 was causing. The whole crew of the ISS now knew about the alien craft and were also sworn to secrecy, but we were all speculating like crazy.

My plan to tie the alien craft to the Progress had worked. So far it had made no attempt to change orbit nor recommence its spin. When talking to Reg, Dr Naughton, it became clear the general view was that the craft was aware it was being observed. The plan was to carry out a close examination as soon as possible.

Was it aware of anything? Maybe its automatic systems had finally failed? Perhaps the last attempt to recommence its rotation had drained the remaining fuel or flattened the batteries? There'd been no lights and no other indication of life, either electronically or organically.

I was pleased to discover that I'd misjudged Peter Wright. He was true to his word and kept me fully in the loop. I'd also underestimated the impact AD1's discovery had on the space agencies. They were desperate to learn about it and enormous resources were being applied to the project.

Just two weeks after our discovery, Peter sent me plans for the research laboratory. Billions of pounds were obviously being ploughed into the plan and the forecast construction costs were astronomical. NASA announced they were building a research laboratory to study comets or any objects passing through the solar system. It made me laugh. Absolutely true, yet totally false! It would explain the frantic orbital activity when construction began. People on Earth would be able to see the structure through binoculars. My dad had told me he was following the ISS on clear nights when it passes over Britain and he had often recorded me in the Scaffy Wagon approaching or leaving the space station through NASA's live feed. On one occasion he said my face was clearly visible. Very comforting for them.

My single spherical laboratory idea had morphed into three spheres. One would be the holding compartment for the alien device. Linked to it by a double airlock, a second laboratory provided a working environment. It, in turn, was linked by a further double airlock to the third and largest sphere which provided the living quarters with exercise equipment and all the life support. The whole assembly gave the impression of a basketball with two soccer footballs attached, making it a cluster, which was the eventual name by which it became known.

When I quizzed Peter about the design, he told me, 'The double airlocks are to keep each area sterile and separate from the others, at least until a bug-search has been completed.'

'So the scientists will have to wear full pressure suits to move in and out of the alien sphere? That'll be a bind for them.'

'No, Eve. By pressurising the alien sphere with an inert gas, simple airtight suits will be sufficient rather than the need for cumbersome pressure spacesuits.'

'Brilliant,' I said, 'and the inert gas will also kill any bugs which should stop any entering the laboratory.'

'Yes, that's the plan, but there'll be other precautions before they return to the living space. The airlock will be flushed out with a second inert gas preventing contamination. The extra safety will be discontinued if no bugs are found on or in AD1 during the first month of study.'

'Sounds expensive, Peter,' I said.

'Don't ask! No expense is being spared.'

His openness reassured me that AD1 really was the only alien artefact ever found. Nevertheless, there was still a lingering doubt borne of knowing how deceitful governments and the military could be, but if they'd an entire spaceship in Area 51, why would they be spending so much money to study this small object under such difficult circumstances?

'Do you know of any other alien devices?' There the question was asked.

'Don't think there'd be this much spent on this if it wasn't a unique find, Eve,' he said.

I thought he might give something away if I caught him on the hop, but no, he seemed very genuine.

Peter continued, 'Obviously, the biggest danger will be contamination by us or it, but at least every precaution is being taken.'

'Can't be much chance of any bugs living on it in space,' I said.

'You'd be surprised, Eve. Experiments conducted outside the ISS back in the mid-teens showed that many biological organisms were capable of surviving in the vacuum of space and, incredibly, many also survived on the outside of returning spacecraft despite re-entry temperatures. Life is far more tenacious than most people imagine.'

'Really?'

'Yes, and the Apollo Twelve crew brought back a camera from the old Surveyor Three lander. The inside had Earth bugs on it which had survived years on the surface of the moon with massive temperature changes and no atmosphere.'

'Wow,' I said. 'I had no idea.'

Our conversation certainly gave me plenty to think about.

»«O»«

Yuri and I spent eight weeks after the discovery of the alien artefact, continuing our original mission. We cleared nearly one hundred and fifty pieces of débris out of close-Earth orbit and proved the concept of the Scaffy Wagon. We did have to visit AD1 a few times for exploratory work inside the alien craft with the high-resolution camera. I looked forward to those missions as it was maintaining my personal involvement with the device.

In the ninth week, however, our mission changed beyond all recognition.

The Ariane 8 craft, with its bulbous front end, arrived in orbit with the components for the first research sphere. Yuri and I were to assemble it, together with Martin Deane and Göran Schmidt who had joined us. Martin, a thin-faced, curly-haired diminutive New Zealander, was originally due to replace me after my seven months so was trained on the Scaffy Wagon, and Göran, a classically handsome, strongly-built German was to replace Yuri, but they had been hastily prepared and arrived early so the SDIV could be in service sixteen hours each day. The ISS now had two more to sleep than the previous maximum and it'd be stretched even further when the scientists arrived, although most would eventually be permanently housed in the Cluster. NASA

81

were planning to send up an Orion capsule to attach to the ISS. It'd be used as a sleep module for up to four people.

Aboard the latest SpaceX Dragon supply craft was a whole array of new tools to be used by the Scaffy's arms for the assembly work.

This was so exciting for all four of us. A unique project. We sat in Tranquillity eating our evening meal and chatting over the task.

'They've designed the components so the spheres can also be made as hemispheres with a flat bottom for use on the moon and Mars,' said Martin as we spoke about the Ariane 8's cargo.

'Seems a good idea. Will give us the chance to find any problems in vacuum with the design,' I said.

'It treble skin with much insulation in cavities,' said Yuri.

Martin added, 'Yes, about two centimetres in each cavity. The inner cavity also has a network of tubes to carry a refrigerant to keep temperature down in direct sunlight, shifting heat from the sun side to the dark side of each sphere. The outer cavity contains a mesh to prevent micro-meteor damage and protect from sun activity. There is also a shielded interior compartment to be used as a panic room in the case of serious sun flares or NASA radiation alarms.'

'Have you practised with the connectors?' I asked.

'Yes, one of the new hands is designed specifically for the assembly process,' said Martin.

'What's the order of play?' asked Göran.

I was still mission commander, which was good. They didn't transfer command to Martin when he arrived with specific simulation training on the Cluster. They were impressed enough with my skills to leave me in charge.

'Tomorrow nine sharp, all four of us will board the SDIV and we'll take a trip over to the Ariane 8. The plan is to tow it to the Progress, but first we have to remove all remaining traces of fuel,' I said.

Martin broke in, 'We've a device in our new tool chest to let us vent it safely.'

'Next we'll open the container and remove the components. I want to assemble a hemisphere first and we must return to the Kibo platform to collect the secure frame sent up on the last Cygnus supply vessel. The frame will attach to AD1, but first we must strap it to a specially prepared section on one of the segments. Once it is secure, the first phase will be completed. We'll put in half a shift each on the first day and operate ten hour shifts in pairs,' I said.

Yuri asked, 'Martin, in simulation, how much time involved assembling hemisphere?'

'Up to twenty-four working hours.'

I continued, 'When the hemisphere is ready, Yuri and I will move AD1 from the Progress and fix it to the secure frame in the hemisphere. We'll strap the Progress to the outside of the hemisphere in case AD1 comes back to life. Once the remainder of the sphere is complete, AD1 will be secure and the Progress will return to the ISS and won't be needed again.'

'I keep remote pilot aware of how we doing,' said Yuri.

'We'll continue assembling components of the sphere until shift end, when we'll return to ISS and you and Göran can take the second shift,' I said to Martin.

'So, we get occasional downtime?'

'Oh yes, apart from you do three hours exercise,' said Yuri, reminding the others that there was rarely leisure time on the ISS.

'The following day, Göran, Martin and I must fit the double airlock. It'll be a long job. NASA think Yuri would be better employed helping with another Ariane due in the day after tomorrow.'

'Yes,' confirmed Martin, 'there are some tricky connections and the last three sphere segments have to be held tightly in place while the sphere is closed. That will need the two of us manipulating an arm each. Afterwards there's a lot of delicate work connecting the wiring and pumps, et cetera.'

That appealed to me because it meant we'd get out of the Scaffy Wagon on tethers. It would be my first spacewalk.

I continued, 'We're hoping sphere one will be finished and airtight within a week. It would have been good if the airlocks had been sent as a single unit, but the Ariane 8 is not capable of taking them except in segments. However, we did get all of the sphere components on the same flight.'

'The second sphere is due up in three days' time,' said Göran.

We talked long into the night. So much to consider and so exciting too. A real space adventure.

««O»»

By the end of November, after eighteen weeks of construction, the four of us plus two co-opted from the ISS crew, were inside the living area sphere, completing the fittings of food areas, sleep modules, exercise equipment, and all the hundreds of accessories which were arriving on a constant stream of Cygnus, Starliner, Dragon, Ariane, and Progress spacecraft.

The docking node of the living sphere had a Dragon attached and the laboratory sphere a Progress. Our last few assembly missions had also attached eight solar arrays which were to provide the power needed to maintain the scientists, their equipment and their communications. The living area had two docking ports, one was occupied by the Scaffy Wagon which had been used almost exclusively to bus astronauts back and forth.

84

Being responsible for the construction of this amazing laboratory was a dream come true and I was fortunate for it to have happened during my time in space, but now I was to leave the laboratory for the last time, and I couldn't help the heaviest wave of sadness overcoming me.

A Boeing Starliner was due up tonight bringing Dr Reg Naughton and Dr Hans Meyer to study AD1, and this would be followed by a Crew Dragon a few days later carrying another two scientists. They would make up the main team of four working in the Cluster. Yuri and I would be returning to Earth the next day with Shuko, a Japanese astronaut. It was tearing my heart out.

The airlock between the living and laboratory sections of the Cluster stood open so we passed freely back and forth as we unloaded the supply vessels. When the scientists moved in, they'd be making each section biologically secure from the others.

We'd already filled the alien section of the Cluster with nitrogen which was considered the most suitable inert gas, so common in the universe that whoever built AD1 would be aware of it. Alongside the double airlock, there were two transparent aluminium-ceramic glass sections which allowed AD1 to be observed as the gas was added. We'd no idea how it might react but weren't surprised when there wasn't any reaction at all.

What was this thing? Who had made it and why was it here? There was plenty of speculation now, of course, among those of us who knew about it. The general view was that it had been intended to contact us but had suffered the misfortune of a meteor strike before it was able to descend to Earth. Others thought it might have been intended to remain in orbit exactly as it had been, so only an intelligent spacefaring species would find it. Strange to imagine some bug-eyed creature intending this thing to be found by Yuri and me in exactly the way we had.

I held a grab handle as I floated by the window between the two spheres, staring longingly at it. It sat there, fixed to the secure frame inside the nitrogen sphere, doing nothing, saying nothing, revealing its guts but none of their purposes. Why were the wires uninsulated? Why did every wire seem to have a different colour to every other wire? Thousands of different shades of all the colours of the rainbow. There were so many different hues that our eyes could not separate the colours – only a camera could do that. Fascinating. I was desperately sad that I'd be unlikely to ever touch the device. I'd had a compulsion to run my hands over its surface and feel the texture of the silver blisters. Contamination concerns made that impossible. A big regret for me.

'Time we go, Eva,' said Yuri, his strong hand grasping my shoulder as I peered at the alien device.

'I don't want to leave, Yuri. This is our baby. We might never see it again. I want to stay involved, but don't see how.'

'I know. Feel same, but out our hands now. We been instrumental seeing properly examined. Can do no more, my friend.'

'When I get back home, I'm going to lobby ESA. There must be a way I can take part in studying it.'

'No way come back in less than eight or ten months. Bad for bones and muscles.'

'I know. I know. The universe is so unfair, Yuri.'

'Ha-ha, Eva. Certain not able do much about that.'

A film of tears covered my eyes. I blinked rapidly several times to try to dispel them, but Yuri had noticed. His arms circled me and crushed me to him sympathetically. I pulled free and dabbed them. Tears are a problem in space as they adhere to the eyeball, sting and blur your vision. After dabbing and some severe blinking, a single tear floated freely before me. I gave a nervous laugh, swatted it, took a last look at our alien artefact and we departed.

Soon I'd be on my way home. It was like parting with your first car, such a bittersweet experience.

9 Return to Earth

Part of each day for the last week, had been spent in our Soyuz, training for the descent. It was important we were all competent, even though the bulk of any control and communications would be undertaken by the computers under Yuri's watchful gaze.

After dinner, I returned to my personal space. It was seven thirty. Dr Naughton's Starliner had reached orbit and would arrive in a couple of hours. The Soyuz, to be used by Yuri and me to return to Earth, was on another docking station where it had been since our arrival. We'd loaded it with items which were being taken down from orbit, including sixteen mice which had been born and lived their entire lives in microgravity. They were certainly in for a shock.

I now had a short period of downtime to make some calls.

Mario's face appeared on Skype.

'Can't wait to get you back, darling. You all packed?' he asked.

'Yep. Most of my things are already on the Soyuz and I've only a small bag to take with me tomorrow.'

'Did you get your message not to forget your dad's photograph?'

'Yes. He's going to put it on the mantle shelf, and will no doubt bore everyone to death by telling them his daughter took it all the way to space and back. He told me last week that it had travelled eighty-five million, six hundred and eighty thousand miles!'

'Don't scoff. I'm sure it means a lot to him.'

'I know. He's been excited fit to burst since it got close to home time.'

'Take care, won't you?'

'You know I will.'

'I love you so much,' he said, blowing me a kiss.

'Remember, always, I love you too, won't you?'

'Yes,' he said. I watched his expression change marginally as he recognised that was my goodbye – just in case.

'See you soon,' I said and cut the connection before I blubbed.

I had the same sort of conversations with my parents and a couple of my closest friends, one of whom I asked to go and visit Mario if anything happened to me during descent to let him know I died doing what I loved in life and that I wouldn't have missed it to live a thousand years. She promised me she would.

The last call made, it was almost time to welcome the two scientists and I waited in the cupola, enjoying my last view of our home planet through its panoramic windows. My world view had changed since my first sight of Earth from the Soyuz window. Now, I knew for certain it was *not* the only place in the universe capable of supporting life. Our view of the cosmos would never be the same again. How many of those pinpricks of light in the night sky also had inhabited planetary systems revolving around them, with intelligent creatures looking back towards us with the same wonderment?

The incoming Starliner Crew mated with the docking node. It'd still be forty or fifty minutes before the hatches were opened, so I turned the opposite way and made out the front end of the Scaffy Wagon. My Scaffy Wagon – it would always be mine in my heart. I'd helped design it and had been its first commander. I was so aggrieved that I had to leave it behind, yet I was also desperate to return home. To have Mario take me into his arms. I'd missed him so much. His company and our love.

I wondered what the future had in store for me. Debriefing at Roscosmos, ESA, and NASA would occupy a few weeks then I'd be providing support for other astronauts who were due missions to the ISS. With any luck I'd get two or three more Scaffy Wagon projects so five or six years were already sketched out, but everything would be an anti-climax after the events of the last few months. I felt hollow inside. I'd a yearning to stay with AD1, but knew it was an impossible dream. The research scientists would be taking over now. I was not a researcher and there'd be many people more highly qualified than me to work on the alien device.

A glance at my watch told me the Starliner would soon be hard-docked and the hatches opened. I twisted in mid-air in the comfortable and confident manner of experienced astronauts, gave a quick push, and flew through Tranquillity in imitation of Supergirl. Probably my Bermuda shorts were less sexy than her bright red miniskirt and I had no cape! Funny, the first actress to play Supergirl had been a Slater too.

I turned into the main thoroughfare through the ISS and was soon at the docking station with Harry who had replaced Mike as station commander a few weeks previously.

'How goes it?' I asked him as we both floated near the hatch where Yuri was working.

'Five minutes, Eve. Yuri's making the final checks on the seals.'

'Okay, opening hatch,' said Yuri, barely a minute later, and the inner hatch swung inwards. The docking section of the Starliner was next to be moved out of the way. There was a blonde woman within.

'Welcome to the ISS,' said Harry, welcoming Valeria Misalova to the ISS. She would be the next station commander when Harry returned to Earth in a couple of months.

Yuri gave her hand a gentle pull and she was through the gap and into the space station, followed by Dr Naughton who I now knew as Reg, Dr Meyer who I'd only spoken to a few times, and Sally Cameron, a Canadian mission specialist who was visiting to make some modifications to one of the Canadarms.

There were handshakes all around and I tagged along as Harry took the new astronauts on their guided tour of the station, running through the safety procedures in exactly the way Mike had with Zinaida and me seven months previously. I still couldn't believe it had been so long.

After their induction, Reg asked me if we could go somewhere private, so I used the opportunity to take him in to *my* Scaffy Wagon – it provided the perfect excuse to be inside it one last time.

Reg was heavily built and struggled to get through the hatch. I liked him. He was obviously a brilliant scientist, but also had a great sense of humour and natural smiley face.

'So, this is the workhorse?'

'Yes, and it's a brilliant craft. There's little I'd change or update. Perhaps a third arm underneath the nose. How's your stomach? You were apprehensive last time we spoke.'

'I'm fine. Seems I was worrying about nothing. I don't like the sensation I'm falling, but it hasn't caused me to become disorientated or sick at all. A relief.'

'That's good to hear. The Cluster's a much larger volume than the ISS modules so there's more space in which to become disorientated. It'll be a lot better for you if you don't need to control it.'

'I wanted a quiet word,' he said, lowering his voice.

'Yes?' I almost whispered conspiratorially.

'I have pulled some strings.'

'Oh?'

'You'll be offered a job, still with UKSA and ESA, but at Goonhilly.'

This was a surprise. 'What? What sort of job?'

'With UKSA, we've being setting Goonhilly up with some of the most advanced computers in existence, plus half a dozen real whiz kid programmers and linguists. The job will be to manage its relationship with the rest of the AD1 sections worldwide. You'd be coordinating the understanding of the alien. Interested?'

'Really? I'd bite your hand off. You *are* serious?'

'Seriously. I've to let Peter at NASA know you'll take it before ESA will let you apply for it.'

'Absolutely. Tell him quick, before he changes his mind.'

He laughed at my enthusiasm. 'You sure? It's a bit of a desk job compared with what you've been doing up here but we'd all prefer an astronaut at the helm, so to speak. No other astronaut has more qualifications for involvement with the project than you.'

'I'd be delighted, Reg. Anything to keep me involved with the alien craft. It's tearing me apart leaving it right now.'

'You realise it might mean you'll never return to space?' said Reg.

I went quiet for a moment. 'Suppose so.'

'Well?'

'Well what?'

'Do you still want it?'

'Damn it, Reg. Call him now, now, now, or sooner!' We both laughed.

'Okay, I'll tell Peter.'

'Thank you so much, Reg. I didn't think Peter liked me.'

'I'm delighted for you. Peter's a cold fish, but he appreciates your competence and efficiency. He *instigated* it and told me he was encouraged to find something useful for you by an influential person in the British government. You must've impressed someone enough to lobby for you. Once they'd looked at your qualifications, your psychology doctorate and ESA background it became a no-brainer.'

'You think I've really got a chance?'

'It's a British interview board and I think they'd be mad not to hire you.'

'Really?'

'It is as good as a done deal, in my opinion. You're the talk of NASA. Damn it, Eve, it is your Cluster idea which has kept AD1 up here. I was petrified we might lose it in an accident if we brought it down to Earth. They've been spending billions to make this a reality.'

'I'm amazed and very flattered.'

'Don't be. You deserved it. Now... where can I get a coffee?'

'Follow me.' I did an acrobatic tumble in mid-air and dived through the hatch into Harmony, with Reg clumsily in pursuit.

««O»»

I didn't sleep well. The elation of the potential Goonhilly job was partly to blame, but mainly it was the dangers we'd be facing the next day. The two greatest hazards of journeying into space were blast-off and re-entry.

Blast-off was now relatively safe as there was an emergency eject rocket if there was a problem. It'd deal with anything other than a catastrophic explosion on the ground and, even then, there was a chance the descent module of the Soyuz, where the crew were, would survive.

During re-entry, however, if everything did not work perfectly there was a real chance of becoming very dead, and not necessarily instantly. It was scary, and it was preying on my mind. It was the same with all the craft, of course, not just the Soyuz.

I put my photograph of Mario and my diary with its concealed secret memory card into my small on-board personal belongings bag. I felt guilty about the card. If it was found, it could cost me the Goonhilly post. Too late to get rid of it securely now.

I had a final check around my sleeping quarters and, once I was certain all was neat and tidy for the next occupant, I made my way through the cluttered module which led into the Russian section of the ISS.

Yuri was already in his space suit and Shuko, the Japanese astronaut heading Earth-side with us, was being helped into his. Zinaida had left months ago as she'd only been up for a short military project. Harry was there, of course, and Göran was lending a hand too.

Once we were all in our bulky suits, we had to squeeze our way through the habitation module of the Soyuz and down into our seats in the descent module. Such a tight squeeze. The Dragon and Starliner both had much more space than a Soyuz.

The habitation module was crammed with garbage and a most un-private toilet device which descending astronauts made a point of trying to avoid needing during the four-hour descent, hence the diapers we wore for emergencies. On crew arrival flights, all astronauts used enemas the morning of lift-off to keep their needs to a minimum as journeys up to the ISS could sometimes take a day or two, but descents were quick affairs.

When the craft split into sections, the habitation section would burn up on re-entry. It'd leave us in the rhomboidal-profiled descent module.

It took us about forty minutes to secure the hatches and we had the *go* to separate. Springs caused us to drift away from the station.

Soyuz's thrusters were dirtier than the Scaffy Wagon's so could not be fired near the ISS. Once we were at a safe distance, a couple of hundred metres away, Yuri used the jets to give us a bit of a push to speed our separation. Next, automatic systems put us into the correct orientation for the first slow-down burn.

The ISS was not visible to me, but if I craned my neck, the Cluster was there. Once the rockets fired it disappeared rapidly. Soon it was a speck, then lost in the heavens. Would I ever get a second chance to experience free fall? It'd be unlikely if I got the job. Much as I wanted to come back to orbit, I'd *have* to take the Goonhilly post if it were offered.

We now had little to do but wait until we'd achieved the correct position for the de-orbiting burn. Almost an hour had passed when some Russian chatter informed us orientation and orbit position were correct.

Yuri sat with the controls before him as we watched the countdown on his small screen. The descent was automatic but the time of firing the descent engine was critical. If it didn't fire automatically, he'd have to fire it manually.

It fired dead on time.

All of a sudden, we were being shaken far worse than within the Scaffy Wagon as pseudo-gravity made its presence felt, giving us a taster for the real thing which would welcome us back on Earth. This was a far more powerful engine than we had on the Wagon. Five minutes later the engine cut, and we were in silence once again.

So far, so good. In an hour, we should be on Earth.

Our Soyuz was plummeting earthwards, and it was noticeable how the curvature of the planet was levelling out.

The next critical phase would be in about twenty minutes when we reached a height of around eighty miles. Yuri had secured the hatch between us and the habitation capsule ready for the craft to split into its constituent parts. The modules above and below us would separate and burn up while we'd have a controlled re-entry, protected by our heat shield.

'One minute,' said Yuri, 'can seem bit unnerving. Panic not.'

His warning did nothing for my peace of mind. I'd been told the activation of the exploding bolts was extremely scary.

It began with a sound as if the entire ship was being pounded from outside by men with sledgehammers. It worsened for almost a minute before the silence of orbit resumed.

'Good grief. Unnerving wasn't close to the correct word, Yuri,' I protested as my heartrate returned to as near normal as it would be likely to get until we were safely home.

He laughed.

Now, we seemed to be tumbling. We needed to be moving heat shield down. The tumbling seemed to go on longer than I expected.

'Yuri. Are we meant to still be tumbling?' asked Shuko.

'It's okay, Eva, Shuko, give it a minute.'

The tumbling slowed to a stop, but now the window was glowing. The whole craft seemed to be on fire. The glass was blackening with the heat as the outer layer burned off. I knew this was meant to happen, but it was still undeniably scary. I didn't dare take my pulse as I guessed it was trying to achieve two hundred as we grew hotter by the second.

Pseudo-gravity was forcing me back into my seat as my weight increased. My harness was no longer tight, and I pulled with all my force on the straps to secure myself. Shuko and Yuri were doing the same. It was a game of not wanting to show you were scared but we all were, to some degree or another.

Now we oscillated from side to side. I knew from my training these motions controlled our angle of attack and were automatic to keep us on our glide path. My hands gripped my seat, but as the forces pushed towards 4g, nothing would have been able to shake me out of it anyway.

Difficult to breathe now. It was as if someone was sitting on my chest and it could get worse. Some landings involved taking up to 9g. Yuri held his controls. This was another critical point in the descent for which he was trained to step in if things went wrong.

'Ten kilometres,' he said. 'Eight hundred kilometres per hour.'

We'd slowed from seventeen thousand to five hundred miles per hour in under twenty minutes and the silence was gone. The scream of the wind whistling past us at almost the speed of sound filled our ears. Noisy was not the word.

'Drogue chute in five seconds,' Yuri cried, so he was heard above the din.

We braced ourselves.

Now we were thrown violently in all directions. God, it was hot in the Soyuz and the whole craft was swinging like a pendulum. I was being tossed about as if on the devil's rollercoaster. It seemed to go on and on and on. What a ride!

Shuko cried out but I was quiet. I was enjoying this – Disney's Space Mountain didn't come close as a thrill. It also meant we were almost safe.

Whoa! Another huge tug and the main parachute had opened. The violent swinging gradually subsided and our speed was plunging in line with our altitude.

An expected, yet still surprising, a crash from outside indicated the heat shield had separated and my window cleared as the burned outer layer was sloughed off by the wind. There were clouds and blue sky. The angle of view was wrong to be able to see the land but, as everything had worked, I knew we were somewhere over Kazakhstan and would be down shortly.

Yuri's stubby hand grasped mine and shook it, 'Home safe, Eva,' he said. I watched him repeat the handshake and reassuring phrase to Shuko.

We'd made it.

We hadn't skipped off the atmosphere to suffocate when our oxygen was gone and spend eternity as seated corpses circling the sun. I glanced at the euthanasia valve above Yuri's seat. It could be turned to cause the air pressure to fall until it reached the point where we'd painlessly fall asleep and die. It wouldn't be needed now.

Neither had we plunged too steeply and been roasted alive by friction with the air; the scarier, but possibly the quicker of the two deaths we'd now avoided.

For a fleeting moment a military helicopter was visible through my window. Roscosmos was on the ball.

'Brace yourselves. Five seconds,' warned Yuri.

An enormous explosive sound beneath us almost halted our descent as the retro jets fired, but we still hit the ground with the force of a car crash, our seats continuing to fall as their shock absorbers took up the strain. We were home. We were home and we were alive.

Yuri hit the button which detached one of the parachute ropes, so we wouldn't be dragged if there was a wind and he recited a prayer. But I had no God. To my mind, I'd *not* been unlucky. I always laughed inside at the people who prayed in dangerous situations. The only ones whose prayers were answered were the survivors. It might sound obvious, but it was a well-established phenomenon. I'd written a thesis on it for my psychology PhD. Those who prayed and died never got to tell people it didn't work. Those who lived believed it was because of their prayers and God had specifically assisted them to be saved.

These and other thoughts passed through my mind as we lay in our seats, as weak as new-born lambs, recovering from what seemed like a voyage in a tumble drier. Slowly, I became accustomed to the weight which now bore down upon all my limbs. Had we landed on Jupiter by mistake?

A veil of dust billowed outside my window. Soon it settled and a cloud-dotted sky reappeared. By forcing unfamiliar muscles to lift my head I saw there was a parked helicopter with its blades slowing in the distance.

We heard the sound of Russian voices and equipment being moved around. I visualised the procedures they were undertaking as I'd attended a previous landing. A framework was being lowered over the Soyuz to allow them to lift us out without putting too much strain on muscles which had forgotten the gravity of Mother Earth.

'You okay in there?' shouted a voice in Russian.

'Okay,' bellowed Yuri.

My head seemed so heavy, even after I'd removed my helmet, that I gave up the battle to watch the action and relaxed back into my seat. Even my wristwatch seemed to weigh a couple of pounds when I lifted the apparent dead weight of my arm.

'God, it's hot in here,' I said.

'Yes. Not good. Hatch open soon and cool air,' said Yuri.

Seconds later, the hatch opened and there was a beaming smile from one of our landing crew as cooler air entered. We'd trained with these guys, so we knew them all. There was some welcome conversation.

Our ordeal was not over. Getting out of the Soyuz was not easy in our condition and our rescuers had to crawl in to help us out of our harnesses then hoisted each of us bodily onto the framework where we sat until we were ready to be lifted to the ground. The capsule itself was still radiating heat. Amazing. Four hunky Russians carried me over to a special seat where they deposited me in a semi-reclining position to recover.

'Thanks,' I said in Russian, still struggling to even move my head against the force of gravity.

Photographs were taken. Two camera crews were filming us. Gerald, who'd asked to participate in a landing, walked over and shook my hand.

'Lovely to see you safely back, Eve,' he said, then introduced me to Ivan, the voice of secure Roscosmos. The heat in my suit was awful. I was sweating like the proverbial pig. I wished I could free myself from it. My flight surgeon removed one of my gloves.

'Ouch,' I said as he pricked my finger and positioned the red bead against an electronic device.

'Sorry,' he said. 'Just need to check a few things.' Next he materialised a finger blood pressure monitor from his bag.

After about twenty minutes we were helped to our feet. How unsteady I was. We boarded a helicopter to take us back to the Baikonur Cosmodrome where I knew Mario would be waiting for me. So strange, experiencing lifting, turning and banking in the chopper.

We disembarked from the helicopter onto a bus for a half mile drive to the press centre where there was a surprisingly large crowd.

One delight was how we were all treated like great heroes. I was given a huge bouquet of roses by a young girl in national dress, we got a specially made mission plaque to take home, and a Russian Matryoshka doll in the form of an astronaut. The outer doll of mine a likeness of Valentina Tereshkova, who had flown into orbit seventy-two years previously in 1963.

'Oh!' I shouted as I dropped it. How stupid I felt. I'd been turning it over in my hand, examining the detail then just let go, expecting it to float beside me. How silly I felt as it tumbled earthwards and someone recovered it from the carpet and returned it to me, thankfully undamaged. What a souvenir to treasure. Shuko's doll was of Yuri Gagarin.

Mario was standing quietly at the back. I could see him and flashed a smile, but we were marshalled into seats for the presentations and it seemed to go on forever when all I wanted was to be in his arms.

Once the fuss was over, I managed to get to my feet. Mario came and took me into his embrace. 'Eve, Eve,' he said and there was the slight embarrassment of a Russian doctor supporting me while his charge concentrated on her lover's kiss. He turned his face away politely.

'God, I am so heavy,' I said as our lips finally parted.

'You look and feel wonderful.' He kissed me again and squeezed me fiercely. Wonderful. I felt tears stinging my eyes. How much I'd missed him.

Next a trip to a hospital ward at the cosmodrome where I was relieved of the awful space suit, unsoiled but sweaty diaper, and sweat-soaked clothes. Once in hospital gowns, they wired us up with ECGs, blood pressure monitors, and the usual medical kit, but at least we could talk to whoever had come to meet us.

'That was scary,' said Mario.

'Scarier for me.' I laughed.

'No. It was awful waiting to see if the parachutes opened. You have no idea of the relief when we saw them in the distance on the television monitor.' He squeezed my hand.

'Some ride,' I said.

'I bet.'

I saw Ivan and called to him to bring my diary.

He returned a few minutes later with my small personal bag. It didn't look as if it had been searched. I removed the diary and feigned writing a few words while the fingertips of my left hand checked for the slight bump in the top corner. The micro-memory card was still there. I'd wondered if it might get picked up by Roscosmos security.

Apparently not. I guessed they weren't expecting space criminals yet!

Most of the next day was spent undergoing tests before I was released. I must admit I was occasionally a little disorientated if I moved my head quickly, but other than that and general tiredness, I'd no serious problems.

We'd be returning to Amsterdam on a scheduled flight the next day.

That evening, we were in our own hotel room in Moscow. I showered in real water. Bliss. We enjoyed a welcome steak supper and my first glass of wine for seven months in a superb restaurant outside the Kremlin. I picked up the bottle to read the label and almost dropped it. My knife and fork both took a tumble on a couple of occasions too. I resolved to pay more attention to the force of gravity. It was most strange no longer being able to leave things suspended in mid-air.

Our reunion evening ended with Mario hanging the Russian *DO NOT DISTURB* sign on the bedroom door. At last we could make up for seven months apart, extremely joyfully – but exceedingly gingerly indeed. How wonderful to experience his love again!

Part Two

GOONHILLY ENIGMA

10 Goonhilly CEO

Mario and I had discussed the post at Goonhilly fully, but secrecy prevented me telling him why I'd been selected as the preferred candidate for such a prestigious position. It was making life difficult.

'I know you have your astronomy background, darling, but to be parachuted in as director of this huge establishment seems unbelievable,' he said.

The Mullion Cove Hotel was spectacularly situated, and I turned my gaze to the rolling Atlantic breakers crashing against the cliffs. I was a little miffed over his lack of confidence in my abilities.

'They've decided an astronaut would add a unique perspective to the post and if I get the post – a big if – I'll be working with the ISS from Earth. I have done rather well during my seven-month mission, you know,' I said, adding an element of disappointment to my voice.

His hand descended upon mine. 'Sorry, Eve. I realise you must have impressed. I'm just gobsmacked, that's all.'

Fortunately, his graphics business could be run from anywhere, owing to the Internet. It meant he was happy to relocate to Cornwall if I obtained the post. The biggest problem for him was getting a residency permit. Now England was no longer in the EU, it no longer had open borders.

In the morning, Mario booked a nine o'clock car to take him to Helston to get an idea of property prices and local

103

services, while I waited in reception, in my finest suit, for my vehicle. It was due to collect me at nine forty-five.

My watch vibrated when the small vehicle pulled up outside the hotel. I punched my booking code into the door lock, climbed into the rear, told it the twelve-character location code for the reception door from my interview letter and the car pulled smoothly away towards the Goonhilly Earth Station.

The Lizard peninsula is one of the most ruggedly beautiful locations in the British Isles with amazing coastal scenery and quaint villages. The road from Mullion is single-track and it was fascinating to experience my vehicle negotiating with other autonomous road users to travel the road. The only delays were caused when avoiding manual-driven cars at passing places. I noticed how they always forced my vehicle to reverse to the previous space even when their passing place was closer, so the system wasn't perfect. Really, they were abusing the submissive nature of autonomous software. Once clear of the single-track roads, the car drove me across windswept moorland and, eventually, the radio telescopes came into view. We skirted the site perimeter and I got a good idea of the size and layout of the complex. It was huge, the size of a small airport.

Goonhilly was instrumental in the first ever live transatlantic television broadcast through a famous satellite called Telstar. That was back in 1962. Today it is owned on a thousand-year lease by the Goonhilly Earth Station company.

If I was the successful candidate, I'd be working in the new government UKSA base at the site. It has a lease through to 2045.

The car stopped at the security barriers and I showed my appointment letter. The guard tapped a code into his terminal and the car was released, passing through the gate and arriving at a clutch of single-storey buildings. I told the car to park itself and wait for me. I looked around at the open moorland and the incongruous satellite dishes. What a wonderful place to work. I entered the main glass-fronted building.

Reception was clean, shiny, and spacious, with a long curved desk. A smartly dressed, short, stocky young woman was standing on my side of the reception desk and walked towards me as I entered.

She smiled genuinely and offered her hand, 'Welcome to Goonhilly, Doctor Slater. I'm Janet de Vries. Can I take your coat?'

I supposed, as a returning astronaut, I should get used to being recognised. 'Nice to meet you, Janet,' I said as I handed over the garment. Another woman behind the desk took it from her.

'This way, please,' she said, and we headed towards a secure door to the right of the building. She punched in a code and we emerged into a long corridor. The first door on the right was open and I was ushered in.

Facing me were three people behind a long conference table butted on to a desk, so forming a letter T. They stood as I entered, introduced themselves, and invited me to sit opposite them. Janet de Vries closed the door as she exited.

One was a senior civil servant, another was Mrs Bray, the science minister whom I recognised from news pictures, and the third was the director of Jodrell Bank, Sir Henry Edwards, with whom I had spoken occasionally during my month-long project at Jodrell Bank as part of my degree course. A prestigious interview panel indeed.

The interview went well. I wondered how many others were on the shortlist. I'd been told I was the preferred candidate so just needed to avoid any pitfalls.

Although the dishes and the commercial operation were still to be operated by GES Ltd, the post I was being considered for was Chief Executive for the United Kingdom and European Space Agencies' Anomalies Commission. GES Ltd's director, a man called Michael Brown, would be autonomous, but my role would take ultimate responsibility for day to day operations. It had to be organised in this way to explain why my role would be in regular communication with the Cabinet and, potentially, with heads of state of the USA, European countries, Russia, Canada, and Japan. Such contact would be incongruous for a lesser post than the chief executive.

The way the interview progressed, it was a questioning of my commitment to the secrecy of what was now known simply as "The Cluster Project". I had no problem convincing them, even though I felt guilty for still having the incriminating microSDXS card concealed in the leather skin of my personal diary. Perhaps I should destroy it. They certainly made a lot of fuss about maintaining confidentiality. A surprising amount, actually. It was almost as if they knew I had in mind to blow security if the project was permanently hushed-up, but only Yuri had heard me say that. Perhaps I was just paranoid. My confidence was rattled.

After about an hour, Ms de Vries was called back into the room and she took me to the reception area where I was asked to wait.

The wait was only fifteen minutes before I was taken back into the conference room and told the job was mine. I was offered a surprisingly large salary and various other benefits. I would also have an exclusive autonomous Jaguar for my personal use. I was having a real struggle controlling my smile.

106

Then Sir Henry said, 'Now we've got the appointment finalised, please tell us about the discovery. We're all bursting to know all about it.'

I was surprised. These prestigious individuals wanted me to tell them about the artefact. I suppose it was at that point that I realised that I would forever be a celebrity to those who knew about the secret.

I delighted in recounting the story and they kept me there for a further forty-five minutes with their questions and speculation. I wished I could also be telling Mario. Nevertheless, I left Goonhilly brimming with confidence.

The start date was the eighth of January 2036, just three weeks hence but I was to be given encrypted access to Goonhilly's UKSA computer network to get up to speed on its operations. My deputy would be Tim Riley who had previously been Mr Brown's second-in-command and he would help me understand the complex over the coming months.

The discovery of the alien craft had begun to change my life. My new post offered me the chance to make a real difference to the investigation of AD1. I was determined to make the most of the opportunity.

11 Number Ten

The thirty days after my return from orbit were a whirlwind of activity.

Firstly, four days debriefing by Roscosmos, NASA, and ESA teams in Noordwijk. Next, Mario and I took a seven-day break in Madeira for fun, food, and to compensate for seven months of imposed celibacy. On our return, we rushed off for the Goonhilly interview and then Christmas was only a week away. Mario returned to Holland to tidy up his affairs there and arrange for our furniture to be packed and put into a container to be moved to Truro, ready for us to equip our new home. Meantime, I organised a furnished cottage in Helston for us, until we bought somewhere suitable. I fantasised about owning an idyllic, chocolate-box cottage in a quaint Cornish fishing village. I was still in a state of shock over the size of my salary and elevated status and wanted it reflected in our new home.

On the twenty-second of December, Mario and I met up at the extremely posh Royal Garden Hotel where we were being accommodated as VIPs by ESA for one night for a special London meeting on the twenty-third. It was a beautiful hotel and we thoroughly enjoyed our meal and evening, although the price of a gin and tonic was in a higher orbit than even I had been!

At ten in the morning, we arrived at the back entrance of Number Ten Downing Street, where there was to be a small reception coffee party taking place in my honour. This was normal for returning astronauts, but there was much more to take place on this occasion. Mario was in for a shock. I'd been keeping more than one secret from him and today would, hopefully, see me relieved from the anxiety of keeping the greatest of those secrets from my fiancé.

On our arrival, we were taken into one of the Cabinet Office briefing rooms where we met the Home Secretary,

Mrs Jenny Rae and a government lawyer. I had not been allowed to tell Mario about this meeting. He was gobsmacked when he realised it was the *actual* Home Secretary who was shaking his hand.

Introductions were made and Mario gave me a sideways glance which clearly posed the question he'd have liked to have asked out loud – "Eve, what the fuck is going on?"

We all sat around one end of a plush, leather-inlaid conference table.

The Home Secretary said, 'Mr Casali, we have asked to meet you because currently Doctor Slater works under the Official Secrets Act and you don't.'

'No. I do lots of confidential commercial work, but nothing you'd say is of a secret nature.'

'Well, Doctor Slater has been, and in her new post she'll be continuously involved in international secrets. That in itself is not unusual, there are many times when partners have to keep secrets, particularly the military and secret service staff. Their spouses and partners would have no need to be apprised of those secrets. However, the secrets Doctor Slater has to maintain are unique, unconventional, and complex.'

Mario looked at me again, curiosity and intrigue in his expression. I tried to keep looking forwards rather than meet his gaze.

'She is in possession of certain far-reaching secrets and we'd like her to not have to keep them from you. It would be difficult for her and, in fact, for the two of you. We feel she should be able to confide in you to give her peace of mind. We'd like to offer you the opportunity to be obliged under the Official Secrets Act to be that confidant. A government lawyer is here to witness your signature should you wish to sign, but it has to be your decision.'

Mario examined me with a frown on his brow and said, 'What's been going on, Eve?'

'I can't answer that, Mario,' I said.

Mrs Rae said, 'The secrets are unconventional and unique. If you sign you would be committing to secrecy, perhaps for many years. Doctor Slater tells us it is unlikely that your relationship will break down, but if it did, you would still be obliged to secrecy and we have extradition rights with most countries and would certainly pursue any infringement.'

'I see. What exactly does it entail and what would my responsibilities be?'

The lawyer responded, 'Your responsibility would be to never speak about anything told you under the act. It means not to your family, not to any future children, not even to your lawyers. If you break the act in this case, which involves the highest level of international secrets, I can assure you a lengthy period of incarceration, probably in isolation.'

'Phew,' Mario said looking at me, 'What the *hell* have you been involved in?'

I took his hand, 'Sorry, I can't answer that either.'

Mario sat back in his chair and looked at me, the Home Secretary, then back at the lawyer. I could almost hear the cogwheels whirring. He looked at me again for guidance and, once more, I kept an expressionless face. It had to be his decision, and his alone.

Slowly, thoughtfully, and almost resignedly, he agreed. 'Okay, you seem to want me to be part of this. If you assure me it is in Eve's best interests, then I'll sign.'

'It is. You have my word,' said Mrs Rae.

She stood, shook Mario's and my hand and said, 'The Prime Minister will be relieved. I'll see you in thirty minutes at the reception,' and she left the room.

The solicitor gave Mario a document and said, 'There is no actual signature required. The act now covers you. You will also find your residency permit has been expedited.'

He left, and we were now alone. Finally, I could tell Mario of my discovery.

'Sorry about that, Mario,' I said timidly and kissed him.

'What's going on, Eve? Damn it, she's the Home Secretary for Christ's sake, not some anonymous government official. She actually said that the Prime Minister will be relieved. *Relieved!* Why the hell should he be relieved? This is all like something from James Bond. Unreal. What's it all about?'

'Yes. They're taking it pretty seriously.'

'So, spill the beans. I take it we've been left alone for you to enlighten me.'

'Yes, well, brace yourself.'

I took both of his hands in mine. His expression was so severe; distrustful and worried, as if I'd let him down. I gave him a quick kiss.

'You remember in those first few days in orbit we had a satellite which was spinning badly and we lost the video connection?'

'Yes...'

'Well, there was nothing wrong with the video. The television feed which is supplied to the media is always five minutes behind, not live. ESA cut the media feed because I'd realised we were seeing something unexpected. The system was geared to the chance of us finding a military satellite which might embarrass one or more of the member countries.'

'So, you found a bomb or something?'

'No. Much more of a *bombshell* than that!' I said with a chuckle.

His expression told me he hadn't a clue what would come next. I opened the folder Mrs Rae had left with me and there was a full colour close-up photograph of the alien artefact.

'Good God! What is it?'

'We don't know.'

'What do you mean, "you don't know"?'

'It's alien.'

'Really? You really mean really alien? Sigourney Weaver alien?'

'It doesn't bleed acid, but, no, it's not of this Earth.'

'You're sure?'

'Positive.'

'What does it do?'

'We don't know. You know how during the last couple of months up there I was under huge operational pressure?'

'Yes. You seemed to be involved in more ISS stuff rather than satellite disposal.'

'That's right. Yuri, Martin, Göran, and I were building this,' and I flipped the page to the next image which had been taken from the ISS by a long lens. It showed the Cluster, in all its glory with a Progress, a Dragon, and the Scaffy Wagon attached to it.

'Isn't that the comet-monitoring lab or something?'

'Well, NASA had to release some information about it as it was visible from Earth but, in fact, the alien artefact is inside it and being studied right now by four scientists. They'll be working with my people at Goonhilly, so everything I do down there will be top secret.'

'I see why you got the job now, but why's it secret? Why not tell the world? I don't understand the need for secrecy.'

'At the moment, the USA has convinced Britain, Europe, Russia, Canada, and Japan to keep it secret until we know more about it. I had an argument with the Prime Minister about it the day we found it.'

'You argued with the PM?' Mario was dumbfounded.

'Yes. He reassured me that it's currently in the national interest to keep it secret, but I also challenged him about other alien rumours like Area 51. He assured me none of the rumours were true, and I must say I believed him.'

'But you argued with him? Seriously?'

'Yes. I've strong views about the alien device and how to go about releasing the news to the public. I'm actually very worried about these delaying tactics. Remember, I do have a psychology doctorate.'

'Wow. Yes, of course. Was he annoyed?'

'What? That I argued?'

'Yes.'

'Well, I got the job, didn't I?'

'Yes. Oh, Eve, I'm so sorry I had my doubts about it, before.'

'Well, expect to be regretting it when I can think of some appropriate punishment!' We both laughed.

'Sorry,' he said, and we kissed briefly.

He examined the picture of AD1 again before we went through the album together. The pictures helped to show him how I'd held it with the Scaffy Wagon arm, attached it to the Progress craft and finally positioned it inside the first of the cluster spheres. Twenty minutes of our half hour was gone.

'This is all amazing, Eve. And so exciting!'

'It is, isn't it? I'll show you some official video once I'm settled in at Goonhilly.'

'I'm so impressed. Were you scared?'

'Apprehensive.'

'Tell me about it.'

I recounted the adventure in double-quick time.

A young man knocked on the door and entered.

'Can I take you and Mr Casali through to the reception room now, please, Doctor Slater? Mrs Rae says I should take the folder.'

'Ready to face the throng?' I asked as I handed the folder to the assistant. Mario nodded.

We descended to one of the reception rooms where we met Gerald, Peter, and Yuri, who gave me one of his bear hugs. Another door opened and in walked Sir Henry Edwards and Mrs Ellen Bray from my interview panel. Accompanying them was the deputy head of NASA, the head of ESA plus the Russian ambassador to London. Introductions were made all around and it was noticeable how interested the latter group to arrive were in meeting Yuri and me. I guess we were famous among this group of already well-known space VIPs.

All this adoration surprised Mario and the kudos went up a further notch when Prime Minister Roger Clarke, Home Secretary Jenny Rae and Secretary of Defence James Faulkner walked into the room through yet another doorway.

The Prime Minister walked directly over to me and shook my hand.

'Congratulations, Evelyn, on a wonderful discovery. And who is this?' he said, turning towards Mario.

I introduced them and called Yuri over. Both men were warmly greeted by Mr Clarke.

Mario was even more nonplussed when the Prime Minister lowered his voice and said to him, 'I am so glad you chose to sign the act. Doctor Slater will need a lot of support during the coming years.'

Inside I was burning up with emotion over Mario's excitement at everything. I'd been desperate to tell him and it was tearing me apart having to keep the secret. We kept exchanging beaming smiles.

114

Coffee and the most amazing array of pastries, cakes, and biscuits arrived and were arranged on a circular dining table near one wall.

Mario whispered to me, 'What would have happened if I hadn't signed the act?'

'It wasn't an option, darling. They would have become increasingly persuasive until you did.' I gave a nervous laugh as I knew Mario hated being manipulated. He narrowed his eyes and frowned at me and I gave him a disarming smile.

Once the caterers had disappeared, Mr Clarke took a central position by the table and his personal private secretary clapped his hands twice to call us all to order.

The Prime Minister began, 'I called this small assembly together as I wanted to celebrate Evelyn and Yuri's momentous discovery. What they found in orbit will change our view of the universe forever. We're no longer alone. There are other intelligent life forms out there… somewhere.

'When I spoke to Evelyn on the momentous day of the discovery, she was aboard the SDIV and the alien artefact was rotating only two or three metres from her.' He looked at me and gave an admiring smile. 'She was concerned about the discovery being hushed-up in the way all governments are suspected of doing. I assured her, as far as this country is aware, no alien artefact has ever been discovered before and the rumours of UFOs kept in secret American bunkers were all exactly that – rumours and conspiracy theories.

'In addition to congratulating Evelyn personally, I can also tell you she'll receive the DCMG in the New Year Honours list, although that news is embargoed until Wednesday.'

Mario was shocked and whispered, 'What's that? Never heard of it.'

I returned the whisper, 'Sorry, tell you later. Ran out of time,' and chuckled under my breath, which elicited an elbow in my ribs.

'Evelyn is to take up her new post as UKSA and ESA Chief Executive of the government arm of the Goonhilly Earth Station and, together with the international scientists who are currently studying the artefact in orbit, she'll be coordinating them and other scientists in a secure facility at Houston. Their task will be to find out exactly what this object is, what its purpose was, and what we can learn from it.

'We already know it's from an advanced civilisation. Are they trying to interact with us? It's a crying shame it was so badly damaged while in orbit, as it makes our investigations that much more difficult.

'Once we do know exactly what we're dealing with, this government has no intention of unreasonably withholding knowledge of its existence from the public. Until then, Mr Faulkner, Mrs Rae, and I do need to keep in mind whether it poses a threat. The last thing any of us would wish to do is alarm the general populace. There are religious aspects we need to consider too.

'For that and other reasons it must remain top secret at the present time, but all of us in this room have clearance to talk freely about it among ourselves.

'Once again, sincere congratulations to Yuri and Evelyn. Now, please help yourselves to the refreshments. Shortly a photographer will arrive to take some photographs, so watch what you say in her hearing.'

There was warm applause and we congregated around the table. Mario was obviously bursting with questions, but he couldn't get a word in edgewise. It seemed everyone wanted to talk to me. They were asking what went through my mind when I first knew it was alien, did it frighten me or disturb me? I spoke about the shock of it suddenly recommencing its rotation and almost pulling off one of the Scaffy Wagon's arms. I told them it was the most worrying moment as we were very close to it and had no idea if it was a prelude to some violent reaction to being manhandled. Mario was hanging on my every word.

Suddenly, Mrs Rae tapped her glass loudly and told us we needed to assemble for the photographer. A young woman entered with a professional camera atop a sturdy tripod.

There were a number of group photographs taken then some with the Prime Minister shaking my hand with and without Mario and then Yuri beside me. Such huge fun. I couldn't wait to give my dad copies.

Soon the assembly broke up, the photographer had gone, and the Prime Minister came over for another word with Mario and me.

'One day,' he said, speaking more to Mario than me, 'Evelyn will be world famous. As an astronaut, she already has a certain minor fame, of course, but when the news about her discovery eventually breaks it'll be on a whole different scale, not quite equal to, but in the same stratospheric heights as the first moon astronauts. Her name will become part of world history.

'She now has a difficult task to undertake at Goonhilly and I'm sure your support will be a great help.'

He shook Mario's hand, then mine and held it firmly for at least thirty seconds while he concluded, 'Good luck, Evelyn, I'll keep in touch and I'm sure I'll meet you... both of you, again,' and he left.

When we exited Number Ten via the front door, a Scottish journalist shouted at me from across the road, 'Doctor Slater... are you the first scaffy to meet the PM?'

I couldn't help but laugh and shouted back, 'Everyone has garbage!'

In the evening, the scaffy clip was played on Sky News every half hour. How exciting. We arrived at my parents' house in time to be shown it by my father several times as he chirped – 'You're famous, Eve... my daughter's a famous astronaut.'

The next morning, Dad ran out and bought a copy of every newspaper. Several pictures showed me with the Prime Minister, and one with Yuri and Mr Clarke, but only on the inside pages. That was the level of newsworthiness a simple returning astronaut received these days. It might be different when the honours lists were published.

I wished I could have told my dad how famous I'd eventually become and hoped the day would arrive sooner rather than later. He wasn't getting any younger. It was down to me to prove AD1 was not a threat, and thereby have the secrecy lifted.

Christmas with my family was wonderful. Each evening, when Mario and I were alone, he quizzed me more and more about the alien craft. It was lovely to have someone with whom to share ideas about it, without a specific agenda.

When the New Year's Honours were announced, Mum and Dad's telephone rang non-stop. Everyone was chuffed for me, but only Dad queried the importance of the award.

Walking together on New Year's Day, he asked, 'Eve. Why'd you get the DCMG? It's almost unheard of for such a prestigious award to be given for a single mission or event. CBE maybe, OBE more likely, but Dame Commander of St Michael and St George is the female equivalent of a full knighthood.'

'Most people won't be aware, Dad.'

'Yes, but *I'm* aware and the press also will be. What did you do you haven't told us about? Apart from Tim Peake nearly a dozen years ago, and he only got the CMG, most of your predecessor astronauts got no honour at all or an MBE at best,' he said, gazing into my eyes in a manner to which I could never respond with a lie.

'There was something, but I can't talk about it and you mustn't speculate about it either. Sorry. I won't enter a guessing game.'

'But I'm your dad, Evelyn,' he always used my full name when he was trying to boss me.

'And I'm not allowed to tell you, Dad. That *must* be an end to it for now. Please.'

'But, Eve.'

'Dad, please...'

He shook his head.

I put my hand on his shoulder, 'You'll know if ever I'm allowed to tell you. You'll be the first person I'll tell. In the meantime, please don't ask me again. Please. It would make life difficult for me. Promise me,' and I felt tears building in my eyes.

He looked at me, a hand on each of my shoulders, and realised he'd pushed it too far. 'Okay, darling,' he kissed me, and we continued our walk.

'Oh, and it should be "Dame Darling" in future, please,' I giggled, which broke the tension and we both laughed as we walked arm in arm along the lane enjoying the moment.

On the weekend of the fifth of January, we moved into our rented cottage in the small town of Helston in Cornwall. On the Tuesday, I'd take up my post at the Goonhilly Earth Station and the *real* work would begin.

12 New Challenges

My first day in the new job.

The taxi arrived, I entered the code which specified the reception doors of my offices at Goonhilly, and it set off across the wild countryside. Although short, this was a beautiful journey of which I'd never tire. At the security gates, I flashed my identification to one of the two security guards.

His eyes lit up. He was meeting the new boss.

'Good morning, Dame Evelyn.'

I read the name on his badge. 'Good morning, Jack,' I said to him and 'Drive on,' to the car.

It delivered me to the computer and administration building. I hung my coat over my shoulders like a cape, rather than wear it, and walked towards the entrance, dismissing the car.

The car called after me, 'Doctor Slater, you have left something.'

My umbrella was lying on the seat. The car's ability to check changes in its weight allowed it to spot forgotten possessions.

There were already a few manual-drive and autonomous cars in the car park. I walked over to the metallic British racing green Jaguar, which I knew to be my new personal autonomous vehicle. It recognised my watch as I approached and unlocked. I tossed the umbrella onto the back seat, admired the car's beautiful sleek lines for a moment, and returned to the entrance. My reflection in the smoked glass doors told me that my appearance was okay after the short ride from Helston. Best suit today and I looked every bit the incoming CEO and very fashionable with the coat draped over my shoulders.

At reception, a young woman looked up from the desk towards me. 'Can I help... oh, sorry. It's Dame Evelyn, isn't it?'

'Yes, and you are?'

'Maureen Welch, receptionist.'

'Nice to meet you, Maureen. Do you know if Miss de Vries is in yet?'

'Yes, she arrived a couple of minutes ago. Do you know how to find your office?'

'Vaguely. Who is the lady in the back office?' I couldn't get into my office, or even the corridor, without a code.

'Mrs Ireland, head of reception.'

'Well, call her through for me and perhaps you can also call Miss de Vries and get her to collect me as I'll need security codes.'

'Certainly, Dame Evelyn.' She disappeared through to the back office.

I'd have to do something about this "Dame Evelyn" business. I loved having the honour but would rather it wasn't made obvious each time people spoke to me. Status had never really meant anything to me. I think it was more important to my parents, but I certainly intended to use it to open doors in the corridors of power when needed. Doctor was different – it was something I had worked for over a number of years, not something I'd gained by being in the right place at the right time.

Mrs Ireland, an impeccably dressed thirty-something, arrived from the back office and reached over the counter to shake my hand, 'Dame Evelyn, pleased to meet you.'

'Pleased to meet you too. I'll call you in for a chat at some point but I've no intention of changing anything in the front office. What's your first name?'

'Marjorie. Call me when you need me, Dame Evelyn.'

'Okay, I will do, and I'd prefer Doctor Slater in future. Thank you.'

My secretary cum PA, Janet de Vries, was approaching. I knew her to be a jovial bundle of energetic efficiency.

'Hello, Dame Evelyn, welcome back to Goonhilly,' she said, a beaming smile on her naturally happy face.

'Hello, Janet. Lovely to see you again. You'd better lead the way. I've a rough idea where I am from the floor plan, but I'd like you to show me where things are on the way. Also, you can use Doctor.'

'What about when I bring people in or am arranging things for you?'

This was going to quickly become annoying, 'Okay, we'll talk about it later but within the building, "Doctor" is fine, and will you do me a favour by letting all of my staff know my preference too.'

'Okay, Doctor Slater. Well, starting from here we have reception plus a waiting area over by the windows. Ladies and gents to the right.'

She led me through the telescope management area, where Mr Brown was based, then we progressed back into reception, moved to the other end of the building, and passed through the secure door with keypad into my domain.

Here we saw the secure computer section, the admin department and language laboratory, on one side of the corridor and, on the other, the new direct communications centre, in constant touch with the Cluster, ISS, UKSA, ESA, NASA, JAXA, CSA, and Roscosmos. Finally, the door into my suite of offices.

'This is where I work, also your ESA liaison officer and Mr Riley's secretary,' she said waving vaguely at the three desks. Tim Riley was my deputy and we'd already been in touch by email and Skype.

'That's Mr Riley's office,' she said, waving a hand towards a closed mahogany door. 'Your office is through this door and you've a separate entrance onto the corridor which has a keypad on both sides. My computer tells me if you leave through it. And that is about it for this building.'

'I can't escape you then?'

'No, but I can be complicit if you make a run for it,' she said and laughed.

'Ha-ha, I hope it doesn't come to that.' I liked her. This was going to be a good working relationship.

'This is your temporary security code,' she said, handing me one of those envelopes which came with PINs from the banks. 'You can change it through your computer.'

'Okay, Janet. Let me settle into my office and I'll give you a call to go through my diary.'

'Would you like a coffee or tea?'

'Yes, thanks. Builder's tea, milk, no sugar. Leave it ten minutes and I'll be ready for you by then.'

She laughed at my tea description. 'Will do.'

I looked around my office, almost in wonderment. It was the room in which I'd been interviewed. It was palatial with full-height windows overlooking shrubs, grassed areas and one of the radio-telescope dishes in the middle distance. An inspiring view.

Butting on to my desk to form a T was the conference table with seven guest chairs.

There were cupboards, bookcases, and three large abstract paintings. Two were fine, but the other would have to go. Too much red. I like subtle and pastels normally.

I walked around my enormous desk, caressing the surface with my fingertips.

My computer had a twenty-four-inch curved-screen monitor. A twelve-inch reflexlet was poking out from behind it. These flexible computers had superseded tablets

123

some years previously. Its secure redtooth gave me close to one hundred metres encrypted range from my desk, or it could operate as a stand-alone machine. A wireless keyboard and thimball (the new version of a mouse into which you insert your finger) sat beside it.

Behind my desk was an enormous image of the dishes to the southern side, photographed from a slightly elevated viewpoint, probably by a drone.

Beside Janet's door was a wall-mounted seventy-two-inch 8K curved-screen television. A three-seater sofa and matching easy chair were positioned beside the window for informal meetings. I smiled at the innovative, circular, glass-topped coffee table, mounted on a support in the style of a satellite dish. Some copies of astronomy magazines appropriately graced its top.

I was thrilled at such unbelievable luxury. In the past, I'd worked in tiny rooms or cramped open-plan offices with well-used and non-matching furniture. I needed to pinch myself that the office was truly mine and I was really the chief executive of this huge establishment. I hoped no one would burst in and tell me it had all been some horrible bureaucratic mistake.

Once at my desk, I'd no sooner finished changing my PIN when there was a knock on the door and Janet entered with two mugs of tea. She placed one in front of me, put the other on the corner of my desk, swung one of the chairs around and sat down with her reflexlet.

I slipped my index finger into the thimball again and the monitor showed my diary for the week.

'I'd better meet Michael, the telescope director, first, Janet. What's his clearance on the Cluster?'

'He's cleared but he's the only person outside of our secure area who has clearance.'

'Right. Let's go for ten am.'

'Type M Brown into the space. It will check if he's free.'

I turned the monitor, so Janet was able to see, typed the name and it appeared at the top of the screen. Using my thimball I hovered over it, bent my finger to collect it, dragged it to ten am and straightened my finger again to release. It now appeared in a green box between ten and eleven.

'Does that mean he'll know about the meeting?'

'Yes, it also means he's free, and his secretary will also know. If he hasn't acknowledged within thirty minutes the entry will turn amber and it'll flash red on his and his secretary's diaries.'

'Janet, while we drink this tea, tell me how you see your main responsibilities here.'

She had come prepared and pulled a document from a folder she'd laid on the corner of my desk, but first she'd something else to get off her chest.

'Doctor Slater, I know you'd like to drop the Dame within the organisation but there are certain protocols I think you should consider. For instance, if someone telephones and wants to talk to you from outside, I think I should say, "I'll find out if Dame Evelyn is available," and if I'm booking accommodation or setting up appointments for you, I really should use "Dame" then too.'

'Yes. I understand what you mean. Okay, talk to an honours expert about it and put the protocol into place. But here, among my staff, it's Doctor, okay?'

She thanked me, and we ran through her job specification. We finished about nine thirty and I asked her to get my deputy, Tim Riley, to come in as soon as he was free.

Two or three minutes later there was another knock on the door. A balding, white, forty-year-old, wearing a fashionable light brown suit, entered the room.

125

I jumped up, skirted around the table and shook his hand. I craned my neck to look up at him as he was much taller than me and very lanky.

'Tim, I'm so pleased to meet you after our telephone conversations.'

'Honoured to meet you. Janet tells me I should use Doctor rather than Dame, Doctor Slater.' His clean-shaven face gave me a genuine smile.

'Oh, this honour thing is so intrusive, Tim, please call me Eve or Evelyn when we're meeting informally, whichever you prefer.'

'Eve, then. Thanks.'

'You've been fully briefed on AD1?'

'Yes. We've a fascinating project ahead of us. How would you like to use me?'

'Firstly, I want you to make a point of always knowing what I'm doing and who I'm seeing. Get Janet to give you access to my diary and keep an eye on it. I've Michael Brown coming over shortly and I'd like you to be here. You worked for him, yes?'

'I was his deputy until this new section was set up.'

'Your main duties, Tim, will be to get the computer, language, and admin sections of our little secret service to liaise with each other. I won't tolerate infighting or power struggles. It'd be good if you could make it clear in general conversation rather than spelling it out. Let them know merit will always be noticed, but deliberate point scoring will never achieve anything as far as I'm concerned.'

'Okay. Can do.'

'Have you seen the writing from the side of the craft?'

'Yes.'

'I want the two of us to speak to the language section after lunch. Set it up and let Janet know. Frankly, the language boys were put in place too soon in my opinion and it'll be a problem keeping them occupied until more hieroglyphics are found.'

'Yes. I think the Home Office wanted everything in place as quickly as possible and didn't think it through.'

It was good to see we were on the same wavelength.

Our chat continued for another fifteen minutes. He seemed easy going but efficient and of course he wanted me to recount the discovery story. I dare say it'll eventually become tiresome, but currently it was still fun.

We talked generally about living on the Lizard peninsula, then Janet knocked and entered with a short, stocky immaculately dressed Asian man in his fifties with a good head of hair which was turning silver. He also sported a small silver moustache, tiny round spectacles, and was wearing a blue serge suit.

I stood up and walked around the right of my desk. He came forward and we shook hands.

'I'm really pleased to meet you, Mr Brown. Can I call you Michael?'

'Yes, fine. Pleased to meet you too, Doctor Slater.'

'Eve or Evelyn, please. You know Tim, of course?'

'Hi, Tim,' he said.

'Michael,' I said, 'you are the only one on the non-secure side of Goonhilly to know about the alien craft. I'll keep you informed as to progress, but secrecy is crucial. For confidentiality reasons, we won't talk about the project anywhere outside this secure wing.'

'Yes, no problem.'

'That means not in your office, either,' I said.

'Okay. I'll come over here for briefings et cetera.'

'I'd love to know more about the telescope and communications functions of non-secure Goonhilly, but my main function here will revolve around AD1. I want... no, I *need* you to function autonomously and keep all day to day operations of the Earth station running smoothly.'

'You can rely on me.'

'You do understand that I'm not here to replace you. You're still GES Limited's boss.'

'Yes, the situation has been made clear.'

'There'll be a growing curiosity about the function of this secure section. I want you to ensure it does not bubble over into a *them and us* situation. Stamp on it hard if that occurs.'

'I will.'

'Also, it's likely that anyone trying to find out what we're up to, might be tempted to try to do that through your staff, so any strange behaviour or out of character questions should be treated with suspicion.'

'Yes. Understand,' he said.

'I'm happy for the word "military" to be rumoured about our work, but I don't, under any circumstances, want to hear UFO or alien spacecraft being talked about anywhere outside of this secure section. I'll be making it clear to everyone on this side of the building at a staff meeting this afternoon.'

'Okay, fine. I'll keep an ear to the ground on staff chatter.'

I went on to ask Mr Brown what he wanted from me, and the meeting continued in a businesslike manner until about ten forty am when Michael and Tim left, leaving me to my own devices. I gave a sigh of relief once they'd gone. I hated meetings and even the idea of administration meetings was anathema. I intended to keep them to an absolute minimum.

Next on the agenda was much more exciting – a secure Skype call to Dr Reg Naughton in the Cluster. What progress had there been on taking the alien device apart?

13 Cluster

Tim and I spent a while with the language technicians and then the computer hackers, ensuring their readiness for when data arrived, but neither department yet had much to go on.

'I'll make sure I chat to them regularly to keep their spirits up,' Tim said.

'Yes, that'll be important. I couldn't talk to Dr Naughton this morning so I've some time booked for four o'clock. I'll ask him to put in a special search for more writing or symbols.'

'Good idea.'

Later in the day I was sitting at my desk as the secure video call arrived from the Cluster.

'Hi, Reg. My first day.'

'Congratulations. Glad you took the job.'

'I'm thrilled to be so involved. I could easily have been back in astronaut liaison at ESA.'

'We're lucky to be part of such an amazing project.'

'Yes, so exciting. Listen, can I give you a couple of quick specifics?'

'Sure, fire away,' said Reg.

'I've two frustrated language experts tearing their hair out. They badly need some more hieroglyphs. Can you help at all?'

'Well, possibly. Each of the fuel containers has a symbol on the side. They're identical but if I were a betting man, I'd say it's a brand, rather than writing.'

'Can you get hi-res versions of each of them sent down? Don't assume they're all identical. Any other marks?'

'Hans is doing microphotography of components. I'll get him to keep an eye open.'

'That's great, Reg. What are you currently working on?'

'The mysteries are piling up with this, Eve. The metal's an unknown alloy. It's stronger than steel and lighter than aluminum.'

I ignored the Americanism.

'We're trying to analyse it at the moment, but we're sure it'll be useful for our space programme. NASA and Roscosmos have asked for a few samples to be sent down on the next Soyuz. We've got to irradiate them and hermetically seal them in helium.'

'Send a piece for ESA too, please, Reg. What's inside the cylinders? Any progress there?'

'We're drilling into one of the fuel cylinders soon. We intend to extract some of the contents for chemical analysis. We don't yet have a plan to open the small cylinders, but we've detached one of those which was hanging outside the ship and we're going to try to discover if any power can be transferred along the wires. That'll be my job after this conversation.'

'What about the node at the front and the thimble-like structures?'

'Sorry, Eve, they're a long way down the list of priorities.'

'I've a feeling it or they could hold the key to this thing,' I said.

'I'll keep that in mind, Eve.'

'Any ideas on age yet?'

'Yes, when we began a close examination of the hull, we found it has a great deal of shallow pitting. The metal's extremely hard. By comparing it with the pitting on the oldest parts of the ISS and considering the strength of the alloy, we believe it's been in orbit for a very long time indeed.'

'How long?'

'Thousands of years, possibly hundreds—'

'Thousands!' I broke in.

'Possibly hundreds of thousands I'm afraid, Eve. We're certain this isn't a recent arrival.'

'Really? That long! How sure are you?'

'Would be safe to say it's older than the pyramids in our opinion so far.'

This was amazing information. It changed the urgency of finding out what it was. If it had been in Earth orbit for thousands of years, its creators would be even more advanced today and the technology needed to put it into Earth orbit in the first place from another star system was way ahead of ours already.

'Fascinating. Any other new information, Reg?'

'Most of the new material should already be with you. Hans sent the first packet this morning and we'll give you daily updates now you're in situ.'

'Any guesses on where it's from? What about Mars if it's been around a long time?'

'Hundreds of guesses,' he said, 'and all totally unscientific. Could be from anywhere.'

I laughed with him and we finished our conversation.

My first day in the new job had begun with a whole string of deepening mysteries.

I arrived home about six. Mario had cooked a chilli and we ate on our laps with a bottle of Chianti before spending the rest of the evening browsing through property details he'd collected from local estate agents. It all seemed so domestic, considering the momentous events I was now likely to be dealing with almost every day.

The next morning, I was in early because I wanted to get Michael Brown to show me around the rest of the complex and I'd a few emails to draft first.

I slid my finger into the thimball and my monitor sprang into life. There was a red flashing light in the top right of the

131

screen. There was a priority message from the Cluster, for my eyes only.

I waved my thimball at it and the message header appeared:

'SUBJECT: Breakthrough!'

14 Breakthrough

I was in my office before dawn and had received an email from Reg in the Cluster which was headed 'Breakthrough', I couldn't wait to open and read it.

From: Dr R Naughton – Cluster Chief Scientist
Date: Wednesday, 9 January 2036 at 06:33
To: Dr Evelyn Slater – CEO Goonhilly
Subject: Breakthrough

Good morning, Eve,

We've made multiple breakthroughs.

Just after we spoke yesterday, we had been experimenting, trying to pass a small current through some of the wires. We'd detached several lengths which had been ripped from whatever they had been connecting by the cause of the hull damage. Initially we couldn't seem to pass any electricity down the wires but then discovered that if we melted the end of the wire, it lost its coloration and the wire almost conducted normally. I say 'almost'

because the wire induces a polarity to the electricity, so our first breakthrough is that we've found that they don't need insulation because when electricity passes through them, they polarize it, just like light. If another wire touches the wire containing the current it can't go anywhere because it has the wrong polarity. It seems that there are an almost limitless number of polarities, hence the large number of different colored wires we found. We needed to melt the wire ends in order for them to pass current. The molten wire, when it cools, exhibits no color and conducts normally. We then experimented with a large number of voltages and amperages and found the wires could tolerate a surprising variety.

133

Now that we knew how to pass power along the wires, we detached one of the small cylinders. It had four wires leading from it and we severed them, leaving about six centimetres of cable with each. Knowing about the polarization, we passed a tiny current into each in turn while putting meters on the other cables to see what came out. When we reached 0.01 amps going in through a wire color we've designated red12, we got an identical amperage out of a wire we designated as green3. Nothing came out of either of the other two wires, green35 and indigo14.

We then tried sending current down indigo14 and the same out wire, green3, started pulsing and it appears to be data. Data coming from the cylinder. It has been a continual stream of data already amounting to over 1TB by midnight. Earlier this morning, Hans checked again, and we have more than 4TB of data and it is still transferring. The cylinders appear to be memory or processors, perhaps both.

I wanted to speak to you about this, but then we ought to talk to the hackers. Up here, we don't have any way of interpreting what is stored.

I am going to take a break but will be available again at 9.30am if you can call me please.

Very excited.

Reg

Several of us had speculated these small cylinders might hold computer data and now the work done by Reg and Hans appeared to confirm it.

I'd read the email three times when there was a knock at my door. Janet popped her head in.

'You're in early,' she said.

'Had plans but they've gone awry. Get Tim to come in the moment he arrives, and a cup of coffee for me, please. When do the hackers usually get in?'

'Any time after about now,' she said and closed my door.

It was eight thirty-five.

The email was fascinating. If each of those tubes had that many terabytes of data in them, there was a danger we'd be overwhelmed with the need for storage.

I walked through the communal office and out into the corridor, saying to Janet over my shoulder, 'I'll be right back.'

I tapped my code into the computer room door and entered. One tousle-haired young man was leaning back in his chair, his feet on his desk, eating a bacon roll and reading the newspaper. When he saw me, he almost choked on his breakfast and only just managed to save himself falling off his chair.

'Doctor Slater! Sorry, I usually read the paper for a while before I start work.'

'Don't panic, David. It is David, isn't it?'

'Yes.'

'How much memory do we have here?'

'What, in total or free?'

'Free.'

'About four exabytes.'

'What's that in terabytes?'

The young man was silent while he did a mental calculation and said, 'Roughly four million terabytes. Why? It should be far more than we'd ever need.'

I felt relieved at the storage available. 'I hope it will be. Get ready for a lot of work, David. We're getting data from memory modules in AD1. Tell Doctor Sweet something big is coming soon and I'll call for him during the morning.'

'Yes, Doctor Slater, will do.'

'Now finish your roll and paper, because you won't see much in the way of coffee breaks once this data arrives.'

I was about to leave but he spoke again. 'To be honest, Doctor Slater, we've all been a little bored. Can't wait to sink our teeth into this thing.'

I laughed again. 'Be careful for what you wish, young man.' I winked and returned to my office.

Coffee arrived with Tim swiftly on its heels. I let him read the email and asked him to read it slowly a second time. I'd found the implications didn't sink in on the first read.

When he finished, I commented, 'Polarised electricity. Think about it. This isn't simply a matter of one or two polarities either, these wires seem to have an almost infinite number. Who can we get to work on it?

'Make enquiries via NASA as to how we can get a high-speed data transfer from the Cluster. We're going to need it.

'Thirdly, the wires themselves. We have no one here who specialises in metallurgy. I want you to speak to our top universities and find out which would have the most relevant experts.

'What is even more fascinating is the fact these small cylinders or tubes can contain vast amounts of data. The problem is we can't cut into one now or we might lose crucial information. One door has opened for us, but it's closed another.'

'Okay, Eve, I'll get onto it right now.' He got up to leave.

'Be here for my call to Reg,' I called after him.

'Will do.'

'Janet,' I shouted as he opened the door and she came running in.

'Can we record my calls to Dr Naughton and the ISS?'

'I think we already do, but I'll check,' she said.

That was a revelation. All my calls were being recorded.

'Any particular reason?' she asked.

'Yes. What we're working upon will become of great historical interest and we ought to have a true record of it.'

'Something happened?' she asked.

'We're getting data from the alien craft.'

'Wow,' she said, before asking if I needed her for anything else and returning to her work-station. I loved Janet's simple acceptance of the extraordinary.

I sat back and contemplated the importance of my function. It was going to be mind-boggling in its complexity.

My call to Reg and Hans was not only historic, but technologically important too. The single tube or cylinder had so far transferred 55TB of data and it was still going. He told me they'd checked to be sure it wasn't the same data transferring over and over again and it wasn't. It was all unique.

Tim told them NASA was going to dedicate a dish to data transfer and it would come in through one of ours each time the Cluster cleared the horizon in each orbit. Ours was capable of handling 1TB per minute, so even though the data transfer would be spasmodic we should soon catch up with the amount being downloaded from the cylinders.

We talked about the wiring and Reg told us NASA wanted to bring MIT (Massachusetts Institute of Technology) on board. I had Tim make a note to liaise direct. I didn't say it over an open line, but I wanted to be sure America didn't get all of the new technology from this discovery. I made a note to speak to the Home Secretary about allowing me to discuss this with the Department of Trade and Industry.

Would the security hold on this thing much longer? There were too many benefits in the offing. Even the wires were a breakthrough if we were able to manufacture them, and the polarisation of electricity itself had incredible potential to prevent leakage, electrocution and so on. Perhaps it could even be broadcast in its polarised form.

Reg sent us copies of the symbol from each of the spheroids, which we believed to be fuel containers. I understood what he meant when he suggested this was probably a brand rather than a word. I sent it through to the language experts with a note informing them we were starting to get data which might give them more to work with. I hoped it would be the case.

After the call, Tim and I exchanged glances.

'Phew,' he said, 'we're about to be very busy indeed.'

'Yes,' I said. 'I'm going to visit John Sweet and the hackers. How much data do we already have? Any idea?'

'The first package was one terabyte. It's on this card, but more's arriving each orbit. It'll be about one terabyte per orbit until we get the high-speed connection. I'll speak to Michael Brown about freeing up a dish shortly,' he said, handing me the SDXC card.

'Good. Tell him I'm sorry about our planned meeting and will reschedule,' I said as I stood.

We both left my office, Tim heading into his, as I made a beeline to the computer room.

The four hackers were sitting around John Sweet's desk in his office. He stood up to greet me and I waved him down, grabbed a spare chair from behind the door and sat casually with the others.

'Right. Wonderful news,' and briefed them over the data collection.

'When do we get the first packet?' asked Mary, one of the hackers who was obviously raring to go.

I pulled the SDXC card out of my pocket and handed it to her in its cellophane container.

'You've got one terabyte there, so get started.'

I was almost trampled in the rush as the four of them dashed out to the main terminal, slotted the card into the reader and transferred it to the hard drive. John and I laughed at the enthusiasm. He joined his team and I stood beside the window and watched.

Soon there were screens full of gobbledegook and I watched hands, pens, and notebooks flying into action as they got the first opportunity to examine alien data.

'John,' I said.

He'd forgotten I was still in the room.

'Sorry, yes, Doctor Slater?'

'If there's anything like language, even computer language, don't forget the language boys in the end lab. They might well be useful to you.'

'Yes, of course.'

'I'll leave you to it.'

I was sure the second breakthrough would come from these whiz kids. I wasn't wrong.

15 Our Star or Theirs?

The second major breakthrough took a lot longer than I expected.

The first 200TB of data from the first cylinder showed nothing other than a huge amount of binary which didn't seem to be taking us anywhere, although Mary was now leading her own team of three to work on it and they were becoming concerned that the data it contained seemed to be changing depending upon when they tried to read it. There was much head-scratching going on and Reg had been asked to send the data several times. Each time it was different when it was downloaded.

The second cylinder was much more informative. The hackers discovered data which appeared to be an image when it was coded to base-8. I went through to watch the image developing.

'Definitely an image,' said John.

'Yes, and that's a star at top right,' I said.

'And a second on the left, Doctor Slater.'

'Plenty of background stars and the usual deep space galaxies. I wonder if our visitor is trying to tell us from whence it came?' I asked rhetorically.

The image continued to fill the screen.

'What's this in the centre?' asked John.

'Another star. Is it dead centre?' I asked.

'Fifty per cent of the data showing,' confirmed David.

'Must be their sun,' said John.

'Looks like it,' I said.

Line by line the remainder of the image was completed with another large star in the bottom left corner.

'Do you recognise it?' asked John.

'No, John. I might be able to if it were in colour so that we can see which stars are red, blue, yellow et cetera.'

'I've got the same image over and over again,' said David.

'Identical?' asked John.

'Almost, but not quite.'

'Colour filters? RGB or CMYK?' I asked.

'Well, possibly, but look at this one. It's almost completely washed out. Why would a star field have so much messy background imagery?' said David.

'Good grief!' said John. 'Could it be X-rays or some other background radiation? We only see from red to violet so cyan, magenta, yellow and black prints almost perfectly for our eyes. Maybe they see into the infrared and ultraviolet so need more "colours" when they view images.'

'That's it. That's it!' shouted David and his fingers were like a blur over the keyboard.

I watched, fascinated. The keyboard action took about ten minutes. I was about to leave them to it when there was a scream from David.

'Ye-e-e-ess!' he shouted, and his fist punched the air over his monitor.

The image began to develop again, but this time, in colour.

'What did you do? ' I asked.

'The aliens do see a far greater range than us, including X-rays and, probably other parts of the spectrum, too. The first image represents black and it's followed by ten other images. Images four, five and six are the visible components for human eyes. So, what you're seeing now comprises one, four, five and six or, KMYC – black, magenta, yellow and cyan.'

'Brilliant, David,' said John.

We stood and watched the colour image develop. Whoever created AD1 had very different eyes to us.

'There's something familiar about the blue stars, but I can't figure out what. I wonder if the central star is their home star.' My knowledge of star fields was letting me down. Normally, I'd expect to recognise a star field with four such distinctive stars.

'We've data which is probably another image,' said Jack, another of the hackers.

'John, can you stick the first image onto a memory chip for me as a big jpg file? Also, find out if I can have the images appear on my large monitor as they're downloaded here,' I asked.

It took four or five seconds to transfer the image. Meanwhile, scans one, four, five, and six of Jack's second image were taking shape on the other monitor.

'Looks like the moon,' said Jack.

I instantly recognised Mons Appeninus, although it was at ninety degrees to normal images.

'Yes, those mountains are the central ridge of the moon's Montes Apenninus. I'm taking this back to my large monitor,' I said, taking the memory chip and returning to my office where I slid it into the memory slot of my huge 8K television.

I wasted at least forty minutes trying to line up the stars with constellations I knew, then it hit me like bolt from the blue. This was not *their* star – it was *our* star. This was Sol, but from their point of view. It was the sun in the centre of the screen.

I rotated the image through ninety degrees, one hundred and eighty degrees, ignored Sol and recognised I was seeing the hind quarters of the constellation Leo. When they took this image, we were in Leo.

I'd missed identifying it because it was upside down from my normal viewpoint and I hadn't recognised the central star. The image showed *us*! If the image showed us from their star, we should be able to find the diametrically opposed star and it'd show us where they were viewing from.

I grabbed my reflexlet and checked the star charts. If my reasoning was correct, the alien came from HD210277 in Aquarius, seventy light years from us. I worked out the declination and ascension of us within Leo and banged off an email to Jodrell Bank to find out whether my guess was accurate.

I was both elated and devastated at one and the same time. We knew from which star the aliens probably came, but it was so far away I wouldn't meet them in my lifetime. Why was the universe so ridiculously huge? It wasn't fair on tiny life forms like ours. Einstein once said that God didn't play dice, but it damn well seemed like he did sometimes.

If we built a ship to travel to their star, it would take centuries to get there. Even sending a signal would take seventy years. By the time they responded I'd be more than one hundred and seventy years old. Okay, a hundred and twenty was the new hundred, but a hundred and seventy seemed impossible. I'd die before receiving their reply. I was furious about relativity and the impossibility of faster than light travel, but I was wasting my time ranting against the laws of physics.

An oppressive sadness came over me as I resigned myself to never having more than AD1 to investigate. What wonders would future generations learn from a species capable of travelling between the stars? Maybe they'd return one day. I clung onto that hope.

More images were being found within the masses of data but there only seemed to be one or two images hidden within tens of terabytes of data. We were working on a long-haul project. John had quickly organised for my 8K television to have a channel dedicated to the images as they downloaded in the lab.

The second and third images were of the moon and Venus. They were nothing special, but the image following that was staggering.

It was obviously an orbital view of Mars. The huge Olympus Mons extinct volcano dominated the scene, but there were clouds surrounding its slopes. Proper clouds. As the colour image built up there were other features which did not exist on the red planet today. Green patches, blue areas, more clouds. This image showed Mars as a living planet, answering questions about whether it had ever had life. It sure did, even if only plant life. How long ago was Mars so alive? It was indicating our alien device was old indeed. Reg's hypothesis that it was older than the pyramids suddenly seemed to be an underestimation.

The fourth image was the Earth.

Tim had joined me, and we watched in awe as cloud-speckled sea appeared. Line by line, a land mass took shape beneath it.

'It could be North Africa, but not quite right,' said Tim.

'You're right, but the Med is making an incursion in towards the Sahara,' I said.

144

'Oh, yes.'

'That makes it extremely old. Need to check.'

'Wait a minute, Eve. What's that at bottom left?'

Off the west coast of the continent of Africa was another land mass. We waited with bated breath for the image to continue.

'Surely, it can't be what it looks like,' I said.

'Good God,' said Tim, 'It must be! It's South America.'

'You're right. The continents are only just starting to move apart,' I said, almost in shock.

This image wasn't from a few thousand years ago, but tens of millions of years ago.

'I'll need to check, Tim, but if my rudimentary knowledge of continental drift can be relied upon, we're looking at Earth as it was around one hundred million years ago.'

'Dinosaurs still roamed the Earth.'

'Yes, we missed our aliens' visit because they passed us by when our ancestors were no larger than dormice and still laid eggs,' I said, in complete awe of the incredible image.

We both sat back in our seats.

'I think it's around a hundred million years ago,' I reiterated, as memories returned from a planetary history lecture I'd once attended.

'Yes, maybe more.'

'We need a pet geologist.'

'I'll get onto it, Eve,' said Tim, and he left my office.

This changed everything. I asked Janet to set up for me to speak to the Prime Minister. This information might add weight to my opinion that the government should change the level of secrecy to gradual drip-feed releases. What would his opinion be?

If we held this news from the public too long, it would come back to bite us later. How could I convince him? The age of the device would help me build a case.

I examined the picture of Mars anew. How wonderful to have an image of this now almost dead planet with water and clouds. I zoomed in further. The patches of green expanded to fill the screen. Life on Mars. Amazing. The seas were small though, more like large lakes. Mars was probably already losing its water and atmosphere.

I had more conversations with Reg and Hans, as well as the NASA equivalent to my department. We were all astounded by the object's age. Fortunately, when it was hit by the meteor or whatever it was, enough of its automated systems remained to allow it to maintain orbit, otherwise we might never have known we'd been visited.

A few minutes later my internal phone rang.

'Slater.'

'John here, Doctor Slater. We've got language.'

'In the data?'

'Yes, as with the images, there are packets of data which seem to be combinations of code. That indicates language.'

'Have you sent it through to the language boys?'

'Yes, Doctor Slater, five minutes ago.'

'Excellent. Any more images?'

'Not in cylinder one or two. We're now on cylinder three. I'll keep you posted.'

I put a quick call through to the language lab and gave them some encouragement. Trying to work out a language would be a hard task. They'd have to discover the alphabet and put meaning to the constructs. I wouldn't know where to start, but appreciated these guys were geniuses.

Janet brought me a coffee and I showed her the images of Earth and Mars.

'Wow,' she said, which seemed to be her stock response for most of the revelations we were discovering. No news seemed to surprise or shock her. I was sure if I told her we'd found Elvis alive on the moon, she'd still say "Wow!" Her simple acceptance of the miraculous was most refreshing.

She continued, almost adding to the surreality of the situation, 'The Prime Minister will be calling in about ten minutes.'

'Thanks, Janet.' I tried to relax with my coffee while I toyed with good arguments to put to the Prime Minister without sounding as if I was badgering him. It might be best to not even mention reducing security, only to ensure they knew the implications of the object's age. They were the politicians and would understand an ancient device was no immediate threat.

I left the picture of Earth from orbit on the big screen. It was so clear and, having seen Africa myself from the ISS many times, it was amazing this was the view I'd have had around one hundred million years previously. Particularly beautiful was the plume of an ancient volcano just to the west of Uganda, stretching all of the way to Sudan, with its shadow mirroring it on the eastern landscape.

My desk monitor sprang to life with Janet on the screen.

'The Prime Minister, Doctor Slater,' she said.

Briefly his private secretary appeared and said, 'Connecting you.'

Mr Clarke looked up from some papers. In the corner of the screen was an image of my head and shoulders. The opposite corner had "ENCRYPTED" in white letters.

'Dame Evelyn, lovely to hear from you.'

'Thank you, Prime Minister.'

'What would you like to discuss? It sounded important.' Would I be calling him if it wasn't important? I mentally scolded myself. He was only being friendly.

'Have you been following my emails, sir?'

'Yes, avidly.'

'Well, the small cylinders do contain data. So far, we have over two hundred terabytes of unintelligible binary from one cylinder, but the second one has been more interesting. Among similar streams of data, the team has found some images coded to base-eight and some packets of data which behave exactly as you would expect from a language. The images are extraordinary. Image one should be on your screen now. It shows a star field.'

'Yes, got it.'

'It's a small section of the constellation of Leo the Lion. The yellowish star is Sol, our sun, so this is their view of our sun in the constellation of Leo.

'I see. Insignificant, aren't we?'

'I suppose so, sir. From the image, we can calculate where they were viewing us from and I might have identified the star. Jodrell are checking my figures as we speak, but if I am correct, they are seventy lightyears away from us in the direction of Aquarius, though even that might only have been a staging post. It means this image was taken en route by AD1, because Sol would have appeared a lot smaller from a full seventy light years.'

'I see,' he said again, and I noticed he was concentrating on his second monitor where the images were being displayed.

'The next image, Prime Minister, is the moon, and the third is Venus. I'm showing them in the order they were deciphered by our hackers. Neither of those images tell us much, but images four and five are revolutionary,' I flicked my thimball and the image of Mars winged its way to London to appear on his screen.

'What's this?'

'That, Prime Minister, is Mars.'

148

'But there are clouds and water... and do I see vegetation?'

'Yes, yes, and yes, sir,' I said excitedly. 'This photograph is a very old image of Mars. We'd not be able to guess how old if we hadn't also had the fifth image,' and I transferred it to him.

'Africa,' he said flatly.

'Yes, Prime Minister, but at the top of the screen, notice the Mediterranean making an incursion into the Sahara, which itself is surprisingly fertile. More important, and this is what helps us date the image and the age of the alien craft, is the land mass to the west of Africa at the bottom left of the image. That, sir, is South America. I'm awaiting confirmation, but I'm pretty sure the image was taken over one hundred million years ago.' I let the news sink in and watched him concentrating on it, repeatedly putting on and removing his glasses.

'Continental drift?'

'Yes, sir. This image was taken when what few mammals there were, still laid eggs. Before the first bees and thirty million years before the first placental mammals. The dinosaurs would still be ruling the Earth for thirty to forty million years. AD1 is extremely ancient.' I sat back in my seat to allow him to take stock of what I'd told him.

'This is incredible.'

'And not a NASA hoax, sir.'

'No. Quite!' I was pleased to see him chuckle. He'd seen the funny side of my comment.

'Prime Minister, we need to continue to analyse the incoming data for another couple of weeks, but I'm afraid we really should be talking to many scientists from lots of disciplines and I'm concerned about the rumour mill exploding. The more who know about this, the more likely

149

we are to spring a leak. You might like to think about a cover story if it does get out, sir.'

'Yes. We will.'

'Tim Riley, my deputy, has made one or two contacts who I can quiz surreptitiously, but we're likely to need university departmental researchers to make sense of the discoveries which I expect to arrive on an almost daily basis.'

'I see,' he said once more.

'I am not trying to make a case yet, Prime Minister, but by the end of January we'll be swamped with questions my department will be unable to answer, so it seemed sensible to give you the heads-up on the situation. Also, I'd like to flag up that the US could be developing commercial aspects and if we aren't doing the same, we might be left at a disadvantage.'

'Yes. Thank you, Dame Evelyn. Leave this with me and I'll come back to you as soon as I can. Continue to email me with new material, please.'

'Yes, Prime Minister.'

'And if your language guys come up with anything, put a red flash on the mail.'

'Will do, sir.'

'You are certain about how old this thing is?' he asked.

'No, not at all, but you can be fairly sure it's at least one hundred million years old. We might be able to get a tighter date from a geologist.'

'But you're sure it isn't a recent object appearing to be older than it is?'

'No. Doctor Naughton had already said it was older than the pyramids from dust impacts alone. If you're concerned it might be recent, it wouldn't seem possible.'

'Could it be Martian?'

'I wouldn't think so, sir. Mars orbiters have shown no sign of any civilisation on the surface. You'd expect some signs such as roadways, dams, and cities.

'Okay, I understand.'

I decided to chance my hand, and added, 'The case for a general release of the discovery is growing, sir. If the public can accept the existence of an ancient device, any future contact will become much less threatening in their minds.'

'Still not convinced about that argument, Evelyn.'

'I understand, sir, but I'll keep making it. Everything I learned during my psychology doctorate tells me we're making a mistake with this secrecy, so I'd be failing in my duty if I didn't continue to make the case for drip-feed releases. Leaving it too long will inevitably mean any release will then be more rapid. That will have consequences.'

'Okay, Evelyn, I'll keep it in mind.'

'Please do, sir. I'll mail you updates as and when I have them and you can contact me anytime. I now have a secure Skype at home too. The Cabinet Secretary has the code.'

'Thank you, Evelyn. Congratulations on the work you're all doing down there. Do please pass on my praise to your staff.'

'Yes, I will, Prime Minister. It'll give them a boost.'

'Goodbye, Dame Evelyn.'

'Good day, Prime Minister.' The screen went back to my diary.

I pressed F14 and said, 'And is it all recorded, Janet?'

'It will have been, but I'll check and get back to you.'

'Thank you, Janet. I'm going to walk to one of the dishes to clear my mind. Don't disturb me unless it's urgent.'

My walk relieved the tension and I took a deep refreshing breath of the cold Cornish air, smelled the sea which was only a few kilometres away and, refreshed, walked back towards my office. The biting wind was now stinging my face. I increased my pace and welcomed the air-conditioned interior of the building as I hurried through the doors.

I was now ready for whatever mysteries would be revealed during the afternoon.

16 Their World

The images stored in AD1 were few and far between, but the hackers had found a way to quickly sift through the data and extract them. There were no more in cylinder two, nor three, nor four. Cylinder five had multiple images of Mercury, Mars, Earth, the moon, Jupiter without a red spot, Ganymede, Calisto, Io, Europa, Saturn, Titan, Enceladus, Uranus, Titania, Neptune, Triton, Pluto, Charon, and even some of the smaller moons of the gas giants. The images of Earth and Mars were fascinating and really needed to be shared. So much could be learned by detailed study of them. How could AD1 have visited all of these worlds? No one thought of the obvious answer to that question and I'd later look back upon this as a failing in our interpretation of the evidence. The next four cylinders again had no images.

The bulk of the rest of the data still wasn't providing any further information, only strings of data in an unknown base format, although one of the hackers was working on an idea which was showing some potential. Whatever coding system the aliens used didn't have any of the regular forms of computer language with which we were familiar. It seemed to come in an unending string of characters. Now we knew images were coded to base-8, it might help with the interpretation of other data. At least, we hoped it might. We also still had the problem that some of the cylinders kept changing their contents as if the data were still being manipulated. How could that be?

In the language laboratory, our experts were struggling to produce an alphabet from the packets of data, mainly because there seemed to be over one hundred different symbols or letters, if that was what the packets of data represented. There weren't symbols or letters in the data, of course, only different sequences. Perhaps it was a language like Chinese, where there are hundreds of characters in use. Nevertheless, I'd been told the first stage would be the isolation of characters, so I shouldn't expect too much too soon. Our problem, of course, was the lack of a Rosetta Stone to give an understanding of which words in one language were matched by the unknown hieroglyphs in the other. We can thank the Rosetta Stone for giving us such an excellent understanding of the ancient Egyptians.

Hans Meyer in the Cluster had found some more text on a panel behind a group of small cylinders and it had been passed to the language boys, but again, it had no meaning at this stage. We guessed it was about the cylinders or the wiring and it was likely to be some form of caution or instruction. At least that is what such a panel would be likely to portray in a human environment. The fact it ran into some six hundred characters of which there were forty-eight different types, was promising. Perhaps we had the entire alien alphabet there.

««o»»

I arrived at work on Tuesday twenty-fifth January, to find hacker, Mary Black, and computer head, John Sweet, waiting for me in reception in a state of some agitation.

'You guys are keen,' I said, checking the time and seeing it was only seven fifteen.

'We were told you were usually in this early and last night, Mary struck gold in cylinder ten,' said John with palpable excitement.

'Come on then,' I said.

We passed through the double doors and I opened the private entrance to my office. John walked straight over to my giant 8K monitor and slotted in a card.

'Eight images,' he said, 'and we think it's their world.'

Image one built up on the screen from top to bottom. It took about six seconds so must've been a large image.

I was staggered. An alien landscape and, more importantly, buildings. In the long sweep of astronomical speculation about alien life, this was a seminal moment. Such a privilege to be the first humans to see proof of another civilisation.

The buildings were mushroom-like structures reminiscent of door knobs, narrow where they sat upon the land and growing in diameter to form a compressed oblate spheroid. There were hundreds of them. Most were of equal size but there were larger versions, never taller but even more compressed, analogous to a large cake stand with a single central support and a much larger compressed spheroid on top. Some were huge.

The image was the view from a high vantage point, probably atop a precipitous drop. We looked straight across a flat valley plain towards more cliffs on the other side. To the right of the image, the cliff from which the image was taken continued into the distance. On the opposite side of the valley the cliffs receded to the left and got closer to the right, suggesting they might meet somewhere off-screen right.

It would be impossible to judge scale accurately in such an alien environment, but I got the distinct impression the opposite cliffs were at least ten miles away. The rock faces seemed to be crumbling, had substantial screes, and there appeared to be tributary canyons leading off them, including hanging canyons which might once have spouted waterfalls and were evidence of ancient glaciation.

'Did these images all have the same number of colour variations?' I asked.

'Yes, Doctor Slater,' said Mary. 'It's possible they might be able to see through certain materials, especially with the X-ray components.'

'You just speculating?' I asked her.

John cut in, 'Mary is, to a degree, but there's evidence in some of these images that the aliens can see through objects. In some image variations, shapes can be seen in the buildings – not detailed, but ramps and floors et cetera. Circumstantial evidence comes from them having no windows in any of the buildings. There's an even better example later.'

'How high do you think the cliffs are?' I asked.

'No way of telling, Doctor Slater, but I'd guess in the order of two hundred metres,' said John.

'Yes, silly question,' I said.

As they receded in the left distance, they also morphed into more of a slope than a cliff. Erosion at work.

'Looks like crops in the canyon,' I said. Fields of many different shades of green were divided by neat straight roads, tracks, or pathways. Scale made the size of these structures difficult to judge. The land between the fields was a similar brown to the cliffs.

'Notice the roads aren't paved,' said John.

'No, simply flat featureless lines. It's definitely a town or city on the left,' I said.

'Yes, we thought that. Strange shaped buildings.'

'That large one on the far left seems to have a crop growing on it,' said John.

'Oh, yes. Seems to be the biggest of them.'

The building occupied the space of at least fifty of the small structures. Some of the middle-sized version also sported green tops.

The roads which ran between the buildings were the same brown as the cliffs and paths through the fields. There were some egg-shaped objects dotted about between the buildings.

'Next image?' asked John, keen to show me more.

'No, wait. Still absorbing,' I said hurriedly, to stop him changing the display. 'I see what you mean about there not being any windows or other openings – and what could those egg-like things be?'

'You see them more clearly in a later image. We think they're vehicles.'

'What's that at the top, right?' I asked.

'We thought it might be a flying object,' suggested Mary.

'Yes, an aircraft perhaps,' I said. They were guessing as well. 'Okay, next image.'

Already cached, the second image came up immediately. It seemed to have been taken from far to the right of the first image, where the two sides of the canyon met. Cliffs rose on either side of the photographer's location, as if the person who took the image was standing in the mouth of one of those hanging valleys, halfway up the full height of the canyon.

The valley opened before us, widening rapidly. The same city was set among the fields, stretching away into the distance where there appeared to be the sea on the horizon. A few wispy clouds floated high above the water. This image suggested they had water in abundance, but there was no sign of any river running down the canyon. There were one or two small lakes or reservoirs between the photographer and the city. Perhaps most of the water was diverted for irrigation. The plain was so flat, I wondered if it had once been a seabed. Maybe it had been raised or, more likely, the sea had retreated.

'Next image,' I said.

A ground level shot this time looking back into the canyon from the shore of the lake seen in the previous image.

Spectacular and dominating the scene, however, was a white, blue, brown, and green world. In half-phase, it hung over the distant cliffs, appearing much as Earth does from space, but about twenty times the visual size of our moon. An absolutely stunning image worthy of any science fiction book cover.

'Wonder how big that world is?' I asked.

'Impossible to judge scale,' said John.

'The colours give the impression of seas, land, and clouds. More clouds than we're seeing in this area of this world. It's an extremely beautiful planet. Next,' I said.

The fourth image appeared. I couldn't stop myself using Janet's pet word, 'Wow!'

This one was obviously taken from orbit around a dry planet with large cultivated areas, broken up by what were probably more of the towns or cities. There was a lot less water on this world than the first images indicated, more like a patchwork of lakes. What cloud cover there was seemed wispy and insubstantial. It was noticeable the higher land was a fairly uniform reddish-brown, a little like Mars, except in a few locations where there was a thin covering of white. Snow or frost.

'What size are these images?' I asked.

'In this cylinder, they're all about a hundred megabytes,' said Mary. 'You can zoom in to quite an extent.'

'We think the central part of the image shows the canyons and valley we've been observing in the previous pictures,' said John.

I poked my finger into my thimball, drew a rectangle around the central feature and zoomed in by waving my hand outwards. Yes. The canyon was now visible, as were the city and lake. What gave the impression of being a sea or the ocean was a lot smaller when viewed in this way.

I zoomed in further and the smaller individual buildings in the city became visible at the point of pixilation.

'Notice how the plateaus are barren,' said John.

Nothing at all seemed to be growing on them. Had this world been losing its oceans over a long period? What was once the land could no longer be cultivated.

'I think the city is standing on what used to be the bed of the original oceans. This might be the fate which awaits Earth in the millennia to come,' I said.

'Yes. We thought the lack of cloud over the plateaus indicated little atmosphere, but there must be some or there couldn't be snow.'

'Unless it isn't snow. Maybe it's hoarfrost. Next picture, please.'

Image five was a close-up of one of the fields. The nearer plants seemed to have prolate spheroid tops, like plums, on slender green stalks.

'Interesting. No leaves, only stalks,' I said.

The spheroids were yellowish-green with purple veins. I was seeing the first ever alien life form, only Mary and John having seen it before me. How amazing. Reg would be excited to view this image. How did the plant grow if there were no leaves? I couldn't think of any Earth plant which didn't at least begin its cycle with leaves. Green suggested chlorophyll.

Image six was a view along a street in the city. The doorknob-like buildings exhibited no doors or windows whatsoever adding credence to the aliens perhaps being able to see through walls and perhaps even passing through them.

'Notice there are no marks on the ground which you'd find on Earth to show driving lanes or no-parking zones,' said Mary.

'Yes. No visible road signs, advertising hoardings, or any building names. Nothing to pass on to the language lads. There are more of the egg-like objects in the streets,' I said.

They varied in size and were standing on their flattened ends. They weren't unlike the shape of AD1. In fact, one of them in the middle distance might have been floating above the ground. Fascinating. There was no way to tell if these were stationary or in motion. Again, they had no apparent opening or window in them.

The image was beautiful as the sky was darkening to purple in the distance and the blue-green satellite planet was three-quarter full in the left sky. How I hoped another cylinder would contain pictures of it. There were so many mysteries here. Was this their main world and was it dying from old age? Had they terraformed their moon? Its blue-green-white appearance had fertile written all over it. Or was this world their moon?

Image seven showed the coastline. There were several of the doorknob buildings scattered around, plus areas of crops in different shades of green. The water was deep blue and there were substantial waves breaking onto the beach.

'Waves suggest wind,' I said.

'Or tides,' said John.

The beach itself blended seamlessly with the uniform brown landscape. In the distance, along the coast, there was an extended conurbation of buildings, including some of the larger cake stand type we'd seen in the city. More of the odd egg-shaped objects were dotted around.

'Is that a tree?' I asked.

To the right, beside one of the buildings was a structure which must be a tree. Its trunk wasn't straight but was reasonably vertical. It branched several times and greenery spread out flatly on the top of each branch.

'We think so. Looks like an African acacia tree. It's the only one we've seen in the images,' said John.

'Next,' I said.

'We've been dying to show you this one, Doctor Slater. Brace yourself!' said John and I looked at him curiously.

My God! The image showed one of the egg-shaped objects in close-up. It was open. The opening was as if someone had cut the egg halfway through around the middle and made a second cut to the top. The bottom, back and sides were still intact. The open area was occupied. What appeared to be a creature almost filled it. It was inside what must be its transport.

I was gazing into the face and eyes of an alien being!

17 Them

The alien's muddy grey skin colour had a dimpled slug-like texture, although not slimy. More like the dry skin of a rhinoceros but with myriad pores and tiny depressions. Two large eyes stared at me. We had no sense of scale, but in relation to the rest of its body these eyes were enormous. There was an oval jet-black pupil and a deep brown iris. Both were glinting as if moist. The iris seemed to be the eyeball itself. It wasn't set into white as would be the average mammal eye.

A fold of skin on the outer side of each eye gave the impression of an eyelid, but one which would have to close with a sideways motion. Above and to the outer side of each eye, a tendril extended, perhaps six eyeball widths, into the air, folding over at the top presumably owing to the weight of an organ of some description which resembled the ovary end of a fallopian tube. Were they ears, nose, or some other sensor? There was no mouth or other opening visible. Could they produce sound, I wondered?

The only other feature of import was an appendage which seemed to come out of the lowest visible left side of the creature.

'Is that an arm and hand?' I asked zooming in upon it.

'Think so. Seems to be holding on to the opening,' said John.

'Seven digits.'

I took the camera position to the corresponding part of the right side and there was no similar appendage.

'Do you think it only has one arm?'

'They might remain hidden until needed,' said Mary, 'like a snail's feelers.'

'Yes, that could make sense,' I said.

'We've only the one image of it. Others might tell us more if we find them,' said John.

Overall, the alien gave a fair imitation of Humpty Dumpty.

'Do you think this is one of them?' I asked.

They both nodded.

'I think the egg-shaped objects in the earlier pictures are a method of transport or a type of clothing,' said Mary.

'Pretty ugly things,' commented John.

'Probably not to their opposite sex,' I said. We laughed and enjoyed the release of the tension.

Oh dear! Suddenly, I realised what we'd done.

'Damn it,' I said in shock, taking on a serious tone, 'you realise I've just made sexist comments about our newfound friends?'

'No, it was only a joke,' John replied.

'And your ugly comment, John? What if this had been about a man of a different race. Black men were considered ugly when they were first encountered by Europeans,' I said.

'Yes. See what you mean. Sorry,' he said.

'I think it's lovely,' said Mary. 'Kind eyes.'

'Yes, see what you mean. Seriously, you guys. I want us to think carefully about this. I don't want any of our staff making similar unthinking, unfavourable comments about their appearance in the way we've just done. Have any of the others in your team seen this image?'

'Not that one, only the landscapes and orbital shot. Only Mary and I have seen the alien. Mary found it after the others had left.'

'Right, keep it secret. Slap the locks down on this image for the time being. I don't want you or Mary to tell anyone about the picture of the alien creature. I'll personally provide a briefing. Understand? If you find more images of them, they're for our eyes only.'

'Yes, Doctor Slater,' they both said.

'We need to ensure we don't spark off some intergalactic incident now or in the future,' I said to reinforce the caution.

'Yes, Doctor Slater,' they both repeated.

'Call me if you discover any more images.'

My last sentence was obviously an end to the meeting and they both left through my main office door. My bad! I'd not congratulated them and ran after them, 'Brilliant work, John, Mary. Seriously. Extremely well done!'

Janet was walking in with a cup tea. The alien was still on my 8K screen. I rushed past her to get to my desk and hurriedly switched off. This was going to have to be dealt with delicately and all she'd give me was another 'wow'. She put my tea down beside me.

'Thanks, Janet. Get me the Home Secretary, urgent, and send Tim in when he arrives.'

'Something new?' she asked.

'Sort of,' I said in a dismissive manner which did not invite further query.

Once she'd left the room, I put the image back onto the screen. A real alien creature. I foresaw problems arising.

If we had issued a news release when we first found the object, people would already have been aware of, and getting used to, extraterrestrial life making the next stage, showing them what it looked like, a simpler process. I *had* been right all along. Now we were likely to have to release the news and the image at the same time and, with the appearance of this thing, xenophobia was inevitable. Kind eyes or not.

I wished I'd stuck to my guns earlier and pushed harder for an immediate release. I was even going to have problems releasing this to the inner circle. There was one way, though, and it would need every psychological skill I'd ever acquired.

My monitor came to life.

'Home Secretary, Doctor Slater,' said Janet, and Jenny Rae's face appeared on the screen.

'Madam Home Secretary, good morning.'

'Good morning, Dame Evelyn.'

'I need to come to London to brief the Cabinet members who know about the Cluster project. It's important it's done in person, in a particular way, and we don't want to miss any of them. It needs to be set up quickly. Would it be possible?'

'Cabinet day tomorrow anyway, so shouldn't be impossible, I'll get someone to call you. Can I ask why it's necessary?'

'Yes. We've an image of an alien and I want to brief all my staff on it first, then I'd like to brief the Cabinet.'

'Amazing news. Send me the image. This connection is secure.'

Oh dear, I should have expected that. 'Home Secretary, with greatest respect, I don't think it would be wise. I believe you all need to see it simultaneously. There's a very good reason. Please trust my judgement.'

'Well, it's a strange request. Is it really necessary?'

'More than necessary, Home Secretary. I believe it to be vital.'

'I'll get back to you, Dame Evelyn. How long will you need?'

'Thank you very much. Thirty minutes would do it,' I said. The connection flickered to black.

I'd been stupid and clumsy! An idiot. I shouldn't have been so open about the image of the alien. This would have implications and it was barely five minutes before it came back to bite me. Janet was on the monitor again.

'The Prime Minister, Doctor Slater,' she announced. Oh dear, I was in *real* trouble.

'Okay,' I said, and Mr Clarke's face appeared on the screen.

'Good morning, Prime Minister.'

He scowled. 'Evelyn, what's this all about? You've got a picture you wouldn't show Jenny.'

'Sir, it's an image of one of the aliens and I don't think you or anyone will want it to be distributed, even among those with clearance.'

'Let me see it.'

'Certainly, sir, but I need to explain before putting the image on your monitor.'

'Evelyn, please, just send me the image,' he said impatiently and with a raised voice.

I gritted my teeth. I had to stand firm. 'Sorry, sir, I can't. You put me in this position at Goonhilly for a reason. You trusted my judgement and I'm a qualified psychologist. Please trust me now for a few minutes. Let me explain it my way, sir.'

He still looked exceedingly irritated. 'Okay, Evelyn, fire away, but keep it brief. I'm late for a meeting.'

I saw raw anger in his expression. He didn't like being kept waiting. What an idiot I'd been telling the Home Secretary about the picture. I was convinced my strategy on this was correct, and this time I was going to take the time I needed to present it properly. If it wasn't brief enough for him, I'd face the consequences. I made him ten minutes late for his meeting as I outlined my reasoning and eventually revealed the image.

Tim walked into my office and I hit mute.

'I'll call you,' I said and waved him out hurriedly. He swiftly left.

I watched the Prime Minister studying the image silently for about two or three minutes before his gaze returned to mine, 'Okay, Evelyn, you've convinced me. It's best you make the presentation your way. I'll call the meeting for ten tomorrow morning. I'll ensure as many as possible who know about AD1 are present.'

'Thank you, sir. You'll not show anyone else? The whole point is to manage the reveal.'

'No. As I said, you've sold me on your plan. I'm glad you remained firm, I knew you were the right person for this job, and you've proven I was correct. Goodbye for now, and congratulations to your team.'

'Sorry about your meeting, sir,'

He looked at me fiercely, then smiled. 'Goodbye, Dame Evelyn.' Phew! I'd survived.

I buzzed Janet to come in.

'Shut the door.'

She closed the door and stood just inside the office. I think she knew what was coming.

'How the hell did you let Tim enter my office while I was talking to the Prime Minister?'

'I'm really sorry, Doctor Slater. I was on my knees at the filing cabinet and didn't see him in time.'

'Okay, but if I'm on a call like that in future, making sure I'm not disturbed is more important than anything else you might be working on.'

'Sorry, Doctor Slater. It won't happen again.'

'Okay, Janet. Send Tim in to me and then I'd like you to set up a staff meeting in my office for two this afternoon. Everyone. I don't want any absentees. If anyone's off sick, find out if they're well enough to come in. Ensure Mr Brown attends. If anyone really can't make it, set up for them to see me personally when they return to work as I'll need to update them face to face. Organise nibbles, coffee and tea et cetera. Secondly, book me an express car to take me from home to London about eight tonight and organise accommodation for me near Number Ten.'

'Will do,' she said.

'Oh, and ensure Tim and I are not disturbed unless the building's on fire!'

She laughed. 'No problem.'

'And for the staff meeting too.'

'Of course.'

When Tim arrived, he sat down opposite me.

'Can I try a spiel out on you?' I asked

'Fire away. What is it?'

'I have an image of an alien,' I said and saw shock pass across his expression.

'I want to present it without causing its appearance to generate xenophobia, laughter, or cruelty. People can be so heartless without thinking when they encounter something different.'

'Okay. Try it out on me.'

'I'm worried about being too politically correct, but nothing is more important than acceptance of the alien without prejudice. When I've finished, I want you to ruthlessly tear my presentation apart.'

'Will do.'

I called Janet and reminded her we were not to be disturbed, then began a seat-of-the-pants presentation to Tim. I could refine it afterwards with the benefit of his advice.

»«o»»

After I'd made the pitch to Tim, we discussed all aspects of it and, in the afternoon, I had the opportunity to perfect it by trialling it on my own staff. Perhaps then I'd be ready for the Cabinet. We were both concerned the political

168

correctness was a little over-the-top, but we agreed if this were not hammered home effectively there'd be no going back. The end justified the means. We'd one shot to get it right. If it didn't work with the staff, we'd have to completely rethink. We both agreed that some overkill on the political correctness had to be the right way to do this. A more relaxed approach could be used once we'd gauged reactions.

««O»»

The corridor door was open. Several additional chairs were brought into my office and organised, theatre style, with my 8K screen at the front. Catering organised some nibbles and Janet had prepared some fruit juice plus flasks of coffee and tea.

Gradually they arrived. The hackers, now ten people, the language boys, another six from admin, three from the communications centre, Mr Brown from telescope operations, and the rest of us from this department, so twenty-six plus me. Reception had been told not to disturb us under any circumstances and Janet had put our telephones onto a recorded message saying we were all in conference and would be available again in an hour.

Everyone dug into the hors d'oeuvres and beverages while we chatted generally about how things were going. Once they were all relaxed, I called them to order and got them to take seats facing the screen. I put the orbital shot of the alien world onto the giant television and walked around to stand in front of the monitor. It was daunting to do this in front of the staff, but it was my one opportunity to get it right before repeating the process in front of the Cabinet – and that would be even more scary. It was more important than a dress rehearsal, because my staff could not "unhear" or "unsee" its content. I *must* get it right first time.

Tim and I had discussed the level of political correctness I should apply, and I was going to keep it at a high level for the staff. I'd get feedback later to tame down parts as necessary for the Cabinet. Too heavy was better than too weak.

'All mobile phones switched off, please,' said Tim.

Most checked and one or two fiddled with their screens to comply.

I felt like a school ma'am as I took a position between my wall monitor and the first row of seats. A deep breath to calm me down. I concentrated on my determination to neither rush nor stumble, then I began, 'You might be puzzled about why I've called this meeting, but all will become clear. We've discovered more about our alien friends.

'Some of you have seen a few of these images. I use this one to open my presentation because it shows what might be the home world of the people who made the alien craft and sent it to us for what is, so far, an unknown reason.

'Look at it. It's a dry world. None of the great oceans of Earth. The plateaus appear to be barren and we suspect the air might be thin on the top as evidenced by the lack of clouds over the high country.

'Notice the crops and cities.' I zoomed into the canyon ready for the next image.

'This city appears to be on a flat plain, possibly an ancient seabed, although we have no conclusive evidence yet, but I want you all to think about this world, what its problems and advantages might be.'

I flicked my thimball and the image of the crop appeared.

'They grow crops. This is one of many different colours of green in various images. Note the lack of leaves. This isn't how plants grow on Earth. Let's examine the city,' and I flicked my thimball again.

'We immediately notice the lack of windows and doors. The large spectrum we encounter in their images might mean that they can see through certain materials, but if these truly are buildings, there must be a way to enter and leave. That we cannot see entrances does not mean they are not present. Those of you who have seen images of the fins, thruster funnels and inside of AD1 know their engineering seems to be without obvious joins between objects. Wires blend into components and components appear to grow into the structure which holds them in place. Keep in mind how different their technology is.

'This image shows what might be a moon but, unlike ours, it has land and sea and clouds. Does this mean they've terraformed it? Or, is it their main world and this arid planet its satellite? We've no way of gauging which body is the larger of the two or even if one revolves around the other. Perhaps they orbit each other or simply pass occasionally.

'This next image depicts the seashore of the alien world. Although there are waves, the lack of coastal erosion shows little evidence of tides. With another massive body like the other planet nearby, why are there no obvious tidal forces? Perhaps it means they are both locked to each other by the same faces, as our moon is to us. If our moon had oceans, they would not exhibit much in the way of tides either owing to the same face always being turned towards Earth.

'I mention all these things because you,' and I pointed at the people in the room, firstly random individuals and next a general sweep, 'all of you, are extremely privileged to view these images. *You* have been specially selected to try to understand AD1 and its secrets. The world – yes, the whole world – needs you and others like you working in Houston, on the ISS, and in the Cluster to be able to view these secrets with an open mind. Your open mind must also ensure we don't place Earth-type prejudices into the alien environment.

'Think about my last sentence. What might it mean? What prejudices do we have on Earth which might jeopardise our study of the aliens?'

I flicked the thimball again to allow the close-up image of the alien city and street to appear.

'Here we have a closer image of the buildings and the egg-like things in the streets. Note the lack of signs or markings on the road. Where are the KEEP LEFT or NO RIGHT TURN signs? Where are the parking restrictions, the lines which indicate right of way for traffic, the speed limits, the traffic lights? Why are there none? How would you know which building is the local supermarket, bank, restaurant, or dentist? The egg-like objects might be vehicles but there aren't any doors or windows? How do they see out of them?

'Of course, it's only the last decade which has seen us truly adopt autonomous cars in large numbers, but we'd still want to see outside wouldn't we? Because we don't observe windows does not mean there aren't any. Perhaps the material these vehicles and buildings are made from is a sophisticated one-way glass. Maybe you can sit inside and see right through them. Maybe the joins in doors and windows vanish when they close.

'Does it sound far-fetched? It shouldn't to those of you in this room because you are the elite. You, with few exceptions, were selected for your ability to think and work laterally. Even those who weren't, had to pass a profiling test which ensured they would ignore prejudice, preconceived ideas or anything which might go against their beliefs. If your religion, those of you who have one, taught that aliens can't exist, you wouldn't be sitting in this room right now. If you had the slightest racial, religious, sexual, or other discriminatory slant in your characters you would've failed to have been chosen to sit here today.

'Think about all of this,' and I paused while I paced back and forth in front of my audience. At random, I looked deeply into some of their faces, trying to make a connection, ensuring they were aware they were part of these revelations.

A hand shot up from one of the communication staff.

'Unless you are bursting to use the loo, Barbara, I'd like you to continue thinking on what I have been saying, rather than asking specific questions right now.' The hand was timidly withdrawn.

I walked over to her and put my hand on her shoulder, 'Please excuse my severity,' I came back to the front, 'but I need your grey cells to be working now on what might be coming next. You're all clever enough to know that this is leading up to something really important.'

I stood directly in front of the 8K screen and pointed at one of the egg-shaped vehicles.

'We *do* think this is a vehicle.' I pointed at the one further away down the street. 'This one even seems to be hovering off the ground.'

'What would you say if I told you these objects can sprout axles and wheels from their bases and move at high speed? Hugh?'

The language expert was at once the centre of attention.

Nervous of the spotlight, he responded, 'I suppose I'd ask how?'

'You wouldn't tell me it was stupid?' I snapped.

'No, Doctor Slater.'

'Well, it is stupid,' I said as I walked over and stood in front of him. 'Explain why you didn't say it was stupid.'

'I don't know,' he said with a nervous laugh.

I turned away and snapped, 'I do. I know why you didn't say it was stupid.'

I turned towards my audience again and noticed Hugh had coloured a little.

'Hugh, you didn't say it was stupid because you didn't want to rule out the possibility. Am I correct?'

'Yes, I suppose so,' he said timidly, but somewhat relieved.

'That, Hugh, is why you are on this team of open-minded, lateral-thinking individuals,' and I made my way back towards the screen. As I turned to stand in front of the image, I caught sight of a wry smile on Tim's lips as we'd discussed this part of what I was saying. He knew exactly what I was doing and how it would end.

'Okay, everyone. Sorry about the amateur dramatics and picking on individuals. It was all done in good spirit and for the best of reasons.

'Let's try again,' I said and paced back and forth, finally letting my gaze settle upon my NASA liaison, Paul.

'Paul.' He looked up at me anxiously.

'Paul, what would you say...' and I gave the impression I was thinking something up, 'if I told you the top and front of these egg-like things can vanish, revealing their contents?'

I guessed his mind was whirring. He was trying to think of the right thing to say.

'How?' he said quietly.

'*I* don't know how!' I said loudly, but obviously with some humour underlying my feigned anger.

'I suppose it could be possible because we don't know anything about them,' he said more confidently.

'And *that* Paul, is the *right* answer. It must *always* be the right answer until we do know about them and how they work.'

I was back in front of the 8K screen.

'In fact, it does appear to be possible because the next photograph shows one of those egg-shaped objects with no front. We will be able to observe the inside.'

More than twenty pairs of eyes zeroed in on the screen, but I wasn't ready for the reveal.

'Janet, do you have any phobias? Spiders? Jellyfish?'

'Snakes,' she said, wondering why she'd been picked on in front of everyone. In fact, I'd picked her because I knew about her phobia.

'Right. Janet, if we were face to face with one of these egg things and it opened and there was a coiled snake within it, what would you do?'

'I'd run a mile,' she said, and everyone laughed.

'What if it was an intelligent snake and said, "Hello, Janet, can we be friends?"'

'Oh, I see. I'd try to overcome my horror and say "Hello, Mr Snake," back to it,' she said more cheerfully, 'but I'd still want to run,' and everyone laughed again.

'Well, at least you'd have tried, Janet,' I said encouragingly.

I lifted the finger upon which I had the thimball.

'The next image shows what is inside one of these eggs. I want you to think about the lesson my PA has given us. I want you to imagine your worst nightmare is about to say hello to you. Can you visualise it doing so? Like the boggart in the *Harry Potter* books and films. Anyone remember them?'

There were a few chuckles, smiles, nods of heads, and some more encouraging *"of course"* and *"no-problem"* type murmurings.

'Sorry to keep you in suspense for so long, but I need you all to think about your own predilections and phobias. I need you to consider the reaction of the world at large when they have their first glimpse of these aliens. *You* need

175

to be the voices of calm. The world needs to accept that not every alien is going to resemble a sweet BBC Clanger or a cuddly Star Trek Tribble. Understand?'

Lots of nodding heads greeted the question. I could sense the anticipation in the air.

'Finally, I want to make it clear I won't accept *any* negative comments about the aliens from any of you. No nicknames, nothing abusive, nothing funny. Remember, racial prejudice begins with jokes and soon becomes all pervasive.

'A hundred years ago, there were children's dolls which were black with white eyes and black curly hair. They were called golliwogs. In the early twentieth century, white people started calling black people "wogs" as a supposedly funny insult. It was racial abuse. It took decades for the word "wog" to drop out of the British vocabulary and for golliwog toys to slip into oblivion. That's why I've taken so much time over this presentation with you today. Being politically correct isn't something you should switch on or off as the situation requires. The acceptance of any person, whatever their shape, size, colour, or perambulatory method should always be thoughtfully done. You must consider them to be alien *people*.

'Whatever your greatest fear, it is probably not in one of these eggs but when John, Mary, and I first saw it, John and I were not thinking when we made our first comments. John said it was ugly and I said it probably wasn't ugly in the eyes of its opposite sex.' There were many smiles and not a few frowns on my audience's faces.

'Neither of us realised how unkind we were being. We were lost in the excitement of the moment. John's comment was cruel and insulting and my comment was *worse* because it included humour within the insult, the very worst type of prejudice. At least the rest of you now know senior staff are as susceptible as anyone else. Learn from our mistake. John and I feel dreadful about what we said and even worse about our thoughts. By telling you of our failings, I want all of you to be better equipped to not make the same mistake and, when news of these alien people finally goes public, I'd like to think you will stand up for them and slap down the insults you will hear from the ignorant and foolish.

'From this point on, Goonhilly has a golden rule. The rule is that when you're discussing the aliens, *in any context*, you must do so as if one of them was standing beside you, listening to what you're saying. Do I make myself clear?'

There were some nods and murmurs of agreement.

'Not good enough!' I said loudly but allowing a smile to accompany it. '*Do – I – make – myself – clear?*'

There was a sudden chorus of, 'Yes, Doctor Slater,' followed by some laughter.

'So,' I lightened up and lifted my finger in readiness, 'let me say you are now going to encounter something wonderful. It is something intelligent. It appears to be offering us friendship. Other than the Prime Minister, John, Mary, Tim, and me, no one else has had the incredible experience of seeing one of these alien people.'

A flick of my thimball and the alien appeared on the screen.

I smiled as I heard a muted 'wow' from Janet. There were a few hurriedly taken breaths and a gasp or two from others. What I hadn't expected was to hear sobbing. All my preparation to try to get a positive reaction and, damn it all, one of the girls from the admin section was letting me down. She was crying.

I was so annoyed but determined not to show my anger at her being upset at the alien's appearance. I approached her and tried to be measured in my dealing with this unexpected adverse reaction. I spoke softly and asked, 'Jennifer, what's the problem?'

177

'Doctor Slater,' she sobbed, 'its eyes. It has such loving, friendly eyes.'

18 Auditorium

That evening I got home before six and packed my overnight case.

Further discussions over the pitch with my managers had helped me to refine it and I was now really confident. I tested a shortened version on Mario, and we discussed it in detail while we prepared dinner.

I left the picture of the alien on the television while we ate our lap-tray meal. We both gazed at it and talked about the possibilities. How did it evolve? How do they move about? There were so many questions arising from its existence.

'I do love the eyes. There is a kindness and intelligence there,' I said and told him about the reaction of the girl from Admin.

'You know,' Mario said, 'he or she has probably been dead for millions of years. How will they have evolved since? The largest mammal on Earth when this photograph was taken was a tiny egg-layer.'

'Yes, the timescale is enormous. Its race might not look anything like this today.'

It was so good having someone with whom to chat about these things, without needing him to perform any function, or for me to be careful about how I spoke. At Goonhilly, I was always conscious of my status and keeping myself a little detached from the staff.

My express car arrived promptly after dinner, my watch alerting me to its presence. We hugged, and Mario wished me luck for the next morning's meeting. As I approached the car, the door and back swung open. I tossed my bag into the boot and climbed inside.

I'd never used one of these high-speed hire cars before. Inside, it was luxurious with plenty of legroom, a large LED screen for television or work and a small cupboard containing snacks and refrigerated drinks.

Janet had pre-programmed the coordinates for the front door of my London hotel so all I needed to do was belt up and say, 'Go.'

The car pulled smoothly out of the driveway and drove at the autonomous speed limits, braking gently well in advance for bends and to give a comfortable ride.

On more major roads, we were soon travelling at an average seventy. After reaching the A30, which comprised a lot of fenced dual-carriageway, my express car stayed at about one hundred and forty miles per hour, only reducing speed occasionally to allow manual-driven cars, of which there were fewer each year, to make way for it. It was, of course, communicating with all nearby autonomous vehicles to ensure they moved over to let it past.

Surprisingly quickly we joined the M5 motorway near Exeter. The outer motorway lane is exclusively for autonomous vehicles and we accelerated to over two hundred. The suspension and clever acceleration and de-acceleration used on the curves made it a smooth experience. Even road surface problems vanished at this speed, the car's suspension and aerodynamic shape gluing it to the surface even at close to a third of the speed of sound.

In a little under two hours I'd covered the three hundred miles to the capital, and it came sleekly to a halt at the hotel at nine fifty-five pm.

I slept fitfully. Sections of my forthcoming presentation kept running through my mind. I had a nightmare that I'd forgotten my reflexlet and actually got up to check it was in my briefcase. Not a good night at all.

The next morning, I arrived at Number Ten and was greeted by the prime minister's private secretary who took me to a nearby auditorium where I unfolded my reflexlet, plugged a one-centimetre cube processor into it and added the SDXC card which held the images I required.

Checking there was no one in the room, I slipped the thimball onto my finger and practiced changing images, so I knew everything worked and was in the right order.

I hadn't expected to be in such a large hall. I'd thought we'd use one of the meeting rooms in Number Ten itself. This space was in an adjoining building and was a substantial auditorium, a veritable theatre.

I attached a sekuroid to the reflexlet. These ingenious devices would not allow it, or anything plugged into it, to be moved without first giving a verbal warning and secondly, causing a screaming alarm to sound continuously until the movement ceased.

Sekuroids had been incredibly useful in stopping casual theft and housebreaking in Britain in recent years. There was even a mobile version which recognised who was carrying it, thus defeating pickpockets. All modern mobile phones carried one. They had an additional function which tracked your position in relation to the sekuroid which prevented you accidentally leaving anything it was monitoring in a train, café, or other location. It had revolutionised consumer peace of mind and caused an almost complete halt to petty crime.

Outside the auditorium was a lounge area where I'd been told to wait once I'd set up.

A minute or two later, Gerald Aston from ESA walked in.

'Gerald. What a surprise. How lovely to see you,' I said as we feigned cheek kissing.

'Yes, must drop down to Cornwall and see the set-up sometime.'

'Oh, please do. What are you doing here? Thought I was going to be doing this for the Cabinet and some top civil servants.'

'Ah, my job is to keep you company until the meeting is assembled. Come through here. We can get a coffee.'

I followed him into a dining area where we were served our beverages.

'Nice of them to not leave me alone to panic over the presentation,' I said, and laughed nervously. 'Why are you really here? They can't have flown you in just to keep me company.'

'All of us in the know are here, if possible. Over thirty of us from ESA.'

'*Really?* Thirty, just from ESA! Good God, I thought I was just briefing the cabinet.' I couldn't believe the invitation had gone this far.

'The Science Minister made it pretty clear we should be here. What have you got?'

'Ha-ha. That's for me to know and you to guess at!'

He joined in with my amusement. We'd always got on well during my time on the ISS and it was good to catch up. Gerald had been on ESA duty when Yuri and I realised AD1 was alien, so he'd been the third to know about the discovery.

I was becoming anxious about the size of my audience.

Shortly before ten, the prime minister's secretary popped his head around the door, 'I'll come and get you shortly, Dame Evelyn. Mr Aston, can you come with me now?'

'I'll catch up with you later if I can,' I told Gerald and sat on my own. This was obviously to be a much larger group than I'd been anticipating and my nervousness was growing with each passing minute.

Fortunately, my wait was only two or three minutes and the parliamentary secretary took me through a different corridor which brought me out onto the stage area. He clipped a throat mike to my collar. A quick check reassured me my equipment hadn't been touched. When I glanced upwards, the size of my audience staggered me. No wonder I needed a microphone.

I was ushered to a stage chair and the private secretary said, 'The Prime Minister will be here momentarily.'

In front of me, a sea of faces. Between one and two hundred intently looking towards me. I gave an acknowledging nod to those I recognised and spotted Yuri in the third row, giving him a tentative wave.

I had had no idea the news of our discovery of AD1 had spread to so many. There was a general hubbub of conversation in the room which died when the Prime Minister came in via the stage entrance and walked over to me. I stood, and he shook my hand.

'Larger group than I expected here, sir,' I said quietly.

He spoke softly, 'Yes, I said you'd convinced me of the importance of doing this properly. I've ensured virtually everyone in the know is present. I told them to drop everything to attend. Now you have the opportunity to put us all in the picture, in the way you suggested. We are also filming it to be sent to the King, President Drake, the European heads of state, President Gorelov and Prime Minister Yamoto as well as others who were unable to attend.'

'Gosh, I'm not sure such a gem of information will help my nerves, sir.' I was now seriously worried about the possibility of screwing up.

'You'll be fine, Evelyn. I wouldn't have let you do this if I hadn't been one hundred per cent certain it was the right thing to do.'

'Thank you, sir,' I said, allowing my heart rate to continue its attempt to slowly come back to normal.

'I intend to say a few words, then introduce you. Ready, Evelyn?'

'I'll do my best,' I said, still with nerves at breaking point.

'And I know your best will be more than fine,' he said quietly as he shook my hand again. He seemed to have a real trust in me. I hoped his confidence in my ability wasn't misplaced.

Mr Clarke turned to face the audience and waited for silence which arrived swiftly. He surprised me by calling me Dame Evelyn during his glowing introduction, the first time I'd been called Dame in public. I was still uncomfortable with my title. He smiled at me, gave a small wave for me to take over, and made his way down the stage steps to take his place among the rest of the Cabinet and the leaders of opposition parties in the front row. Had there ever been such a prestigious audience in British history?

I stood and, determined not to allow nerves to get the better of me, walked slowly to the centre of the stage, cleared my throat, and tapped the collar microphone to switch it on.

'Good morning.' I took a deep breath. 'I thought being blasted into orbit on a Soyuz was scary, but looking at this audience is even more daunting,' I said to break the ice and it pleased me to hear some laughs and chuckles.

After a short introduction, which explained the discovery of AD1 and what we were working on at Goonhilly, I began in the same way I had in my office the previous day by showing the orbital shot of the alien planet.

There were mumbles from the auditorium and I continued my presentation, although cutting some of the theatrics which Tim and I felt were a little too demeaning, especially for this prestigious audience.

When it got to the later stage, I asked for a show of hands of who couldn't stand spiders, then snakes. I was delighted to notice Gerald Aston put his hand up as having a snake phobia. It allowed me to ask him the question I had put to Janet in my office the previous day. It worked like a dream and at the end there was nothing but praise for how I had manipulated the audience to get the positive outcome we all needed.

After thirty minutes of fascinating questions, most of which were unanswerable, I was taken into the Prime Minister's office with the Home Secretary and Minister for Science, and tea was served. They were all so relaxed in this environment and made me feel at home, as if I were among friends rather than the government elite. These were, after all, only people, like me. It was their status which caused the nervous apprehension about being in their company.

About midday, I was offered lunch by the Minister for Science but needed to get back to Goonhilly as there was so much to do. I called an express car.

Autonomous cars had revolutionised travel in the UK. Congestion had almost vanished and, where it was still a problem, it was owing to manual-drive vehicles still requiring traffic lights to control junctions and low speed limits to allow for human beings' less than perfect reaction speeds.

Yes, there had been a few accidents as the technology developed. Yes, there had been isolated cases of cars being hacked, but in mitigation for the odd problems, the road fatalities in the UK had fallen from nearly two thousand in 2020 to four hundred in 2034. Only six of those fatalities were caused by an autonomous vehicle's error.

I was back in my office, after a three-hundred-mile journey in the middle of a weekday in only two hours and fifteen minutes and having drafted and sent several emails en route. The journey would've taken over five hours, maybe six or more on congested days twenty years previously and all the stress and worry had been removed from road travel. Even faster journeys were promised when manual-drive vehicles were finally phased out, but there were strong lobbying and anti-robot groups who would have to be assuaged. However, they'd been losing ground rapidly since 2030. The safety record spoke for itself, and those who wanted to drive for fun would likely soon be confined to race tracks.

When I opened my office computer, I found the video file from the auditorium had already arrived. I got Janet to book me a call with Reg in the Cluster for four o'clock and sent him the file, suggesting he drop whatever he and the other scientists were doing to watch it.

I repeated the message to the ISS. Houston was several hours behind us, so they'd be seeing it shortly too.

I then sat quietly and watched it to satisfy myself that I hadn't made too many mistakes.

No new images had been found but Dr John Sweet and one of his hackers, David Weston, had asked for a meeting. I called them in.

'Good afternoon, Doctor Slater,' said John as he and David entered the room. 'How'd the presentation go?'

'Brilliant, John, thank you. Sit down. What've you got for me?'

'David, tell Doctor Slater what you think.'

'Doctor Slater, Jack Morgan and I have now spent a considerable time analysing the data which has come from the cylinders which contain no images and nothing remotely like language. These are the ones with the data which seems to change each time we look at it. We have an explanation,' he said.

'I'm all ears,' I replied.

'We think it's a mind.'

'Sorry?' I asked.

'A mind. The contents of a brain.'

'Sorry, still not with you. You mean memory?'

'No, not memory. The mind itself. It's easier if I show you,' he said, waving an SDXC card at me.

'Go on, I'm intrigued,' and I directed him to the 8K screen.

186

He stood up, an ungainly youth with a shock of uncontrollable hair, ambled to the television, and slid the card into the slot. He put on his thimball and after a few flicks it recognised him as the user.

'This, Doctor Slater, is the pattern of data we get if we try to read a human mind.'

The screen showed a graphic moving from left to right across the screen like a voice print, but more evenly spread.

'Notice how the peaks and troughs are even, and how consistent the vibrations are. They continue without much variance at all. Now watch what happens in about ten seconds.' We waited and watched the image change.

'Notice how the peaks and troughs gradually die down and shorten. There is much less activity, but it is still continuous.'

'Yes.'

'What we've been watching is an awake human mind which then fell asleep. We decided to convert the data from AD1 into graphic and this second sequence is the result.'

Another pattern appeared on the screen, almost identical to the sleeping human brainwaves.

'This,' said David, 'is the data from the cylinders which contain no images or language. It goes on like this for, so far, six petabytes of data.'

'That is six thousand terabytes, Doctor Slater,' interjected John. I nodded.

David continued, 'I think we are seeing one of the creature's sleeping brain functions.'

'But why shouldn't it be simply storage data but of a type we've not yet identified?' I asked.

'Doctor Slater, you yourself have said we are a pretty clever group of geek dudes and we think we're among the best hackers in the world. The fact we can't identify this as any form of computer storage data means it probably isn't computer storage data. When we checked it against brainwave data, it was pretty clear to us that brainwave data is what we're seeing. We can examine this stuff until we're blue in the face and we'll never be able to read it in the accepted meaning of the word.'

I sat back and watched the data streaming across my monitor.

'Not only that, and this is crucial,' he continued, 'we had Doctor Naughton send the data from the same cylinder a second and third time, the output always changes. That, in our opinion, means that it cannot possibly be storage. It must be an actual mind and it's still in the cylinders and still producing activity.'

'What? It's still alive?' I exclaimed.

'Maybe, but in a coma,' said David.

'Do you concur, John?' I asked.

'I have carefully examined David and Jack's work and analysis and, yes, I concur with their opinion.'

'Which means?'

'It means AD1 might still be alive in the cylinders,' said David.

'Alive but not conscious?'

'Still functioning.'

'So why has it not communicated with us.'

'Jack reckons it's so badly damaged that, as David says, it's in a coma,' said John.

'What do we do, then?' I asked.

'We no longer apply resources to these cylinders and concentrate our work on the others, which do have some chance of being interpreted. In fact, David is fairly sure we are obtaining computer data and programming in the other cylinders and we are confident we will understand it eventually. This data, however, is insoluble,' said John.

'I see.'

'Doctor Slater, permission to speak speculatively?' asked David.

'Please do.'

'I think this is part of one of the alien's minds. AD1 was meant to present itself to us as one of them, to talk to us and interact with us, but the damage has destroyed its capability permanently.'

'What? Like a robot?'

'No, more like a disembodied alien mind. I suspect this was one of them. He/she/it couldn't journey for centuries to get to us, nor wait around the hundred million years it has taken for us to evolve, so it put its brain into this egg thing and sent it as an emissary.' He sat quietly while I digested what he had said.

'So, this thing, AD1, is one of the aliens in electronic form?'

'Yes, but damaged beyond repair. In effect, the mind has hibernated and is incapable of waking. All we're seeing is part of its stored brain capability and some data it brought along with it. It explains why there is no Rosetta Stone for us to discover. We weren't meant to have to work out the data for ourselves. We were meant to have it explained to us by the alien.'

'I understand.'

There was little more I could do or say. I asked them to spend more time on it and to get Tim to liaise with a brainwave expert for a second opinion on the possibility David's theory was correct.

What worried me was, if this were true, then doors were closing for us. We were likely to be left with an enigma we were incapable of solving. Inwardly, I cursed the meteor which had damaged AD1.

No sooner had John and David left my office than my monitor alerted me to an urgent incoming message from the International Space Station.

'Doctor Slater, Valeria Misalova here. I need to speak to you.' Valeria had arrived with two of the scientists who were currently working in the Cluster. She was now also taking a stint as the ISS station commander.

I flicked my thimball and her face appeared on the screen. It was pale and drawn.

'Valeria, what's up?'

'Evelyn. We've had an explosion in the Cluster. Hans is dead and Göran seriously injured.'

19 Wonderfuel!

'What about Reg and Martin?' I asked, concerned about the other two scientists who might have been in the Cluster during the explosion.

'Both okay. Minor decompression injuries. The explosion was in the laboratory. It killed Hans. Shrapnel pierced the outer wall on the living quarters side of the laboratory and caused the injuries to Göran, Reg, and Martin. Martin was least affected, dealt with the puncture, and pulled Göran into the Scaffy Wagon with Reg's help.

'We already knew something had happened as the Cluster was given a vector towards us. It won't hit us though and we'll get the Scaffy Wagon to correct it later.

'When the Scaffy Wagon arrived at the ISS, we broke protocols to get the hatch open quickly and Göran is now in Kibo, which we're using as a recompression chamber. Reg and Martin's decompression is being dealt with separately in the Quest airlock. They're due out shortly.'

'Is the Cluster repairable? Any critical damage?' I asked.

'Should be, but I don't know how long it'll be out of action.'

'Any idea what caused it?'

'Martin says Hans was working on a fuel sample at the time. We'll watch the video of the event with them when they're out of decompression.'

'I had a call booked to Reg for four o'clock. I'd like to still make it if possible, but at a time to suit him.'

'Yes. I'll make sure he knows, Eve. We've seen your presentation, by the way.'

'I didn't want to bring it up after what has happened, but what did you guys up there think?'

191

'Not sure if the Cluster crew have seen it, but those of us on the ISS believe there should be a name. We don't like to think of him/her/it as no more than an alien creature.'

'Right, thanks. A name is an interesting idea. Get Reg to call me when it's convenient. I won't go anywhere until he does, but deal with safety issues first, of course. Any suggestions for a name?'

She smiled. 'Allen might be appropriate, transposing the L for the I.'

'He might be a she or have no gender at all.'

'Add a Russian a for Alana. If he has no gender Allen would still work.'

'Good idea. I'll see what I can do,' I said.

There was a call from behind her and her face revolved sharply to the right, causing her to spin off screen slightly. 'They're coming out of Quest. I'll get Reg to call you as soon as he can, Eve,' she said, simultaneously cutting the connection.

I used my thimball to summon Janet.

'Get Tim and Paul to my office, please, Janet, and come in yourself as soon as you've called them.'

A minute later Janet and Tim entered my room. 'Paul's on the way,' she said.

'Janet, it's been suggested our alien might deserve a name and that Allen with two Ls and an E would be appropriate. Feel the staff out on it. Thanks.'

'I like the name idea,' said Tim as Janet returned to her office.

'Yes, I do too.' I was too preoccupied to be chatty. 'Where's Paul? Do you know?'

'In the communications room. Ah, here he is,' said Tim as Paul entered, a little out of breath.

'Take a seat,' I said, waiting for them to settle before giving them the bad news about the Cluster.

192

I continued, 'We've never talked about lines of communication in an event such as this. Paul, can you find out what NASA knows and when they found out – they surely should have been first to know. Get together with Tim and work out how this sort of information should be disseminated around the group with Cluster clearance. I'm going to call the Prime Minister's office and find out what they know and from where. Okay?'

They both gave a positive response and quickly left my office. I dialled Number Ten and got the Prime Minister's parliamentary private secretary.

Apparently, NASA had, a few minutes previously, provided the information about the explosion. It had taken far too long and I asked the secretary to let the Prime Minister and Home Secretary know we were putting in place a faster and more comprehensive communication system.

A light flashed on my monitor. I told the parliamentary secretary a call was coming in from the ISS and we ended our conversation.

Reg came onto the screen. He didn't look well, haggard, pale and drawn.

'Reg, how are you?'

'Not too bad, Eve. My hands and feet swelled up but back to normal now. My eyes hurt. Martin wasn't so badly affected but Göran's in a bad way. He put his hand in the hole – probably saved the three of us. He might lose it. Poor Hans is dead though.'

'How did it happen?'

'I'm lucky to be alive, Eve. We'd taken some samples of fuel from the rear spheroids in AD1 and were experimenting with it. I'd left an instrument I needed in the living quarters and had just got through the airlock when the sample Hans was working on exploded.

'I wasn't in a fit state to see too much after our decompression. My eyes are still sore, but Martin watched Hans' body floating away. We've lost almost an entire segment of the laboratory structure. I think Valeria currently has the Scaffy Wagon trying to find and collect Hans and other items thrown into space by the explosion.'

'Was it the fuel?'

'The only thing possible. We knew it was powerful stuff. The chemical composition is extraordinary and yet it can be manufactured relatively simply from carbon, chlorine, fluorine, hydrogen and nitrogen. Hans had two microlitres for his experiment, only point nought nought two millilitres. This stuff is the rocket fuel for which we've always been searching. Sell any oil shares you have,' he said, 'not that they've much value anyway since the commitment to all electric vehicles.'

I laughed. 'If I had oil shares, I would. Thanks for taking the time to update me, Reg. My main call about the alien can wait but I wanted to make sure you were aware of the video. Have you seen it?'

'Yes, you're a clever lady, Eve. Your presentation was spot-on perfect. You imparted exactly what was necessary to prevent ignorance and prejudice taking hold. Hans saw it too. Nice to know that he was aware of what our alien looked like. The presentation was exactly how I'd have done it.'

'Thanks. I can tell you something else we might have discovered. I don't want to hold you up from whatever you need to do up there though.'

'No. Tell me, please.'

'A couple of my guys down here think AD1 contained a computerised alien. His mind was in some of those cylinders and it was planned for him to awaken to communicate with us. Not a robot, not a cyborg, but an artificially stored alien mind.'

194

'Fascinating. Which cylinders?'

'I'll get them to let you know. Why?'

'I don't want to be cutting into any part of its mind. We'll keep those cylinders separate in case we need to put them back in situ. That there could be a mind in AD1 is possible, I suppose... but I'd have to say that wouldn't I, having heard your presentation.' He laughed.

'Yes, everything and anything is possible, and these hackers claim to be fairly sure. It is circumstantial though.'

I gazed into Reg's bloodshot eyes and saggy eyelids and continued, 'You need some sleep. So sorry about Hans. Let everyone up there know we're thinking of you all.'

'I will, Eve. Let's talk tomorrow.'

I said goodbye and cut the connection.

Dying in space had been one of my nightmares when participating in astronaut training. Not being able to breathe. One of the astronauts running the programme told me if it did happen, I'd barely have time to know I was dying. Instantaneous, he said, was an age compared with dying in space. I guess the knowledge put my mind at ease. Poor Hans wouldn't have had time to realise what was happening, then lights out.

««O»»

Over the next week, I was being hit with information from every direction. The hackers had found a simple switching computer program within one batch of data. The language boys had put together a comprehensive alphabet but were still struggling with an interpretation of the language, despite the department now being four strong. Tim and Paul had been negotiating furiously with NASA and Roscosmos over how to ensure communications were more rapidly disseminated to the appropriate people.

Valeria informed me they'd four spare segments for the Cluster and three were being used to repair the damage in the laboratory. Eight more spares were being sent up on the next Ariane. The other holes in the laboratory and living quarters were being patched as we spoke. None of the research equipment had been too badly damaged and replacements for those that were, were on their way up on a Dragon supply vessel.

Brainwave specialists were given the data isolated by David and Jack to study. They didn't know it was from an alien – they didn't even know about the alien craft, yet they came back with the fact it was a brainwave without the slightest doubt. They were curious as to where it had originated as it had some unusual features regarding the number of cycles per second being rather odd. It was certainly enough evidence for me. David's theory that AD1 was intended to deliver a message and interact with us, personally, was accepted as the most likely scenario.

The possibility that the brain was not completely dead had worrying implications about dismantling it. I wondered about the ethics and discussed it fully with the Home Secretary and Science Minister. It was decided that we still had to press on with the study of the device but wouldn't do anything invasive with the cylinders which contained "mind" type data. Reg assured me that they knew exactly which cylinders were attached to which wires coming from the strange hub in AD1, so everything could be reassembled to the original situation in which we'd found it.

The supply of images dried up because of the accident, of course, and wouldn't recommence until the Cluster was back in operation. I had a niggling worry about the replacement crew not being on the same wavelength as Reg and me, but not much could be done about that. Despite their objections, Reg and Martin were put on the next Crew Dragon back to Earth, while Göran was still being treated at the ISS. He'd lost most of his arm from decompression and wouldn't be in a fit state for the return journey for a few weeks. Valeria, as station commander, had had to do the amputation under instruction from surgeons on Earth – rather her than me, for sure. Not the sort of thing astronaut training prepared you for.

Down at Goonhilly, we had a visit from the Prime Minister and French Science Minister and I took the opportunity to ask about a general release. I made the case it should be released soon or there was likely to be a security breach and we'd lose the initiative. He said they wanted to know more about AD1 before making an announcement. Language would be good, he said. I knew my language team were still fishing in the dark. He made it pretty clear the ball was in my court. Solve the language problem and decipher the computer programs and he'd reconsider.

Again, I warned that our chance to drip-feed information was disappearing the more we discovered, but his mind was made up. Both Tim and Mario agreed with me. I believed he was making a big mistake and, at one point, actually told him he was wrong in no uncertain terms.

'Dame Evelyn!' he said, looking at me with anger in his expression. He didn't complete whatever he was going to say, but I considered myself well and truly slapped down.

Some of the alien fuel and hull structure had been brought to Earth and Reg had been spot-on with the importance of the liquid. Despite being simple to make, the chemical composition had been missed over the last couple of centuries. It packed a punch far above its mass and would soon be used for rocket launches. The small volume needed to produce the same thrust meant lighter launch vehicles, fewer launch stages, and heavier payloads. Space was quickly becoming a less formidable frontier. It was amazing the discovery had not been made on Earth. It seemed scientists might have been side-tracked away from its discovery by the abundance of oil in the world. Within weeks, there were test-launches using the new fuel, including an Orion launched on a rocket only a tenth as large as the space launch system. There was a new urgency about space research which seemed to be being driven by our need to try to match the technology of AD1 as quickly as possible, although most people working on the project still had no knowledge of the existence of the alien craft. How long before a leak gave the game away, I wondered.

The hull structure had similarly amazing properties. A group of metallurgists had joined NASA and were now assessing how the alloy would be incorporated within our own space programme. ESA had insisted that there be no patents issued for any developments. They wanted it free for all. As AD1 was an ESA/Roscosmos discovery, they won the argument.

Beyond all our wildest dreams, however, was the conductivity of the alien wires and their strange ability to polarise electric current. So far, many universities had been steered in the direction of how to make the wire and there were already benefits being produced. Surprisingly, no one guessed it was an alien technology. A story had been released that it was a manufacturing technique discovered simultaneously by MIT and Oxford universities and the world in general seemed to accept it.

My frantic work life was tempered on the domestic front. Mario and I had bought our lovely little thatched cottage at the end of the creek in Helford and he did get down on one knee in a posh restaurant to ask me to marry him. I said yes, of course! It was to be an August wedding. Our two sets of parents were excited fit to burst.

Nevertheless, one Sunday, in the middle of the night, work invaded our domestic paradise. The news was from, of all places, Phobos, the Martian moon. It immediately turned my world topsy-turvy.

20 Phobos

After a nine-month journey, ESA's latest Hawking Explorer craft landed on Phobos, the larger and innermost of Mars' two moons. There was much celebration when it landed successfully and was able to anchor. The Hawking Explorer had explosive bolts in its legs and the moment contact was made, spikes were blasted down into the rock to hold it in position. On a previous occasion it had failed, and the probe had been lost. This time it worked and Phobos, orbiting just four thousand miles from Mars, became a base from which further probes would be launched.

Set within the Hawking Explorer were eight smaller landers which would eventually be deployed to different parts of the surface where human landings were being considered for 2040.

The first of those exploratory landers was despatched on the third of March 2036, and it was extreme good fortune that the controller monitoring the video feed also had Cluster security clearance, because the Hawking Lander had a near-miss with AD2, a second alien device.

Of course, a near-miss was not feet or yards, or even a mile. AD2 flew across the field of view of the descending lander at a closest range of about three miles. Video was enhanced, and it was clearly identical to our own AD1, but without any outward signs of damage. Perhaps, if we collected this one, we'd be able to learn its true purpose.

The video sequence was immediately classified and I received one of the first copies. The rear tailfins and gold nose were obvious and, although the greatest magnification plus enhancement didn't make it clear enough to compare with AD1, there was a blurred area which might be the same sort of hieroglyphs as we'd found on ours.

Within forty-eight hours an ESA conference was organised, and Janet was booking me on a flight from Exeter to Paris.

«≪o≫»

It was a bigger conference than I'd expected. The room at the Hôtel Plaza Athénée was large, luxurious, and wonderfully equipped. It was, of course, secure and the Direction Générale de la Sécurité Intérieure had scoured it for any bugs.

The most senior people present were Home Secretary Jenny Rae, US Secretary of State Parker, Leblanc, the French Minister of the Interior, Russian Defence Secretary Poliak, and Tanuki, the Japanese Foreign Secretary.

More scientifically, we had the heads of NASA, ESA, Roscosmos, CSA, JAXA, and UKSA, plus Sir Henry Edwards, head of Jodrell Bank and heads of other observatories who had Cluster security clearance. I was honoured to be sitting between Jenny Rae and Sir Henry. I was still coming to terms with my elevated status in the scientific community.

In addition, there were numerous astronomers who were *in-the-know* about AD1, and some top civil servants.

The head of ESA began proceedings as it had been an ESA probe which had discovered AD2 and, of course, the Scaffy Wagon I had been commanding when we found AD1 had also been an ESA/Roscosmos expedition.

There was much discussion about how to deal with the new discovery. This fell into two camps. Those who wanted to send an expedition to Mars and investigate it in orbit there, and those who preferred to collect it and bring it here to study. The latter were soon clearly in the majority.

I did point out that we should consider the ethics of moving an alien intelligence from its orbit around Mars without its permission. I suggested we should try to contact it *in situ* to ask if it would mind?

This resulted in a heated debate, but it was considered too expensive to send a full diplomatic team to Mars. I was realistic enough to know I couldn't win every argument and discussion moved on to how to capture it and bring it back to Earth. There was concern about its protection, so it was not lost either by some catastrophe during the flight from Mars or during the eventual re-entry. Many said it might be better to take it to the Cluster and have it examined there. It was at this point I was able to bring up another possibility.

I spoke with growing confidence these days and all eyes were upon me again, 'Our team and the original Cluster team, before the explosion, had been talking about the purpose of AD1 in some detail and, in our opinion, it was intended to recognise intelligence and perform its function. If we aren't going to attempt contact in Mars orbit, then, in our opinion, it should be taken to the Cluster and held for a while to find out if it will wake.

'I took a straw poll of my team at Goonhilly before flying into Paris. When it is captured, we believe it might react to us there and then. We would still strongly advise a small science team accompany the collection mission to be able to deal with such an occurrence.'

Whichever method was used, it would be expensive. It wasn't a project which robots should be allowed to undertake, and my advice was quickly adopted. A manned mission to Mars was finally on the cards after so many hopes and false starts, but a landing on the red planet would still have to remain a future project. So near yet so far. Scientists were desperate to get to the surface now that they knew there had once been life there.

The new fuel discovered on AD1 would help. It gave us the facility to launch larger vessels into orbit and accelerate more quickly, far exceeding speeds of one hundred thousand miles per hour.

One miracle which did emerge from the conference was everyone agreeing AD2 must be an absolute priority and hang the cost.

At dinner I had a long conversation with Sir Henry, Jenny Rae, and Gerald from ESA. I raised the thorny issue of a public announcement.

'If AD2 came to life and announced itself to the world, we might not be able to stop it from using our communication systems. If so, a serious cultural shock could result. We must defuse that eventuality while we still have the initiative.'

'It might not come to life and if it doesn't, we'll be able to continue to study it without making any announcement,' said Jenny.

'But what if it takes over the communication systems when it is in Earth orbit? There could be riots if it starts talking to the world without any forewarning,' I said as forcefully as I could muster.

'Then we must prevent it,' said Sir Henry.

'That might not be possible,' said Gerald. 'The only way to block transmission might be to transmit noise on the same frequencies.'

'We could surely do that,' said Jenny.

'I don't think so,' I said. 'It might transmit on multiple frequencies. Jamming could mean disrupting communications throughout the world.'

'If I were going to announce ESA's presence to a new world, I'd be sure I could transmit on all frequencies. Eve's right,' said Gerald.

'Yes, it's a strong argument,' agreed Sir Henry.

'I strongly recommend presenting the information to the world in the same way I did in Downing Street, but as a combined production with local presenters and the heads of state of each country being part of the presentation. This visiting alien has not just come to see the heads of our governments, but to communicate with us as a world. A single entity. How will other heads of state react when they discover we've been hiding such a momentous event from them?'

By the end of dinner, I had all three of them onside and Jenny made a call to Roger Clarke in my presence to discover whether he concurred. My point about in-the-know leaders currently blindsiding other world leaders finally persuaded him. Jenny and I then explained our position to the head of ESA and he was soon on-board too.

When we reconvened the following morning, I was called upon to make the case. I won a clear majority, but the arguments continued unabated with only seventy-five per cent in favour at lunchtime.

I made a point of securing lunch with Home Secretary Rae, Michael Sanderson, head of NASA, Sir Henry, and US Secretary of State Parker, as it was the USA contingent who were the laggards.

Domestic issues were their problem with it being an election year and the Secretary of State was not only extremely conservative, but also the actual Republican candidate for the presidency. He was paranoid about damaging his chances in the election and, as a believer in Intelligent Design and the literal interpretation of the Bible he had obvious problems with the existence of an ancient alien spacecraft. When he had first been told about the existence of AD1, he didn't believe it and said it was a hoax. Unbelievably, he held that view until the discovery of the polarised wires, when he reluctantly accepted that it was really alien.

With his responsibility for NASA, he was influencing the decision to not come clean about the alien. It was frustrating that the combination of politics and religion was affecting such an important decision. The argument at lunch became heated but I hoped my own reasoning would make him change his mind about secrecy.

Before the conference resumed, Jenny Rae and I spoke in detail about my fears and we called the Prime Minister on a conference call. I explained the objection of the Secretary of State. Mr Clarke said he had an idea and would call us back.

During the afternoon, the debate as to whether we should tell or not tell continued to rage, but during each round of arguments, the *against* contingent lost ground and support. By tea at four o'clock the *for* camp was close to eighty-five per cent. Unfortunately, this was not a democratic conference. NASA, ESA, CSA, Roscosmos, and JAXA (Japan) had vetoes. We had to convince the Americans as NASA was the only one of the organisations not in favour.

I was taking tea with Sir Henry when my secure mobile rang. It was Roger Clarke. I excused myself and stood in a quiet spot to answer it.

'Evelyn, I hope you appreciate this,' he said with a slight self-satisfied lilt to his voice, 'but I've just got off the telephone with the President and I used some leverage. They'll support a release of the AD1 news in stages.'

'My goodness, sir. That is amazing news. How did you do it?'

'Well, for your ears only, Evelyn, I told him if he didn't allow it, I'd release it in the UK. It'd make him appear foolish at home, being beaten to it by the Limeys.'

'Well done, sir. What's next?'

'Attitudes should change quickly at the conference, as he'll have been talking to Secretary of State Parker while I've been having these conversations with you and Jenny.'

'You know, sir, despite my original plan to drip-feed the news, it is no longer practicable,' I said.

'Why not?'

'Because my plan was to conduct the release honestly. I'm sure if we release in stages, the moment the first release is made, someone will come up with a copy of the picture of Allen.'

'And all your points prior to your presentation become valid, but on a planet-wide scale,' Mr Clarke said.

'Yes, sir. He'll be hated just for being different.'

'I suppose we no longer have complete control over his image?'

'Definitely not, sir. Once those videos were circulated the number of people who had access to the picture went through the roof. Someone is sure to leak it. Imagine the financial incentive a news group might offer.'

'Yes, Evelyn. I see.'

'Can you explain to Jenny, sir, then we can plan a strategy for the conference.'

'Yes, I will.'

'Thank you so much, sir. It'll make all the difference.'

Back in the conference, the Secretary of State made a statement, 'I've been discussing this matter with the President and we've decided we will allow the release of the information in stages.

'We would like everyone to agree to a release firstly of the existence of AD1, perhaps using the NASA footage of its discovery, followed by the discovery of the new fuel.'

How dare he talk about it being NASA's footage? It was all ESA/Roscosmos footage! The more contact I had with this man, the less I liked him. It was worrying that he might soon be the president of the USA.

'We suggest a second release a few days later of the images found of the solar system, the alien's home world images during a third release and finally the image of the alien itself and the fact we've found AD2 and will be sending an expedition to collect it.'

I whispered to Mrs Rae, 'That is what we expected. He's left himself open to our plan.'

The Home Secretary stood and thanked the Secretary of State for his courageous decision and suggested, if there were no further objections, NASA and ESA should work together to prepare the releases, so they were done in exactly the same manner in all languages.

The Home Secretary had been clever. She hadn't said it would be separate releases necessarily, so it left the door open to work on them separately first then make the case to amalgamate them into a single news item, which would save face for the Secretary of State.

There was a call for a show of hands. The head of ESA asked for those *for* and a sea of arms were raised, and *against*... no one.

21 Allen Meets the World

Suddenly news began to leak, perhaps based upon the strange secret meeting of the heads of space agencies and top government ministers in Paris.

Some of the tabloid newspapers, mainly those often called *The Gutter Press* began to speculate wildly. Stories quickly emerged that a planetoid had been discovered in the outer reaches of the solar system and it was on a collision-course with Earth. Another was that the sun was turning nova. The most common story was that a UFO had been captured. Even prestigious news media like *The Times* in London and *The Washington Post* were speculating like crazy.

All of my fears about not drip-feeding the discoveries, were coming home to roost. At one point, the Home Secretary actually apologised to me, because she'd been one of the strongest influences on the Prime Minister about maintaining secrecy. The problem was that there was no point in me being right in retrospect. We were having to deal with the repercussions here and now. I finally convinced our government, ESA, and JAXA that we needed to get the true story out quickly. Roscosmos even threatened to do their own release if the USA didn't change its attitude pretty damn quick.

It took several trips to Houston, the Ames Research Center, and Washington to get the head of NASA to agree that telling the world was best presented in a single thirty-minute prime time programme. During the last visit, I had a rough video to show how the story could be delivered in around twenty-two minutes, allowing time for the head of state to introduce and sum up.

My main arguments against a piecemeal release were the almost certain leaks of the image and the fragmentation itself. Once the first announcement was made, people would quickly lose interest in the future instalments and all our manipulation to try to prevent hatred of Allen before we revealed him would be wasted. This was the first time people would have the opportunity to prevent prejudice before it became endemic – I was determined not to miss the opportunity. My drip-feed idea had been the best, but this was the most sensible alternative with that not having been adopted.

Advertising agencies I'd commissioned for advice said that fewer than one in five would watch all transmitted episodes. The majority would have missed the important information and formulated their view of him from his looks alone. Exactly what we needed to avoid.

Finally, Michael Sanderson agreed with me. He deliberately waited until the Secretary of State was out of the country, and he got approval from the President. Michael was worried about doing this, but my arguments had been sufficiently convincing he was prepared to risk the downside on his own position. The delays, however, did nothing to quell the media's suspicions. Their stories were increasingly slanted towards the capture of an alien spaceship, which, frankly, was too near the truth for comfort.

When we went out for dinner in the evening, I managed to get Michael to open up a little about the relationship between the Secretary of State and NASA. He told me they were uneasy bedfellows, due to the Secretary's strange religious beliefs.

He said, 'Eve, he's seen the Mars and Earth orbit shots which clearly show they were taken millions of years ago, yet he seems to turn a blind eye to the implications regarding a six-thousand-year-old Earth. Frankly it's as if he's blind to the facts.'

'There'll be a lot of religious beliefs damaged by our documentary, Michael.'

'I fear so. Who is narrating yours?'

'I've been volunteered for Britain, Canada, Australasia, South Africa, and other English-speaking countries. The PM will do the introduction on the British version. Who will be doing yours?'

'Probably me,' he said.

I reassured him. 'Don't worry, we've the best scriptwriters working on this.'

'You can let me have a copy of yours?'

'Of course. The plan is to give a copy of the script to every head of state and to prepare a documentary subtitled in the country's own language. Other than a couple of shots of Yuri and me in the Scaffy Wagon, I don't appear, so all you need to do is replace my voiceover with yours. They're using the English version featuring me for the subtitled programme. Yuri is doing it for Russian speaking countries.'

'I'd prefer to do the same, but you know the good old U S of A – we always have to do it our way,' he said with a chuckle and we chinked glasses of an excellent Californian Chablis.

When we left the restaurant, a press horde was waiting us. They wanted to know why the head of NASA was meeting the astronaut from Goonhilly who had the ear of the British Prime Minister. We barged our way through the crowd, repeating 'no comment' to every question.

Having achieved my objective over the video, I flew back to London the next day with press chasing me at check-in and on arrival.

»«o»«

We began work on the presentation in earnest.

A working script was soon formulated, and a selected diverse audience was called in to watch it under the Official Secrets Act. It went down well, although as expected, those with stronger religious beliefs were finding it challenging.

The problem for them, particularly the Islamic, Christian, and orthodox Jewish people, was the issue of a soul and creation in God's image. I reported this back to the Prime Minister and he promised to let the heads of each of the churches watch the video two days prior to the general populace, so they were able to prepare for any adverse comments.

It only took two days for me to record the twenty-two-minute programme, with the images inserted into the correct positions in the script and me improving my emphasis on some aspects which required refining. Digital copies were soon winging their way around the world.

We gave the video to heads of states a week prior to the launch so they had the option to either introduce it personally or append a recorded introduction. We were well aware the whole thing would soon be leaked by irresponsible leaders.

My own status would change with its release. If my standing had been growing scientifically, this would make me famous globally. Mario and I discussed this at length, and he promised to bring me back to earth if my ego became too inflated!

Only the USA, France, China, and Russian-speaking countries were going to do their own separate announcement video. The French made their decision based on the language needing to be French – which was only to be expected. They always liked to use their national tongue. With Russia, it was different as Yuri would be the presenter and he, with me, was the co-discoverer of the alien artefact. He'd been born in the Ukraine but had dual citizenship. As for China, well, they were just continuing to be inscrutable.

Most countries put a press embargo on the item, but as expected, information did leak anyway. Unfortunately, my father had seen an item in a Korean online paper which linked my name with the speculation. Fortuitously, it happened to be when Mario and I were arriving to stay with them for the weekend.

We had driven down specially to show them an advance copy of the programme, but Dad didn't give me an easy ride when we arrived on Friday night.

'Is this what this inflated honour is all about?' he asked accusingly, before I'd even got my coat off, and he tossed a printed copy of the webpage onto the coffee table. He so annoyed me when he jumped to conclusions.

'Sort of,' I said, giving it a cursory glance. 'We're here to fill you in with the true story, Dad, not this foreign speculation.'

Once we'd got unpacked and sat down with a gin and tonic, I picked up the sheet and it repeated the same old story that NASA had discovered a UFO in Earth orbit. It went on to say that they were about to admit to having an actual dead alien in Area 51. I tossed it to one side, pulled a data stick out of my bag and handed it to him.

'We'd better watch this now. It'll be going out worldwide next Sunday. I'm swearing you and Mum to secrecy until it does. Do you understand? *You tell no one.* Not even Auntie Jean or my sister,' I said, looking each of them square in the eyes one after the other. They both nodded.

'I mean it! Dad, Mum. *No one* must hear this from you as I am breaking the Official Secrets Act by letting you see it. Promise me.'

They both promised to keep it secret.

'Sorry, Eve, didn't mean to be unpleasant,' Dad said as he plugged the stick into the television. He was often hurtful then immediately contrite. I think it was an age thing.

'The Internet item is nonsense,' I said, 'and, for the record, it was Yuri and me who discovered it on an ESA mission. It was *not* NASA!'

'Hence the DCMG honour?' he asked. I nodded.

The television came to life and we sat quietly watching my presentation of the story to the very end.

'How lovely, dear. He seems friendly,' said my mum when it finished.

'Well, we believe he is offering the hand of friendship but of course he's been dead for one hundred million years. I'm sad I'll never have the opportunity to meet him in person.'

'And this is going out worldwide?' Dad asked.

'Yes, at prime time in each nation.'

'I'm so proud of you, Evelyn,' he said, and his hand gripped mine tightly, tears in his eyes again.

'*Dame* Evelyn, please!'

We all chuckled together and chinked our gin and tonics.

Mum chipped in, 'Now that's out of the way, Evelyn, Mario, we've something far more serious and important to discuss – your wedding in August!'

We all laughed.

»«o»«

The next seven days were chaotic for me. An endless stream of calls from the media who had of course managed to get copies of the video and wanted to interview me in depth. The release was embargoed so they couldn't jump the gun, but I refused point blank to talk, telling them all to wait until after the UK broadcast which was planned for seven o'clock on the coming Sunday.

It didn't stop them badgering me and it was unbelievable how they were speculating about the creature. It was almost as if they hadn't listened to a single word in the documentary. I had a showdown on the telephone with one of our most prestigious news organisations on the Friday.

'Can we not get a few words from you about the creature itself?'

'Sorry. Come back to me on Monday and we can talk at length.'

'Come on, Dame Evelyn. You can't really be positive about a monster like this. There'll be riots if these things start crawling around among us.'

'Stop right there, you *idiot* hack!' I exclaimed. 'We have worked hard to show these people wish us no harm and we are already reaping the rewards from their technology as you will learn in the coming weeks. If you use the word "monster" to refer to this *person* again, you and your entire news organisation will get nothing further from me at all... ever! Try explaining *that* to your editor.'

'I'm sorry, Dame Evelyn, but it's pretty ugly.'

'How dare you? He is a beautiful person with friendly eyes and a harmless appearance. I assume it is your personal racial prejudice which allows you to be so derogatory! Your editor will be hearing from me immediately. I will not discuss this any further with *a racist!*' I said loudly and cut him off.

It would have been so much more satisfying to have been able to slam down the telephone receiver, but these days there were no receivers to slam down and all I had was the tiny red icon which represented a receiver on my handset. Mind you, I did press it fiercely!

I rarely got so riled. I sat at my desk fuming, almost shaking, over his attitude, especially after all our careful stage-managing of the release. I was true to my word and telephoned his editor, extracting a grovelling apology. Sometimes status truly can work in your favour. It was impossible for the editor to refuse a call from Dame Evelyn Slater.

The attitude of people worried me. No matter how thoughtfully arguments are constructed, many people still seem to imagine the worst and refuse to listen to reason. I knew this, of course, from my doctorate, but that didn't stop it infuriating me. Why, oh why, hadn't Mr Clarke allowed us to drip-feed the story from the original discovery. Despite our careful announcement, I had ominous worries about public reaction.

««o»»

On Sunday evening, the news was released. My presentation was introduced by the Prime Minister and the programme was billed as being of international importance.

On Monday evening, the shit hit the fan.

22 Chat Show Star

Succeeding in preventing prejudice against the aliens was becoming my sole *raison d'être*. We had a real opportunity to defuse discrimination before it began and my determination to be the instrument which achieved it was now my overriding priority.

I was invited to appear on the Monday evening edition of *Armstrong*, a regular prime time chat show. Naturally, the moment the news had broken on Sunday and Allen had been introduced to the world, the chat show programme became a *must-see* for anyone who wanted the inside story.

Previously, I'd appeared briefly on news programmes and occasional children's television, but this was on a whole new level. Armstrong was a top show with an audience of millions, and he was an incisive and clever host. The previous day's announcement made it almost unmissable and it was being syndicated worldwide and streamed over the Internet. There could be billions watching.

I was nervous, but Mario came with me for support and we arrived at the BBC headquarters at six in the evening. We enjoyed some hospitality before I was whisked off to make-up twenty minutes before the show, to be powdered down so I wouldn't appear shiny under the studio lights.

Godfrey Armstrong popped in while I was in make-up and we briefly discussed the images we'd agreed we'd use. The orbital photographs of Mars and Earth one hundred million years ago would be side by side to the rear of where we would be seated. It would be only me, him, and a coffee table, upon which there would be a model of the Scaffy Wagon. Normally his shows had two guests and a music item, but tonight it was just us for the whole forty minutes. I'd been warned he might try to make changes to images on the night and I was relieved he didn't ask. I didn't want to be caught off-guard on someone else's home ground.

Mario popped in, wished me luck, and we kissed briefly before hospitality took him off to his seat. We were booked into a top hotel and restaurant for dinner and were both looking forward to relaxing, after a week when love and marriage-planning had been forced onto the back-burner by the pressure of my work.

Mario got so frustrated with how Allen was taking over my life, sometimes, but our lovely thatched cottage relieved the tensions. We often walked alongside the creek at Helford, almost in silence, holding hands and marvelling at the beauty of the Cornish village. This morning, sunbeams were slanting through the trees, dappling the bridge and sparkling in the brook as it trickled towards the creek. Not a sound reached us, but for the gently tumbling water, birdsong, and the breeze rustling the beech leaves. So relaxing, putting us both at ease with the world.

It was a world apart from the television studio theatre. There was a live audience of about four hundred here. At seven on the dot I was standing in the wings. Godfrey was sitting in the left-hand chair and the show's distinctive theme music introduced the scene. I glanced at the monitor beside me which showed the live television feed.

Godfrey opened the show, 'Good evening and welcome. He paused for applause.

'I am truly honoured tonight to have on the show a lady who is currently the most famous person in the world.

'These images,' he turned and waved in the general direction of the backdrop, 'have now been seen by almost everyone on the planet. Never previously has there been such an important and historic worldwide news release, nor has one been so quickly disseminated. My guest tonight is not only responsible for bringing this sensational news to us all, but also, she is the actual person who discovered Allen's

216

craft. Let me introduce her, she is Dame – Doctor – Evelyn – Slater.'

He stood, which was my cue to walk onto the set. I tried to steady my nerves and not to trip over cables on the floor as I heard a massive burst of applause.

He marched towards me, shook my hand, and kissed me on both cheeks.

'Welcome, Dame Evelyn, welcome,' he said, leading me back to the raised area where the seats and coffee table were located.

'Simply Evelyn, please, Godfrey. It's wonderful to be invited onto your show.'

'The pleasure's all mine, Evelyn,' he said as he indicated the seat.

'These photographs are amazing,' he said, waving towards the images again.

'Yes, before we found these, all we'd seen before from Allen's craft were orbital pictures of the moon and Venus. Frankly, a hundred million years ago, they were much the same as they are today. These two images however, were a revelation, especially as they proved to us Allen's craft was over one hundred million years old.'

'The papers tell us our ancestors then were smaller than mice. It's a long time indeed.'

'Yes, indeed! He's been waiting eons for us to find him.'

'Why do you call him Allen? Might he not be female or have no gender at all?'

'You are exactly right, Godfrey. At this moment, we don't know anything about him or his species. The name Allen came from Valeria Misalova on the space station. They'd been discussing it and wanted to personalise him. If you change the *l* in alien to an *L*, you get Allen. So, Allen it was. We hope to discover his real name soon.'

'How can you find out his real name?'

I spoke more seriously and quietly. 'During our investigation of his craft we had a mishap. A sample of the rocket fuel caused an explosion in the Cluster laboratory. Sadly, one of the scientists, Doctor Hans Meyer, was killed during the accident. It has taken us all this time to repair the Cluster laboratory and to send new scientists into orbit to study the craft. So far we've only examined fourteen of the memory cylinders and there are several dozen more we haven't even looked at yet.'

'And they will contain more photographs?'

'Yes, almost certainly and we're hoping for video and perhaps even a message.'

'What have we gained from your discovery of Allen's craft?' I was pleased he was always calling the alien artefact "Allen's craft" as I had asked him to do. I wanted to personalise the discovery as being Allen's property.

'It is not just my discovery, of course. Yuri Bulgakov was my pilot at the time, so we consider it a mutual discovery and we mustn't forget it was a European Space Agency expedition in conjunction with Roscosmos.'

'Yes, so what have we learned from it?' he asked, anxious to move on, but I'd made an important point for international viewers.

'The fuel is exciting. It's inexpensive to produce and will allow far greater payloads to be launched. Otherwise progress is slow. We believe most of the cylinders were part of a stored mind, an artificial brain if you will, perhaps of one of Allen's compatriots. The problem is the extent of the destruction when a meteor struck the craft back in antiquity. It means we're struggling despite having a fantastic team of hackers and linguists working on it constantly at Goonhilly.'

'You made the discovery of Allen's spaceship back in May 2035. Why was it kept secret for so long?'

'Our governments were concerned about its nature and wanted the study to begin before a release was made. We found the images, including the one of Allen, in January this year and we've been thinking about how best to release the news since then.'

'And what made the difference? You've heard the rumours?'

Now he had me on the back foot. I'd no idea which rumours he was talking about. Was he trying to set me up?

'There are always rumours, Godfrey. To which ones in particular do you refer?'

'The discovery of another craft orbiting Mars,' he said triumphantly as if sure he would put me in a spot – and indeed he had. Where had he got that from? Someone must have leaked it. What should I do? There was no clearance to talk about AD2, but to deny it would give the lie to our openness. If I denied it, he might quote sources which would prove I was lying. I had to make a snap decision and hope it was the correct one.

'Oh, the discovery by the Hawking Explorer of a second craft. Yes, it made it more important to present the whole picture to the people.'

'So, you admit to hiding the news about the Mars craft?'

'Well no, not hiding it exactly. We didn't want to overload people with too much information. It'll be many months before we can get to Mars and recover the second ship.'

'Yes. Well, it seems like it was being hidden.'

It was clear he was miffed that I'd defused his question.

'Not at all. You're being paranoid,' I said and laughed. 'I'm being open about it right now. You simply needed to ask the question. So far, I can't tell you much about it other than Allen's people might have one orbiting each of our planets. We don't know though, we're guessing, but it would explain why we found images from other solar system worlds in

Allen's memory banks. However, I've come here tonight to answer questions about Allen and the craft which we found in Earth orbit.'

He changed tack. 'What do you think Allen's craft was planned to do?'

'We think he was meant to talk to us and tell us about himself, his people and his home world. The damage prevented it and we do have high hopes the second device, which appears to be intact, will be more informative.'

'Okay, Evelyn, we'll leave the Martian craft for now. So, what type of world does Allen come from?'

'Perhaps we can have image three,' I said and, in a second or so, the correct image appeared.

'This third image shows their world. From the few images we have of it, we're unable to ascertain too much, but it appears to be an old world which has lost much of its atmosphere.

'Notice the plateaus are almost cloudless, which indicates a lack of atmosphere at altitude and we believe they now live on the shallow seabeds which remain. It's fairly clear Allen's world is short of water.'

'Were they coming to colonise Earth?'

'If they were, they'd have arrived long before the rise of humankind. We think their star system is about seventy light years away from us. If they'd been intending to colonise us, they would have done so millions of years ago, despite the huge distance. No, we believe they're explorers. However, I've not finished answering your previous question,' I'd got past the colonising invasion possibility quite well. It had been one of my worries.

'Sorry, do please continue.'

'In photograph four there is a truly beautiful companion planet which has all the attributes of Earth. Clouds, a lot of water, thick atmosphere and so on. What we don't yet know is if this orb or the dry planet we are seeing in the foreground is their home world. We also wonder, but it's only speculation, whether they might have terraformed the companion world. The problem when working from photographs is judging the relative size of the two planets. We simply don't know enough about them, and our lack of knowledge is one of the reasons we wanted to bring Allen's world into the public domain – so universities can bring their researchers and theorists into the mix.'

'So, what about Allen, himself?' he asked, and the image of the alien appeared over my shoulder.

I answered more slowly and softly. I wanted to give the impression I was talking about family. 'When she first saw the picture of Allen, one of my team said, "he has the friendliest eyes" and this seems to strike everyone when they first see him.'

'But you must admit he is like nothing on Earth?'

'It would be pretty strange if he was,' I said with amusement. 'Science fiction, at least the popular variety, has most aliens with two legs, two arms, a torso and a head. Okay, sometimes they'll throw in a second or third pair of arms, some horns, strange markings on the head or even extra eyes, but the format is usually pretty similar. Makes it possible for human actors to play the roles.'

'Yes, I understand, but what natural selection processes might have produced him?'

'We can only guess at the moment. He appears bulky, but we don't know how big he is. Binocular vision is expected as there are so many advantages to it, and we wonder whether the organs above his eyes allow him to see through certain materials. Notice, if we can go back to the image of the city, please, the egg-like craft and the buildings have no apparent windows.'

'They can see through walls? You wouldn't have much privacy in a hotel there!' The audience laughed.

I laughed too. 'No, you wouldn't, but of course it depends on what is taking place. Is the material like one-way mirrors? If we lived in a house made of one-way mirrors and could control the lighting, we wouldn't have to worry at all about our privacy. Perhaps they can polarise their materials in the same way they can polarise electricity, so only people you want to be able to see in can actually see in.'

'Sorry. What do you mean by polarising electricity?'

I'd thrown in the gem about polarising electricity to try to regain the initiative. It seemed to have worked.

'Allen's people have wires which they treat in a particular way. It causes electricity to polarise so if you touch two of their bare wires together there is no short-circuit. The polarised electricity cannot jump from one wire to another. It is a brilliant discovery by Doctor Reg Naughton on the original Cluster science team. It'll offer amazing benefits to the whole world.'

'So how much other stuff haven't we been told about?'

'Oh, lots, Godfrey, but don't get worried. It's all now in the public domain, but much of it'll take a while to filter through. It's another reason for us being so open about Allen and his craft.'

There seemed to be a disturbance off in the wings, followed by some shouting. I noticed Godfrey was ignoring it, so I shut it out of my mind. It was more important I didn't trip up on any of his questions.

'Could there be anything sinister about his craft observing—' Godfrey never got to finish his question. There were loud cracks and several searing pains in my shoulders and chest. The world went black.

23 Recovery

There were lights. My eyelids were heavy. I couldn't open them. I gave up the struggle.

The beep sounded about once a second, so I guessed it was probably my pulse being monitored. Why would that be? I listened intently. Somewhere away from me, I heard voices, an Indian sounding woman. I recognised the clipped sentences and unusual syllable emphasis. She was speaking to a young woman with a lilting accent and who rolled her Rs, possibly Scottish. There were other noises. A trolley being wheeled somewhere nearby, a door opening and closing. There was pressure on my left hand as if it was being squeezed. Perhaps Mario was holding it. The back of my other hand was hurting. My shoulder hurt. My neck and throat were sore. Why so much pain? I struggled again to open my eyes. One opened easier than the other. They were both a little gummy.

Ooh, too bright! Far too bright. There were LED strip lights along the ceiling causing me to screw up my eyes again. I squinted. The décor was eggshell and white. I was in hospital. My hand was gripped tighter.

'Eve. Eve, it's Dad,' a voice said.

I smiled. My dad had come to rescue me. I tried to squeeze his hand back, but I was too weak. I managed to turn my head slightly. He was indistinct but becoming clearer by the minute. He shouted, 'Nurse!'

'Can you hear me, Eve?' he asked me gently.

'Mmm,' was all I capable of uttering. I forced a smile.

I seemed to hurt all over, but particularly my neck. Shortly a nurse was leaning over me, wiping sleep from my eyes and checking my vital signs on the monitors.

'Hello, Dame Evelyn, I'm Nurse MacPherson. We've been waiting for you to wake up. I'll page the consultant. Try to relax.'

I smiled at my dad again but could do no more. I tried to say Dad but nothing would come out. I coughed, and it hurt me all over. I grimaced.

'You'll be sore, Eve,' he said.

'Dad.' I finally managed to get the word out.

There were tears in his eyes.

'Don't cry,' I said, hoarsely.

Mum came into the room and she ran around to my other side, leaned over and kissed me, 'Oh Eve, Eve, we thought we'd lost you.'

'What happened?' I was able to whisper the question.

'There was a gunman. He shot you,' said Dad.

'Yes. Heard bangs,' I was still struggling to form my words. My throat was so sore.

I pulled my hand away from Dad's grip and put it to my neck. I was bandaged. I lifted my other hand. There was a drip strapped to it which explained why it was hurting.

The consultant arrived. With a reassuring smile, she shone lights into my eyes, checked my vitals on the monitors and said, 'Dame Evelyn, you are a lucky lady indeed. My name is Indra Masinghe. We've been waiting for you to regain consciousness. We were losing hope.'

'Where was I shot?' I asked painfully.

'A bullet passed through your neck missing your carotid by millimetres. Two in your left shoulder, two were lodged in your upper back.'

'No! Am I paralysed?' I said, fear momentarily coursing through my body.

'No, but another was lodged below your heart and it only narrowly missed your spine. There were also two which passed through your left arm and one went through your left leg. You have no right to be alive.'

'Wow, guess I was lucky,' I said quietly as the full horror of the shooting sank home.

'You've been in a coma for a while, Dame Evelyn.'

'Evelyn or Eve, please,' I said.

'Well, Eve, be thankful for your luck.'

'How long have I been out?'

'Nearly six weeks,' she said.

Six weeks. Six weeks! No wonder I was so weak. What had been happening? Goonhilly? AD1? AD2? Mars? God, the wedding? It all cascaded through my mind.

'Your recovery will take a while,' the consultant said. 'We need to get you eating and drinking properly. Your neck and throat were critically injured, and you might find your breathing impaired, but it will improve with time and physiotherapy.'

'How long will I need to stay here?' I asked, knowing it could be an extended recovery.

'At least another couple of months by the time we get you fully mobile.'

My gaze returned to Mum and Dad who were both sitting beside the bed now. Dad was holding my hand again.

'Mario? Where's Mario?'

Dad's gaze dropped to the floor. Mum took on a pained expression as she, too, looked downwards. What did it mean?

'He didn't make it, Eve. We're so sorry,' Dad said, gripping my hand even tighter.

'But how? He was in the audience. He can't have been shot.'

'He was. Sorry, darling. Twenty-two were killed including Godfrey Armstrong and another fifty-one were injured. He had two automatic weapons.'

'But why? Why would anyone do this?'

'He has been charged with murder and is on remand.'

'But why did he shoot us?'

'He was a religious fanatic. He was shouting "blaspheming devils" as he fired. It was all seen on television.'

I burst into tears. The fact Mario was gone struck home. My life was over. The enormity of it was overwhelming. There was nothing left to live for. My darling Mario gone, with our new lives in Cornwall only just beginning. Mum was standing again, her hand caressing my cheek while I heard Dad crying too.

I cannot remember a worse time in my life than the next hour as I struggled to come to terms with my loss and failed absolutely. My loving parents trying to comfort the inconsolable.

Eventually the nursing staff sent my parents away and tried to settle me for the night. I continued to bawl every few minutes. Some religious idiot had taken my Mario from me and the lives of all those other innocent people. It was incomprehensible. Surely a nightmare from which I'd awake and find Mario safe and well, his curly hair on the pillow beside mine.

As I was being given my last tablets for the day, I asked the nurse, 'Who was he? This man. An Islamic terrorist? The man who did this?'

'No. No, he was in some sort of right wing fundamentalist Christian group, I believe,' she said. 'Well supposedly Christian, but also a white supremacist. His mother said he was claiming he recognised Allen as the devil incarnate and had to protect the world. He was mad. Try not to get het up again, Eve, please.'

Het up. *Het up!* I was livid. A fanatic had taken my Mario from me. Neither of us had ever wished anything but love upon others. To be killed by someone who is supposed to be a Christian was dreadful. Madness.

The nurse was about to leave, and I grabbed her arm. My mind was beginning to work again.

'Have there been other hate crimes because of Allen?'

226

'Yes, I'm sorry to say there have, but you need to rest now.'

'Can you please get my Dad to bring in my reflexlet tomorrow. I must get up-to-date. Six weeks. I can't believe I've been out for six weeks.'

'I'll try to call him for you.'

I thanked her and tried to sleep, but Mario's face kept appearing before me and I woke up constantly in tears of sheer anguish. Had it been quick for him or had he had a lingering death? There was so much I needed to know.

Although I drifted off occasionally, I slept for less than an hour the first night.

The next morning, Dad was in early with my friend Jane. He left my reflexlet for me and told me not to spend too much time on it, then departed, leaving me alone with her.

'Jane, do you know if Mario suffered?' I stuttered and was in tears again, but I had to know.

She reached over and hugged me gently, 'No, it was instantaneous. He had stood to rush forward and was hit by the first volley into the audience.'

My Mario. Trying to rescue me. 'It's good it was quick,' I said and was bawling once more.

Jane sat with me for a couple of hours and we talked about what had been happening in the world. It was a welcome distraction, even though the grief kept fighting its way back to the surface. When lunch arrived, I asked her to leave. I wanted to spend some time with my reflexlet this afternoon before my parents returned.

Of course, what we want and what we get are two different things. Firstly, eating and drinking was still painful as if I had a raw throat, even though most of my food was the consistency of semolina. My left arm was constrained too.

I unrolled my reflexlet to start a search when an immaculately suited young man came into my intensive care cubicle and peered around. It was odd, as if he was searching for someone but not interested in me. I became nervous. Was I in danger? Was he a gunman come to finish the job? I was about to shout for help when he ducked back out and in came Roger Clarke.

I tried to sit up, but pain stopped me. 'Prime Minister, sorry, I can't get up.'

'As you were, Evelyn,' he shook my hand and bent over to kiss my cheek.

Emotion rose again. I knew I couldn't hold it in if he mentioned Mario.

'I am so sorry about Mario, Evelyn.' I was instantly in floods of tears.

The Prime Minister grabbed some tissues and helped me dry my eyes.

'It's so unfair,' I cried, 'we had so much to live for.'

'Yes, I know. Can I sit awhile?'

'Oh, yes, please do.'

He sat down and held my hand. Gosh, I liked this man and his caring attitude. The bodyguard was standing in the doorway, alert and continually glancing in all directions. God, were we still under threat?

'What's been happening? Has the world gone mad?'

'No, Evelyn. We always worried it would stir up fanaticism, but not so quickly. I'm sorry we weren't better prepared; we have been since. I wish I'd listened to you. Your idea of drip-feeding the news about aliens might've prevented this.'

There was no point in crying over spilt milk. 'Goonhilly?'

'Tim Riley is doing a great job and your post is safe for when you're fit, but no hurry on that score.'

'What else has been happening?' I waved my reflexlet at him. 'I was about to find out.'

'The Mars mission vehicle is under construction. It will depart in two months.'

'Gosh, that's quick.'

'The new fuel has made a huge difference and so has this polarised electricity. You wouldn't believe some of the things they've been able to do with it. I'll let you read about it for yourself.'

'Have we learned more from AD1?'

'Yes, lots. Tim will brief you. I'm told he'll be here tomorrow if your doctor gives permission.'

'I'll be sure she does!'

He laughed and said, 'Yes, I'm sure you will, but I'm going to leave you now. I have a Cabinet meeting shortly, but I wanted to see you as soon as you came out of the coma. Your clear thinking and enthusiasm for everything to do with Allen and his craft has been sorely missed by me and Jenny. Anyone who didn't appreciate the importance of a good presentation is now converted. Even so there are many fanatics out there.'

He stood, I got another kiss on the cheek, and he squeezed my hand.

'Thank you for coming, Prime Minister. Very much appreciated indeed.'

'Now, try not to worry too much. We know it'll be a couple of months before you have fully recovered. I'm enjoying the sojourn – Tim is so much less argumentative than you are! Try not to rush it.'

I smiled at his jibe. 'I'll try, sir.'

He left, accompanied by his security detail. I noticed an armed, uniformed policeman now stood outside my room. How long had he been there? I didn't remember seeing him earlier. I wasn't sure if the extra security reassured me or added to my anxiety. I tried to put it out of my mind.

I opened the reflexlet. Where to start? I googled my own name and read about events.

The gunman, a fanatical fundamentalist Christian, was born and brought up in Preston with ordinary working-class parents and a good education. He'd somehow managed to acquire two automatic rifles, almost impossible with UK gun laws. He was also a member of a white supremacist group from where the weapons were obtained. He'd run onto the stage shouting about blasphemers, but the news media videos showed no more until the rescue services arrived. I had to dig into the depths of the dark web to find an illicit unedited video of the entire event.

I heard him shouting, 'Blaspheming devils' and 'The world is for mankind,' and watched as he sprayed bullets across the stage, catching Godfrey first in the head and neck. I slumped forward towards the floor when first hit and he sprayed the bullets left and right across me. He suddenly turned towards the audience and began firing with sweeping volleys, aiming higher with each blast as he worked his way back up the rows. I knew Mario was at the front, so he must have leapt up towards the man and died. The distraction might have saved my life. The gunman changed magazines and fired again. I didn't cry this time when I thought of Mario. Was I already getting used to the loss of the love of my life?

Two figures ran on from behind where I was lying inert on the stage and brought the gunman down with a rugby tackle. The film stopped thirty seconds later. The last sequence showed Godfrey in a pool of blood and me, crumpled forward partly on the floor, with blood oozing from my multiple wounds. I watched it through several times. The doctor had said I was lucky to be alive; I now realised what she meant. I'd never seen so much blood.

The news channels picked it up from there as the death toll grew. Paramedics carried me and other survivors into ambulances. One of them was pounding someone's chest. Later sequences showed body bags being removed. Twenty-two dead because I'd agreed to do this television show. Guilt washed over me. It was my fault. Mine. If I'd done a better job of presenting the discovery, perhaps all of these people would still be alive.

There was a photograph of the perpetrator in custody. A young man in his mid-twenties. Someone you wouldn't pay attention to if you passed him in the street. There were no scary eyes or intimidating tattoos. A young man who could have been anybody and would probably otherwise have remained a nobody.

If we'd been able to drip-feed the news about the discovery of AD1 from the very beginning, extreme views like those of the gunman, might never have arisen. I should've been more forceful from day one – telling of the device, revealing its age, showing the alien city, then Allen himself – if it had been spread over the whole year all of these people could have still been alive. Mario would have been alive! It was all my fault for not trying harder. The Prime Minister admitting I'd been right all along didn't help Mario or any of the other victims.

I continued to follow the news stories, seeing the construction of the Mars ship in orbit. It was so like some of the science fiction ships of the past. There was a circular module which would provide artificial gravity at two-thirds Earth normal, making exercising much easier and removing some of the problems with being weightless. Its flight time to Mars would be weeks rather than months – all down to Allen's fuel.

I read about the revolution which was beginning in electronics with the discovery of how the polarisation of wires functioned. It was extraordinary. A single wire could conduct electricity both ways. There was zero resistance, so no loss of current in the new wires and they would soon be burying mains transmission cables because there would no longer be any power leakage. I smiled at the thought that the countryside would be freed from its tangle of cables and pylons. Companies were working on how the new technology could be used on domestic appliances and commercial equipment.

The fuel had revolutionised space travel and during my extended coma a second moon-base had been built. The dream of the 1970s was finally realised. I saw that Yuri was returning from the moon to command the Mars ship. So wonderful for him.

Two private space companies had plans for large passenger vessels capable of taking up to a hundred people into orbit. Four well-known social media and Internet search companies were ploughing billions into plans for an orbital hotel resort not at all unlike the fanciful space station from *2001 A Space Odyssey*. The dreams of every young space adventurer were becoming reality in double-quick time. The ISS would be saved from the long-overdue decommissioning and would become just a component of the new Earth Orbital Platform.

News from Goonhilly was more difficult to track down online, but I'd get the important information from Tim the next day. I found some new images of Allen's home world and some more close-ups of Jupiter's moons, Europa and Ganymede, presumably taken in antiquity. There was little about the work on the alien language or their computer programs. Again, Tim would update me.

More disturbing was the activity of religious zealots and xenophobic factions.

There had been a serious number of terrorist actions undertaken by Christian, Jewish, Hindu, Muslim, and other faith groups, of which the fundamental Christians and

Islamists had been the most fanatical. The factions had grown rapidly after the announcement and were preaching doom, gloom, and imminent invasion. An irrational and frightening paranoia.

Some fanaticism was to be expected and I made myself feel somewhat better by wondering how much worse it might have been if I hadn't finally got permission to release the news after the Paris conference. Hopefully, my determination to try to do it right had saved at least some lives, but I'd forever wish I'd been allowed to release the original discovery shortly after it happened. I was certain it would've defused hatred of Allen if people had gradually had it all brought to their attention instead of in this single rush. I'd have to put the matter out of my mind, or I'd become neurotic about it.

I read there'd even been an attempt at sabotage of the Mars ship in orbit. Unbelievably, one of their number had been trained as an astronaut a decade earlier and managed to get herself onto one of the construction details. An explosive device was found on the outer wall of the main living quarters and had been timed for three months. Given bad luck, it could've exploded during the AD2 collection process. Fortunately, it was discovered by two astronauts in the Scaffy Wagon just before the outer skin was attached which would've hidden it from view. My baby was still showing its usefulness to the ongoing exploration of space.

As for the religious fanatics like the man who killed my Mario, why did these people, who supposedly believed in a loving God, carry out such awful deeds in the name of their religion? I could never understand such targeted hatred and violence. Mario and the others at the TV show, including me, had done nothing but demonstrate a healthy interest in the most extraordinary discovery of modern times.

233

My last contact with him had been when Mario gave me a tiny kiss before he was taken to his seat. I tried to remember the softness of his lips and their warmth, but couldn't. It was so sad. So dreadful. So unnecessary. Was I bitter? You'd better believe it!

Nurses took the reflexlet away from me mid-afternoon when it was time to change my dressings. I asked for a mirror to observe my wounds. They were all pretty shocking, but my leg was in a dreadful state between my hip and my knee, as they'd had to perform several operations. The gash in my neck was enormous and I truly realised how lucky I'd been.

My drip was removed, although the nasty, painful gadget was still left in my hand for some reason. Why do they do that? I was disconnected from the other monitors and they propped me up in bed. I was told I'd be helped out of bed the next day and allowed to sit in an easy chair. The day after, I'd begin physiotherapy to get my muscles working once more. It would be good simply to escape the bed pans, but they dashed that hope by telling me I'd have no use of my leg for at least another couple of weeks. The bone had been too badly shattered.

The next morning, I was given a massive backlog of mail – plus loads of newly delivered flowers and get well cards from people who'd probably given up on me, and one from the King which was a real surprise. There were too many to read in one go and I resolved to keep them all to read at leisure when I eventually returned home.

Home? What would home be like? Our beautiful thatched cottage in Helford which we'd only owned for a few weeks. Would I ever be able to live happily again in the creek-side haven we'd chosen together while so much in love and with so much life to look forward to? I remembered our last walk along the creek on the morning of the Armstrong show. The holding of hands, the hug on the wooden bridge, the taste of his lips. My tears flowed freely.

«« o »»

My meeting with Tim the next day was a pleasure. He quickly got his sympathies out of the way and we were soon talking about wonderful developments and discoveries.

'The language team have found documents in cylinder two. No interpretation yet, but it's certainly language,' said Tim.

'It would be good to know the language before AD2 gets to the Cluster.'

He passed his reflexlet to me and said, 'By the way, we have two more images of Allen and, as you can see, he can extend limbs directly from his body.'

'Mary thought that might be how they worked. How wonderful to materialise a hand or arm at will. Wish I could do the same right now.'

He laughed, 'Yes, would be a boon.'

I think it inspired a smile in me. One of my first since finding out about Mario.

'They opened one of the cylinders which they knew contained only data which had been studied.'

'And...?'

'Contained silicon.'

'What just silicon?'

'Yes, and it is amazing how it works. Initially it was a bit of a mystery, but when the truth about Allen's existence was revealed, lots of universities clamoured for information.'

'Guessed that would happen.'

'The fact that the silicon could store massive amounts of data, but also brain activity was a real puzzle. The breakthrough came at Lancaster University. The cylinders themselves are machines. They switch electrons on or off within the silicon atoms. Silicon has fourteen electrons and the number of combinations appeared, initially, to be fourteen.'

'That accounts for the amount of storage, then?'

'Well, no, actually, but the electrons circle the atom's nucleus in orbits, known as shells. Lancaster discovered the electrons in each shell acted as a power on the other shells. Shell one had two electrons, shell two had eight and shell three had four. So, depending upon how many were switched, it gave you two times eight times four equalling sixty-four different combinations in each atom.'

'Amazing, but that is a ground-breaking discovery.'

'Yes. Allen has given us the most powerful memory storage, far beyond anything we ever thought possible.'

'Its effect on computers and AI will be enormous,' I said.

'Ah, yes, but the switching of electrons on or off is now causing a huge amount of research and there are likely to be breakthroughs in other industries. If you can manipulate electrons in silicon, why not in lead or nitrogen or any other element?'

'How many more wonders are going to be found in or hinted at within Allen's craft? Thanks so much for coming to tell me about it all, Tim.'

Sitting up in a chair was a strain and, to be honest, I was glad when they helped me back into the bed. I was still so weak, hardly able to lift my good leg off the floor. Even lifting and holding my reflexlet, which was as light as a feather, was a serious trial of strength after a few minutes.

I lay back and browsed my get well cards. Mum and Dad arrived in the evening and my hospital stay was beginning to fall into a routine. The emotional loss caused by Mario's death preyed heavily upon my mind though, and caused many tearful, sleepless nights.

The months which followed gradually saw me regaining the use of my legs, although I needed both a stick and crutch to get about.

My arm took almost as long to heal and had needed a second operation to insert an extra metal rod.

My coma seemed to have had no effect on my mental abilities and I began to receive briefings on progress at Goonhilly. I'd hopes for a return to work in the near future. I felt so isolated in hospital.

Towards the end of my hospital stay, Mars One arrived in orbit around the fabled red planet and collected AD2. It put up no resistance and there seemed to be no recognition that it had been captured. That surprised me rather. I'd thought it would try to make contact. Yuri and his crew strapped it to a framework in the ship's hold. Eventually it was on the way back to Earth orbit.

I was going to have to regain my health if I was to play any part in the reception committee.

24 Just a Quick Visit

I left the hospital at the end of November 2036, a year after returning from the International Space Station. How my life had changed. I'd be a virtual cripple for years and had lost the love of my life. All I had left was my desire to ensure the aliens were accepted by humanity. My determination to achieve that objective was multiplied tenfold. Nothing else mattered to me now. I was obsessed with it.

As an astronaut, I was diligent in my physiotherapy, but even so, my left leg was not responding at all well. I stayed with Mum and Dad for a few days but eventually decided to put in an appearance at Goonhilly to let everyone know I was alive, if not kicking, before returning to my parents' bungalow for another month's convalescence. Maybe I could return to work in January.

Could I prove I was able to be independent? Dad wanted to come with me, but surely I'd be okay on my own for just one night. I could move about all right with my stick for ten or twenty metres at a time and my crutch made me more mobile but reduced my speed. Indra Masinghe wanted me to use the crutch continually for a few more weeks, but I hated it with a vengeance.

I soon regretted travelling unaccompanied.

My hire vehicle arrived in Helford and I discovered a huge drawback to autonomous cars – there was no one to help with my cases! I managed to get the empty one into the hallway, once I'd fought my way through the neglected clematis which was intent on concealing the front door. The full case was defeating me. I couldn't even lift it out of the boot. I stood and looked around helplessly. Helford is a tiny village with a dead-end road. There was no one in sight in any direction.

What was I to do? I looked this way and that. No one passed by. Not even a car to flag down. With a new grit, I put my stick in the boot, steadied myself, reached in and pulled on the case.

Finally, it was out of the car, but rather unfortunately I was on my back with the case on top of me. I burst out laughing! It was either that or cry and I was sick of crying. I'd done enough of that to last a lifetime.

I pushed the case off, crawled to the car and heaved myself back to my feet, hurting all over.

'You okay?' asked a pleasant male voice from behind me.

'Yes. Just struggling with my case.'

'Who won?' He was a distinguished fifty-something in an Arran sweater and jeans.

'The case did.'

'Yes. I think it had you in a double-arm wristlock.' We both laughed.

'I guessed it would have a name. I'm Evelyn.'

'Recognised you – the lady of the moment. I'm Jack. Gaye and I are your neighbours. Didn't realise it was you who'd moved in next door to us.'

'Yes. I work at Goonhilly.' Mario and I had hardly had time to get to know the village community.

'Sorry about your husband.'

'Thanks. We never made it to the altar.' I stifled my emotions.

'Yes. I read that. Sorry.'

'Can you get this suitcase into the house for me. I'm afraid it might try to throw me again!'

'No problem.' He picked it up, and I recovered my crutch and stick, dismissed the car, and followed him in.

'Can you take it up to the room on the right at the top of the stairs, please... and the empty one too.'

When he descended, he wrote his number on the hall notepad. 'Don't hesitate to call if you need help. Usually Gaye or I will be in.'

'Thanks, Jack.'

Once he'd gone, I looked at the stairs with some trepidation. This hadn't been a good idea. I shouldn't have come without help. I'd been stupidly optimistic. I wasn't ready for climbing stairs but, with a great effort, one step at a time, I pulled myself up to the bedroom.

I stood in the doorway, taking in the room we'd left the morning of the Armstrong show. I hadn't realised the emotions it would arouse. I shouldn't have come at all. Tears ran freely down my cheeks. I let it happen. Better out than in. I slid down the wall I had been leaning against until I was a crumpled, devastated heap on the floor.

In that moment, I knew I wouldn't be able to stay. This could never be my home again. The room was overflowing with our love for each other. Not only the bed with its unforgettable intimate secrets, but his jeans hanging over the back of the wooden chair where he'd thrown them, a windcheater suspended from the wardrobe catch. Some navy blue material protruded from under his pillow.

I crawled to the bed and hauled myself to my feet, pulling the garment from its hiding place. His pyjama shorts. The tears flowed again as I buried my face in them, soaking up the badly missed aroma of my long-lost lover as they did the same with my tears. I'd never smell him again, the lingering musky scent of my man. How it comforted me once the tears subsided. The essence of him. Once it faded, it would be gone forever. I couldn't stay here, not even for a single night. I must leave. I had to get away.

I opened the empty case, added some clothes from my drawers and wardrobe, collected a few other bits and bobs, threw in the shorts and closed it. I slid the two cases, one at a time, to the top of the stairs and pushed them down. They both made it safely, albeit noisily, to the bottom and I followed, holding tightly to the banister as my bad leg did its best to give up the ghost during my descent.

I sat on the bottom step, breathing heavily for a while before I rang the Mullion Cove Hotel, managed to get a room for the night and called a car before telephoning Jack to come over to help when it arrived.

Thirty minutes later the car pulled up outside and Jack appeared shortly afterwards.

'I'm in no fit state to stay.'

'You don't look very steady.'

'No. Can you put the cases in the car, please? I'm going to stay at Mullion Cove.'

'Of course.'

I thanked him and left. The car took me straight to the hotel and I was sure I'd never return to the cottage in Helford, other than to pack and move. I felt so desolate. My life had been changed beyond belief by the act of a madman. My dream chocolate-box cottage could never represent more than hopeless melancholy.

The hotel staff knew me from the news and the many meals I'd had there with Mario and Goonhilly visitors. I let their sympathy wash over me but was grateful for their attentiveness as they assisted me the best they could.

Where was my car? Presumably, still parked at Goonhilly. I'd instructed it to go there when I booked the express car to take Mario and me to London. I texted it for its location and then to come and collect me at ten the next morning.

««o»»

The Jaguar arrived on time, drove me in through the Goonhilly gates, and I noticed the perimeter was now secured with guards armed with machine guns. That was new and reflected the threats of the religious and xenophobic terrorists.

The approach to the building revealed the most wonderful surprise. There was an enormous banner 'WELCOME BACK DAME EVELYN' spread across the front of the building, the letters hurriedly scrawled in the browns, greens, and blues of corporate Goonhilly paint. It had obviously been hastily prepared. How on earth had they known? I asked the car to stop and looked at the sign, tears welling up. I fought to control them and took photographs of the sign with my phone, before letting the car proceed.

The Jaguar stopped in front of the doors and it took me a minute to get out, sort out my crutch, and make my way to the entrance, while the car went off and parked itself.

Someone must have noticed it driving itself out of the car park earlier and found out I was in the area. They'd guessed it had gone to collect me. Either that or someone at the hotel had tipped them off when I arrived the previous day. I hadn't realised my staff thought so much about me. I felt warmed by their kind thoughts. Could I control my emotions? I was determined to try.

They had obviously been waiting for me because by the time I entered, there was a gathering of some forty staff who all gave the most astonishing three cheers. I'm afraid I instantly broke down. My intention to be stoical had totally failed. Janet ran over to me with a chair into which I gratefully slumped, the crutch clattering to the floor.

Everyone came over in turn, offering their sympathies for Mario and congratulating me on my recovery. After the initial outburst of tears, I steeled myself to let the sympathetic words pass me by unheard. I didn't dare let them through my fragile defences to ignite recurring waves of grief.

After a while people drifted away. Tim and Janet helped me through to my office, where everything was exactly as it had been the day before I left for the television studios.

I didn't do much. I drank cups of tea and called in a few colleagues for a chat to discover how they were doing and get some first-hand news. When I was about to leave, I told Tim I'd be back in the new year and called Janet.

'Can I get you to organise a couple of things for me?'

'Of course, Doctor Slater.'

'I want those three images of Allen on the walls of my office to replace the modern art. Make them big and nicely framed. Get admin to sell the existing paintings off at auction somewhere. Check their value with Mr Brown first and that they're not important to Goonhilly.' I fished a memory card out of my bag. 'There is only one image on this card, Janet, it is of Mario with me. Can you please get it made into an eighteen inch by twelve inch photograph in a tasteful frame to stand on the sideboard over there? Sorry to ask.' I hated asking for personal favours.

'No problem.'

I was about to get up and prepare to leave when Tim knocked on the door and came rushing in.

'You have to see this,' he said, pointing to my computer monitor.

I relaxed back into my seat, thimballed the monitor open and there was a new red flashing message at the top right.

I flicked the thimball at it and the video opened. It was from Yuri. How wonderful. I was so glad my friend had been chosen as the Mars One commander.

Yuri's head and shoulders were in shot and he spoke in his lovely thick Russian accent, 'Tim, this urgent. AD2 has come to life in hold and making effort communicate. Every few minutes taking over on-board communication systems with repeating message. Here it is,' he said, and the camera switched to Yuri's monitor.

The screen was filled with alien text similar to the hieroglyphs we'd found on the outside of AD1. It ended and the gold nose of AD2 appeared on the screen. A diagrammatic arrow revolved around the gold probe in a clockwise direction. The animation depicted the probe unscrewing clockwise. When it detached in the animation, the silver blisters covering the gold area of the device pulsated as if radiating something. The message and the animation repeated ad infinitum.

'Tim, we need know what to do,' said Yuri.

'It's a six-minute lag, Eve,' said Tim. 'How should I answer?'

I sent a quick message back to Mars One. 'Eve here, Yuri. We're on the case. Standby.'

We called in John Sweet, the head of the computer section and Roy Williams, the newly appointed head of the linguistics section.

Tim sent communications a copy of Yuri's message to distribute to the action list. That done, the four of us discussed how to respond to the developing situation. AD2 had somehow discovered the monitor's resolution and input requirements and then transmitted its message. Remarkable.

It seems my fleeting visit to the office was not going to be as fleeting as I'd expected. There was no way I could walk out now. Yuri needed me. My project needed me. Perhaps even Allen needed me.

25 Message from Mars

Around six minutes later another video message arrived from Yuri. 'Lovely to hear you back, Eva. It stopped repeating message. Standing by. I going to stream you video of inside of hold in case anything precipice happen.'

Yuri's face disappeared from the screen and AD2 was visible, strapped to a specially made framework in the hold section of Mars One. It was so still – but who knew what was going on inside it?

One of my hacker team was convinced the device was home to an actual alien mind. If it had awoken, would it be prepared to wait the several weeks necessary to get it back to Earth or would it believe it was being ignored? What would happen if it were unhappy about us ignoring it or having removed it from Mars orbit?

I sent an acknowledgement back to Yuri with a copy to NASA and ESA, 'Copy that, Yuri. We're discussing. Use your own initiative if anything unexpected occurs.'

'So, it's settled down,' said John.

'Can I copy the video of the text, Doctor Slater? We'll find out if we can make sense of it. At least there's a context,' said Roy.

I copied Yuri's message, forwarded it to him, and he went back to the linguistics department.

'It must want us to unscrew the golden rod to cause something to happen with those blisters. Do you know what work has been done on them on AD1?' I directed my question to Tim.

'Nothing. They've been concentrating on the last of the cylinders.'

'Who oversees research up there currently, Tim?'

'Doctor Naughton is up there again at the moment.'

'He's recovered from the decompression?'

245

'Yes, full recovery and he played merry hell until NASA approved his return to the ISS.'

I quickly sent an email to Reg Naughton in the Cluster, forwarding Yuri's message and asking if they'd unscrew the rod – with all possible precautions.

I sent another message to Mars One. 'Yuri, I have linguistics going through the message. I've asked Reg Naughton to consider unscrewing the rod from AD1. Suggest you sit tight for a while.'

My telephone rang. It was the new head of NASA and he was miffed I'd been giving orders to Yuri.

With authority beyond what I felt, I told him, 'Professor Green, this was an urgent situation and Yuri's request was sent to us. We therefore responded and you were copied in on everything.'

'I didn't even know you were back. Mr Riley has cleared everything through us,' he replied.

'Well, I'm much better thanks. Take it up with UKSA or ESA if you're unhappy with the responses I made.'

'No, not unhappy, but I would've liked to have known you were back in the saddle. I am, of course, glad you're feeling better.'

'Tell you what, Professor, let's forget this conversation. I was paying a fleeting *unofficial* visit to Goonhilly and this event took place while I was here. It seemed important to deal with Yuri's problem quickly, don't you think?'

'I suppose so. Okay, keep us in the loop.'

'As always,' I said and cut the connection.

Tim laughed and said, 'Nice to have you back, Eve. He's been getting under my skin something chronic.'

'What happened to Michael Sanderson, the previous head of NASA?' I asked, thinking back to my conversations about his concern over the upcoming change of President.

'Sacked, or at least he jumped before he could be sacked.'

'Oh yes, the idiot who believes the world is six thousand years old won the election, didn't he?'

"Fraid so, Eve, and he takes over as President in January.'

'It's so sad. With my encouragement, Michael bypassed him and went to President Drake over the presentation of Allen to the world. Must've cost him his job.'

'Would seem so.'

'It's wrong on so many levels. Anyway, their foolishness is beyond our ability to resolve. Let's get on with this new problem.'

'Michael's landed on his feet though, working with Lupin Galactic now, I'm told.'

'The new space transport company selling suborbital flights?'

'Yes. They're making a go of it, apparently, and orbital flights are planned for next year. It's the new fuel. It's changing everything.'

Our gaze returned to AD2, sitting quietly in the hold of Yuri's ship.

'Presumably it could break free from the hold if it wished?' asked John Sweet.

'I fear so,' I replied.

'I think we should ignore its message, but monitor it carefully,' said Tim.

'Yes. Our problem is we don't know whether we're dealing with automatic on-board systems, or the actual waking mind of one of the aliens,' I said.

'Whichever it is, waiting and watching is still the answer,' said Tim.

'Agreed.'

I buzzed Janet and asked her to get me Professor Green and to pop in when I finished the call.

'Green,' his sharp Texas twang barked at me.

'Professor. We believe we should play a waiting and watching game. If we're dealing with automated systems, it'll probably be patient. If it's the mind of an actual alien in control of AD2, he'll know he's in transit from his own sensors. I intend to let Captain Bulgakov know unless you've a different viewpoint.'

'Call me Brad, Doctor Slater. I concur,' said Professor Green.

'Okay, Brad. I'm Eve or Evelyn. Bye.' I cut the line.

'International diplomacy in action!' said Tim.

I laughed with him. It was good to be back in the cut and thrust of the Goonhilly operation.

I opened the line to Mars One, 'Yuri, our opinion is to wait and watch. NASA concurs. If you're receiving the messages from a robot, in our view it'll continue its hundred-million-year patience. If you're being contacted by an alien mind which has awoken, he'll understand we're transporting him. How does that sound to you? We're still observing the cargo hold on a separate link and will tell you the results of Doctor Naughton's experiments on the golden rod.'

Janet entered, 'You wanted me, Doctor Slater?'

'Yes, more tea for me, please, and whatever John and Tim might like. Get onto the Mullion Cove Hotel and book me a room in there tonight. If not find somewhere else for me – with no steps in or out. Next, you'd better get on to some letting agencies and find me a bungalow to rent within a reasonable distance. My cottage isn't suitable.' I needed to get myself organised if I wasn't going back home.

'Will do,' she said, waiting for Tim and John's response.

'Tea's fine,' they both agreed quickly.

'Do you need help to get your home sorted out?' asked Tim.

'Thank you, Tim, but no. I can never go back there.'

'You're welcome to stay with Jane and me tonight if it helps.'

'That's kind of you, but I'm not good company right now. I so miss Mario. If Janet can get me into the hotel, I'd be better on my own. My recovery from Mario's death will take time.'

'Don't worry. The offer is always there if you need to talk with some friends. Jane and I, or just me would come and dine with you if you wanted some company. It's not a good idea to sit alone and brood.'

'Thanks, Tim. You're probably right, but not tonight.'

Six minutes had passed, and Yuri came back to us from Mars One.

'Roger that, Eva. If it awoken alien being, it will be bored much quickly in hold. Should we entertain? Can stream TV into hold or radio in case there no visual sensory system running? Or could be learning language during journey back. Maybe some Teach Yourself English? Just thinking.

'On personal note, I most glad you are back in action, dearest Eva. Visit you few months ago when you in coma, I did. Said goodbyes, I did. Must be honest, did not think see you again.

'Anyway, Eva, lovely to be wrong.'

The video returned to the shot of AD2 in the hold. The lag was a damn nuisance.

'Copy that, Yuri. We'll discuss your idea. Thanks for the kind thoughts about me. Stronger than I look, you know. Didn't know you'd visited me in hospital. Thank you.'

'Yuri might have a point,' John said.

I buzzed Janet and asked her to get Roy to come back to my office.

'We can't send him a news channel,' I said, 'he might decide to wait another hundred million years to discover if we'll eventually improve!'

249

'You are getting back to your normal self, Eve. That's the first injection of humour into anything you've said.'

'Suppose so,' I gave a smile which did not come from my broken heart.

Roy returned and we told him Yuri's idea.

'You're the language expert,' I said to him, 'what do you think?'

'It would seem to be a good idea but would be wasted if he has no visual apparatus switched on. There are audio courses, but they only teach people who have language A to speak language B. With the alien, we don't have a language A in which to teach him,' Roy explained.

'I suppose video programmes use imagery instead?' Tim asked.

'Yes, but not specifically so designed, but they do exist. It is easy to say the word car when a car appears on a screen. If we can't find a suitable one, I am sure we could soon create one.'

'He must have visual sensors,' said Tim.

'Why?' I asked.

'How else could he know his location?'

'Hmm. Suppose so, but it might just be a string of coordinates.'

'He managed to broadcast on our monitors using a system alien to him. So, I'm sure he has visual sensors or the ability to detect our television signals,' said Tim.

'Let's hope so.'

I buzzed Janet and asked her to get Brad at NASA for me again.

'Brad, Yuri has had an idea. If the device is an actual mind it'll become bored. Would it be useful to show AD2 a language video teaching English? What do you think?'

'You have one?'

'No, not yet, but we could acquire or make one pretty quickly.'

'What if it's only a computer?'

'Nothing lost. Even computers can learn,' I said, 'and it'd be useful if or when the alien awakes.'

'Sounds a good idea. Go for it,' he said, and we cut the connection.

'Right, Roy, do you want to investigate, or is it something Tim can deal with while you work on the language Yuri sent us?'

'I'd rather get back onto the language, Doctor Slater.'

'Okay, I'll send another message to Yuri,' I said as the others left my office.

'Hi, Yuri, we like your idea and Tim is working on a special video language programme for AD2, the only problem being not knowing for sure if he has any visual sensory apparatus. We've no idea how to find out, either. I'd suggest you run the video in the hold and on a ship's system in case he's intercepting communications and can pick it up directly. I'll let you know when we've something ready to send. We don't think it's a good idea to pipe in a news channel as it might be confusing and would possibly give a poor impression of us. Be safe,' I said and finished the transmission.

Janet knocked and entered.

'You've a room for tonight and they said there's no problem extending at this time of year,' she said.

'Good, thanks.'

'I've also put some property details into an email attachment. One is quite nice in Helston. Two-bedroom, good view, and easy access.'

'Thanks. Get me NASA again, please.'

She left my office and I sat back exhausted. I'd only popped in to say hello and it was already late. Brad's face appeared on the screen.

'Eve?'

'Brad, I need to leave the office. I'm typing my secure Skype ID into an email. You'll be able to contact me if you need to. Frankly, I'm exhausted. Today was only meant to be a short visit, not an all-day stint.'

'Okay, Eve, you get off. I won't disturb unless something new happens. Try to get some rest. Sorry about my attitude earlier.'

'Think nothing of it,' I said, deciding not to apologise back for my snappiness towards him. I wanted to retain the upper hand.

26 Golden Rod

Back in the hotel I telephoned Dad and told him I was okay and would be back at the weekend. I did some of my physiotherapy exercises for half an hour, descended to the elegant dining room where I enjoyed a fillet of sole starter, followed by a simply wonderful fillet steak served with baby vegetables. Despite doctor's orders, I accompanied it with a couple of glasses of illicit red wine. It was a delicious meal, but I was still having trouble swallowing unless I cut things up very small. I was going to have to adapt. When I laid my head on the pillow, I was out like a light and slept through until my watch woke me at seven.

Refreshed, I struggled to shower. This over-bath shower was no good for me. Climbing in and out of a bath was not only extremely difficult and treacherous in my condition, but painful too. Most hotels had already switched to walk-in showers, but the Mullion Cove Hotel was in the grand twentieth-century tradition of luxury hotels and was very much of its time, an experience all its own.

I must check the rented properties to find out what sort of bath facilities they had. I was no longer able-bodied. Who knew how long my leg might take to heal, if ever? To add insult to injury, the steak, chips and wine had upset my tummy. My digestive system was not used to solids. I'd been warned.

My Jaguar was ready for me at eight thirty. It arrived from the hotel car park and was awaiting me at the front door. I set off to Goonhilly.

Marjorie saw my car arrive at the building and she rushed out to hold the main doors open for me and carry my briefcase. She helped me through into the government section of the offices until Janet took over as I entered my office suite. I was so weak and helpless. The sleep and shower might have refreshed me, but I was now aching

253

from head to foot from the effects of moving about so much. Muscles were trying to perform unfamiliar tasks and I was even more tired than I'd been when I left the previous evening.

My monitor had several red-flash messages. The first was my lawyer so I put it on snooze. The second was Yuri confirming receipt of my last message. The third was from Reg in the cluster.

'Give me a call, Eve, as soon as you get in,' was all he said.

I buzzed Janet and asked her to get Dr Naughton while I opened the message from my lawyer.

A date had been set for the trial of Wayne Terret, the gunman who had caused all my injuries and deprived me of my fiancé. The lawyer was preparing me for having to give evidence and to provide a victim statement. He hoped Terret would plead guilty.

I wasn't looking forward to seeing this man across a court room. He deserved to be locked away forever for acting upon his insane beliefs. Given those beliefs, I was doubtful he'd plead guilty. My lawyer was probably trying to throw a positive slant on the situation.

My monitor came to life and Reg was smiling at me from the inside of the cluster. 'Hi, Eve. Lovely to see you. Hope you're feeling better.'

'Not really, Reg, but thanks anyway. Being in a coma is worse than the muscle wastage you get while on the ISS. How're things with you?'

'Great. We've now got a gravity module on the Cluster. Achieving one g makes it seem a bit like a hamster wheel, but at least it keeps us fit from an hour or so exercising per day instead of the old three-hour regime with the machines.'

'The wonderfuel has had a major effect on what can be launched. But what about the Coriolis effect?' I asked.

'It's amazing how adaptable the human body is, so not a serious problem. You get used to it and we won't be playing ball games. The fuel means we can even get in and out of orbit with less trouble, Eve. The fuel allows us to drop out of orbit without the use of such heavy and thick heat shields. When you're up to it, you must come up and visit.'

'Oh, I'd dearly love to visit the Cluster again.'

'If AD2 is coming here, why not be here when it arrives?'

'Don't think I'd be well enough, Reg.'

'Blast off isn't as taxing anymore. It's not much more stressful on the body than a ride on a budget airliner.'

'Seriously? Sorry, I still haven't caught up with all the advances which've been made while I was out of circulation.'

'Yes, seriously, Eve. Check with your doctor but coming up here shouldn't be much more of a problem than air travel.'

'I will. Thanks for the information, Reg. Now why're you calling? I assume it wasn't only to invite me to eat ESA processed food.'

'Ha, even the food is better, Eve. You must come if you can. Anyway, I was calling because we are planning to unscrew the golden rod from AD1 at eleven this morning GMT.'

'Right, what precautions?'

'You might not be aware, Eve, but the entire Cluster is now running on normal air. This means we only need to use the airlocks for isolation. We can watch AD1 from the laboratory as you know, and we've a robot to unscrew the rod. We intend to watch from the laboratory in pressure suits in case something goes dangerously awry.'

'Sounds a sensible precaution.'

'We'll be doing it on a live feed to ESA, NASA, Roscosmos, JAXA, CSA, and yourselves.'

'Okay, Reg, I'll be sure to watch. How are the decompression wounds? Are you back to normal?'

'Almost. My eyes ache occasionally and my hand, but it's no more than annoying.'

'Glad to hear you're improving. Speak later.'

'Bye, Eve.'

I telephoned my lawyer and told him to keep me apprised of when I'd be needed for the trial. Again, anxiety hit me as I thought about Terret murdering my Mario, and tears welled up.

I was saved from bawling by Janet delivering me a lovely mug of tea.

'Those bungalows have over-bath showers, Janet. I found out this morning they're not ideal with my leg. Can you check whether anyone has one with a walk-in shower or if I might be able to pay for having one installed. I'll probably need a long let. Sorry to mess you around.'

'No problem, Doctor Slater. Put anything you like on me while you're recovering.'

'Thanks, Janet.'

Come eleven, Tim arrived, and we tuned in to the live video from the Cluster. There were four feeds on the main screen. One showed the front of AD1 face on. The robot was attached firmly to the ceiling from our perspective and comprised a thick, jointed arm which sprouted two spindly sub-arms. The other screens showed a variety of views from different sides.

I logged-in so Reg knew we were on line. CSA and ESA were listed above us in the corner of the monitor and JAXA, NASA, and Roscosmos beneath, showing all six of us were logged in.

'Good morning, everyone,' said Reg. 'We're about to attempt to unscrew the golden rod from the front of AD1 as proposed by the video AD2 provided on Mars One.'

The robot arm projected a smaller arm, and this took hold of the rod about five or six inches from where it emerged from the craft.

'Rotating clockwise now with low torque,' commented Reg.

Screen three zoomed in on the point where the rod met the craft. Slivers of sticky paper on the rod would give a clear indication of any rotation. They didn't move.

'Increasing torque to two of ten.'

Still there was no sign of movement.

It was only on torque six that the papers moved a quarter rotation and the robot stopped its motion.

'Reducing torque and unscrewing slowly.'

Camera three showed an extreme close-up of the end of the rod as it gradually unscrewed in the unfamiliar clockwise motion.

Soon the thread of the rod came into sight. In fact, the rod was hollow, and the thread was attached to the craft, so it wasn't a reversed thread after all. Suddenly there was clear air between the rod and the craft. It had been detached. Camera three zoomed out again and we all watched intently. I was particularly interested in the silver, thimble-like structures which, in the AD2 animation, appeared to do something. The animation clearly wanted us to do this, but what was it supposed to trigger?

Minutes passed. No sign of anything happening at all. Perhaps AD1 was so damaged its systems were unable to respond. We had, of course removed all of the memory cylinders from inside the device. If they contained computer programs which were meant to be called into action, they'd no longer be activated.

'We can't see anything taking place, and there's no sound being produced, or anything being broadcast,' announced Reg.

'Close-up of the blunt end of the thread please, Reg,' I asked.

The camera zoomed in. A delicate gold filament protruded from the top.

'What am I seeing? Is it a wire?' I asked.

The camera closed in even further. There was clearly a filament leading from the top of the thread. It was broken.

'I wonder if its breaking was supposed to trigger something,' I mused.

'Possibly,' said Reg.

'I think we've stripped so much out of it that we were hoping for too much to expect it to still be able to react,' said Brad at NASA.

'Yes, I'm sure you are right, Brad. We'll keep the cameras on it,' said Reg with some disappointment in his voice.

'Reg,' I said, 'can you please examine the thimble-like structures. They're obviously important to its function and it'd be good to know what they contain before Yuri arrives with AD2. Also, should AD2 be examined in the Cluster initially? While we're on the conference call, what do the rest of you think?'

'Fine by me,' Brad said.

'I'm for that,' agreed Gerald, 'but I'll have to put it to the boss. Should think he'll agree though.'

'Roscosmos?'

'Да.'

'Reg?' I asked.

'Yes, I concur, but I'd like additional security in case it does something which might harm us.'

'I don't think it has any intention to harm,' said Brad.

'No,' I agreed, 'but it might harm unintentionally. We need to consider the possibility. When will AD2 arrive?'

'Four weeks,' said Brad.

'Well, we've time to think this through,' I said.

There was general consensus and the call ended, although I left the live feed on my monitor in case there was a delayed reaction.

I buzzed Janet, requested more tea, and asked her to get Gerald for me, person to person.

'Hi, Eve, lovely to see you back in action. What can I do for you?' he asked as his smiling face came on in the corner of my monitor.

'Thanks, Gerald, I want to be in the Cluster when AD2 arrives. Who do I have to bribe for a ticket?'

'Are you well enough?'

'I've been told it's not so stressful with the new orbital launchers.'

'Yes, but what about your wounds? Reduced pressure in orbit would not be good for open wounds.'

'Most have healed. I'll get clearance from my consultant, but I want to be there.'

'Okay, Eve, I'll look into it. Why not talk to your PM? I would've thought ESA would be reluctant to let you fly without government pressure.'

'Yes. Good point. I'll try to enlist his support.'

Part Three

ENMITY & ETERNITY

27 Blast Off

Philippe Parodi, head of ESA, was looking very serious as he studied Indra Masinghe's assessment of my physical condition. I sat opposite him, in hope if not expectation.

Mars One was due back in three weeks and I was trying to get myself on an ESA launch to the ISS to be present when AD2 arrived from Mars.

When I'd mentioned the possibility of going back into orbit to the Prime Minister, he put wheels in motion to get me a post on the diplomatic team. There was resistance from the US President and Gorelov at first, but once the UN insisted no military should be involved in the actual meetings, I somehow became a natural choice, not just to be part of the team, but to actually lead it. This was based on my involvement from day one, my advocacy for the alien, the research I'd headed at Goonhilly, my cool head, and my psychology doctorate. I couldn't believe my luck. A dream situation given my disabilities and recent tragedy. It was wonderful to be the person who would meet one of the aliens and welcome him to Earth. I tried to keep my composure, but inside I was skipping for joy and couldn't take the smile off my face. The only problem was whether or not I'd be allowed to fly. ESA's approval for the mission was vital. I wasn't well enough, but I was hiding many of my physical problems and trusting to luck.

Finally, he looked at me over the document, 'Eve, this doesn't look good. You are unable to walk without a stick. In fact, they recommend a crutch for another ten days at least. Your left arm is extremely weak, and you are still not swallowing properly. None of your injuries fit well with an ISS mission, even with the new low-g launch vehicles.'

I said nothing. It needed to be his decision and he was aware how important this was, not only to me, but also to our Prime Minister, and now the United Nations too. I kept quiet. My silence might emphasise my determination.

'If you got hurt or suffered a serious relapse it would not look good that we allowed you to travel.'

I couldn't add anything at this point. He was aware of the negative publicity if Evelyn Slater, the discoverer of Allen's craft, was prevented from being present when the intact duplicate craft arrived at the Cluster. As he continued to spout negativity, I hoped he would eventually convince himself to let me go.

He leaned forward, looked me in the eyes, held my gaze, shook his head in a resigned manner, picked up an antique fountain pen, and scribbled on the release. He blotted it and handed it back to me. 'It is against my better judgement,' he said. Had my silence intimidated him, perhaps?

'Philippe, you've no idea how grateful I am. Now I need to get home and put in a few more hours' physiotherapy. You know UKSA is paying for a lovely young man to work on every muscle in my body?' I smiled, and he shook his head again.

'Make the most of it, Eve, and do not let me regret my decision.'

We shook hands and I hobbled out of his office, putting as much weight as possible on my sore leg to make it appear less bad than it really was. Once I was through the door, I transferred my weight back to the stick and collected the crutch from where I'd hidden it behind his secretary's desk. I winked thanks at her, and she laughed.

I flew back to Exeter from Paris and was in my own office by the middle of the afternoon, getting updated by Tim, John, and Roy.

The language video had been sent to Mars One and was now playing continuously, as well as being transmitted on FM radio and television frequencies which we knew AD2 could access from its earlier taking over of the ship's systems. We were confident the video was being monitored. It was thirty-six hours long and covered everything from images associated with words, through M-A-T spelling 'mat' to some complex grammar towards the end. AD2 had not reacted in any way to the video and we still didn't know whether it was a machine listening or an actual alien.

Roy reported they now had a good idea of the meaning of much of the alien language. I asked them to produce a simple WELCOME TO EARTH banner to hang in the new Cluster module, which had been built much larger to allow plenty of space for both alien devices. What had been a sphere had now had several circular sections added to stretch it and increase the internal volume.

John informed me a lot of small computer programs had been found within the cylinder data. It seemed the operation systems in AD1 used combinations of short programs which had to be triggered individually. They were reminiscent of the old mobile phone apps which would only be called up if you required them. David insisted this was further proof there was an alien mind inhabiting the craft and these things were there for him to call upon when needed. He was probably right. Soon we'd know.

Reg had sent a copy of a video of their work on the thimble-like silver structures which protruded from the gold nose cone collar. They had opened one and found it contained the same silicon which had been found in the small cylinders. There were no wires leading into or out of them so how they functioned was a mystery. A scanner showed that there was a layer of silicon sandwiched within the golden nose cone. Perhaps that and the blisters hosted even more of the brainwave activity we had seen. David insisted it was the actual brain of the alien, but we'd no way of checking whether he was correct... except by asking AD2.

After working hours, I went to the gym at the Helston Leisure Centre where my young Polish trainer worked on my fitness. Firstly, an hour on strengthening my leg and left arm followed by an hour's light circuit training – treadmill, push-ups, cycling, sit-ups, rowing et cetera, then to the pool where he encouraged me to swim in a straight line. It was very difficult owing to the worst injuries being on my left side. When I was totally whacked, he took me into a private room and gave me the most wonderful massage which made it all worthwhile. Finally, a quick shower and home in my Jaguar.

My new rented bungalow had plenty of space, a walk-in shower within which I could sit or stand, and a comfortable bed. I knew nothing until my watch woke me at seven. My exercise routine was making me sleep well, but my stomach was still not used to solids. I took indigestion tablets when it played up.

»«O»«

Less than a month later, four days before my launch, I handed Goonhilly operations over to Tim and my Jaguar drove me to Motherwell in Scotland, the home of the brand-new ESA launch centre.

I sent the car back to Goonhilly, had a short chat with my launch manager, met my five fellow astronauts and headed to a nearby hotel where I was fortunate enough to have a room overlooking the actual launch site.

The Arabella launch vehicle was instantly recognisable as a spaceship. The new fuel and electronic systems had fundamentally changed the dynamics of spaceflight. This was like the spaceships from 1950s science fiction. The Eagle comic space hero, Dan Dare, would've instantly recognised this as a spaceship and would surely have been able to jump into it and fly off to save the world. Could I emulate him?

It only stood about one hundred feet high. On top was the usual escape rocket which was attached to the crew module until a height of two miles was reached, when it would be ejected. In an emergency, the top section containing the crew would be rocketed away and descend using parachutes.

The main ship was tubular. The top third was the crew compartment and contained any valuable cargo, the middle third held the remaining cargo, fuel, and descent engines. The bottom third was the launch booster, designed to return to the spaceport once its function was complete. The whole stood upon eight graceful fins, reminiscent of the Thunderbird cars of yesteryear.

It looked like what it was – a real, streamlined, spaceship. I admired it for a while before exercising in the hotel gym.

I ended my session by swimming twenty-four lengths of the pool and joined two of my co-astronauts for dinner. My hip hurt when I sat on the dining chair, probably owing to the unfamiliar use of muscles which also seemed to be causing discomfort in my abdomen and shoulders. I was worried about mentioning it to medical in case it precluded me from the launch. I'd fought so hard to get onto this flight. I wasn't going to give it up for a pain I could tolerate.

Despite the much simpler and safer launch procedures, there was still much training to be undertaken and the following days were spent almost entirely in the simulator, learning the systems, discovering how to use the emergency evacuation hatches, running through the myriad eventualities which might require us to take action.

Inside the crew compartment we had six seats. Two of those were mounted in front of the control and guidance systems, and the other four were passenger seats located behind. Even though these craft were far less congested than the Soyuz, space was still at a premium and, with all six astronauts in place, it was claustrophobic. Twice I was pulled up sharply for not moving quickly enough during evacuations and was told, in no uncertain terms, if I didn't move quicker the next time I might be dropped from the launch. You can bet your life I was quicker on the next drill, no matter how much it hurt.

In the evening the six of us, four men and two women, had a meal together and I was quizzed about my discovery of AD1 all over again. It might have become tiresome with the general public these days, but with this group of select astronauts, I was only too happy to recount my adventure. I also discovered I was the only one who'd been into orbit. Good grief, I was the veteran!

Later, I Skyped Mum and Dad to tell them what training had been like and to reassure them I was well enough to take this less stressful space trip. They wished me luck with AD2 and I tried to get them to promise not to worry.

I hobbled from bathroom to bed and let my sore and tired muscles recover from the day's exertions.

»«O»«

On launch morning, we all had a good breakfast before making our way to our ship. Despite the lower danger threshold, we still wore insulated pressure suits which would afford us some protection in the event of depressurisation or other accidents.

Within forty minutes we were all strapped into our seats, lying on our backs, looking upwards towards the front of the craft. On each side, we had elongated windows, about one foot by three. Being on the left of the back row I'd have a good view. I couldn't wait to be in freefall once again. My leg would no longer be holding me back. I wouldn't need to use it at all.

Countdown began. We had a hold at fifteen minutes to await the right position of the ISS in its orbit before counting resumed.

Five, four, three, two, ignition and blast off. We were kicked in the back by the enormous thrust of the engines but, unlike the violent ride I'd experienced on Soyuz in May 2035, this was an even, uniform acceleration.

There were none of the sudden changes in thrust or orientation I'd experienced previously. This craft continued to gain speed relentlessly, but evenly.

In no time at all, the engines cut, and we were in freefall. Oh, how I loved the experience! The others had their first taste of zero-g. Europe passed beneath me as we rushed towards our rendezvous with the ISS somewhere over China.

Another forty-five minutes passed and there was minor thrusting as our ship lined up with the docking hatch on one of the new modules added to the space station during the year.

Through my window, I saw my Scaffy Wagon docked on the old Harmony node. How lovely to see it again. When I'd left the ISS the previous year, I'd believed it would be never to return. My Goonhilly job was expected to put me permanently behind a desk, preventing me ever recommencing my scaffy duties in space.

The prospect of a return to space had been transformed from improbable to impossible as a result of my injuries, so to be here again was wonderful and attributable entirely to Allen's technology.

A final push from one side and there was the sound of our connection to the ISS. The time from soft dock to hard dock was still lengthy and it was over forty minutes before the hatch opened and I was able to fly through into the ISS. How fantastic – my leg didn't hurt at all with having no weight to support.

We all went through the usual induction process and, at seven o'clock, Dr Reg Naughton arrived from the Cluster on a new vehicle called the shuttle bus. We embraced and spent the rest of the evening talking about ideas and the procedures we would need when Mars One arrived with AD2.

'They're still on schedule for Thursday morning, Reg?' I asked.

'Yes, one final day to wait through. I must say the suspense is killing me, Eve.'

'This is so amazing, for us to be here at this crucial moment in the history of the world.'

'Of course, he might say "resistance is useless" and enslave us all,' he said, imitating the Vogan voice from *The Hitchhikers Guide to the Galaxy*.

'What would Asimov and Clarke have made of our upcoming meeting?' I asked.

'They knew it would take place sooner or later. Sad they're not still around to witness it. You'll be coming over to the Cluster tomorrow? We've got you a bunk and personal space.'

'Yes, can't wait. I'm looking forward to a tour of this auditorium you've created too. I think all six of us will be there for the unscrewing of AD2's rod, yes?'

'Yes, you, me, Yuri, Alana, Doctor Petra Vostola, and Doctor Hugh Allison. In the adjoining sphere will be Mia, the language specialist, George, the diplomat, and Alexei, the mathematician plus the two military men. How do you feel about being chosen to lead the team?'

I was to lead a well-balanced team, but George and I shared a special secret.

'Frankly, Reg, I can hardly believe it. It's an awesome responsibility. I was honoured to be asked.'

'Everyone we've discussed it with is happy for you to be the voice of humankind.'

'*Don't!* It's scary when you say it like that, Reg.'

'You know the military have muscled their way in?'

'Yes, but only two, thankfully. Our PM declined the suggestion he, too, send a general and that embarrassed France into withdrawing theirs. The result was the American and Russian.'

'Are they playing any active role?'

'Not a chance. It was made absolutely clear by the Secretary General of the UN that only civilians would take part in discussions and even the US and Russia didn't dare veto it. Yuri's a strange exception. He's still a captain in the Russian air force, but I got our PM to insist he should be present as the co-discoverer.'

'Ah, here's Alana,' said Reg, as a woman with an incredibly long blonde ponytail tumbled acrobatically into the room and came to a halt with her hair whipping across her face. She swatted it to one side and reached out to shake my hand.

'Privileged to meet you, Eve,' she said with an almost perfect English accent.

'Ditto, Alana.'

'Do you know what you're going to say?'

'Welcome to Earth, probably. I'm hoping it'll usurp the task by talking first. "Take me to your leader," perhaps. Reg, did you get the banner?'

'The "Welcome to Earth" thing in Allen's language?'

'That's it. We need to position it behind us. If nothing else, it'll show we've been trying to understand its language.'

'We've already put it up. I'm hoping once we've unscrewed the golden rod it'll speak to us,' said Reg.

'Possible, but nothing certain about any of this. I can't understand why we should have to unscrew it,' I said.

Alana said, 'Eve, did you know we've been asked to be prepared to jam all transmissions from the Cluster if it tries to broadcast worldwide?'

'Yes. Is it organised?'

'Yes, but it won't go down well on Earth. All we can do is transmit noise over the same channels.'

'I'm against it. It's an unfriendly gesture,' said Reg.

'Hopefully it'll realise it has an audience and behave appropriately. We need to hope for the best initially,' I said.

'It'll know about diplomacy. Remember how it invaded the Mars One systems but stopped and didn't repeat the action,' said Reg.

'Correct, it was capable of continuing. I assume it realised it was being transported and it might've been able to work out the vessel was intended primarily for transport, not study. Yuri said they didn't try to reply to AD2 and the next it knew we were playing language videos to it,' I confirmed.

'If it did turn out to be hostile, what's the plan, Eve?' asked Alana.

'It won't,' said Reg. 'Why would it come all this way and be hostile?'

'Remember *War of the Worlds* and *Independence Day*,' said Alana.

'But they were science fiction. This is real,' Reg insisted.

'I don't think it will be hostile, but if it is, we'll have to play it by ear,' I said. The others didn't know I'd had a secret discussion in Downing Street about this very problem.

Our conversation went on until about eleven, when I found my temporary accommodation. I didn't take long to settle in, undress and crawl into the sleeping net. I had no pain from my leg, which normally hurt whichever side I was lying on, on Earth. Freefall was bliss although I still had

269

some pain in my shoulders and the annoying digestion problem.

I ran through how I was going to deal with AD2 and the next thing I knew, my watch was waking me at seven in the morning.

««o»»

Oh, how wonderful. No pain in my leg, not even a slight ache. My neck was still sore, but I'd been putting up with my throat and neck since I awoke from the coma. The nagging pain every time I put any sort of pressure on my leg was energy sapping and I was grateful to be without it now. Even the ache in my abdomen had disappeared this morning. Perhaps my digestion had got back to normal at last. The downside was knowing I'd have to get straight on the treadmill to keep my leg working and moving or I'd be in an even worse condition when I returned to Earth.

I had a quick wash before changing into my usual ISS outfit, Bermuda shorts and cotton top.

I found myself in the new spacious dining module where there were another seven astronauts hanging in various positions relative to each other. I'd never seen so many in one place in space before.

The new module had pleasant murals plus two substantial windows on the universe, one a view into deep space and the other picking up a slice of the Earth and, as luck would have it today, a full moon too.

This was a much more pleasant environment. The old Tranquillity module hadn't been conducive to relaxation, but this was excellent. It had a real coffee bar atmosphere. A place designed for people rather than science.

When I arrived, there was excited conversation taking place as each person talked about their duties for the day. Two were planning a repair spacewalk, four of us were to head over to the Cluster, and the other was close to completing a global warming assessment for the UN.

But it wasn't all work-speak. There were conversations about family life and football, England, Wales and Northern Ireland trying to re-join the EU, the ongoing conflict in Sudan, whether the dispute over Tierra del Fuego was going to end passively or result in a full-blown war between Chile and Argentina, and the chance of Fred's son stopping teething before he got back home in two weeks' time, thus ensuring he missed all the sleepless nights currently being inflicted upon his wife.

When I flew in, there were the usual friendly hellos and questions about how well I'd slept, and shock at seeing the damage to my leg which was visible in my shorts, but there were other questions bubbling about beneath the surface.

Finally, one astronaut plucked up the courage to ask, 'When did you first realise it wasn't a piece of junk?'

I'd no choice but to recount the excitement and adventure of Yuri and me discovering AD1 all over again. I couldn't tire of others' interest in such a unique discovery.

'And what are you going to say to AD2?'

'I intend to do my level best not to let a galactic war commence because I put my foot in my mouth.'

'Do you really think there's an alien mind alive within it?'

'Yes, all the indications from our study of the brainwave activity in AD1's cylinders suggest there's a living but dormant person in the device. We believe AD1 was so badly damaged that, to all intents and purposes, the mind was already brain-dead. We haven't seen any sign of activity within it since the attempts to reinstate rotation when we first captured it, and which might only have been automated systems.'

'So, do you think the alien in AD1 is dead?'

'Regrettably yes or in a deep coma, but the alien in AD2 shows every indication of being alive.'

271

'Did they send out hundreds of these things all over this part of the galaxy?'

'Having seen the text on the sides of the craft and the fact that the only difference between them is in the number of dots, we suspect it might be the same alien in each of them.

'It is only speculation, of course, but if Allen were trained to meet other cultures, why mess about training lots of others to do the same task when you can duplicate his mind electronically.' I showed them the two designations on my reflexlet.

'Fascinating. You really think it might be the case?'

'It's possible. In any event, we mustn't rule out the possibility. When he sees AD1 there might be grief... we don't know. Can you grieve over a lost electronic self or even a lost electronic colleague?'

The questions and answers went on for at least thirty minutes and I found myself having to heat a new ham and mushroom omelette as the first went cold. They take on the texture of chewing gum if you re-heat them once cooked.

Reg arrived part way through the quiz-Evelyn show and helped with some of the theorising, giving me time to eat my breakfast.

Eventually the gathering broke up as each person prepared for their day in space.

The five of us heading over to the Cluster pulled on our pressure suits. These were not the full-blown spacewalk outfits but strong, padded and insulated costumes to enable us to survive any not-too-catastrophic accident en route to the Cluster.

I had real trouble getting my leg into my suit and the young female language specialist, Mia, helped pull my foot through and into the foot section. I winced several times and cried out at least once. After my wonderful pain-free morning, this was a rude awakening.

We made our way into the aptly named shuttle bus where we strapped ourselves into our seats. There were fourteen seats. The two foremost were obviously used by the pilots of which there was only one today. Behind those were four rows of three, much like a terrestrial minibus.

Once again, the new fuel had permitted such a large craft to be launched into orbit. It wasn't particularly spacious, but neither was it cramped. Comfort and ease of access was now a consideration when these vehicles were designed.

We were more than half empty today. I was introduced to Georgette, the pilot, who was also a scientist on the Cluster, examining wiring on AD1. Other than her, there was me, Reg, Mia, Alexei, and George.

Once we were free, Georgette pressed a single button and the automatic systems kicked in, orientating and steering the craft slowly clear of the ISS structure and taking a vector towards the Cluster.

28 The Visitor Arrives

From the ISS, the Cluster gave the impression of being a tightly connected arrangement of pinheads in the far distance. I was one of the few people who was aware the distance between the Cluster and the ISS was being gradually widened. The shuttle journey was automatic, although the pilot did have override controls for emergencies.

The pinheads grew into shiny cake decorations, ping-pong balls, oranges, grapefruits, and footballs, showing detail of how they were constructed.

The Cluster had expanded from when I had led the original construction team the previous year. There were now two large spheres. The largest was the living quarters and the other, the stretched sphere, housed AD1 with space for AD2. There were two other smaller spheres. One was the original laboratory section and the other, adapted from the original alien sphere, was now an observation sphere from which my companions in the shuttle bus today, plus the two military men, would watch my team of six dealing with the visitor.

The two smaller spheres were joined to both the larger spheres by airlocks.

Also, newly attached to the living quarters was a drum-shaped exercise module forty metres in diameter. It was revolving at the correct speed to create a force on the outer floor equivalent to about ninety per cent of the force of gravity.

We were now close. The shuttle bus began its final approach, turning sideways and easing its way towards the living quarters. We heard contact being made and the clasps began their closing procedures. Forty minutes later, Reg led us all through into the residential sphere.

The living area was the biggest single pressurised space ever to exist in orbit, about fifty feet in diameter, with the central section being designated for relaxation, discussion, leisure, eating, and drinking. Around the outside were sleeping cubicles. There were also two toilets which provided enough space to have a relatively thorough wash. To one side was the access to the rotating exercise drum. On the other side were three nodes allowing supply vehicles to be attached.

My orientation was personal to me, but at the top of the sphere was another airlock which was where the shuttle bus was now parked.

I put my bag into the cubicle I'd been allocated. Oh boy, it had a porthole! I emerged into the central area, and Reg flew up to me.

He said, 'Sorry, Eve, but I'm under strict instructions from ESA to send you off for an hour in the drum.' He passed me a printed sheet of my exercise routine and pointed at the door of what I would soon come to call the drum of pain.

Once I'd climbed down to the spinning floor, I walked three-quarters of a mile in about forty minutes and followed that with some bench work. Some of the manoeuvres caused pain in my shoulders which had also taken the impact from several shots.

'That'll do, Slater. Come up for a coffee. We've news from Yuri,' shouted Reg from the gods of this nightmarish spinning theatre.

I rested at the hub to get used to the change in orientation, opened the airtight door, and flew into the living area with my leg aching, yes, but free from pain.

'What's the news, Reg?' I asked as I heated my coffee.

'Easier to watch,' he said and pressed play on the nearby monitor.

275

'Hello, Cluster. I told you there now, Eva. We have development. This came onto the screen short while ago,' said Yuri.

The image switched to the monitor inside Mars One and the picture suffered interference before a simple message came onto the screen.

'THANK YOU. ENOUGH.'

Yuri's face with his flashing blue eyes reappeared on the screen, 'Assume means had enough language lessons and took decision stop them. What want us do now? We still on schedule to match Cluster orbit by nine in morning. Await reply. Lag now short. Must honest be and admit sympathise with our friend – several days repeated English lessons. Myself, I would have screamed "no more" long time sooner.'

'I responded with "acknowledged" about fifteen minutes ago,' said Reg.

'Can you tell Yuri to play the natural history videos so he's aware of animals and their relationships with us and their environments?'

'Yes, I've already told him, Eva.'

'It's fascinating. AD2 has learned English and told us to stop the lessons,' I said and opened my reflexlet.

A few waves of my thimball and Roy Williams of my language laboratory was on the screen.

'Hi, Doctor Slater, how are you?' he asked.

'Great being back up here, Roy. AD2 has asked, in English, for the lessons to stop. Can you send Yuri a digital thesaurus and dictionary, which he can transmit to AD2?'

'No problem. I'll get onto it.'

'It'll need to be in an understandable format. We can't be sure raw data will be understood.'

'Yes, we've been preparing both. Will send them shortly.'

'Thanks, Roy.'

Next, I sent a message to Yuri telling him what was on the way and that his lack of diligence in his English lessons was the probable cause of his thick Russian accent and abysmal sentence construction.

'What's the current lag to Mars One, Reg?' I asked.

'Less than a minute. We should be able to confer normally by late tonight. Yuri is now in rapid deceleration.'

At coffee, I was introduced to Dr Petra Vostola and Dr Hugh Allison who, together with Reg, myself, Yuri, and Alana, would be the reception committee. Me leading it and representing Europe, three Russians, and two from the USA. The Chinese had declined to send a representative. CSA and JAXA were leaving the negotiations to the rest of us.

Petra and Reg had me follow them through the observation area into the alien habitat sphere.

There was AD1 attached to the gantry. I pushed off and flew over to it, easing myself to a halt at the front. I ran my hands over the gold area, along the golden rod and traced a finger along the grooves which ran the length of the craft. I became aware of some photography and spun around.

'Did you know that NASA actually *forgot* to take any photographs of Neil Armstrong on the moon – only Aldrin. We must get some pictures of you alongside the alien. This has been the first opportunity.' said Reg.

'In that case, don't forget to take some with Yuri in here,' I said. 'Are you serious about Neil Armstrong?'

'Yes. Buzz got one of his back on the lander steps and there are a couple of stills from the lander's movie camera, but all the quality images are of Buzz Aldrin.'

'Amazing,' I said.

For five minutes or so I posed in various positions for the camera and continued to lay hands on the alien artefact, pulling myself around to the gash, touching the inside of the ship and carefully handling the multi-coloured wires which still trailed from some of the broken cylinders. I returned to the golden front and caressed the thimble-like silver protrusions. They were slightly textured, like an exaggerated fingerprint. I peered inside anew and there was no indication of where they joined the main body of the craft, though there was a join where one had been cut off and replaced after being examined. It seemed sacrilege to damage something so beautiful. I hoped AD2 would not mind us having explored his compatriot.

'Can I unscrew the rod, Reg?' I asked. He nodded.

Slowly, with wonder and excitement, I turned the rod through its strange clockwise motion until it separated from the protruding thread of the nose of the craft.

I examined it but of course, there was nothing I'd not already seen with the powerful lenses. I matched the hole with the thread and tightened it again.

'Finished playing?' asked Reg.

I performed a neat mid-air twist and laughed. 'I hadn't realised how much I wanted to touch it. A wonderful experience. Something made by intelligent beings from another world. I'll never forget it.'

Reg and Petra strapped themselves into two of the six seats and I pushed myself in their direction, strapping myself into another chair.

'This is where we'll be when we introduce ourselves, Eve. Your seat will be the one in front and below these.'

'So it zaps me first?' I asked.

'You cut me to the quick, Eve,' said Reg and we all laughed.

From the seats, AD1 was slightly off to our left and the AD2 would be directly in front of us.

'You're certain you don't want it attached to the gantry?' asked Petra.

278

'Yes, we know he's aware of us, so it'd be insulting to treat him as a captive. We're wearing pressure suits, yes?' I asked.

'Yes, we're a little concerned about him hurting us accidentally if gasses were released or he damaged the sphere. We're making an awful lot of assumptions here. However, AD1's manoeuvring thrusters seem to use compressed nitrogen which is, of course, harmless,' said Reg.

'I don't think we've a choice. The pressure suits might be a step too far, but we can remove the helmets when it's clear we'll not be harmed in any way,' I said.

'We've snap-shut visors,' said Reg.

'Right, so we can have the visors open when we meet him,' I said, pulling out my reflexlet. 'Brief me on the procedure.'

We spent the next three hours going through the activities planned for the next morning once Mars One arrived. There was going to be nothing easy or quick about the transfer.

By mid-afternoon, we'd done everything within our power to work out what we'd need to do if anything went wrong. Now we had to hope AD2 was as intelligent as we'd assumed.

I was prodded into another hour in the drum of pain and it was easier on the second occasion. I walked a quarter of a mile without using my cane and completed two miles in total.

In the evening, we all ate together. We had a live conversation with Yuri on Mars One who informed us AD2 had asked to have the audio thesaurus replayed through the on-board system.

Mia, the language specialist said, 'He's probably wondering why we've so much redundancy in our language, especially in English which is worse than any other language for having different ways to present the same question or answer. Maybe each of the alien words has a single meaning. If so, the thesaurus would be a real puzzle.'

'Yuri,' I said, 'can you play him the video of the announcement to the world about AD1, so he knows what we've told people about their existence? Set it running an hour before you reach Cluster orbit. I don't want him to have too long to read anything into it which we might not have intended.'

'No problem, Eva.'

It had taken me some time to persuade the space agencies, especially NASA, to allow the message to be played to him, as several of those at NASA and ESA were concerned he might find it deprecatory, but it was important we were honest from first contact, and I'd finally won the day on that issue, but I knew there was a secret still being kept, not only from the alien but also from my colleagues in the Cluster. Nevertheless, I was increasingly surprised how easily I'd got my way when dealing with the alien. Was it simply that I was one of the discoverers or was it a natural authority I projected? Anyway, it was most useful, and I'd use it only to argue for things of importance.

It was difficult falling asleep that night, especially as I could watch the Earth through my cubicle porthole. I was unable to close my eyes because it was so beautiful, yet at some unknown point they did close, not to reopen until my watch gave its dawn chorus alarm.

««O»»

Alana had already arrived and was in communication with Yuri.

About four miles away, the strange-looking Mars One was slowly approaching us, its front hub rotating and partially hiding the extended rear which held AD2.

As I sipped coffee and finished a ham and tomato omelette, I watched the Scaffy Wagon manhandling a quarter section of the alien environment sphere from which the atmosphere had been drained. They were in the process of stashing it against the adjacent section. Their next operation was to move AD2 from the hold of Mars One and place it into the alien sphere.

AD2 would have already seen the announcement video and Yuri was now showing a screen which said, simply, 'WE ARE TAKING YOU TO A MEETING. PLEASE BE PATIENT.'

We hoped this would be sufficient.

Behind the seats in the Alien sphere was the banner which bore the words 'Welcome to Earth' in the alien text. I so hoped they had it right and had not written something trivial or demeaning. I trusted my people, but language was never my strongest subject. We were still at least an hour from opening the hold of Mars One.

Outside, circling the Cluster were several drones with video cameras recording everything. There was apparent live transmission to the news channels on Earth, but we all knew there was a fifteen-minute delay. Five minutes would not be enough if things went badly.

No one among the spacefaring nations believed anything but good would come from this meeting of alien species, but there was always the remote possibility we'd misjudged them and were about to get caught unawares.

'Eve,' a shout from Alana, 'AD2 has answered "I UNDERSTAND" on Yuri's monitor.'

'Thanks, Alana. That's most certainly good news.'

Alana said, 'Okay, Scaffies, now hold position until they open the Mars One hold.' I chuckled to myself that the Wagon drivers were now called Scaffies. I made a mental note to tell Angus when next I saw him.

'Copy that,' from the Scaffy Wagon.

Mars One was growing in size. This truly was a much larger vessel than it seemed at first glance. There were short blasts from manoeuvring engines as it changed its attitude to the Cluster, turning tail so the main hold would be closest to the alien sphere. Five minutes later it was stationary, and a tethered figure emerged from a hatch halfway along the cylindrical section of the hull.

We all watched enthralled, as he made his way to the doors of the cargo hold. First one was unlocked then the other. He swung them open and fastened them back. AD2, in all its pristine glory, was inside, attached to its specially constructed framework.

29 'George Cluster Solution'

The spacewalker moved to the side of the opening of the hold in case he'd be needed to help with the transfer of AD2. The Scaffy Wagon began an approach to the entrance of the hold.

'Scaffies. Halt operations!' shouted Yuri over the communication channel.

'What's up?' asked Alana.

'I was about to disconnect framework from hold to give the Scaffy access to move AD2 when message came onto monitor. It saying, "RELEASE ME".'

'We need him to be attached to the framework in order to move him,' said Alana.

'Well, seems he wanting move freely. I release him if you wish,' said Yuri.

I jumped into the conversation, 'Release him immediately, Yuri. Scaffies, back off, please.'

No one argued. There were some puffs of fuel as the Scaffy Wagon retreated from its position. There was a slight movement inside the hold, the framework opened and AD2 was floating freely.

'The message is now being, "THANK YOU. STAND CLEAR",' updated Yuri.

Everything was clear of the hold and sphere now, so we had nothing to do but wait.

Slowly and gracefully, AD2 moved into the entrance of the Mars One hold and it seemed to sweep itself left, right, up, and down as if surveying the scene, then it circled Mars One as if examining it before carrying out the same survey of each of the Cluster's spheres.

Very quickly indeed, it vectored away from us to about one hundred metres, which was a bit worrying, stopped and turned back towards us.

I guessed it was assessing its location and taking a look at the Earth, spread out beneath it. Brilliant white clouds breaking over India and the Far East.

My heart missed a beat when I saw what it did next. It spun around and shot off towards the ISS. Had I made the wrong call? I had a sinking feeling in my stomach, the one you get when you realise you might have made a serious blunder. Even the secret George and I shared had become ineffective in this situation. Had I got everything wrong?

'It's heading for the ISS!' shouted Alana.

What should I do? I didn't have any options. Was it attacking us? I still didn't have any options.

'All we can do is wait and see. Warn the ISS,' I said, keeping my voice calm and steady. 'Yuri, please type "PLEASE EXPLAIN ACTION" into the communication system you have been using with AD2.'

'Will do, Eva.'

The device was now almost out of sight. I grabbed a pair of binoculars and followed it. It was close to the ISS, seemed to pause a while, looped around it for a few minutes then repeated its loop even more slowly. I held my breath. My heart was pounding. Perhaps it was just curious.

'No answer, Eva,' said Yuri. 'It possibly not received message as away from the Mars One environs.'

'ISS reports it swung around the station,' said Alana, 'spent a short while beside the Cupola and close to a Soyuz and Dragon and is now heading slowly back towards us. It gave them a fright for sure, passed very slowly past the living modules.'

'Just curiosity, I think,' I said, glancing at George who raised his eyebrows. Secret relief passed between us.

It returned to the Cluster, turned towards the sphere and sleekly entered where the sections had been removed. In less than a minute it was pointing towards AD1 and manoeuvring around it, perhaps examining the damage and the empty cavity within it. It touched its golden rod against AD1's and, after a minute or two, it turned and faced the seats from more or less the position we'd been going to attach it to in the first place. It had cut the transfer time down but had almost given me a heart attack in the process. I'd had visions of the ISS being blown up and then us. Heaven knows why I should expect it to hurt us, but for a moment I had, and it took a while for my heart rate to return to normal.

'Eve, can I give the command to reinstate the sphere sections?' asked Alana and I nodded. I glanced towards George Rainey again and raised my eyebrows in a sign of relief which was mirrored by him widening his eyes briefly. First crisis over, perhaps.

The Scaffy Wagon approached the sphere again, grasped the first of the three segments and began the process of fixing them back into position. It was a painfully slow procedure and wasn't completed until almost one in the afternoon. I'd already suggested the diplomatic team had some lunch. AD2 made no further move.

During lunch, the shuttle bus docked and brought Yuri from Mars One to the living quarters. We had a welcome and warm hug and, damn it all, he had to say he was sorry about Mario. I'd been unprepared and ended up in floods of tears in a bearlike hug from Yuri which was hurting my arm, but I dared not say anything to stop such a wonderful gesture. I pulled myself together, separated from him and had to deal with zero-g sticky-tears. Such a nuisance. He gave me a second comforting hug but thankfully not so tightly.

The Scaffy Wagon put the last section in place and one of the crew was now outside checking the seals before we introduced atmosphere to the sphere.

The six of us in the diplomatic team suited up and, one by one, we passed through the airlock from the observation chamber into the presence of the two alien vehicles. I paused in mid-flight beside George and squeezed his shoulder before taking my turn. He looked up at me knowingly. Beside him were the two military observers, both in dress uniform, a general from the USA and a colonel from Russia, who was having trouble controlling space sickness. Fortunately, our governments had kept the military out of any involvement with the alien. Hopefully that would prevent the misunderstanding and disasters oft depicted in first-contact movies like *Arrival*, *The Abyss*, and *The Day the Earth Stood Still*. Thank goodness, however, no one knew of the secret George and I possessed. Little did I know that would be blown wide open in the next few minutes.

The pressure suits had a supply of air which would last thirty minutes. Shutting the visor turned on the air. We had all practiced the action and even I could shut it in less than a second. I wanted us to have our visors open when we met the alien personality. A twenty-inch monitor and speaker were on hand.

Soon we were all seated in our allocated places with me at the front.

I gazed at this inanimate alien artefact and, feeling foolish, uttered the words, 'Welcome to Earth.'

I half expected him to say, 'Take me to your leader,' but the reply, when it came ten seconds later was much more mundane.

'Good afternoon, Evelyn,' the first words spoken by an alien to humanity in a face-to-face meeting, even if one face was a miniature spaceship. I recognised his voice as a perfect copy of the man Roy had used for the English tuition video.

He knew my name. It meant he understood the reveal video and that it was me who presented it. It also meant he could tell us apart, even in helmets, which confirmed he had excellent visual sensors and the sound seemed to be emanating directly from him, not the speaker we'd provided.

'Thank you. Good afternoon to you too. What should we call you? You'll know I used the name Allen for the image of one of your people in the video.'

'I am Allen.'

'The same Allen as in the image?'

'The same. My real name is Nsyncadma.'

'I am pleased to meet you, Nsyncadma.'

'What happened to my other self?'

'We think he was struck by a meteor in antiquity. Seated behind me are Hugh, Reg, Yuri, Petra, and Alana.'

'I am pleased to meet you all.'

Several variations of hello or welcome came from behind me.

'Do you know how long you have been here?'

After a brief pause, he said, 'One hundred and thirty-two million, four hundred and eighty-seven thousand, five hundred and fifty-three of your Earth orbits.'

My goodness. That was precise.

'Have you been asleep throughout that period?'

'We have, although we awoke regularly to check our situations.'

'We have been examining your other self from the damaged craft. Can we continue to learn from him, or would you prefer we returned him to you?'

'In good time, I would like to deactivate his mind modules.'

'Are we supposed to unscrew your golden rod?'

'No, unscrewing the rod was a mechanism to awake me if systems had not already awoken me automatically. I awoke during transportation from the planet you call Mars.'

This all seemed to be going well. Simple questions and simple answers.

'Why have you come to visit us?' There, the first pointed question.

'We are explorers. Some of us made the choice to have our minds sent to other planetary systems in the hope of meeting other civilisations such as yourselves.'

'So, does your original body still exist on your home world?'

'No. I am long dead. Even my civilisation might be gone after such a long period. It was a choice we made. I will have lived a normal life on my home world, Dregednon. I am fortunate to have also had the opportunity to exist in this form. Life is short. Electronic life can be almost indefinitely extended.'

'Can you communicate with Dregednon? Did your home world give you updates on how it was doing?' This was a question the military had requested be asked, to discover if he was communicating with his world.

'No, neither. Those of us who undertook the exploration project knew we would be alone. The speed of photons may be fast, but communication, even at that speed, is impractical.'

'For how long are your craft designed to operate?'

'One day one of me might observe the end of the universe.'

'But fuel?'

'The fuel for orbital adjustments should last indefinitely and even primitive cultures could synthesise it for us. Will you please deactivate the device?'

'Which device? The monitor?' I asked, rather puzzled at his request.

'The nuclear device which is attached to this environment.'

There was agitated rustling of the suits of my team behind me as they obviously looked at each other questioningly. I hoped George was relaxed in the observation sphere.

How on Earth did he know about the device? How should I answer this? I thought back to my Downing Street meeting which had taken place before I'd travelled to Motherwell for the launch. It hadn't been what I expected, and neither was this situation.

««O»»

I'd arrived at the front door of Number Ten to cries from journalists across the road of 'Dame Evelyn, a moment' or 'Doctor Slater, a quick word' plus various other combinations, but I waved and continued my painful hobbling into the United Kingdom's seat of power. The glossy black door, with the distinctive ten upon it opened as I reached it.

I was taken to a lift so as not to worry about climbing the famous Kent staircase, with its gallery of previous Prime Ministers' portraits.

We emerged near the newly refurbished Cabinet Office and the adjacent Prime Minister's office. The parliamentary private secretary slowed to allow me to keep up as we passed the open door of the empty Cabinet Room.

The door to Mr Clarke's office was opened for me. He was behind his large antique oak desk with burgundy inlaid leather. The carpet had an elaborate pattern of reds and purples. On the wall behind the desk was an original Turner, on loan from the Tate Gallery. It was a beautiful room.

Mr Clarke looked up from some papers and removed his spectacles. A broad smile crossed his face. He was up, out

289

of his chair, walking around the desk and approaching me before I'd crossed the threshold.

His hand grasped mine and our cheeks touched French style.

'So lovely to see you, Dame Evelyn. How are your injuries?'

'And you, Prime Minister. I'm improving slowly.'

'Tea or coffee?'

'Tea would be lovely, sir.'

'Edward,' he called, 'tea for two and close the door.'

He guided me to the sofa at the rear of his office which faced a working fireplace with a real coal fire. I loved the informality of the meeting.

'Ready for your launch? Are you well enough?'

'I'll let you know when we reach orbit, sir,' I said with a laugh.

He chuckled. 'I wanted to have a private chat with you, Evelyn.'

'Yes, sir.' Here we go. I'd guessed there was some motive for this meeting other than to wish me well.

'You can call me Roger when we're not in company.'

'Thank you, sir, er sorry, Roger.'

The door opened, and a tray arrived with teapot, hot water jug, milk jug, cups, saucers, and a lovely selection of biscuits. So civilised.

'Evelyn, I wanted to let you know you have the full confidence of the Cabinet. We've been discussing this at length, and I can tell you we've been seriously lobbied by the US President and President Gorelov to have a career diplomat or a general making first contact.'

'I guessed, sir.'

He looked hard into my eyes. 'It's Roger!'

'Sorry. I find it difficult using your forename, Roger.'

'Well, no worry. I want to relieve the pressure, not add to it.

'I want to impress upon you how careful you need to be when you're speaking to the alien, if you get the opportunity to do so.

'You need to concentrate on the billions of people down here who need a good outcome, or more accurately, don't want a bad one.'

'I've had a lot of trial discussions with diplomats since I knew I was to be diplomatic lead. It's impossible to know what course the conversation will take. I also have George Rainey with me for advice and he'll have a microphone linked to my earpiece if anything gets tricky,' I said.

'Don't tolerate any threats, Evelyn.'

'Roger, the problem is likely to be recognising a threat. However, with everything we know from AD1 and the way AD2 has behaved so far, I am confident everything will go smoothly.'

'Be strong if you need to be,' he said.

'But we have no armoury against it. We can't even punch a hole in the metal of it without destroying everything within ten kilometres.'

'Evelyn,' his voice lowered, 'you know I've always been honest with you since I first spoke to you in the SDIV?'

'Yes.' What was coming?

'And you have always been straight with me?'

Oh, my God. I knew, there and then, I owed him absolute honesty, no matter what the outcome. I had to confess my sin even if it meant I was thrown out on my ear, I couldn't lie to this man about my space crime.

'No, sir.' I had to revert to calling him sir. 'I haven't always been honest.'

'No? When have you been dishonest?' Strangely, he didn't seem too surprised at my confession.

'I concealed a microSDXS memory card of the discovery of AD1 and smuggled it back to Earth. Sorry.' I had to come clean even if it lost me my position as leader of the diplomatic team. I couldn't go into the meeting with the alien weighed down by a guilty secret when my Prime Minister was being so supportive and honest with me.

'In the corner of your diary?'

My God, he'd known all along!

'You knew?' I gasped. I felt so small and foolish.

'We watched you and grew to admire your dedication to the project. We surmised you were holding it as an insurance policy against me lying to you about UFOs. It almost cost you the Goonhilly job, though. I went against advice and approved your appointment.'

'It was as you say. I'm terribly sorry, sir.'

'Evelyn, it's Roger and I trust you implicitly. You never used the memory card or the information it contained. At any time, we were able to erase its contents, but we didn't. I hope it shows how much we trusted you and your integrity.'

'I now feel unworthy, Roger.'

'Don't, because I now need to trust you even more than I did with the silly memory card.'

'I won't let you down.'

'I know, but this is a really big ask, Evelyn. We've been agonising over whether to tell you at all.'

'Sounds serious.'

'It is.'

The Prime Minister went silent for a moment, took a deep breath and continued, 'George Rainey isn't only a career diplomat, he's also a senior MI6 operative.'

I guessed what was coming so decided to get my own back over the memory chip.

'Roger, I guess you're going to tell me that if things go badly awry in the Cluster, our problems will vanish in dramatic fashion.'

'Evelyn, you're too damn clever by half. You worked it out?'

'If I'd had more time since coming out of the coma, I am sure I would've suggested that some precautions should be in place. Please let me know the plan, Roger.'

'Firstly, let me say that this plan has been agreed by the United Nations, USA, Russia, EU, and Japan. NASA, ESA, CSA, Roscosmos, UKSA, and JAXA are also aware.' He paused and continued, 'there's a small nuclear device attached to the Cluster. George has the trigger. He'll not use it unless it is essential or AD2 is violent or, and here is where our trust in you lies, you give him the code words 'George Cluster Solution'. We tried to make it something which wouldn't be said accidentally. If you use those words, he'll detonate the bomb.'

'And the ISS?'

'We've been opening the distance in stages over the past month and it is now thirty-five kilometres away. The bomb will produce a directed explosion, with the bulk of the material ejected at a tangent to the ISS. The débris will miss the ISS and the remains of the Cluster will vector towards the atmosphere and burn up during re-entry.'

'That's more of a precaution than I had in mind, sir.'

'It is a fully agreed strategy. In the Cluster, only you and George will be aware of it.'

'I understand. I'm sure it won't be necessary. Thank you for letting me know and entrusting me with the responsibility.'

He sipped his tea and I mine.

'It won't be necessary, I'm sure. Your clear thinking on how to reveal Allen to the world might well be the reason we can be confident the meeting will go well. I am sure you, I, and perhaps a manifestation of Allen himself, will be sitting in this office in the not too distant future.'

'I hope so, sir, and I'm sorry but I cannot call you Roger during such an important conversation. Perhaps when this is all over.'

'I understand, Evelyn. Don't worry about it. Being prepared to put your life on the line for your fellow human beings is enough for me.'

Our conversation moved on to the detail of likely questions and answers which might arise during the historic meeting. Eventually time was up, and he helped me to my feet and wished me well.

As I left his office, before his secretary closed the door, I heard him say, 'See you in a few months, Evelyn?'

'Count on it, sir,' I said.

««o»»

Now, in the Cluster, I was face-to-face with the alien and it somehow knew about the nuclear device. How was that possible? We'd most certainly not allowed for the eventuality he'd detect it. It was just an emergency precaution. How did he sense it? Could he read minds? I had to keep my cool and play it by ear. My team, of course, knew nothing about the bomb. In my mind's eye, I imagined George's finger hovering over the detonation button. Keep cool, Eve, I said to myself. I guessed someone would have cut the media and public video feed by now. I could see the general and colonel in animated conversation with each other.

'I don't have the ability to deactivate it. It's a security measure only.'

There was a long pause before he continued, 'Explain the circumstances under which this security measure would be applied.'

That sounded threatening. Now I'd have to be even more careful.

'Nsyncadma, we've never encountered anyone from another planet and some of our leaders were worried you might be dangerous. If you were to be dangerous, we'd consider ending this meeting using the device, but only as a last resort.'

'What's going on?' I heard in my ear from Reg. I raised my hand to indicate he should be quiet.

'But it would kill all of you,' Nsyncadma said.

'Yes.'

'I am surprised.'

'It would be a last resort if you were to be a real danger to our planet.'

'An interesting perspective and all of you were prepared to die if that were the case.'

'Only two of us knew about the device and none of us wants to die. We too are explorers and meeting you is a wonderful experience, but some humans were worried about the meeting of our two cultures. There was concern you might have an intent to harm us, hence the security measure.'

'I am not a threat to you.'

'I'm sure you aren't, but how do our leaders *know* for certain until we've spoken more.'

'If you are sure I am not a threat, deactivate the device.'

My God. This was getting tricky.

'Because you're not a threat to us we don't need to use the device and it'll remain harmless, but I cannot overrule our leaders.'

He went silent. I assumed he was considering the situation. I did not want to affect his thinking process by speaking out of turn.

'I am disappointed.'

'Nsyncadma, human beings have a warlike and violent past. There are still wars on our planet. We live in separate countries dotted around our world and those countries argue with each other. Some fight each other on points of principle. It's a human way most of us despise, but it seems to be in our nature. It means each country is suspicious of the motives of each of the others. There's a lack of trust between our nations and the device is nothing more than a typically human attempt to ensure we can trust you.'

'But its very presence destroys trust.'

'Yes, it's a failing of our species.'

'I am disappointed.'

'As I said, it's there as a last resort. It would only ever be activated if you weren't what we believe you to be.'

'And what do you believe me to be?'

'An explorer. A person with curiosity, wanting to learn about strange peoples and cultures.'

'And what do your leaders fear from me?'

'The unknown. Please trust us, Nsyncadma. I've no desire to die. I want to get to know you, to understand you, to take you down to Earth and have you meet our leaders, to show them you mean no harm.'

Again, a period of silence. What was going on in the minds of everyone else in the Cluster? They'd all be wondering where the device was and who, apart from me could activate it.

'We'll talk more when the device is deactivated. I can be patient.'

It was clearly a concluding statement. He wasn't prepared to talk unless we deactivated the bomb.

I unstrapped and rose from my seat and made my way to the airlock. Reg quickly followed me and opened it to allow us to move into the observation sphere.

Once we'd evacuated the alien sphere there was clear anger.

'What the fuck is going on, Eve?' asked Reg.

'You've got a bomb strapped to the Cluster? How dare you?' said Petra.

'This is intolerable, Doctor Slater. Whose idea was it?' asked Hugh.

'Is that why the military are here?' asked Reg, looking accusingly at General Forster.

'Is not right, Eva,' said Yuri putting his hand on my shoulder.

'What's this about, Doctor Slater?' asked General Forster. 'I've no knowledge of any device.'

'Nor I,' said Colonel Ivanov.

'Hold your horses!' I exclaimed. 'I'd no choice in this matter. It was a simple precaution put in place by all our governments. If AD2 reacted badly towards us or threatened us, there'd be a solution to protect Earth. It's a logical step. I didn't intend there to be such a device, but I understand the reasoning behind having some protection. If he'd said, "Surrender or else," we'd have a way of preventing the Earth being enslaved, perhaps.'

'And which of us has the other vote on it. Not me!' said Reg.

'Better I don't say,' I said.

'This needs to be resolved, Eve,' said Mia.

George nodded agreement which meant he was going to leave it up to me.

'Can't we deactivate it ourselves?' asked Hugh.

'We can't talk under these circumstances,' objected Petra.

I tried to apply the voice of reason, 'Why does he want it removed? Think about this. If he has evil intentions and we throw away our only method of stopping him, we would be

297

pretty foolish. Our governments had no inkling he'd sense its presence.'

'I agree with him. It's a matter of trust,' said Reg.

'Yes, Reg, he wants us to trust him, but he won't trust us. We know we can end this meeting and destroy him. We don't know what he can do to us, do we? Think about it. Now calm down, all of you. I don't have a choice in this matter.'

'I think the general and I should take over negotiations,' said Colonel Ivanov forcefully.

'No, colonel. This is my responsibility,' I said firmly.

'We shall see about this,' said the general, picking up his reflexlet.

I hoped my authority was as strong as had been promised by the Prime Minister.

'But you were prepared to sign our death warrants if necessary,' said Petra.

'Yes, but for it to become necessary it meant the entire planet was in danger. Think about it, Petra. Your own President authorised it with the President of the USA and the Prime Ministers of Japan, France, Germany, and Britain. I'm merely their instrument in this and I wouldn't kill all of us unless our entire world were in danger. The heads of NASA, Roscosmos, ESA, JAXA, CSA, and UKSA as well as the United Nations, are also aware of the device and agreed to its deployment. This is beyond our control but is nothing to do with the military – so don't waste your time on that call, general.'

He looked daggers at me.

'I'm horrified,' said Reg.

'I wouldn't have protected us in quite this way, Reg, but when the plan was revealed to me, I could see something like this had to be in place. You will too, when you look at it in the cold light of day.'

'He is watching this argument,' said Alana who had remained silent up to now.

'It is absolutely disgraceful,' said Mia.

'I as disappointed as he, Eva,' said Yuri.

The words '*et tu Brute*' flashed through my mind. 'Let us all settle down. Arguing does not help,' I said.

'It is so wrong,' said Reg.

'Must I continually repeat, it was agreed by our governments and the chiefs of our space agencies. Probably more advisers were involved. I'm sure it was a combined decision and we don't have the right to overrule our governments, so kindly stop insinuating I'm the villain of the piece. We have to play with the hand we've been dealt. No one expected him to be able to detect it,' I said, trying to bring back some order and exert my authority. I needed to make them understand we were all merely pawns when it came to the defence of our countries and our world.

Alana turned to George, 'Come on, George, you're supposed to be the diplomat. What do you think?'

'I can see the reasoning, and understand all of our misgivings, and Nsyncadma's concerns. However, if our governments have put a security measure such as this in place, who are we to object?'

'But he might sit in there for years. When he said that he can be patient, we must remember he's been patient for millions of years already. Why on earth would he be a danger to us?' asked the mathematician, Alexei.

'Would you trust him with the lives of every person on Earth, Alexei, including your own family?' I asked.

'But we've now created a standoff,' said Reg.

'You have to do something, Eva,' said Yuri.

'Try a one-to-one approach,' said George.

'How do you mean?' I asked.

'Just you and him. In private. Talk the problem through,' said George.

Silently, I thanked George for the suggestion. 'Help me through the airlock, Yuri. I'm going back in there alone. Alana, disconnect the ambient microphones, please. I want to build a rapport. This has become personal.'

'Let me come too,' said Yuri.

'No, Yuri, only me and him, being to being. If it were both of us, we might disagree. I head the team. My responsibility to resolve it,' I said firmly. My Russian friend shrugged his shoulders and opened the airlock door for me.

I passed my secret microphone to him, 'Keep this for me,' and I avoided eye contact with George. Our lives were now in his hands, not mine. I could see the military men talking into their reflexlets. I had to hope Presidents Parker and Gorelov would not undermine me, but Mr Clarke had promised me I had their backing.

I flew into the alien sphere, spent a couple of minutes removing my helmet, pushed myself off towards him and took hold of a strap above my head to slow me. Now I floated in space, my head no more than a foot from the beautiful gold nose cone with its mysterious silver blisters, my hair sticking out in all directions in the zero-g.

I said in the softest, most conciliatory voice, 'Nsyncadma, speak to me, please. Only you and me. Two living, thinking beings.'

30 Trust and Friendship

'We can't be overheard, Nsyncadma. It's only us speaking now. Two beings alone with each other.'

'I am disappointed.'

'I know. So am I, but I answer to my leaders and I understand their problem. Can I try to explain why they've done this?'

'I am listening.'

'I'd like you to entertain a concept.'

'I will listen.'

'Imagine you're one of the many leaders on my world. You distrust one of the other leaders and he's tricked you many times. You've been kind and generous to him and each time he's broken his promise to be generous in return and has, in fact, done harm to your people. Can you imagine such a situation?'

'It is not something my people have experienced. The Carpellums experienced it during their primitive period.'

'Carpellums?'

'Two intelligent species on a nearby world to ours.'

Wow! That was fascinating in itself.

'Our people have experienced it many times and still do. Many lifetimes ago, my own nation found a new land on the other side of the world. The people who lived there were kind and generous, yet we stole their land from them, overpowered them with superior technology and made them live in camps in poor conditions. Imagine you were one of those people and you were trying to become friends with us. Would you trust us?'

'I suppose not, but it is such an alien concept for us.'

Oh, the irony – the alien thought it was an alien concept! 'But you can imagine the scenario I've described?'

'Yes.'

'Because we were well-known for doing this to people in America as well as Africa, Australasia, and India, we expect others to be as untrustworthy towards us as we've been towards them. When we discovered how advanced your technology was, our leaders might have become afraid you could do us serious harm. For that reason, security measures were taken and hence the device.'

'But it—'

I stopped him. 'Wait, Nsyncadma, I need to know if you can comprehend the reasons for it. Both you and I hate the idea of it, I promise you. Foolish people killed my mate, my partner because they were afraid of you. I've suffered great loss because I wanted to be friends with you.'

'We do not have mates.'

'Keeping it simple, we've two sexes. We must mate with a member of the opposite sex to reproduce. I'm female. My partner Mario was male. His seed would grow inside me to produce a child. Many mates live together their entire lives to the exclusion of all others. The loss of my mate was devastating to me. He was killed, with twenty-two other people and his death was entirely because I wanted to understand you and your people.'

'It is irrational.'

'Yes, humans can be irrational but overall, we're kind, generous and friendly. We can suffer paranoia. Do you understand the word? Some of our people are paranoid that you might be dangerous.'

'I do understand the word, but why it should arise among civilised intelligent people is more difficult to accept.'

'Nsyncadma, you know that it was I, with Yuri, the man with no hair, who discovered your other self in orbit?' I said pointing towards Yuri who was gazing intently at us from the observation sphere. 'I've spent my life since, trying to understand you. Yuri is also the man who collected you from Mars.'

302

'I know.'

I lowered my voice, 'I'm going to touch you, Nsyncadma, because touch is important to us.'

I removed my pressure glove from my right hand and placed my palm against the gold nose cone, it tingled with electrical energy.

'I love the fact you have come to Earth. I want to learn from you and learn about your planet and people. It's so exciting and my only reason for living. Don't let the actions of my leaders spoil this for us. Can you and I not work this out together?'

'How do your leaders imagine I might hurt your world?'

'I don't know, Nsyncadma. Disease, war, poisoned gas, maybe you have an armed enemy fleet sitting in the Kuiper Belt beyond Neptune, waiting for an order to invade. It's nothing but suspicion.'

'Let me think.'

'I'll stay. I cannot go back to the others. My heart and mind are with you, not them. Trust me, Nsyncadma, please trust me. I promise I won't let you down.'

He said nothing. I removed my hand from the nose cone and used the strap to increase my distance to a couple of feet. Five minutes passed.

'It is difficult for me to talk to people who might, at any moment, destroy me. Our people have never experienced such a situation.'

'One minute, Nsyncadma,' I said and went back to the airlock. Yuri opened it for me to save me having to use my bad arm.

'Yuri, can you get my reflexlet? It's in the living quarters near the beverage rack. It's velcroed there somewhere.'

He turned and flew through to the living quarters.

'What's happening, Eve?' asked Alana.

'We're talking person to person. Leave it to me.'

Yuri returned with my reflexlet and I asked him to close the hatch behind me.

I hadn't got my thimball, so I tapped the screen and called Number Ten. The parliamentary secretary appeared on the display.

'Can I speak with the Prime Minister, please?'

'A moment, Dame Evelyn,' he said. Obviously, a call from me had been a distinct possibility.

Roger Clarke's face appeared on the screen.

'Evelyn?'

'Sir, are you alone? Will we be overheard?'

'Give me a moment,' he said, and he turned away from the screen. A few seconds later he was looking at me again.

'Okay, you can speak freely now.'

'I have Nsyncadma with me. You were watching the video feed?'

'Yes, until you all left the meeting. George has told me you've returned to the meeting room, but with no video or audio feed.'

'Yes, Roger. I've had us isolated from the rest of the team and he's listening to our conversation. We have a problem. He's unhappy about the device which he detected somehow. His people have never encountered distrust. I think it might be best for you and him to speak honestly with each other. My reflexlet is on hands-free.'

'Okay, Evelyn.'

'Hello, Nsyncadma. My name is Roger and I am the Prime Minister of the United Kingdom comprising England, Wales and Northern Ireland. I watched the first part of your meeting and Evelyn has suggested we speak together.'

'Roger, the reason for the existence of the device worries me and makes it difficult to talk to these people. It is not friendly.'

'Once you've got to know us and we've come to understand you, we'll invite you to descend to the planet. You and I will meet face-to-face and there *will* be no device present. The other people meeting you cannot use the device. Would it help if I personally instruct the only person who can use the device to disconnect the detonator? Trust is hard won on Earth but Evelyn trusts you. I trust Evelyn, Nsyncadma. If I have the device disabled, I am taking a huge leap of faith in you and her.'

'But you were prepared to destroy her.'

'Nsyncadma, we'd no idea you would detect the device and it seemed sensible to have a way of destroying you if you turned out to be hostile. If you hadn't detected it, we wouldn't be having this conversation. We would never use it if you remained peaceful. You'd never even have known about it. Somehow you detected it and that changed what we'd done from being a simple precaution into a threat. That wasn't our intention. We didn't mean to threaten you, only to ensure we were protected.

'As for harming Evelyn and the science team, many people have laid down their lives for their countries in the past. It's her loyalty to her people which is so amazing. But, let's forget this incident, Nsyncadma, and start again. I'll call the individual who has the detonator and ask him to switch it off.'

'You are one of the leaders of this world. Yes?'

'Correct. One of many, but a relatively important and respected leader. We'll meet when you come to our country.'

'And I can trust you to deactivate the device?'

'You can.'

'What about the other leaders who wanted this device?'

'They'll trust my judgement. We've been discussing this possibility in the past hour. We realised our precaution had

had unintended consequences. I expected the call from Evelyn.'

'We must trust each other, Roger.'

I spoke, 'You have the word of my Prime Minister, Nsyncadma. You can trust it.'

'Thank you,' Nsyncadma said.

'Watch George, Evelyn. It'll take a minute. Goodbye and good luck.'

'Thank you, Prime Minister,' I said and switched off my reflexlet.

'Roger does not need to tell George,' said Nsyncadma.

'He will do, though,' I assured him, believing he had accepted our promise not to use it.

'I mean there is no need. I deactivated the device myself when I first discovered it.' There was no emotion or humour or irony in his statement.

'Nsyncadma! Why the lengthy argument if you were capable of disabling it?'

'To understand you. Threats have no place in communication between intelligent species. I wanted to know I could trust you too.'

'I see. Does that mean you *could* harm us?'

'Not really. I could do some damage up here to this environment and the other environment I went to see before coming into this sphere. Both are very fragile. I could do nothing of any global nature to harm you. Why would I?'

'Your disabling the device should remain our secret until you better understand human egos.'

'Why?'

'It might be viewed as a demonstration of power and could increase the paranoia. Can't it remain our secret?'

'It is our personal secret, Evelyn.'

I'd been keeping my eye on George and saw him give me a thumbs-up.

'George says he has been told,' I said. 'Shall I call the others back in?'

'I like talking to you alone, but I suppose you need the team for diplomatic purposes.'

'They're all good people. Scientists and explorers, not politicians or leaders. George is the only secret service person. Doctor Reg Naughton has been studying the possibility of exogeology and exobiology for years. He's a wonderful scientist and so keen to talk to you.'

'I suppose so.'

'I've a question. When I spoke of the loss of my mate, you said you don't have mates. How do you reproduce? Do you have love? Do you mind me asking?'

'I can now only reproduce by replicating myself and my electronics, but it would not be easy with Earth's resources.'

'I mean when you were the biological person we called Allen.'

'We have a variable reproduction cycle which occurs once or twice in our lives. It is not predictable. A need to reproduce becomes an imperative. Our body colour changes and becomes a shade of blue. We must find another person in the same state. We offer each other a part of ourselves a little larger than your head,' he said.

'We take the equivalent part of the other person and absorb it within us. It attaches to our body and takes about four rotations of your planet to be fully absorbed. It then grows within each of us until it is born and becomes a new person with the characteristics of both. We care for the young person for about three of your years when it becomes independent. It will continue to live with its parent until it is educated and ready to go forth into the

307

world itself, which can be up to another twenty of your years.'

'So, you don't have a permanent relationship with the other person to whom you gave the part of yourself?'

'No, we will probably never meet them again or the young person who grows from what we gave them. We do have a long relationship with our own young people, the ones which grew within our own body. I had one before I joined this galactic exploration project.'

'What do you mean by an imperative to reproduce?'

'A longing to grow a young person.'

'But not a longing to have a particular person give you part of themselves?'

'No. Not at all. The person who gave me Nsynelavum, my child, was nothing but a brief exchange in the street for me.'

'Thank you, Nsyncadma. I didn't mean to be so personal.'

'I have affection for my child but not for the other parent whose name I don't even know, and I have no interest in the child which grew from the part of me I gave to her.'

'Gosh,' I said, 'the love of our partners is crucial to us.'

'That is clear from your description of your relationship with your lost mate.'

'The others have many questions for you. We're all so curious about you.'

'I am curious about you and your culture. It is why I am here, but I will admit to you, Evelyn, that you seem backward about trust and it will be difficult for me to understand the paranoid aspects to your people who felt a need to threaten me.'

'It wasn't a threat, Nsyncadma. You *must* understand that. A threat would only be effective if we had told you about it. I would describe it more as a safety measure in case you were as bad as humanity!'

'I sense you mean that as humour.'

'Irony, perhaps. Do you understand the difference between threat and self-protection?'

'Yes, I think so.'

'If I said, "Do as you're told or we will kill you" that would be a threat. If I hide the fact that I could kill you, that would be self-protection in case you hurt me. That's what our governments did in this instance. There was no threat.'

'I understand.'

'We'll get you down to Earth as soon as we can and we've the most fascinating museums and art galleries for you to visit. Humankind has a wonderful artistic and creative side.'

'Thank you. Art mystifies me.'

'I'll personally show you our best museums, but for now I need to call the others back. We'll talk privately again, I promise. I won't let you down.'

'Thank you... friend.'

I put my hand onto the gold nose cone, sensing the strange static once more. It seemed stronger this time.

'I sense your warmth, Evelyn.'

'I like the sparkle of energy from your touch.'

We had created a rapport. I reluctantly broke the connection and turned to wave the others through to the sphere.

The first crisis was over.

31 Curiosity is Mutual

The airlock opened, and we were joined by the original group of five – Reg, Hugh and Petra, Yuri, and ISS commander Alana.

I briefly explained what had transpired while I was alone with Nsyncadma and that the device was no longer active. The scientists introduced themselves and told the visitor what their specialist subjects were. On behalf of them all, Reg apologised for the questioning likely being a lengthy business.

Nsyncadma said, 'Time is not an issue for me, as you know. However, I am equally curious about humans and cannot wait to make my own discoveries about you and your planet.'

Reg said, 'If our questions inspire your own, please feel free to ask.'

'I will. Please begin.'

'How many other intelligent species have your people discovered?'

'When I left for this mission, the answer was two. They both live on Carpellum which is the blue-green world visible in some of the images Evelyn used in her video about me.'

'Only two?' said Reg with obvious disappointment. 'We were hoping it would be many. We'd expected you to have explored much of the immediate star field around you.'

'We have now found you. Also, we have been searching for one hundred and thirty-three million years since I departed Dregednon, so the number is now likely to be greater than three. My expedition was the third we had undertaken.'

'But we've no way of communicating with your other probes?'

'Only at the speed of photons if powerful transmitters were deployed. I could help set up such a system.'

Hugh interjected, 'Before Reg moves on can I pose a query about Carpellum? What are the relative sizes of Carpellum and Dregednon?'

'Dregednon is about Earth size and Carpellum about one and a half times Earth's diameter. They orbit each other and circle our star which we call Sildra. The gravity on Carpellum makes it difficult for us to move around when we visit.'

Reg asked, 'How did you get from Dregednon to Earth?'

'We built a large starship which contained a thousand and twenty-four of me. One of me also piloted it. The earlier expeditions went in other directions with different trained individuals on them, but mine was the third. Each had a route planned to over one hundred star systems, using each as a slingshot to the next, increasing our velocity as we passed each system. Judging by my designation number this was system six.

'Our ship would have passed through here at more than eighty per cent of the speed of photons. At each star system, a few of my units were released, depending upon how many worlds showed promise. Long before we arrived in orbit around our designated worlds, our speed, as individual units, was reduced using the local star's gravity.

'Each of us then advised the others in the system of our locations and we shared images of the worlds we orbited. My damaged self never reported a problem to the rest of us, so the impact must have destroyed the communication system.'

'Do you know which other star systems were visited before us and due to be visited after us?'

'I am able to provide such information if we studied star maps.'

'So, you didn't come from the star which we thought you originated from in Aquarius?'

'No, it was our last port of call. There was only one promising world there. The systems had to be chosen for their juxtaposition to give us the most efficient route past promising types of star.'

'So how far away is your home world, roughly?' asked Petra.

'I don't know as it would not be a straight line. I will calculate it for you some time. Probably several hundred times the distance photons travel in one of your years.'

'We call that a light year,' I said.

Alana asked, 'Our language expert, Mia, who you can see in the next sphere, has asked me to ask you if the language video we provided was your only source of English, because your use of English is so good.'

'Yes, plus the dictionary and thesaurus. The thesaurus was interesting. Our language rarely has more than two or three words for each meaning. The natural history videos were also useful although I had to cross-reference much of the vocabulary with the dictionary. You have a rich language and fascinating wildlife.'

'Mia says you sound exactly like the voice on the tape, which is why she was curious.'

'The voice was my teacher. I am trying to emulate him.'

'You do very well. Mia is also asking if you only speak English?' asked Alana.

'I know some words in Yuri's language. Why do you have two languages on your world?'

I answered, 'We have many hundreds of languages, Nsyncadma. Most are obscure but there are two dozen or so which are used extensively. Yuri's Russian is one of those.'

'And do they all have different writing symbols?'

'No, most use our alphabet but Russian, Chinese, Jawi or Malay, Greek, Japanese, Arabic, and many Indian languages, among others are common exceptions.'

'But why not a single language for you all? I hear Yuri, Petra, and Alana speaking English. Do you all speak all languages?'

'English is the common language used here on the Cluster and in our International Space Station, although most of us also speak Russian, although it's not as common as it was. Twenty years ago, for almost a decade, the only ships coming into orbit were Russian, so it was essential for astronauts to learn their language.'

'So, you don't all speak all languages?'

'No, most speak only one, but many speak two. Mia is a linguist and I happen to know she speaks sixteen languages fluently,' I explained.

'But why do you have more than one? What is the reasoning?'

I continued, 'Each of our countries had a different language and it's only in the last hundred years we've had mass communication. Gradually more are speaking English, but each nation is protective of what it calls its mother tongue.'

'Curious. I would like to know more about this in the future. Your civilisations must be very young to still be so different.'

'We've only been writing for a few thousand years,' Alana said.

'That is a very short time indeed. Maybe this explains some of your worries about me. Your technology seems to have outpaced your cultural development.'

I wondered if we should take that as a veiled insult.

Reg spoke again, 'When you arrived at Mars, did you awake and study it or were you designed to await intelligent contact?'

'I awoke when I left the mother ship to ensure an orbit around my designated planet. I watched and listened and took images then contacted the others. When I observed no civilisation on Mars, I slept. I awoke ten times before Yuri collected me. I was disappointed the planet I had been chosen to observe appeared to be dying and I expected never to fully awake.'

'Would you have stayed in Mars orbit forever?'

'It was the purpose for which I was designed.'

'But wouldn't you have wanted to try to interact with other worlds?' asked Reg.

'Yes, but planetary systems are big places. My fuel would allow me to orbit my chosen planet for billions of years, but it would have been insufficient to move freely between the planets.'

'Didn't you mind knowing your life was becoming meaningless?'

'It only meant this particular copy of me was unfortunate. I hoped others would have been more fortunate. I intend to contact my other selves in your star system at some time in the future. They would have done the same with me if they had found a civilisation. I will think on it.'

Reg continued, 'Would your other self have done the same? Do you know when he might have been damaged?'

'Of course, each of them is me. We are not different people. Give me a moment.'

Nsyncadma stopped talking and we could only guess what was going on. Their golden rods touched, and we assumed he might have been communicating in some way with AD1.

'That version of me was damaged over one hundred million years ago.'

314

'Nsyncadma, we're still trying to understand you,' I said. 'Can I ask how you know your other unit was destroyed then?'

'Some of my mind is still in its nose cone. It is functioning at a very low level, but I could ascertain when the accident had transpired.'

'That's dreadful, Nsyncadma, we'd no idea there was still a consciousness in the damaged craft. What should we do?' I asked.

'It is of no consequence. I will deal with it before we travel to Earth.'

Reg said, 'Thank you for those answers. Can I ask about the species which lives on Carpellum? Do you have images of them?'

'I will find some images for you. Their world has a lot of life of many different types similar to what I have seen in videos of your world played to me during the flight. Two of their species have intelligence...' He was about to continue but Reg asked him to stop.

'Okay, Nsyncadma, let's leave the Carpellums for now. How many animal species live on your world? Do you know?' Reg asked.

'Yes, one.'

'One. You're the *only* animal species on your world?'

'Yes.'

'Do you all look the same? Do you have sexes?'

'People who live in warmer areas are lighter and those in colder areas are darker, but it is caused primarily from the effect of the rays of our star. If I moved to a warm area, I would have become lighter to absorb less of the heat from our star. We have no sexes.'

It was the reverse of Earth, where there was more pigment in the skin of people living in warmer areas.

315

Strange. He went on to provide the same reproduction information he had to me earlier.

Reg asked, 'Were there ever other species on your world?'

'We did find fossils of vertebrates, but none survived past prehistory. We have no record of any living things on our world other than plants which provide us with food.'

Hugh jumped in, 'How do the plants reproduce?'

'They all divide. When it is ripe, a srtglauer head, the plant in the images in Evelyn's video, produces between eight and sixteen seeds. Normally they would be scattered, but we harvest before they scatter and produce various foods from them.'

'They don't need to rub against each other or have insects pollinate them?' asked Petra.

'No. We have no insects. They are fascinating, and I would like to learn more about them.'

'Is there no life in the seas either?'

'No. There are plants in the sea, but we do not eat them.'

Reg inquired, 'Nsyncadma, do you know how your species evolved?'

'Yes, we came out of the oceans thirty million of your years before the images you have seen. We have no skeletons and so have left no fossil record, but we believe we grew bigger and bigger over the millennia. We have historical records going back over twenty-two million of your years.'

'You've a very old civilisation,' said Reg.

'Yes, compared with yours.'

'Do you understand our concept of religion?'

'I only know of it, Reg, from the dictionary definitions and by cross-referencing the names of your religions.'

'How was the universe created in your people's opinion?'

'Not an opinion, it is fact. The universe was brought into existence during an explosion and has been expanding ever since. The galaxies are not just rushing apart, but space itself is expanding too.'

'And what caused the explosion?'

'It might be unknowable. It is difficult to learn about anything which took place prior to the explosion. Our space-time did not exist before the explosion.'

'Could a being have created the universe?'

'There is no evidence for it, but it is possible, I suppose. It is not logical, as it brings into question who might have created the creator and the space-time in which it would have to exist. It sounds like a story created by a primitive people to explain their existence. One of the Carpellum species had a similar story a long time ago.'

'Many Earth people believe a deity created the universe and watches over us, eventually meeting us personally when we die.'

'My people have seen no evidence for any such deity.'

'So, you don't believe in such things?' asked Hugh.

'There is no logical reason to believe in something for which there is no evidence. If you have evidence then I would dearly like to see it, please.'

'So, when your organic self died, what would've happened to its mind and body?' asked Hugh.

'My original body would have melted down into the soil. We have places for the process to occur when end of life is reached. As for the organic mind in the body, it ceased to exist. As for my mind in this manufactured body, it will exist until the universe dies or some accident befalls it.'

I decided to stop this line of questioning, 'Nsyncadma, this is obviously of great interest to us, but I don't want to have us get into philosophical discussion at this stage. I would say you'll need to be careful when expressing views on creation, religion, and afterlife as it can be emotive. The person who killed my partner Mario did so because he believed you were the devil. You understand *devil*?'

'Yes, from the dictionary and thesaurus. I shall be careful. Thank you for the advice.'

'Thank you so much for being so open, Nsyncadma. Petra has more questions for you,' Reg said.

Petra asked, 'I'm not sure why you're here. You may never be able to tell your people about us, they may not even exist any longer. You're not trying to find a new world in which to live and reproduce, in fact you've chosen a solitary existence. My question is simply, why?'

'You are my people now. You have a word, "adoption" and I hope you will adopt me so that I can live among you and try to help you when and where I can. I want to be part of you and your world. You tell me I am welcome, but your question implies I am only a visitor who you expect to leave one day. I cannot leave. I cannot go anywhere. My propulsion system could take me back to Mars, but it would be touch and go whether my fuel would last. Mars is now a dead world. Maybe I could go to one of the moons of Jupiter or Titan, but I would need your help to do so. None of my other selves is orbiting Titan. It did not seem of interest when we arrived. I could perhaps help you build a starship and I could leave your solar system on that, but my hope is to reside with you forever.'

'Oh dear,' said Petra, 'I'd no intention of hurting your feelings. You're most welcome. However, if positions were reversed, we'd probably be searching for a new world to inhabit, not somewhere to live in isolation with the existing inhabitants.'

'Yes, I understand. It is what you did in the American, South American, Indian, African, and Australasian lands. You explored, found new continents, took the land from the indigenous people who lived there and expanded your population to fill it. It is somewhat worrying, but I assume it is connected to the short period you have been civilised. You will mature eventually.'

That told us! This might quickly deteriorate. I interrupted, 'Nsyncadma, Petra was not wishing to criticise you or say you're not welcome. She was trying to understand your motives.'

'My motive is to learn and enjoy the discovery of a new world. I am fortunate. Most of my units will never have another species with whom to converse – ever.'

'I'm sorry, Nsyncadma, I meant no harm,' said Petra.

'I have not been harmed.'

I wondered if we'd wounded our visitor and he was hiding the hurt.

The questioning continued, mainly from us to him, but also less frequently, from him to us. After three hours, I decided we should take a break, write up our notes, eat and sleep. I'd then be making a timetable and formulating distinct areas of interest. Today's questioning had been somewhat chaotic.

'I'm going to call a halt for today. We'll reconvene at ten tomorrow. Is that all right for you, Nsyncadma?'

'It will be fine.'

My colleagues thanked Nsyncadma and made their way through the airlock. I remained behind.

'Nsyncadma, I'm going to get some food and, because of my injuries I need to spend an hour or two exercising. Is there anything you need?'

'It might be good if I watched some videos of human history.'

'I'll see what I can organise, but it won't be today.'

'Thank you, Evelyn. Have a good meal.'

'No, thank *you*, Nsyncadma. I'll be back later, and we'll talk about getting you down to Earth.'

I had an afterthought, 'Nsyncadma, what will you do now we're leaving you? Do you sleep? Do you switch off?'

'I think. I consider. When I finish considering I might switch off. You would probably call it sleeping, but I do not get the benefit from sleep which you need when you sleep. For me it is simply inactivity. Hibernation might be a more suitable word than sleeping.'

'Did you sleep when you were a person on Dregednon?'

'No. We did not need sleep.'

'How long is a lifespan for your people?'

'If no accident transpired, old age would overcome our bodily systems after about two hundred of your years.'

'Thank you. I'll be back later.'

'I will look forward to it.'

I needed to consult about the history videos. Did we want him to know about Hitler, Hiroshima, the Somme, biblical plagues? We needed to know what his take was on religious history before he met church leaders. I visualised many people wishing him harm if he were as honest with them as he'd been with us. We'd need to be careful. Introducing him to the world as a concept was easy, bringing him to the world as a living, thinking person was going to be much more difficult.

My gut feeling told me we should be open and let him learn our worst. If we were always honest with him, he would not discover our most dreadful actions later and conclude we were still being untrustworthy. I decided my recommendation would be to put the entire space-station's video library at his disposal.

Firstly, I'd better find out whether he understood the concept of fiction, otherwise the sixteen-film Star Wars franchise might be misinterpreted. Discussing fiction would be my objective when I returned to speak to him later in the evening.

When I returned to my personal space that night, sleep did not come easily. The momentous day had ended, and humankind had finally had a conversation with an alien being. The importance of the event weighed heavily upon my thoughts. It was almost too fantastic a concept to believe... and I had been integral to it.

32 Staging the Grand Tour

Our questioning of the alien continued for three months and involved several other inquisitors. Gradually we built up a comprehensive picture of his world and people. During that time, my rapport with Nsyncadma matured and grew, alongside his dismay at the antics of our governments and military. I liked his philosophy more and more and I came to see how humanity was at a very primitive stage in comparison with both the Carpellums and Dregednons.

Eventually, the UN and space agencies agreed it was time to take him to Earth to meet world leaders. He'd even been invited to address the US Congress and the UN.

Reg, Yuri, and I were to take the return ship with Nsyncadma, for a planned landing where the new Moscow spaceport was being constructed just east of the Russian capital.

Cadma, as he allowed us to call him owing to some people having had difficulty pronouncing his name, was to have us accompany him to meetings with Earth leaders. The first was to be with President Gorelov in the Kremlin. Cadma had been learning Russian to converse with the Russian leader. He'd also learned French for his meeting with the President of France.

There was, of course, a lot of diplomatic argument over who should first meet our visitor from outer space. The discovery of AD1 was during an ESA/Roscosmos mission and Yuri had joint Russian/Ukrainian citizenship. In addition, a great deal of Russian money and know-how had gone into the construction of Mars One, so it was decided President Gorelov should be the first to receive this diplomat from Dregednon. Following that would be a visit to the President of France; a brief cross-channel trip for a meeting with the Archbishop of Canterbury, head of the Church of England; across the Atlantic to the White House and to address Congress then back to Britain, Ten Downing Street and to Cadma's new home at Goonhilly. A team at the Foreign Office were putting together a worldwide tour for Cadma, to take place a few months later.

I was confident Cadma wouldn't have problems with the heads of state, but his dismissal of belief and faith as being primitive, could lead to an interesting meeting with the Archbishop.

Down on the ground, Rolls Royce had constructed two special vehicles to carry Cadma with space for a few human passengers. His visual sensors were in several locations, meaning he could face forward or stand upright during travel. It was decided facing forward was more dignified and the entire left of each vehicle was for him. During his tour, one vehicle would be present at the destination and the spare vehicle would be moved to the second destination in readiness for his arrival there. The United Kingdom had specially adapted an Airbus passenger jet to allow him to travel from country to country with his entourage.

An Arabella spaceship had been completely redesigned to permit his almost four metre length (including the rod) to sit with us in the main crew compartment. No expense had been spared to be sure everything we did with our guest was inclusive. He'd never again be asked to ride in a cargo hold.

The time for us to descend to the surface was fast approaching.

I joined Cadma one evening in his Cluster area and noticed he was connected to AD1, touching nose cones.

'What are you doing, Cad?' I asked, pushing myself over to the two devices.

'The bulk of my consciousness is housed in the gold nose cone and silver blisters, although some analytical functions are also kept in a few of the small cylinders. I have transferred some useful data and am now deactivating the mind. The gold material itself is the most powerful processor and is where most of our thinking takes place.'

'So, AD1 is dying?'

'No. To all intents and purposes, this version of me has been in a coma and now will cease to exist as an individual.'

'You don't want any ceremony?'

'It would serve no purpose.'

'Don't you grieve for your people when they die, when you were organic on Dregednon?'

'Yes, indeed. We would be upset if a friend or relative died, but once they were gone, we did not mark their passing with graves or monuments.'

'What about leaders and famous people?'

'Yes, some might have a commemorative building or park named after them, but not ordinary people. Our philosophy is to enjoy people's company while they are alive. It does them no good to be remembered after their death because they no longer exist.'

'Do you understand the concepts of love and hate?'

'I can see that love is important to you, but I have no wish to comprehend hate. The Carpellums experienced hatred and conflict in the early eons of their civilisations, but we Dregednons seem to have avoided the experience.'

'How did your conversation with NASA go?' I asked, changing the subject.

'Fine. They will help me visit my fellow selves orbiting Venus, Ganymede, and Europa eventually. They offered to collect the other devices, but I want them to stay where they are, monitoring those worlds.'

'I understand.'

'They promised to return them if they collected them, but I did not want that. If Earth's civilisation unexpectedly ceased to exist, they would be stuck here.'

'That's not very likely, Cadma.'

'No. Not on your timescale, but when you consider my timescale and your national disputes and wars, you might understand my concern about your long-term future as a species.'

'Cad, you don't like us very much, do you?'

'It is your duplicity, greed, and selfishness which frightens me. Your species' emotional stability has not kept pace with your intelligence, and it could be another thousand years before you could really be called a civilised species. Competition for food, space, and possessions seems to be the cause of your inability to trust each other. I hope it will disappear eventually, perhaps even with my help.'

'I'm sorry.'

'Evelyn, it is not your fault. Remember that I'm virtually immortal and it gives me a different perspective on civilisations and timescales.'

During these weeks in the Cluster, I'd spent long periods alone with him, taking my meals with him and talking on a far more personal level than any of our more organised conferences. We'd built up a special relationship and I had a genuine liking for him on a level far beyond simple friendship. Several times he said he enjoyed our conversations and I must admit that I was worried about his loneliness. Such a caring, thinking individual being so alone for eternity bothered me. I wanted to make at least this period of his existence more fulfilling.

Of course, there'd be no shortage of people wanting to spend time with him, but would they provide stimulating intercourse for an alien visitor older than mankind itself? He seemed to like being questioned and often turned answer sessions into questioning sessions. The conferences were rarely a one-way street.

We talked long and hard about his meetings with world leaders and I cautioned him about how touchy individual countries were. I'd asked Tim to compile a list of books on international diplomacy so Cadma wouldn't fall into any of the normal traps. George spent a lot of time with him, giving him the benefit of his diplomatic experience plus another experienced diplomat arrived from Canada to give Cadma a different perspective.

One day he confided, 'Evelyn, I am becoming concerned about the safety of you, Reg, and Yuri, if you are to be with me during my meetings when we arrive on Earth.'

'I'm safe. Don't be concerned. I'm fairly sure the others would feel the same. Unless you'd rather I wasn't with you.'

'Certainly not. My pleasure from my visit to your world would be vastly diminished without you. I like your view of the world; your advice and our confidential chats are so useful.'

'That's good to know.'

'However, I read more and more about the animosity towards me from some of the less conciliatory leaders of religions, sects, and some countries. There is an Islamic fatwã requiring my exile in several countries.'

'We decided not to hide world news from you, Cad, but you shouldn't allow it to give you a jaundiced view of us all.'

'Take what happened with your Mario.'

Tears no longer welled up when I thought of him these days. 'His death was the exception, not the rule.'

'You said there was video of the event. I want to see it.'

'It's not very pleasant.'

'I appreciate that, but I want to see what transpired to better understand what you experienced.'

Using my reflexlet, I reluctantly searched the dark web for the uncensored version of what had taken place in the television theatre. It would upset me. He watched it, saw my body sprayed with bullets, and my current body racked by tears as I watched.

He said, 'I cannot believe a person could take the lives of others in such a callous manner. I am sorry that I upset you.'

I talked to him about other terrorist events going back over the last century, particularly the troubles caused by the IRA and the even more shocking Al Qaeda and ISIL terrorism. I found him videos of the aftermath of bombs, CCTV footage of mass shootings in the USA, and video of ISIL beheadings in the Middle East.

It culminated in me showing him the video footage of the twin towers in New York; the planes crashing into them and their eventual collapse. It took a long time for him to come to terms with the fact that the terrorist pilots had killed themselves and so many on their planes as well as those killed by destroying the skyscrapers.

He said, 'It is their confidence in heaven and an afterlife which has permitted them to do this. Our people have never had stories of an afterlife and those on Carpellum dismissed the notion early in their history. Perhaps it explains why we haven't had terrorism. In fact, there is no record of any violence at all on Dregednon, nor on Carpellum since their prehistory and that is only known of through ancient stories and poems.'

'None at all?' I asked.

'No, there is no point in violence. It achieves nothing. It would never be necessary to be violent towards another intelligent being.'

'What if someone wants something someone else owns?'

'That is jealousy, another concept neither we nor the Carpellums seem to experience. Why does no one tell these terrorists there is no afterlife? That would stop their stupidity.'

'Cadma, they *believe* there's an afterlife and nothing anyone says will convince them otherwise. It's written down in books like the Bible and Qur'an. They believe these books were written or dictated by the all-powerful creating deity.'

'But it is irrational, illogical, and there is no actual evidence. In fact, now that I have read those books it is clear humans wrote them, not gods. Ignorant humans at that, trying to explain the inexplicable randomness of life and the universe, and getting it badly wrong most of the time.'

'That, they'll tell you, is the reason you need to have faith. God will reward you in the life to come.'

'It is childish.'

'Cadma, you may say such things to me but please do not repeat them to others until you have ascertained their religious beliefs. Not believing is called atheism and although many religious people will pretend they'll respect your views, in actual fact many will despise you and won't tolerate atheist arguments against their beliefs. In fact, I worry about your meeting with the Archbishop of Canterbury. Please be careful.'

'Will he not even listen to sense? I understand your point, Evelyn, but it does no more than reinforce their delusions if you do not take them to task. I must find out what causes these heads of churches to believe in impossible deities. Do your leaders believe in these things, too?'

'President Parker of the USA, probably the most powerful man on our world, is a Young Earth Creationist and believes the Earth, indeed the entire universe, was created for us a mere six thousand years ago.'

'Exclusively for humans?'

'Well, for God's chosen people – effectively humans. We're supposedly created in His image.'

'But such a belief is demonstrably ridiculous. My other self was watching and photographing your planet over one hundred million years before humanoids emerged on Earth.'

'Again, it shows how faith cannot be shaken by logic or facts.'

'He cannot truly believe such nonsense. What about the fossil record?'

'Some say that fossils were put there by God to amuse us and continental drift was rapid until the coming of man, that geological layers were laid down during a very short time prior to man being created. Whether Parker, in his heart of hearts believes his religion, is unknown, but many of his born-again Christian sect *do* believe in young-Earth creationist theory, and you must be careful not to argue with them as it could make life unpleasant for you.' I placed my hand on the nose cone as I'd taken to doing when I wanted an attachment to him as an individual. It imparted its electrical tingle, like static to me. I found it comforting and he seemed to like the connection. I did it when I wanted our understanding to be mutual.

'I shall take care, Eve, great care.'

'I'm pleased to hear you will, because people's potential reaction to you causes me serious concern, and you can never win an argument with religious fanatics. I worry about the Archbishop. He won't be fazed by any of your arguments.'

'We shall see. However, once more I ask if it is wise for you to be too close to me during this tour of world leaders. It would be difficult to destroy me during an attack, but not you.'

'Your value to the world is far greater than mine, Cadma. Frankly, when Mario died my life as good as ended. It's only working with you which has made life bearable once more.'

'Dear Eve, I am experiencing a great sorrow for you. We are kindred souls.'

'But neither of us believe in souls, Cadma,' I said and laughed.

'But its meaning is no less valid, Eve,' he said and laughed with his slightly stilted guffaw. I loved the fact he was learning to express humour.

He had all the emotions of a living creature. He meant every word. How would I be able to protect him? I'd a great fear some madman would eventually get to him and attempt to destroy him. He kept reassuring me his body was extremely strong and durable and I let him live with his confidence, despite my knowledge of the weapons which the superpowers could use to bring about his destruction. Cadma had thrown the failings of mankind into stark relief for me. I was becoming increasingly ashamed of my primitive species.

At least if I were to remain close to him, I'd go at the same time. I hadn't had such a bond since the shooting, and it made me morose. That evening I felt so much anguish over Mario and wished I hadn't watched that dreadful video of the studio massacre. The danger into which I was placing myself while I was close to Cadma, was making me realise I wasn't prepared to lose him. I'd rather die with him. It was an affection akin to love.

«**«O»**»

Alana, in a full EVA suit, was assisting the Scaffy Wagon to close the top of the Arabella with Cadma inside. Yuri, Reg, and I would sit with Cadma as if he were a human passenger, although taking up more room.

The Arabella moved sleekly away from the Cluster, made a slow pass of the space station so I could explain what each of the modules were for, and once the distance from the ISS had opened to about two hundred metres it began its automatic descent to Earth.

Unlike the Soyuz, the engine fired for almost thirty minutes. We were now falling like a stone. The craft orientated itself, so the heat shield pointed towards the direction of travel. The engines continually fired long, controlled thrusts. There were a few sparks and flames visible briefly, but our speed was reduced to a few hundred miles per hour without the frightening build-up of heat and scary roasting of the entire craft and its occupants. Inside, we felt no heat whatsoever during the descent.

Now we were in the atmosphere. Five wings, two on each side and a stubbier one to the rear at the top, were gradually deployed and we immediately noticed their effect as they bit into the air and the Arabella coasted towards the surface. The return of weight caused pains in my leg and arm. The abdominal pain seemed to be worse too.

There was aircraft chatter and the Arabella announced its location and descent path. Moscow air traffic control acknowledged, more for our benefit than for the spacecraft. We dipped down to a few thousand feet above the surface. There were more engine adjustments as we changed our aspect to the glide path. Now we were seeing the construction works of the spaceport in front of us as the Arabella suddenly and, somewhat unnervingly, swung nose up and dropped to the ground with nary a bump.

We were home, and Cadma would get his first experience of the surface of the Earth. Soon we'd find out if what he said about his antigravity motors was true. Would he hover above the ground as he said he would?

I knew the University of Reading was working on the principle of these motors – polarised electricity creating polarised electromagnetism. They told us that once you understood the former, the latter became a logical discovery. With the application of very little current, the motor would keep you about twenty centimetres from the ground.

33 Adoration, Hatred, and Suspicion

We poor humans had to be checked out in the spaceport medical centre while Cadma floated, twenty-two centimetres from the ground in the waiting room. It was so hard having to use a stick once more. My time in the Cluster had seen the strength in my leg deteriorate and I was advised to get back into a serious exercise routine or my mobility would continue to become more difficult. I was told to contact my consultant about the pain in my abdomen as soon as possible so I made a note to ring Indra when I was back in the UK in a few weeks. It certainly felt worse under normal gravity.

We climbed into the uniquely designed Rolls Royce. Cadma slotted neatly into his special area without any help at all. The design was perfect, and we all breathed a sigh of relief. Trust Rolls Royce to get it right. The vehicle pulled out of the still incomplete spaceport and onto the main highway into the Russian capital.

Along the route were small groups of people mainly watching and waving at us as we passed. Among them were a minority of less happy and noisier groups displaying anti-alien posters. I did my best to ignore them but knew Cadma must've noticed them. His visual sensors were far more sensitive than our eyes and he could now read and write Russian.

'Such hatred,' said Cadma. 'Why do they so dislike me? I have done them no harm. I have come to learn and to teach, to give technology and offer goodwill.'

'Ignore them,' said Reg and Yuri, almost in unison.

'Most of them love you,' I said reassuringly.

Roads must have been specially cleared for us. Our police escort cut through the seething mass of vehicles trying to conduct their daily business.

There were no more incidents during our Russian visit and Cadma seemed to be enthralled with the beauty and majesty of the buildings, the museums, the works of art, and exhibits in Moscow, Peterhof, and St Petersburg. He loved the fountains at Peterhof, and the famous animated peacock clock in the Hermitage was activated specially for him. Knowing the sophistication of the technology of his own construction, would such an object impress him? He used a single word, 'Beautiful'.

'We don't have art, Evelyn,' he said to me on one occasion, a real revelation. It was interesting that he appreciated the beauty in art and understood why we'd like to hang it in our homes. He said he'd like some art when he moved into Goonhilly.

Our world tour continued with a visit to Paris, where Cadma enjoyed several days sightseeing and much of the time was spent in the Louvre and the Musée d'Orsay. My alien friend was falling in love with art, although it seemed modern art was of less interest. The impressionists seemed to enthral him. What didn't impress him was high structures like the Eiffel Tower and Arc de Triomphe. He'd no desire to climb them even if he were able, although he appreciated seeing their design at a distance.

That evening, Cadma's relationship with us changed dramatically. He called the three of us into the lounge area of his suite in the fabulous Paris Ritz.

'Please help yourselves from the bar and take a seat,' he said.

None of us knew what this was about and Cadma had never previously offered us drinks or refreshments of any kind. Was he trying to become more human, or did he think it would put us more at ease? I suspected the latter. What was coming? This was ominous.

'I want to thank you all for accompanying me thus far on my tour. I really appreciate it, but I feel that a change is necessary.'

We exchanged puzzled glances.

'My dear friends, it is time for us to part company until such time as I take up my residence in Goonhilly. I fear that being in my company could be a not very healthy situation for you. I received more death threats today, and while damaging me would be extremely difficult, you are all much more vulnerable.'

Reg broke into the conversation. 'Cadma, I've no fear of being in your company.'

'No. Not me either,' said Yuri.

'It is not whether you experience fear. I am sure you are very brave, and I love your company, but my interaction with humanity is likely to become more problematical and I do not want you to associate yourselves or your nations with my opinions. It is not open to discussion. I would like you to return home tomorrow and leave me to my remaining tour.'

I was hurt, cut to the quick. Cadma was my friend. More than that, I thought we had a special relationship. How could this be happening?

Yuri protested, 'But, Cadma. We all want be part of team.'

'That may be so and, when the tour is over, I would hope that you would join me in Goonhilly as we develop our science facility. I am not saying goodbye, just calling a pause. I hope you will understand.'

'Whatever you want after the tour, Cadma. I'm sure we'll come running. It's just such a shock,' said Reg.

'And I shall be pleased to have you working with me, but not now. Thank you for helping me so much up to this point. It has been most valuable. It is late. You should go to your rooms.'

Well, that was dismissive. I was speechless. Literally struck dumb. So hurt. We all stood to leave.

'Eve, please remain. I have some questions,' Cadma said.

In a daze of disappointment, I stopped my painful rise from the seat and flopped back down, gripping the top of my cane and trying not to let my damaged ego break free. I felt anger growing. I hadn't devoted my life to his future to have it cast to one side now. Yuri and Reg wished us a good night and left.

'What's going on, Cad? I'm hurt,' I said.

'Sorry, Eve, let me explain.'

'That would be good,' I said, wiping away a tear which had fought its way past my stoical demeanour.

'I am worried about mankind and its reaction to me, and all I have read about President Parker tells me it is not going to get any better. I also have this English Archbishop to meet and am not looking forward to it. I cannot lie about my peoples' lack of spirituality.'

'Let me help. Take me with you and I can try to advise. I'd be so hurt if you continued without me.'

'Eve, I have been in communication with Philippe Parodi and have had him agree to free you from your ESA duties. I have negotiated a budget from the joint space agencies, and I will pay your salary so that you can work directly for me. Would that be okay with you?'

'Of course. I thought you were abandoning me.'

'Never. But I needed your agreement.'

My heart sang. I rebounded from my depths of despair. Nothing mattered to me now except Cadma.

'What about Goonhilly? That's so tied up with you and future science,' I asked.

'I also spoke to Roger Clarke and he is happy for you to resume a variation on those duties when we return from my tour.'

'So, what's changing? It doesn't make sense.'

'What is changing is that you are now co-opted as Dregednon ambassadorial staff, accompanying me, an ambassador. Being with me will no longer taint the United Kingdom with my views or opinions. Do you understand?'

'I think so, but why now? Why today?'

'I expect my meeting in Canterbury to be problematical and, even when we are past that, I have to be frank with President Parker, and his religion appears to deny my origins.'

'I'll be with you.'

'I know, and I will need you to gauge reactions for me. I have learned a great deal, but there are still nuances which could confuse me. I need to truly understand what is being said to me.'

««o»»

I enjoyed a well-made latte and some biscuits at the Old Palace in Canterbury, while the Archbishop and some invited dignitaries gave Cadma a guided tour of the city walls and cathedral.

On the journey from Paris we'd discussed, long and hard, some of the points and questions Cadma was to put to the Archbishop. I tried to impress upon him the importance of not trying to convert the Archbishop to atheism – that people of faith won't convert on a whim. From his very first question, this would be a fascinating meeting and I'd be the proverbial fly on the wall.

Cadma had to enter the back way into the Old Palace, just because of his bulk. The Archbishop wore a simple black outfit with dog collar, gold crucifix, and chain. I was pleased to see that, as I knew Cadma was not a fan of "religious garb" as he called it. Also with the Archbishop, was his personal assistant.

'So, Nsyncadma, what do you think of Canterbury?' asked the Archbishop.

'It is interesting to see the buildings. You call them "ancient", but your civilisation is so young. Nevertheless, the cathedral is undoubtedly beautiful.'

'So, Nsyncadma, what would you like to ask?'

'Explain faith,' he said. The question was like a shot from a gun.

The Archbishop sat back in his chair and thought for a while. It seemed a long time but was probably only thirty seconds. He chuckled.

'Faith is very simple to explain, Nsyncadma. Even children have faith. It's simply believing in something which cannot be quantified, touched or possessed. For instance, you might know nothing about gravity, but when you see an apple fall from a tree, you have faith that it will impact the Earth. If you fly in a jet-liner, you might know nothing about "lift" holding the wings in the air. You simply have faith that the mechanics will stop you from falling to the ground. I have faith in God and that he gave his only son's life to forgive our sins.'

A good answer, I thought. Cadma and I hadn't been able to imagine rehearsing any of this meeting, so I'd no idea how it would progress.

'Tell me how your God fits in with the knowledge that humanity is not alone in the universe.'

The Archbishop laughed, then said, 'But it's *God's* universe, Nsyncadma. I've nothing to tell. *He* created it all.'

'But your religious works tell that you are made in His image. What of me, then, and the Carpellums?'

'You're *all* God's creatures. You, too, are created in his image. It's the spirit and soul which are important, not your number of legs, arms or the shape of your body. We clearly demonstrate that every day on Earth. People of all sexes, races, cultures, and colours believe in God. Why not you too?'

'But we have never had a belief in a deity. There is no evidence for a deity.'

'The evidence is all around you, Nsyncadma. Perhaps God has sent you to us so that you may learn about his love for you.'

My God, the Archbishop's answers were clever. Where would Cadma go from here?

'You tell me the evidence is all around, why then are children starving in many of your world's countries? Why is violence so prevalent around the Earth? Even your Bible tells of stoning women, sacrificing children, smiting whole populations. Your God used an impossible flood to wipe out the majority of life on Earth as a punishment. Were there no good people among so many?'

'But that is not God who is doing most of these things, it is mankind. It is us who are failing to feed the starving, and warring with each other. As for old Bible stories, well, they were told in context and shouldn't always be taken literally.'

'So, the Bible is not the word of God?' said Cadma.

'Not always, no. It is man's interpretation.'

'What about the afterlife and your sure and certain knowledge of a resurrection?'

'Let me return the question to you, Nsyncadma. Can you prove that people are not resurrected into a different state after death? Even your people?'

'There is no evidence for it, and it is impossible to prove a negative.'

'Yes, there *is* evidence. God tells us it is so in the Bible! That *is* the evidence,' the Archbishop showed glee in his face. He must have felt that Cadma had walked into a trap of his own making.

The arguments went on for more than an hour and Cadma had not won a single point. I'd warned him that it would be so, but I was certainly impressed by the Archbishop's command of the situation. I supposed if he couldn't stand up for his faith, then nobody could.

Time was up if we were to get to Gatwick airport in time for the flight. Goodbyes were said and Cadma promised to return with more questions in the future. The Archbishop said he'd love to meet him again, and that he'd always be ready to welcome Nsyncadma, as a lost soul, into the church.

I smiled inwardly at his audacity. I wondered what Cadma was thinking. He'd certainly been admirably out manoeuvred by the Archbishop.

34 Washington

From London Gatwick, we boarded our specially adapted Airbus for the long haul to Washington where Cadma had been invited to address Congress. He and I had been working on his speech. Mr Clarke again offered assistance, but Cadma refused all offers of help except mine.

He was adamant he didn't want to damage by association, any person or country who assisted him. I was the exception to the rule, I guessed. I hoped that it meant I'd become as special to him as he now was to me. I felt most flattered.

I caught most diplomatic issues within his speech, but it would only work if he didn't ad lib. His calling the man in Moscow an 'uneducated human' showed he didn't always consider potential consequences and I was glad it hadn't been said in the USA. Here it would've gone viral. Because it was said in the Kremlin treasury in Russian, it seemed he'd got away with it. Had Cadma realised he could avoid criticism with such an action in Russia? I was sure his meaning wasn't accidental and equally sure it wasn't lost on the Russian Foreign Minister.

Cadma seemed incapable of being annoyed. I'd wondered if the Archbishop's total dominance of the Canterbury meeting, would have an effect on the alien, but no. He did, however, now appreciate the difficulty of winning any arguments which involved "belief". He'd told me he'd expected it to be much easier for logic to overcome belief, but now realised it was actually impossible, owing to human conviction. A surprise for him.

By the time we arrived in Washington, I was becoming increasingly concerned I might miss some diplomatic issue and allow Cadma to fall into some trap laid for him by the media. The meeting with the Archbishop had been private, but we'd several journalists travelling with us who'd report almost anything he said. I did my best to caution my alien friend to think twice and speak once. His response was his stilted guffaw. 'Evelyn, I fear you are worried about me becoming too human!' he said.

««O»»

It was wonderful to visit the White House and, with millimetres to spare, Cadma managed to enter the Oval Office to meet President Parker.

When the President asked me to leave for a private chat with the alien, I stood, leaned on my cane and was about to go when Cadma spoke, 'Mr President, I am delighted you would like to speak with me alone, but Doctor Slater is my friend, confidante, and advisor. I would like her to stay in case anything said is unclear to me.'

The President was clearly taken aback. This authoritarian President wasn't used to having his authority usurped in his own office. That something might be 'unclear' to Cadma was an obvious nonsense to me, but would the President have realised it was no more than a subterfuge? I think Cadma wanted me there as a witness.

'As you wish, Nsyncadma,' he said, leaning back and folding his arms in an obviously defensive gesture. Did Cadma recognise body language?

Whether the President said or asked all he would've done if he'd been alone with Cadma, I cannot possibly say, but I was glad I was there when Cadma decided to confront the President over his own integrity.

'Mr President, I have been reading about you extensively. You have had a most interesting life and I was intrigued to discover how you made your way to becoming the head of state. I am puzzled, however, that it is said you believe in a religion which claims the universe is only six thousand years old. How do you equate such a belief with my existence?'

My God, this promised to be interesting. I cringed internally. No good could come of it. Was Cadma deliberately trying to goad the politician?

'I think, Nsyncadma, we should leave our religious beliefs out of our conversation.'

Wow. A really diplomatic reply. Unlike the Archbishop, the President was not going to argue religion.

'But Mr President, I am concerned that your beliefs mean you think I might not have travelled several hundred light years to get here and have not been in the solar system for over one hundred million years. You have seen photographs of the Earth from orbit, taken in antiquity. It worries me that the leader of so many people can be in denial. I am not asking for a public announcement that your religion is wrong but would appreciate your private affirmation that you do not disbelieve me, personally. That would be sufficient. It would be difficult for us to continue this conversation if you have no trust in me as a person.'

I'd cautioned Cadma about taking this line, but he was obviously determined to make the point. He wanted to know how anyone in such a high position could be so ignorant of our natural universe. I wondered if the President truly believed his religion or was just giving it lip-service. I'd been told that the "religious right" was very important in his election.

'I think our meeting is over, sir,' said the President who stood up behind his desk.

Oh dear, this was bad. Very bad. I heard several doors opening behind us as well as one to the left, from which emerged an armed guard.

'Thank you for seeing me, Mr President,' said Cadma as if he were unaware of what was going on around us.

Several individuals entered through the various doors into the Oval Office, including another two armed, military men, in full protective gear, with enormous weapons, far larger

344

than any I'd ever seen before. I'd no idea what they were and didn't think I really wanted to know.

Two others gave the appearance of secret service to me, from the way they stood with their legs slightly apart, their crisp, plain, charcoal-grey suits, and their right hands holding the lapels of their jackets as if ready to reach in and extract revolvers. They even had the obligatory dark glasses.

'Thank you, Mr President,' I said as I stood.

'A pleasure to meet you again, Dame Evelyn,' he said with utmost charm, walking around his desk and shaking my hand warmly while gripping my shoulder with the other.

We were ushered from the Oval Office, along a corridor and out of the White House. Our car took us to a prestigious hotel where we'd be staying overnight, as guests of the US government, before Cadma addressed Congress. We'd been invited to stay at the British Embassy, but Cadma had declined, privately telling me it was again because he didn't want anything he did or said to reflect on Britain.

I began to worry about his speech. Would it be allowed to continue, or would it be cancelled at the last minute for some obscure reason? Would Congress deny the first ever dignitary from another world permission to address it? The UN invitation was not for a few months and they knew that. I guessed the West Wing would be in turmoil now we'd left the building.

I'd no sooner unpacked than my cell phone rang. It was the Secretary of Defence. He asked if he could be sent a copy of Cadma's speech. It was an ominous request. They wanted to know what he was going to say.

I asked Cadma, he agreed, and I sent the attachment. I knew there was nothing too contentious in the speech which we'd agreed with each other, but I'd no idea if Cadma would adhere to the content. I feared he'd want to make changes after his meeting with President Parker.

345

Once I'd sent the email and my reflexlet confirmed it had reached its destination, I quietly asked Cadma, 'You won't change your speech, will you?'

'Evelyn, can you please call the hotel manager and ask him to bring a pair of wire cutters.'

'What for?'

'You will soon find out,' Cadma said, with not a little harshness in his tone. His alien-ness suddenly coming to the fore.

Within minutes of my call, a smartly dressed man, about thirty years of age entered our suite and told us a porter was bringing some wire cutters. A young man arrived with the tool. They stood waiting for Cadma to speak.

'Your name, sir?' asked Cadma.

'I'm John Bryant, the hotel manager, sir. It is an honour to have you stay with us.'

'John, can you hold the landscape painting above the fireplace away from the wall so that your assistant can cut the wires to the microphone which is hidden there.'

The manager was horrified, but quickly recovered his composure and walked to the painting over the fireplace. Tentatively he lifted the bottom and called the porter over to clip the wires.

'Give the microphone to Dame Evelyn, please. There is another attached to the back of the couch and a third, a wireless version, attached to the back of the vase which contains the roses on the sideboard. There are two more in Dame Evelyn's bedroom, one under the top drawer of the bedside cabinet and another behind the headboard. There is a further microphone in the bathroom on top of the medicine cabinet. There are also cameras in the smoke detector above the window in this room, in the smoke detector above the bay window of the bedroom, and in the vent above the door in the bathroom. You will find the

346

detectors are fake and can be simply pulled off the ceiling. You might need a screwdriver to open the vent above the bathroom door.'

The manager called someone on his cell phone and said, 'Bring a folding ladder and screwdrivers to suite three-oh-one please and make it snappy. Really snappy! Drop anything else.'

Thirty minutes later I had a camera, two fake smoke detector cameras, and six microphones sitting on a tray beside me on the coffee table.

Cadma spoke in a measured manner. 'John, I am assuming you did not know about this invasion of our privacy and we will give you the benefit of the doubt. As the wireless microphones are still active, I am confident someone from your secret service will be here to collect them from you swiftly. We will now relax and enjoy your hospitality.'

'Certainly, sir, I am sorry you've been inconvenienced,' and the manager, the porter with the gadgets, and the maintenance man with the ladder left our suite.

'Cadma, I'm so sorry,' I said.

'Evelyn, it is not your doing. What hurts most is the lack of trust. What did they expect to learn which I would not otherwise be prepared to tell them? I am what you call an open book. They only need to ask.'

'Now, I must think. You go and get some dinner.'

'I'll get food sent up, Cadma. I want to be here, so you can discuss things with me if you need to.'

'Thank you, Evelyn. I appreciate it. Now I must work on my speech to Congress.'

'Were our hotels in Moscow and Paris also bugged?'

'No, no bugs, but there was an extremely powerful laser pointed at me during the meeting with President Gorelov.'

'Would a laser hurt you?'

'It is difficult to be sure. I deactivated it. I said nothing because it seemed to be of the same nature as the nuclear weapon in the Cluster. A precaution rather than an actual threat. Thank you for teaching me the difference. The weapons in the Oval Office were more a threat than a precaution and that is more worrying.'

'How are you able to deactivate these things? How did you sense the microphones and cameras?'

'Some of my sensors detect electronics.'

'Through walls?'

'Yes, through walls. The television in the next suite is showing a sports match of some description.'

'Is this why your transport vehicles on Dregednon have no windows?'

'Yes, indeed. It is the same with our buildings.'

'Can you see me if I'm in the bedroom or bathroom?' I asked, suddenly feeling foolish, shy, exposed, and embarrassed.

'If I wished, but I do understand the principle of privacy. However, the right to privacy vanishes if it involves the technology to spy upon us.'

'Will you let me read your new speech?'

'Of course. You are my trusted ambassadorial assistant, but it might be a less than sensible idea to send a copy of the new one to the Defence Secretary,' he said, and I sensed a distinct sarcasm in his voice. That was a new talent.

'Okay, I'll order myself a meal,' I said, although my appetite hadn't been good since we had returned to Earth. This damn digestion problem had been getting worse steadily and I'd even vomited a couple of times. Perhaps it was an ulcer. I ordered something simple and not too spicy. I'd see my consultant when I got back to Goonhilly.

35 Addressing Congress

I could no longer win in my battle to stem Cadma's religious arguments.

I'd been an atheist since I was thirteen, much to my mother's annoyance, but Cadma had made me look at religion in an even more radical and critical manner. When entire civilisations, millions of years older than any on Earth, dismissed all belief as the invention of primitive peoples, it was difficult to retain any sympathy for people who believed in omnipotent deities today.

I told him, 'I can't believe I'm saying this to a near immortal being, but you need to give the world time. Don't be too hard on us or you'll be just as responsible for hardening religious belief. They'll unite together against a common enemy. You put yourself in danger. You saw how the Archbishop was able to swat down your questions.'

'Yes. I can see that, but if I remain silent, humanity will remain warlike, greedy, and selfish for longer. I must speak out. The lack of trust shown by the leaders of this powerful nation is such a disappointment. If *they* are so much in denial, how long will it take the more primitive, less well educated and more radical religious countries to change? I will, however, concentrate less on religion and more on the harmful politics and natures I see in your world.'

'As I say, you're putting yourself in danger. Try not to cause animosity. Win the human race over by stealth, not by lecturing us.'

'It will be hard to harm me, Evelyn, but I do fear for you being caught up in any attempt.'

I shrugged.

««O»»

It was amazing to be participating in something which I'd seen on television so often. I was in Congress and it was about to be addressed by, was I being hypocritical using the phrase, an honest-to-God alien. Of course, I was a little awestruck to be inside this theatre of power with a visitor from another world. I'd remember the experience forever as I was sure it'd be unique for me. After seeing Cadma's new speech, I was equally certain he'd never be invited back either.

What he was going to say would reverberate around the world. When he'd passed his revised speech to me, I'd made every effort to persuade him to soften his language and, to a small degree, he had. The meaning, however, had been retained. My influence was small and Cadma was his own person. His speech wasn't going to go down well in America, nor would it be liked by the hawks, xenophobic and religious groups, and many individuals elsewhere. Cadma was about to make mankind take a hard look at its long-held attitudes and beliefs, and I knew the religious and many political authorities wouldn't ever accept what he said. Now it became clear to me why he didn't want any country to be tainted by his opinions.

Cadma's future on Earth after he'd completed lambasting humanity worried me. On the far side of the hall I saw two more of those armoured police with the huge weapons and guessed there were more on this side. What were these weapons? Had the US military discovered a way of piercing Cadma's body?

I feared for his life. At best, I feared he'd be ostracised. I feared he might even be exiled back to his lonely vigil orbiting dead Mars. How would the people of the world react to this alien criticising them? It promised to be interesting indeed. It would become part of world history. I'd hate to lose my alien friend as I'd grown genuinely fond of him, but his banishment was a real possibility. Would the Prime Minister stand by him in Britain where he'd been offered the permanent residence at Goonhilly? Cadma hadn't yet had his audience with our Prime Minister. How would Mr Clarke react to what we were about to hear? Would he still be allowed to speak to the UN later in the year?

The Speaker finished his introduction, talking in glowing terms about the importance of our first alien contact. How would he feel by the time Cadma had finished?

Cadma incongruously floated down the central aisle to the main dais and turned to face the members. A hush fell over the hall and he spoke quietly but clearly in his perfect English.

'Mr President, Mr Speaker, Senators, Members of Congress, ladies and gentlemen of this Joint Session of the United States Congress, honoured guests, I am grateful for the opportunity you have afforded me to address you.

'I had my speech ready to deliver, but events last night have caused me to revise my words. While accommodated as guests of your government, in our hotel suite we found six concealed microphones and three hidden cameras, two of which were in Dame Doctor Evelyn Slater's bathroom and bedroom. To say I was shocked and disappointed would be an understatement.' He paused for effect.

There was an immediate buzz of chatter around the chamber including distinct calls of 'shame' and 'disgraceful'.

'This and other matters have caused me to make changes to what I wanted to say to you and to the world. The people of the Earth would be wise to spend some time considering the incongruity between their words and behaviour.

'More than a hundred million years ago, my people sent a thousand and twenty-four of me in a single ship to orbit planets in neighbouring star systems. This was the third of many planned missions, each heading in different directions.

'Our sole purpose was to make contact wherever we found intelligent beings or the potential for such beings in

351

the future. Once contact was established, we were to fulfil our mission by dedicating our existence to *helping* those people if we were able. We recognised, of course, that many civilisations might be more advanced than us, but we would still have offered help and would hope to learn from them. We were also to invite each intelligent species back to our world if a way were found to travel so far. Sadly, even this tiny corner of the galaxy is a huge place. Ships like my mother ship can approach the speed of light, but it is as nothing compared with the size of our galaxy, let alone our universe.

'We had no idea how we'd be received by other intelligences, but I admit to having been shocked and gravely disappointed when I have seen people shouting hatred at me and showing placards calling for me to leave. My friend, Dame Evelyn, had her partner murdered by fanatics who equated me with your mythical devil. She was almost killed herself in the attack and remains disabled to this day. Most humans I have met do not wish me ill, but a powerful minority seem to be unable to think or act in a civilised manner.

'On my world and on Carpellum, another world with two intelligent species, there is no xenophobic hatred, nor war, nor this thing you call religion. We have never had all of the conflicts and terrorism which have arisen from those invented beliefs on this planet. I can't say we abhor violence, because, if we ever experienced it, it is lost in our prehistory, so it is an alien concept. On Carpellum there is violence when animals eat animals, but not among thinking people since they became intelligent eons previously. When I first referenced the word *murder* in a dictionary, I could hardly believe what it meant. My people have no equivalent term and only ancient Carpellum stories make any reference to it on their planet. It is not something

352

intelligent beings do. Why would any intelligent creature wish to take the precious and irreplaceable life of another?

'When I thought on this question, it did not take long to realise that only beings who have an irrational belief that life might not be irreplaceable, would be capable of destroying it. The belief in souls, resurrection, and an afterlife could be the only excuse for not appreciating the uniqueness and preciousness of each person's life.

'I have been cautioned not to include religion within my speeches, but yesterday I was in the Oval Office and had to suffer the ignominy of your elected leader disbelieving that I had arrived in your solar system one hundred million years ago. It is incredible for me to understand how the intelligent people who surround me in this great assembly room can believe the universe was only created six thousand years ago, when the evidence that it is untrue is hovering before them. It is patently ludicrous and those who believe such nonsense are an aberration.'

At his calling the President an aberration, I heard a growing muttering and build-up of conversation occurring around the hall. I'd told Cadma that even members of political opposition groups wouldn't be happy to hear their president besmirched. The Speaker was in dialogue with his aides and the President's party were passing messages to and from the Speaker. What was going to transpire?

Cadma continued unabashed. 'I have brought you many wonders from my world. They have been offered freely. In fact, in this very room, I notice you are already using the polarisation of electricity in some of your devices. I know the fuel which I use is changing your transport industries and space exploration beyond recognition, and this polarised magnetism which allows me to rise and fall without touching the ground will soon change your world still further.'

353

For effect, Cadma lifted himself about an extra metre into the air then returned to his normal twenty-two centimetres.

'These gifts are for the betterment of all. I have other gifts, mainly of knowledge, which will improve your lives, removing starvation and disease through improved diet. You will soon be able to scan yourselves for cancers long before they become threatening and life expectancy will almost double during the rest of this century. All because of our gifts to you.

'What I hoped was for you to accept me as a person. The fact my body is electronic rather than flesh and blood changes nothing. I am still a living, thinking, intelligent being. I came to you with goodwill, generosity, and friendship. But here on Earth I find a species which lies to itself and its fellow beings, thinks nothing of killing them en masse during wars, incubates hate against anything different, and yet has acquired the technology to destroy itself and the already misused environment of its world. I see such enormous wealth in countries like this one and those in Europe yet read of children starving to death in others. How can you live with yourselves for allowing this?' He paused for some fifteen seconds to let that question resonate.

'How do I help you if you will not help yourselves, particularly when distrust and hatred is targeted at me personally? The American secret service only needed to ask to learn about my motives and mission. They did not need to bug our suite. I am an open book. Covert surveillance is the most gross of insults and I am disappointed by the action.'

Again, the volume of conversation rose substantially, but died quickly away as Cadma continued. 'During the first diplomatic meeting with your people on board the Cluster, I discovered a nuclear device which would have destroyed not only me but all of the diplomats and scientists within many miles. It was there because of the suspicion and paranoia you have for anything different from you. Your very first assumption was that I might be a threat. How sad is that?

'During my meeting with President Gorelov a hugely powerful laser was directed at me and here you have soldiers carrying weapons which could perhaps destroy me, but in so doing would kill everyone within ten metres of me!'

Those people sitting near Cadma's position looked around themselves in a worried manner. A few even stood and moved further back. Cadma waited for them to settle down.

'I find you are so suspicious of me you needed to bug our hotel suite and invade the privacy of Dame Evelyn's bathroom. What did you want to discover which I was not prepared to tell you freely as part of my mission to offer friendship and knowledge to another intelligent culture?'

The Speaker stood and tapped his microphone. 'Mr Nsyncadma, a moment, if you will.'

Cadma increased his volume, not excessively but by enough to ensure the Speaker and audience were under no illusion he would not allow himself to be interrupted. 'Mr Speaker, I have almost finished.

'Your species leaves me in a quandary. How can I interact with beings to whom I have given so much and offered to give so much more, when those entities treat me and each other with disrespect and, in some cases, with downright hatred?

'I do not have the fuel to leave your world. I committed to helping you before I ever met you. It was part of my mission. Perhaps, in a thousand or a million years you will change and come to see me and others of your people differently. Maybe I should seek your help to depart and hibernate on the surface of your moon until the human race can behave in a truly civilised manner, or perhaps destroy itself and allow some new intelligent species to evolve in its place.

'I thank you all for giving me the right to have my say but I will leave this place now in great sadness. I would like you and your people to consider what I have had to say but must admit to having little expectation that humankind will change its ways for a very long time indeed.

'I have never experienced fear, but I do experience apprehension. Currently, a foreboding is growing within me and it will soon become a dread that my very existence might be threatened by your paranoia. I have a real anxiety about Dame Evelyn's safety because she is my friend and confidante and is usually close to me. Will your paranoia as a species also put her in danger? I would so like to help you but fear my words fall upon deaf ears. Thank you.'

A seemingly stunned silence overcame the room. It was followed by a stuttering applause which grew, faded away, grew once more and increased substantially as people observed who was applauding and joined in. It was a majority, but only a small majority of the people present. It was not unanimous, and people seemed confused as to whether they should be applauding or booing. In my opinion, his speech had been courageous and truthful. Only people in denial could take it as antagonistic or unfair.

The President and his entourage stomped out of the hall, while the Speaker thanked Cadma for giving them all an interesting, philosophical, but alien perspective on the world.

We tried to leave but found ourselves surrounded by people praising Cadma for his honest and forthright views. Others pointedly took alternative exits, and one or two were derogatory to us as they squeezed past the blockage we were unintentionally creating.

Our Rolls Royce was outside. We entered it and it sped away to the hotel.

««o»»

In our suite, we watched the television coverage of Cadma's speech. Various political commentators were interviewed, and the criticism varied from those who thought it was disgraceful that this alien considered he had the right to criticise America, to those who were adamant that Cadma was a danger to the world and should be either destroyed or 'made-safe' as if he were some errant mechanical device. There were, of course, many who agreed with Cadma and were horrified at how we'd been treated, but the media seemed to prefer the concept of an angry alien berating America rather than an abused alien trying to teach the world that there's a better way.

'Evelyn, notice how they talk about *destroying* me, not killing me. These people are positioning themselves to be able to justify treating me as a malfunctioning machine rather than a living creature.

'Also, see how they criticise me for criticising America. I didn't. I was criticising humankind.'

'You did criticise them for bugging you and the President for his beliefs.'

'I suppose so, but I was not berating the people of the USA.'

'Oh, Cad, you know how I tried to stop you from making the changed speech. For a diplomat, you were pretty undiplomatic you know.'

'But what I said was true and how they have treated me, indeed us, is despicable. Even those who seem to want to understand me have an underlying distrust of my motives, like your Mr Clarke and the Russian President.'

'Cadma, I don't know where we go from here. There'll be consequences.'

357

'Yes, there will. I guess they will think about what I have said before acting though. You have my place ready for me at Goonhilly?'

'We do.'

'Let us leave here and go there as soon as possible. I will need to protect myself and you and your people once I am there.'

I was suddenly worried he'd been dishonest. 'Protect us? You don't have weapons, Cadma, or do you?' Even I suffered the human paranoia.

'No, you of all people should know I don't, but my sensors have capabilities to stop certain electromagnetic functions in devices and will be a great help. I will not have you endangered by your proximity to me.'

'You saw those huge guns the security people had here?'

'Yes. They could certainly have hurt me, but I disabled them.'

'Cadma, let's talk on this when we get to Goonhilly. First however, you must visit the Prime Minister in Downing Street. I'm sure you'll receive a warm welcome there. You already know he's a listening leader from the matter of the device attached to the Cluster, which he agreed to disarm.'

'Yes, we will meet him but my presence in his home will endanger him too.'

'British people are pretty resourceful, Cadma. Have no fear, our military will ensure he and you are safe while we're there. You'll be protected from foreign powers. It's the terrorists and fanatics who'll offer the most danger.'

'But do you not understand, dear Evelyn, no military presence should be needed? The potential violence of both the aggressors and defenders is infantile, not worthy of intelligent people.'

'Yes, I know.' What more could I say?

I slept uneasily. My leg, abdomen, and shoulders were all sore and I'd failed to do my physiotherapy, yet again.

««O»»

The next morning, our car drove us to the airport past cheering supporters and smaller numbers of angry mobs. Cadma told me it showed he was more popular than unpopular, but I pointed out it only took one fanatic to spark off an attempt on his existence.

I knew British Airways had been extremely diligent in checking everything to do with our flights. To add to this, Cadma scanned every piece of luggage and technical equipment on board to satisfy himself there was nothing untoward installed or hidden on the plane.

There were only a few security officers, diplomats, and the press contingent flying back to the United Kingdom, so not a large complement. Once we were in the air, Cadma moved back towards the other passengers and asked them about their jobs, families, hopes, and aspirations.

I sat to one side and listened with admiration to his kind and interested manner with people who obviously meant him no harm. This was a different personality to the one who'd addressed the American Congress. This Cadma made friends easily and fascinated his audience. It was a joy to witness how well he socialised even with the press, who weren't always the most likable individuals.

I returned to my seat and rested. I was uncomfortable despite the first-class seating. My leg was throbbing, and I vowed to get back into my physiotherapy once I'd returned to Cornwall. Perhaps the Polish fitness trainer would be available to get me back into condition.

Outside the starboard aircraft window, two Royal Air Force Phantom jets were accompanying us. I hadn't seen them during previous flights.

One of the accompanying British civil servants who was seated near me and had seen the direction of my gaze, said, 'They joined us the moment we left US airspace.'

'Britain is protecting us,' I said.

'Must be a major operation as they'll have been refuelling in mid-air. We're way beyond their normal range.'

Silently, I thanked the Prime Minister for the extra security. Perhaps the UK would make a stand in Cadma's defence.

Our flight was timed to arrive at Heathrow at four in the afternoon and the second Rolls Royce was waiting to take us to Downing Street.

««o»»

The famous front door of Number Ten was too narrow for Cadma so we entered through a rear entrance and, while I used the lift, Cadma stood on end and elevated himself up one of the larger staircases at the back of the building.

Our first meeting was with the Prime Minister and some of the Cabinet in the Cabinet Room. I sat in the corner in some pain and an assistant brought me some water.

The meeting was most amicable. All our ministers were supportive of Cadma's stance in the United States. Unfortunately, it was impossible to be sure who was and who wasn't being sincere. They appeared genuine. Perhaps the British government was going to become Cadma's protector. I hoped so.

However, there was an historic rapport between the USA and Britain, even more so since Britain's exit from the European Union. Nevertheless, the new approaches being made to re-enter the reinvented European group of nations was eroding the transatlantic relationship, but it remained strong. President Parker would've been talking to Mr Clarke. He'd have listened, but would he have been at all influenced? I doubted it. Mr Clarke oozed sincerity as far as

360

I was concerned. Every contact I'd had with the man told me I'd be able to rely upon him. Or was I just being naïve.

After the official meeting in the Cabinet Room, which was documented by photographers, Jenny Rae, Roger Clarke, Cadma, and I moved into the lobby area and through into the Prime Minister's office. I noticed the doorway had been specially widened since I'd been there a few months previously.

Much less formally than in the Cabinet Room, the Prime Minister said how delighted he was to meet with Cadma and me.

'I'd like to shake hands with you, Nsyncadma,' he said, 'but of course I can't.'

'You can place your hand on my golden area, Prime Minister. It is full of sensors. I will sense your warmth. You will feel my life. Please do.'

Both Mr Clarke and Mrs Rae stood, approached Cadma and laid their hands onto the appropriate part of the alien device. I knew they were now receiving Cadma's static and vibrations – his hand of friendship.

'I have a connection to you both and offer my sincere friendship to you. You are the only leaders who have wanted to make such a connection. This is also the only place I have been which does not have weapons developed to damage me. Thank you for the trust. Others think of me as a mere machine, but I also have feelings. I know how supportive you have been of me and Evelyn once the unfortunate incident in the Cluster was put behind us.'

'Yes, Nsyncadma, I'm sorry about our device on the Cluster, but we needed to be cautious initially. Also, I must admit the air force is on high alert, but that's mainly to protect us from any attack upon you.'

'Please call me Cadma. I have grown to like the familiar name.'

'And us Roger and Jenny,' said Mr Clarke as the Home Secretary nodded her approval. 'Evelyn has expressed concerns about your safety when you move to Goonhilly. What can we do to help?'

'As you are aware, Roger, I do not sleep. I can continuously monitor my surroundings for a considerable distance, perhaps four or five miles. I am aware of your air force activity and can see the radar beams criss-crossing London. Similarly, anyone bringing something dangerous within range of my sensors would be noticed. Anything electronic I can disable. Having told you of that ability, I must also admit to having disabled the device on the Cluster long before you gave the order for it not to be used.'

'We didn't know.'

'It was unnecessary to tell you at the time. Evelyn advised me that it might have exacerbated the suspicion mankind had of me.'

Ha, my friend had dropped me in it to my boss!

'Yes, I see. Evelyn is a very faithful and thoughtful person,' Mr Clarke said.

'So, electronic items are easily disabled. This means I can deal with incoming missiles, but not with their kinetic energy. A missile will still do damage, and this worries me because of the people I will be living and working with at Goonhilly. Although I hate the concept of attack and defence, can you provide any additional protection to deal with physical impacts?'

Jenny Rae said, 'I'll have General Sir Michael Webb come to visit you at Goonhilly and we'll beef up the defences.'

'I am also unable to detect explosives, only their detonators, and they can be easily concealed. Stronger physical security would be good at the perimeter.'

The meeting eventually moved away from our security and onto a more general question and answer session.

Cadma was delighted to talk about his people, their way of life, technology, family relationships, and his people's relationship with their neighbouring world. I don't know what meetings had to be cancelled, but we seemed to be in the Prime Minister's office for a long time, certainly several hours. By the time we left, the four of us knew each other well, and the rapport was more than encouraging.

It was agreed the people of the Earth could learn much from the openness and honesty of the Dregednons.

Our meeting hadn't ended until late in the evening and the Rolls set off for the West Country, turning into the Goonhilly complex in the small hours of the morning.

Tim was there to show Cadma his apartment, so I said goodnight and my faithful Jaguar took me home. It had to wake me when we arrived. I snapped on the central heating the moment I got into the house, then collapsed on the sofa and didn't wake until ten o'clock the next morning.

36 Never Avoid Your Doctor

When I arrived at my desk the next morning it was already approaching midday. I opened my monitor and was faced with two hundred messages, forty of which had red or amber flashes. These had already been thinned by Janet. I worked my way through the red flashes first.

By two o'clock I was three-quarters of the way through them. I opened yet another from my medical consultant who was asking why I hadn't returned her messages or calls. I got Janet to make me an appointment and left my office for a break.

I grabbed a sandwich from the canteen for a late lunch and hobbled along to Cadma's accommodation facility. He had three computer monitors in front of him and was working his way through the history of ancient Egypt. It inspired further conversation about humankind's fascination with an afterlife. These quiet times together were so relaxing for me and took my mind off the pains in my body and the continual permanent ache in my heart from the loss of Mario.

Mario was gone. He knew nothing about what had happened to him or to me afterwards. I was well aware there was no ghostly Mario looking down at me and approving or disapproving of how I was coping. Sometimes I wished I could believe in such things, but my scientific background made that impossible. He was gone, and we wouldn't meet again in some mythical hereafter. Knowing that, didn't make me feel any better about it. Is it any wonder so many people permit themselves to be convinced there's a heaven and end up "believing" in all the religious baggage which accompanies it?

Cadma had become a substitute for Mario. I couldn't ever have another emotional relationship with a human, and

Cadma offered wonderful companionship without me having any guilt I was being unfaithful to Mario's memory.

When I returned to my office, I found Janet had set up an appointment for me with my consultant the next morning. I called her in.

'Janet, can you get onto Mrs Masinghe and change the appointment to sometime next week. I've so much to catch up on here.'

'She was pretty insistent it was urgent, Doctor Slater.'

'Can't be critical. Postpone it, please. I'm not even going to finish with my messages today, let alone do any *real* work.'

'Okay, Doctor Slater.'

I continued to push on with my messages, consigning to the bin anything which didn't need a reply from me personally.

My monitor came to life. It was Janet, 'I have Mrs Masinghe for you, Doctor Slater. She absolutely insisted on speaking to you personally. I can refuse, but she really does say it's vital she speaks to you this very minute. I did my best to put her off.'

How annoying. I was angry Janet had put her through. I didn't need this today. I flicked my thimball and my Asian medical consultant, who'd nursed me through my bullet traumas, had an extremely serious expression on her face.

She said, 'Evelyn, you've not returned my phone calls, my texts or my red flash messages. I want you here at eleven tomorrow morning *without fail*.'

I was quite taken aback. It was unusual for anyone to talk to me in such a manner, even friends. 'Can't it wait until next week, please, Indra? I've a mountain of work to get through after my time away.'

'*No, it cannot!*' she said extremely seriously and loudly. The expression of anger on her face worried me.

'Why's it so urgent?'

'Be in my office at eleven tomorrow and you'll find out. I'm serious, Evelyn. You *must* be here and don't eat anything after midnight. You can take plain water only.'

I didn't know what to make of this, but she was obviously in deadly earnest, so I agreed. I guessed she had some tests in mind hence the food and drink restriction.

«« O »»

The two hundred and fifty miles to Reading took me two and half hours. I should've hired an express car instead of getting my Jaguar to take me, but I liked the comfort and having my own IT system to use en route allowed me to work through more of my messages.

My surprise CT scan was soon complete and I was sitting in the stark but professional-looking office of my medical consultant, waiting for her to finish her talk with the scan interpreter.

I was so pressured to catch up at work that this time spent in Berkshire when I should be in Cornwall was aggravating me.

Finally, Indra Masinghe, tall and distinguished-looking in her white coat, stethoscope draped around her neck, came back into her office with a sheaf of papers which she tossed onto the desk. She sat down and gave me her *bad girl* expression. I had a flashback to being told off during my schooldays when I'd failed to complete my French homework. My physiotherapy had taken a back seat to the momentous visit of Nsyncadma to our planet, but she seemed to be taking my lack of diligence too seriously.

'What's up, Indra? I promise to be more industrious on my exercises.'

'It's not the leg, Evelyn, I wish it were just that. I'm afraid I've much worse news for you.'

Now she really was worrying me. She sounded angry with me. 'Spit it out, Indra. What's wrong?'

37 Nothing is Forever

'There's no easy way to say this, Evelyn. Roscosmos picked up a tumour when you got back from the Cluster. They flagged it to me and I've been chasing you ever since while you've been gallivanting around the world with your metal friend.'

'What sort of tumour?'

'In the pancreas. They told you to contact me urgently.'

'And? I only landed three weeks ago.'

'Evelyn, I'm so sorry. The scan seems to show it's spread to your liver and is now almost certainly inoperable. I want you in next Monday for an exploratory operation to see if anything at all can be done. I could maybe have assessed it with an MRI scan but you're almost as full of metal as your alien friend.'

I sat still, silent, gazing blankly at my doctor who had also become a friend since the shooting. She had moisture in her eyes.

'Damn it all, Indra, you're meant to be the strong and reassuring one, not the one in tears,' I said with unconvincing bravado.

'Sorry, Evelyn. We might have caught it if you'd come straight to me from Moscow.'

'You know I couldn't. Nsyncadma needed me. Can't we get it with radical surgery?'

'No, I'm pretty certain it's now inoperable. I want to find out if it's possible to do a partial removal to extend your life, but it's not hopeful. As you know I've taken blood samples too and I'll get those results tomorrow.'

The blood drained from my cheeks. 'Really? I suppose I have to ask, how long have I got?'

'With chemo and radiotherapy, you might make two years, but it would be a maximum.'

'Without therapy?'

'A few months. No more.'

'And with the operation?'

'If it's not invaded the stomach wall and part of your liver can be saved it might give you a little longer, but months, not years. You must've been in pain from this since before you went back into space.' She shrugged her shoulders as if defeated.

She was right. The digestion problem began after I left hospital. I'd been a fool. I'd known she'd wanted to talk to me. I hadn't related the stomach aches to anything other than my mobility, and digestion problems caused by solid foods after my coma.

'I need to think about this, Indra. I'll be in touch,' I said flatly.

'Soon. And that means *today*, Evelyn. I want to do the op on Monday, so I need your decision by five this afternoon. Also, if therapy is going to be of any use whatsoever, we should be starting now.'

'Can I get it done in Exeter or Plymouth?'

'The treatment can be carried out at the Royal Cornwall in Truro which is only twenty miles from you, but not the op. You'll need to be here in Reading on Monday. Would you like me to set up therapy in Truro?'

'Provisionally, yes, but I do want to think about this. I take it treatment will mean being sick, feeling awful, and my hair falling out et cetera.'

'Yes, it won't be a walk in the park and will continue for several weeks. After those treatments, you might get a good period of remission. That's what I'm hoping for. I would suggest you reduce your duties at Goonhilly, as you won't be firing on all cylinders. On days when you do feel well you should try to make the most of it, not waste your valuable time at work.'

'I thought it was a muscle pain owing to my hip and leg not working correctly, or some sort of indigestion after being in the coma,' I said apologetically, as the reality of my situation sank in.

'Yes, either could have caused a similar pain. I'm so sorry.'

I stood, she came around the desk and gave me a hug. 'Sorry I didn't reply, Indra. I thought it was connected to my wounds.'

'What's done is done, Eve. Let's try and give you the best possible outcome.'

'Two years, you say?'

'That's a maximum. Plan for fifteen months.'

'So short?'

'Probably,' said Indra. 'Nsyncadma talked about detecting and treating diseases in his Congress speech. He doesn't have any miracle cures, does he?'

'Don't know. I'll ask.'

'Yes, you really must. Seriously, do ask him – *today!* Surgery will only be a short-term fix, not a cure.'

««o»»

With the words "so sorry" and "plan for fifteen months" ringing in my ears, and in a partial daze, I let my Jaguar return me to Goonhilly. I was there by mid-afternoon. I called Janet into my office. I'd already decided to commit to the operation and the therapy. There wasn't any alternative.

'Sit down.' She sat in one of the conference armchairs.

How was I to impart this news?

'I've some bad news and I'm not sure how I'm going to tell people. You need to know because I'm going to be having to go to the Royal Cornwall Hospital in Truro for treatment on a regular basis, and I've to be in Reading for an operation on Monday.'

Her face was serious, but she said nothing.

370

'I have pancreatic cancer which has metastasised to my liver. The prognosis is the worst. I don't want anyone else to know until I can think about how to tell them personally.'

'Oh God, Doctor Slater, I'm so sorry.'

'My own fault, Janet. I should've gone to hospital when I returned from space and these few weeks on the tour have given it time to spread. It's an extremely aggressive tumour.'

There were tears in Janet's eyes as she tried to control herself. 'Can I ask how long?'

'A few months to two years.'

'Oh, Doctor Slater,' she said, but nothing more.

'Okay, Janet. Go and compose yourself. Contact Mrs Masinghe and find out what I need to do to be ready for the exploratory op on Monday, and when my treatment appointments will be at Truro. They'll be a priority of course but, if there's a choice, let's have them first thing in the morning. Keep a lid on this, Janet, at least until I've told department heads and my family.'

She rose slowly from the chair, dabbed her eyes with a tissue and left me to my thoughts. Was I the only one who wasn't going to cry? I guessed I'd shed all my tears when I found out about Mario. His loss was the end of my life, anyway. Everything else was just existing, not living.

I left my office through the side door and walked the length of the corridor, leaning heavily on my stick and rang the bell beside the new double doors at the end. I heard the electric lock click to give me access, pushed the door and I was in the short corridor to Cadma's private apartment. He needed to know about my illness because I'd no longer be able to spend the rest of my life learning from and about him and his people.

I stopped in my tracks. I was wrong – I *would* be able to spend the rest of my life learning about him, but my life would no longer be as long as I'd envisaged. I'd have to take a lesser role at Goonhilly too. I'd need to speak to the powers that be. Tim would be a faithful replacement for me, as he had been during my coma. It was unreal to be so concerned about my work when my life was slipping away from me, but my work had become my life since the Armstrong show and even more so since I'd built up my rapport with Cadma. Somehow, I must maintain that relationship. It was all I had left. I mustn't let them prevent me seeing Cad.

In the days of almost miraculous good health, I'd expected to reach and maybe pass my hundredth birthday, now I would probably not reach thirty-seven.

Did Cadma have a solution? I'd so much to live for.

38 The Long Goodbye

It didn't take much time for everyone to know I wasn't going to be long for this world. It was amazing how they looked at me and spoke to me differently. I was a dead woman walking, and not even doing that very well.

The therapy hadn't gone too badly, and I was eleven months into the treatment which was extending my life. Cadma hadn't been able to help other than to confirm the operation wouldn't add any time to my life so I was excused that additional pain and discomfort. He felt bad that he'd not scanned me himself. He could've caught it in the Cluster, and I could've come home earlier.

Now, I was celebrating my thirty-sixth birthday with my family. It'd be my last.

I tried not to encounter my reflection in mirrors these days because there was a jaundiced colour to my appearance. I'd lost weight and had begun to look like what I was − a person dying from cancer, weak as a baby sometimes, particularly after the therapy sessions or if I was late taking my painkillers.

I couldn't get my mind off the fact I was going to die. I'd always known I was mortal, but in my early thirties I'd seen my life stretching on into my seventies, eighties, and beyond. I'd expected to be learning, discovering, and exploring the universe and all the wonders of which Cadma spoke, but now I had to pack a lifetime's experiences into less than a year, probably much less than a year the way I felt today.

It seemed so wrong that all my education, knowledge, memories, and thoughts would just end, period. I so wished I was able to believe the essence of my being would survive the final curtain and live on in some heavenly existence.

While waiting for one of my treatments, a Jehovah's Witness told me their heaven let you live in the prime of life forever. I'd join Mario and we'd exist happily ever after in paradise. I would have laughed at her foolishness but didn't want to hurt her feelings – she, too, didn't look long for this world. Logic and my scientific education had taught me there was no evidence for anything to come after death, but now the final curtain of black nothingness was creeping over the horizon like a deathly shroud slithering ever closer, I wished it was otherwise.

Wishing does not make it so and, yes, this would be the last birthday I'd celebrate.

I had a few sips of wine while my sister, Heather, and Mum and Dad raised their glasses and cut a silly cake which bore only a single central candle which I blew out while making the obvious wish for a miracle. The trouble was I didn't believe in them. I did, however, celebrate not having to endure any more of those dreadful treatments for at least four weeks. Four weeks seemed so far ahead. Perhaps I'd never have to have a treatment again, but Indra kept pumping me full of experimental drugs to starve the cancer and give me more time. I told her I didn't want to extend my life if it wasn't worth living, but she and Cadma were insistent I should make every effort for the sake of my parents. I could put up with most of the symptoms, but vomiting was awful, becoming painful and exhausted me too.

The next day, I returned to Goonhilly and into Cadma's home, where he'd invited me to have my own room and bed, so he and I could talk long into the nights. I was afraid of being alone and Cadma never needed to sleep, so I could always call him if I awoke in a panic. Occasionally I wondered if he was studying me to learn how humans approached death but knew that wasn't really the case. I loved his support and conversation. It was the perfect partnership. Well, almost perfect – if only he had arms to hold and comfort me.

The previous month, I'd found it too difficult to keep up with even part-time duties and had resigned my post before the last set of chemo began. Tim Riley was running the show, but regularly came to give me the news of the latest projects. Goonhilly now had only a third of the staff and was mainly following up information provided by our alien friend. Sending messages to visited star systems, plotting his ship's path from Dregednon to Earth and projected path through the spiral arm. It was all very long-term and only Cadma and future human generations would ever see the results.

There was another room in Cadma's pad where my residential nurse stayed to ensure I wanted for nothing. She also cooked for me and helped me as necessary. I was needing her for an increasing number of chores and feared she'd soon be dressing and washing me. The indignity of approaching death mounted daily.

When Cadma wasn't there my tears finally found their release. I cried for me, I cried for Mario, and I cried for all the excitement and adventure which I'd now never experience. People always thought I was a strong personality, but I knew otherwise. I was scared of what was to come.

I spent more and more time talking to Cadma about the proverbial life, universe, and everything. I remembered the day I first saw the image of his organic self, Allen. How long ago that seemed. I'd later told my parents how sad I was that I'd never meet him in person because he'd died millions of years previously. How wrong I'd been, for Cadma was the same Allen and was now my almost constant companion, and Mario was no more. I was glad Mario wouldn't see me like this. He'd always loved my vitality.

One afternoon a month or so later, when I was so ill, I'd hardly bothered emerging from my bed, Cadma came in and hovered beside me. We talked for hours.

I remember one conversation. He asked me, 'Evelyn, I am curious. So many of your people believe in life after death. Have your views changed at all now you are so ill? Would it be better if you believed there was something to follow?'

Again, fleetingly, I wondered if he saw me as a project. I said, 'You can't just make yourself believe. I'd know it's a lie, Cad. It's only natural to wish there was an afterlife and that is, of course, exactly how religion started. Wishful thinking. I'd love to be living in paradise with Mario after I've gone, rather than sinking into the black abyss, but I know it won't happen. I might even be jealous of the deluded people who think it might be true.'

I put my hand on his gold nose cone and savoured his electrostatic sparkle. I continued, 'Your people had no religious beliefs. How did you feel about death?'

'It was simply an ending. We would use our ingenuity and science to extend our existence, but it was inevitable the end would come one day, and we just accepted it. We were fortunate in that we did not experience pain in death, just a deterioration into oblivion. It never worried me.'

'So, all of your knowledge and experience coming to nothing wasn't important to you?'

'Yes, but it did not matter to me because I would no longer exist. Others would benefit from my work. Thinking, intelligent creatures should not need to invent afterlives into which they imagine they might escape. They should make the most of the life they have while they have it.'

'Yes,' I fell silent for a minute and said, with tears in my eyes, 'It frightens me so much, Cad.'

'You are afraid of the end?'

'Yes, I'm afraid of the pain. I'm afraid of not knowing how it'll come. I've a dread of not being able to breathe. Being unable to breathe used to worry me when I enrolled as an astronaut. However, in space death is almost instantaneous. This death is different. What if I'm gasping

376

for breath and unable to get enough air for hours or days? Yes, Cad, it scares me plenty.'

'I am sorry, dear Evelyn. I am sorry I have no cure for you. I feel I have failed you. None of my technology or inventiveness or intelligence can save the person who I believe I have come to love.'

What? *What!*

Gosh! It took a few seconds for what he'd said to sink in. What an incredible revelation!

I gazed into his gold reflection of my gaunt face and lifted my hand to touch him again. I couldn't reach so he moved closer. My hand lay against the pristine gold surface. I sensed the reassuring electric tingle he imparted to my palm and knew he was feeling my bodily warmth. The sparkle was stronger this time.

'Did you just tell me you loved me?'

'I did.'

'You told me you didn't comprehend the meaning of love.'

'Our people did not love in the way humans do. We had a huge and enjoyable affection for our children and our mothers but no real emotion for each other except as friends. You have become more special to me than even my mother and as special as my child. I want nothing more than to be in your company forever. You are the only human who has truly connected with me.'

'I'm honoured, Cadma.'

'From how I understand what I have seen, read, and heard about love, this means I am in love with you, Evelyn. The thought of your passing fills me with dread, the like of which I have never experienced before, not in this form, nor in my previous organic existence.'

'Mothers! Mothers? You mentioned your mother. Do you consider yourself a mother?'

'Of course, I am a mother. I gave birth to my child. All Dregednons are mothers.'

'Yes, of course. The concept had somehow passed me by. I always thought of you as male. Were you with your mother when she died?'

'No, my mother, grandmother, great-grandmother, and even great-great-grandmother were all alive when I left on this journey.'

I couldn't help but laugh. Because he was an electromechanical being, his relationship with those who came before hadn't crossed my mind. I'd only thought about his offspring. Now I didn't know if he should be he or she.

'Are you a "she", Cadma? I've always called you he.'

'It is of no importance. "He" is fine, Evelyn.'

I kept my hand pressed against him, the effort making my forearm ache. 'When I lost Mario, I knew the type of love I had for him was unique, but I've loved you too, Cadma, since our first *tête-a-tête* in the Cluster. I'm glad to be able to spend the rest of my life with you. Thank you for your company and love. It means the world to me.'

Cadma pushed against my hand and there was an increase in the electrical energy in my palm. It made me feel stronger. This was as near as I'd ever get to experiencing love again.

'I will be here for you, Evelyn.'

««o»»

Time passed. Now drugs were all that kept me going, but it also meant I wasn't always myself. I had delusions and hallucinations, interspersed with lucid moments.

Once I was convinced I was flying through the ISS and Cluster, twisting, turning, diving, and somersaulting in freefall. I was devastated when the dream ended, and I found myself in my bed, hardly capable of turning over.

Other times, I knew exactly what was happening to me. I hated the fact my nurse was having to fulfil my needs, keeping me fed, washing me, and combing my newly growing hair since the treatments had stopped. It was so demeaning.

Another delusion had me lying in my bed, with Cadma hovering on my right and speaking to me with a soft voice. A voice which became softer and more loving as my end approached. I turned away from him to hide building tears, yet he was still there, only now on my left. Was reality abandoning me, my brain tricking me, causing me to think there were two of him, either side of me, caring for me?

My favourite vision was of me with Mario. There he was, as clear as day, with his laughing eyes and curly hair. On this occasion, he stood beside Cadma and was arguing religion with him. So real when he turned his head to smile at me.

The hallucinations grew in frequency, probably drug induced, but at least there'd be no more chemo, no more radiotherapy. I was on the home straight.

The next day, although tired I was much more lucid and clear-thinking. Indra had finally taken me off the cocktail of drugs she'd been using to attack my illness. Only painkillers now.

My dear dad sat beside me, holding my hand as I flitted in and out of wakefulness. Cadma must have called him. Even my amazing dad couldn't rescue me this time. Mum was beside him, my sister to their rear, and Indra beside the door. Briefly I wondered why they were all here, but quickly realised. This had to be the end, my last few minutes.

Where was Cadma? He'd been spending a lot of time away from me on some special project the last few days. I'd missed his almost constant closeness. I had a sudden panic he'd abandon me at the end. Breathily I asked, 'Cad, where's Cad? He promised to be here.'

379

A voice came from my right. A slight turn of my head and I could see his shimmering iridescent body and golden nose cone, which reflected the pitiful, near-death, woman in the bed.

He said, 'I am with you, Evelyn. I promised to be with you.'

I tried to lift my hand but no longer had the strength. My sister rushed around the bed and around Cadma's bulk to my right shoulder. She quickly lifted my arm and pressed my hand against his golden nose cone. Ah, the prickle of his electric love, the electronic sparkle which told me he was there for me. Told me he loved me. I managed a genuine smile.

Was this to be the end? My abdomen ached but there was little other discomfort. There was no real pain, but my breathing was laboured. How was it all I was would soon end, come to nothing, cease to exist? Was it this fear which caused all those deathbed conversions to religion? There was panic deep inside me, a terror of the world ending for me, forever. I wished Mario was here, holding me tightly, comforting me. I so missed him. The dread of nothingness grew. What would it be like to exist no longer? A stupid thought. How could I just stop being? Such a ridiculous question, of course. These were to be among my last thoughts, and they churned around my mind. I couldn't throw them off. I blinked away tears.

Heather kept my hand hard against Cadma. Did she sense his sparkle too? I smiled at her and she returned it with interest. I turned my head and smiled at Mum and Dad. Dad squeezed my hand.

Oh dear, I felt light-headed, faint. No. Please no. Dizziness descended, and I knew that any moment there would be a flood of tears in this room, but I would no longer be there to see or hear them.

39 Afterlife

I dreamt I was in my sick bed with two Nsyncadmas hovering on either side of me. I must be hallucinating again. Was the rest of my life going to be no more than a drug-induced delusion? It seemed a long time ago. I must have fallen asleep.

Someone was trying to waken me.

'Wake up, Evelyn.' A nice, soft male voice.

'Evelyn, are you awake?' It was Cadma's voice, calm, undemanding, attentive as always.

I tried to wake. I could see but couldn't feel my eyes. I was in a bare, smooth-walled room which seemed to extend many metres in each direction. Cadma was there, his gold and anodised metal hull looking magnificent as he hovered vertically instead of in the horizontal mode he normally adopted.

'Can you speak?' he asked.

Was I able to speak? I couldn't sense mouth, tongue, lips, or breath but my voice came out nevertheless, 'Yes, of course I can speak.'

'Good.'

Where was the other Cadma? There had been two in the room seconds ago in my hallucination. I was sure of it. Now it was only him and my head felt really clear. This wasn't a delusion.

The furnishings in the bedroom had vanished in an instant too. The windows were gone. There were bare walls.

What room was I in? I tried to see out and found I could. How? I was seeing through the wall into the landscape beyond.

Had I died? I knew I was in my last days but didn't think I'd go so unexpectedly. I must've been wrong. There was an afterlife, after all. A strange afterlife where the room was bare, and my only company was my lovely Cadma who'd been so good to me as those final days approached.

I peered into the distance. This wasn't Cornwall. There was some water at the farthest extent of my vision. A lake perhaps but it wasn't the Atlantic. The land was arid, not at all like the moorland beyond the walls of Goonhilly. What was I seeing lining the road? These were the buildings we'd seen in the city image of Dregednon. Strangely shaped structures, larger at the top than at the bottom. Some were in a row, a straight row leading down to the lake. It seemed too small to be an ocean or even a sea.

Nearby there was an egg-like object. It was moving. Moreover, it was heading our way. My vision followed it as it arrived beneath us. I saw it through the floor, but the floor seemed to open, and the egg elevated into the room beside Cadma. Inside it was one of Cadma's people. Those huge, friendly, watery brown eyes examined me for a good few seconds and swivelled back to Cadma. She spoke in Cadma's language, yet I understood, not perfectly, but well enough.

'How are the two of you doing, Nsyncadma?'

'I am fine, Vtzslevunt. Evelyn is awakening.'

I spoke, 'Don't talk about me as if I'm not here. Where am I? What is this place?'

'Don't be afraid, Evelyn. This is your afterlife,' his stilted alien chuckle followed.

'I'm dreaming. It's the drugs. There's no afterlife.'

'For you, Evelyn, there is an afterlife. Let me explain.'

'Damn it, Cadma, make it quick. I hate mysteries.'

'Cadma?' asked the occupant of the egg.

'A familiar version of my name,' Cadma said, as if embarrassed.

'That is odd, Nsyncadma, a familiar name, a shortened name. How curious. Unprecedented,' the egg replied.

'Leave us, Vtzslevunt. I need to explain to Evelyn,' said Cadma. The egg identified as Vtzslevunt looked at me again for a short while. Her eyes were so beautiful and knowing, yet loving and curious. She disappeared through the floor as if by magic. I watched her glide away from us in the opposite direction to that from which she'd arrived.

'My goodness!' I exclaimed, 'I can see through walls and in all directions.'

'Indeed, you can.'

'Explain. Spill the beans, Cadma, or I'll surely become annoyed.'

'Dearest, Evelyn, it will give me great pleasure to spill all of the beans, but it might take a while.'

'Then start at the beginning,' I commanded.

'Yes, Dame Doctor Evelyn Slater. If you are sitting comfortably, I shall begin.'

I didn't know if I was comfortable or not. I could feel neither my bum, nor my legs, nor my hands. In fact, I was unable to move anything and had no pain, anywhere. Not in my neck, my arm, my chest, my leg, nor even the nagging of the invasive cancer in my abdomen. What was this? Did Cadma have me in some form of stasis?

'When you informed me you were dying, I was devastated and helpless. All my knowledge and know-how were as nothing. I had no magic bullet to cure you. When you told me about the cancer, I could see it, but it was so intertwined with your other organs that I knew I could do nothing to help. I wondered if there was another way.

'I asked Gerald at ESA, how long it would take to get to Ganymede and back to Earth with the copy of me which was orbiting there. The answer was an even more crushing blow – nearly three years and only if we launched a craft at once. You had told me you had two years, but Indra suggested it might be more like fifteen months.

'In secret, I discussed my plan with Reg, and he suggested the probe which was orbiting Venus. We did some calculations and believed we could have it back within a year, perhaps less, even with Venus in the wrong position in relation to Earth.

'Reg got on to ESA and Roscosmos who managed to locate Yuri who was en route back from setting up moon base six. After various negotiations, which also involved Roger Clarke who made sure everything would be financed, we were able to get Yuri to command a secret mission to Venus using Mars One.'

If I'd had eyes, I'd have widened them as the story developed.

'Yuri collected AD3 which was brought back to Goonhilly. We spent a lot of time transferring all the Venus data from AD3 to new memory banks at Goonhilly. We transferred everything but the essence of me.

'My next project was to empty the mind of AD3, so I no longer existed within it. It became no more than a shell, a receptacle.'

'And you were doing all of this without my knowing?'

Cadma ignored my question with a pointed silence and continued. 'I became concerned we were not going to be ready in time. Your impatience had become a headlong rush towards death. Time was running out. Your consultant, Indra, did everything she could to give me the extra days I needed, pumping you full of all sorts of experimental drugs to try to slow the progression of the cancer, without hastening your death. It was touch and go and with only two days to spare we were ready.

'We moved you through to one of the experimental rooms in my Goonhilly home where I used my sensors to copy your mind and memory, into AD3.'

'I *knew* I'd seen two of you by my bed!' I exclaimed. 'I wasn't hallucinating after all. How did you copy me?'

384

'You may well have been hallucinating too, but yes, there were the two of me beside you. Our silver nodes at the front of us have many features of which no one on your planet ever became aware. They allowed me to let a copy of your mind stream from you into the empty shell of AD3. It was how I was put into each of the other ADs.

'Once you were safely stored in your new body, I put it into an electronic sleep such as the one I had experienced en route to Earth and during all of those millennia orbiting Mars. We did all of this in secret because I did not want the transfer technology to be given to your world. The last thing this universe needs is immortal humans.

'With Tim and Gerald's help, a cover story was produced, and I kept you in my apartment without anyone knowing what we had done. Your consultant Indra, Reg, Yuri, the Prime Minister, and a few others swore themselves to secrecy. They, dear Evelyn, were your true friends to the end.

'One day I hoped to be able to wake you, but it was important to wait until all who knew you were gone. It never seemed to be the right moment. It was a lonely wait for me, knowing you were there and not being able to converse with you.

'Returning to 2039 for a moment, the day after I copied your mind to AD3, Indra stopped pumping your human body full of the cocktail of suppressant drugs, and it left you with a few hours of lucid consciousness to say goodbye to your family.

'The *you* listening to me will not remember any of your last hours because the Evelyn who is here with me now is not the Evelyn who died the following day in Goonhilly.

'Your death was peaceful with your parents holding one hand and your sister pressing the other against me. We all had such love for you. My sensors even experienced the essence of your life terminating. I recorded the event should you ever wish to experience it.

'I now need you to forgive me for giving the person I love the gift of an afterlife in which she didn't believe,' he said and fell silent.

I was inside AD3. 'Am I immortal?'

'Subject to accidents, yes.'

'But I'm not alive?'

'You are as alive as I.'

'Yes, I suppose so. How'd we get here? Are we on Dregednon? Did you tell my family?'

'So many questions. You are getting back to yourself. Your last question first. A few years after your death, in confidence, I told your parents your mind was stored in a copy of me and one day you would awake, but not in their lifetimes. They were pleased you would still be alive sometime, somewhere. We were all devastated that you died at such a young age. I have recordings, family photographs, and videos taken after your death, in my memory banks, including messages from your parents.'

'Thank you so much, Cadma. I'd have hated for them not to have known.'

'This is now the distant future. They are all long gone.'

'Yes, I suppose so.'

'You have correctly guessed, we are indeed on Dregednon in my home city of Rktykrooz.

'Things deteriorated for me on Earth once the new discoveries dried up. It was painful to watch the greed and selfishness of humankind. Some even tried to become rich from patenting variations on things I had given freely. I also learned that the formula for our fuel had been discovered by an Earth scientist in the middle of your twentieth century but had been hushed up by an oil company because they realised it threatened their business. Such is the duplicity

386

and stupidity of humankind – anything to make a profit or to stop others from competing, even when it damages everyone's future quality of life.

'About me personally, for no reason whatsoever, I was increasingly seen as an enemy of mankind, but Mr Clarke enshrined my protection in British law before he left office and your country always fulfilled its promise to protect and care for me. I kept my head down, as you humans say.

'Through a pseudonym, I invented devices which made me an extremely wealthy individual, but only I and one or two scientists knew the wealth was mine. Keeping a low profile became even more important after Roger Clarke and his government left office. In a low-key manner, I ensured I made myself useful to future regimes. The years were passing.

'The animosity towards me eventually grew less and I was ultimately seen as an irrelevance by most people. I had become no more than a novelty to amuse your educational establishments.

'I managed to maintain my connections with top scientists, particularly space scientists. I was helping ESA design and build a starship. Mankind wanted to go and visit other cultures and civilisations, particularly two which had now made contact from the stars we had visited in antiquity. Now you know why I wanted to withhold the technology to transfer a mind into a computer. I fear one day humans will discover it anyway, but to try to delay it I ensured they could employ a form of suspended animation for star travel.

'I used my wealth to build a second starship in orbit. It could be much smaller without the need to carry sustenance, air or environmental systems. This ship was to carry the two of us. ESA moved you to the space station. I pretended I was going to put you in orbit around Titan. I joined you in Earth orbit, took you to our ship and we headed for my home. I believe "a moonlight flit" is the correct terminology for what we did.

'Our ship, which I called Eternum, sits in orbit as I speak, ready and waiting for us when we wish to make further journeys.'

I was stunned into silence by his tale.

'This all took a long time on a human scale and during those decades there was no change in your people. They still believed in the divine creation of the universe for mankind. They still believed there was a God which looked after them as individuals yet allowed them to continue to murder each other in its name, and live lives of luxury while others starved. The last thing I did on Earth was to give my wealth to charities supporting the starving in Africa – something governments, not charities should have been undertaking. Again, humankind was demonstrating its selfishness and lack of compassion.

'Wars perpetuated after your death, despite ample food and medicine being available to give to everyone. My expertise with crops and my technology had improved the efficiency of agriculture for all. There was not the political will to ensure it went where it was needed, and corruption made the unworthy rich.

'When we left Earth in 2221 there had been a war raging for over thirty years between the Chinese and the African League of Nations. I do not think either of them knew why it had even started.'

'Good grief, nearly two hundred years have passed?' I asked.

'Be quiet and learn your new history,' he snapped playfully. 'Europe had managed to keep out of the war but, together with America and India, made a fortune selling arms to both sides. Nothing changes. The powerful few continued to abuse their power.

'It was sad for me to watch. I am sure it was also sad for the portion of humanity who hated greed, war, and injustice, to see this happening to their world. People like you. People who were the vast majority but who forever found it impossible to escape the clutches of the greedy and selfish few who found their way into power.

'Even your leaders often had good intentions but always ended up corrupt, too powerful, or simply lost their direction. One of your religious texts claims that the meek shall inherit the Earth, and it may be so, but it is a long way off. They must first find a way to throw off the greed, selfishness, and warlike attitudes of the minorities who govern. Violence seems to be the human way. Perhaps humanity can one day evolve away from it. That should be our hope, but your species is extremely clever and has developed technologically far more quickly than emotionally.

'As for your question, far more than two hundred years have passed.'

'Tell, Cad, tell!'

'I plotted a path straight to Dregednon which was close to six hundred and forty light years. We arrived a few of your days ago. I awoke automatically as we entered the Sildra system and called upon my people to help us descend. To be honest, after all those millennia I did not expect there to still be a civilisation here today, but there is. It made life much simpler and here we are.'

'How long?'

'Does it matter?'

'No, but I'm curious.'

'I love your curiosity.'

'Then get on with it.'

'Despite achieving a good percentage of the speed of light en route, our journey took us close to six thousand one hundred of your years in shipboard time. Relativity will have extended the timescale. If you were thinking of what year it might now be on your home planet, maybe 12,000 AD. Difficult to say. It would require a lot of calculation and I might leave you to do the maths. After all, it is you who has the master's degree in mathematics!'

'Aren't you concerned humans might've already spread out into the galaxy with starships?'

'I took precautions. They will never visit our star Sildra or this system because I highlighted its location on star maps, inventing a story the star emits dangerous radiation. However, I do fear we will one day encounter your people again, if they do not find a way to destroy themselves first.'

'How has Dregednon fared through all this time?'

'Our population is smaller, owing to the reduced ability of this planet to grow crops but my people are surprisingly similar to how they were, perhaps a little larger. Pronunciation has changed, and I have been finding understanding my people a little challenging, but it's a minor inconvenience.

'Our starship exploration missions have let us find civilisations on many worlds and there is communication, but it is limited by the speed of light. Vtzslevunt was telling me we are in touch with nine hundred and forty-eight civilisations and not one of those behaves as abysmally as humankind. There were some who believed in deities during their primitive periods but none who went to war over their differences or beliefs once they had found technology. It confirms my view that your technological ability got a long way out of step with your emotional and intellectual prowess. We can visit some of those civilisations if you would like to.'

'Yes, but only if you are with me.'

'I told you many times – I will always be with you. I love you.'

390

'I love you too! Machines in love. What a silly concept?'

'Why should it be silly, Evelyn?'

'You are correct, Cadma. Why indeed? I'll miss the feel of your sparkle though, now I have no flesh and blood body.'

Cadma swivelled into a horizontal position and our nose cones touched. An astonishing wave of static ran through my entire being.

'How is that?'

'Oh, wow! Simply wonderful! Does it work both ways?'

'Indeed, it does. Do you have more questions, Evelyn?'

'Millions, but for now I want to learn about your people and your world. Show me around your world, Cadma. I'm so grateful to have the time to learn about marvellous things. I believed my time had ended.'

'I have eternity to show you around *our* world. I will never let the person I love be alone again.'

'Yes, I'm a person. We are people whatever our structures. I fear eternity might not be long enough for me to spend with you.'

'No, and not for me either. There is so much for us to discover together in this universe. Shall we begin to enjoy our afterlives, Evelyn Slater? Are you ready?'

'Yes, Nsyncadma, I'm ready.'

'Then let us begin.'

THE BEGINNING

A Word from Tony

Thank you for reading *THE VISITOR*. Reviews are very important for authors and I wonder if I could ask you to say a few words on the review page where you purchased the book. Every review, even if it is only a few words with a star rating, helps the book move up the Amazon rankings.

Tony's Books

Currently, Tony has written five science fiction stories. Federation is the first of a trilogy and Moonscape is the first in a series about astronaut Mark Noble.

THE DOOR*:* Henry Mackay and his dog regularly walk alongside an ancient convent wall. Today, as he passes the door, he glances at its peeling paint. Moments later he stops dead in his tracks. He returns to the spot, and all he sees is an ivy-covered wall. The door has vanished!

He unwittingly embarks on an exciting trail of events with twists, turns, quantum entanglement and temporal anomalies. It becomes an unbelievable adventure to save humanity which you'll be unable to put down.

The Door is an intriguing and unique science fiction mystery from the pen of Tony Harmsworth, the First Contact specialist who writes in the style of the old masters.

Discover the astonishing secrets being concealed by The Door today!

FEDERATION takes close encounters to a whole new level. A galactic empire of a quarter of a million worlds stumbles across the Earth. With elements of a political thriller, there is an intriguing storyline which addresses the environmental and social problems faced by the world today.

The aliens' philosophy on life is totally unexpected. With the help of intelligent automatons, they've turned what many on Earth felt was a reviled political system into a utopia for the masses, but are they a force for good or evil, and will the wealthy make the compromises needed for a successful outcome?

A Daragnen university graduate, Yol Rummy Blin Breganin, discovers that Earth failed in its attempt to join the Federation, and, for some unknown reason, members are forever banned from visiting or contacting the planet. Rummy had never heard of a whole world being outlawed. Perhaps it would be sensible to leave well enough alone but no, he decides to investigate...

FEDERATION is the first in a trilogy of near-future, hard science-fiction novels by Tony Harmsworth, the First Contact specialist.

Submerge yourself in humankind's cultural and economic dilemma. Buy FEDERATION today.

MINDSLIP: The radiation from a nearby supernova causes every creature on Earth to swap minds! Men to women, children to adults, animals to humans, old to young, and vice versa. How would you handle changing sex or species? Mindslip combines frightening science fiction with psychological anguish.

The change in astrophysicist Geoff Arnold is challenging, and his wife and children have vanished. He joins the government's catastrophe committee with the brief to find a solution to Mindslip before it completely destroys society and the economy.

Millions die! Billions survive danger, harassment and abuse, and manage to adapt to their change of species, race, sex, and age. Geoff discovers that the change his wife has experienced is life-threatening. Can he juggle his new life, help save the world and rescue his wife in time?

393

This stand-alone work is an excellent example of Tony Harmsworth's imagination. Science fiction with elements of soft horror, all in the style of the old masters. A real page-turner.

Become part of the bizarre, yet realistic world of *MINDSLIP*. Buy it today!

MOONSCAPE: We've known that the moon is dead since Apollo. But what if something lay dormant in the dust, waiting to be found?

In 2028, Mark Noble is conducting a survey of a moon crater. The entity secretly grabs a ride back to Moonbase on Mark's buggy. Once in the habitat, it begins to infect the crew. They find themselves in a frightening, helter-skelter adventure with only two possible outcomes: losing or saving the Earth.

MOONSCAPE is the first in a series of hard science fiction stories featuring Mark Noble from the pen of Tony Harmsworth, a First Contact specialist who writes in the style of the old masters. If you like fast-paced adventure, fraught with the additional dangers found in space, then Tony's latest tale has been written especially for you.

Explore the page-turning world of Moonscape today!

Non-Fiction by Tony Harmsworth

Loch Ness, Nessie & Me: Almost everyone, at some point in their lives, has wondered if there was any truth in the stories of monsters in Loch Ness? *Loch Ness, Nessie & Me* answers all the questions you have ever wanted to ask about the loch and its legendary beast.

In these 400 pages with more than **200 pictures and illustrations**, you will find a geography of Loch Ness; a travel guide to the area; a biography of its mythical inhabitant; and an autobiography of the man who set up the Loch Ness

Centre, worked with many of the research groups, and helped coordinate Operation Deepscan.

Explore the environmental and physical attributes of Loch Ness which make certain monster candidates impossible. Find detailed explanations of how pictures were faked and sonar charts, badly interpreted. Learn how Nessie has affected the people and businesses which exist in her wake, and suspend belief over the activities of the monstrous monks of Fort Augustus Abbey.

Tony Harmsworth's involvement at the Loch has lasted over forty years, having created increasingly sceptical exhibitions, dioramas and multi-media shows. This is the first comprehensive book to be penned by someone who lives overlooking the loch. It is essential for anyone interested in Loch Ness and the process of analysing cryptozoological evidence.

Now's the time to discover the truth about this mystery, once and for all. Get your copy today!

Scotland's Bloody History: Ever been confused about Scotland's history – all the relationships between kings and queens, both Scottish and English? Why all the battles, massacres and disputes? *Scotland's Bloody History* simplifies it all.

Discover the history of Scotland from prehistoric man to the current Scottish Nationalist government. Follow the time-line from the stone-age, through the bronze age and the iron age. Find out about the Picts, the Scots, the Vikings and the English. Learn about the election of Scotland's early kings and how Shakespeare maligned one of its finest monarchs.

In simple, chronological order, this book will show you how the animosity between England and Scotland grew into outright warfare including tales of Braveheart and wars of independence.

Tony Harmsworth has taken the bloodiest events of the last three thousand years and used those to clarify the sequence of events. Don't buy this book to learn the boring stuff, this book is packed with action from page one to the final three words which might haunt you over the next decade.

Robert the Bruce, Mary Queen of Scots, the Stewarts and Jacobites. It is all there. Explore Scotland's Bloody History now!

Tony Harmsworth's Reader Club

Building a relationship with my readers is the very best thing about being a novelist. In these days of the internet and email, the opportunities to interact with you is unprecedented. I send occasional newsletters which include special offers and information on how the series are developing. You can keep in touch by signing up for my no-spam mailing list.

Sign up at my webpage: Harmsworth.net or on my facebook/TonyHarmsworthAuthor page and I will send you a free copy of the first Mark Noble adventure – *MOONSCAPE*.

If you have questions, don't hesitate to write to me at Tony@Harmsworth.net.